For more information, or to book an event, contact:
reneedolanauthor@gmail.com &
http://www.reneedolanauthor.com

Cover design by Nicole Elizabeth Smith

ISBN - Paperback: 979-8-9875150-0-6
ISBN - Ebook : 979-8-9875150-1-3

First Edition: February 2023

AMONG THE GRAY

Renee Dolan

CREATIVE

For Jesse
With you, this story found a home.
Without you—I have none.

THEN

THE HOST

A COUGH ignited her throat like a firework as she brought the towel to her lips, a spatter of red blotting the cheap cloth from the airport lounge bathroom. She caught a few sideways glances from a young family sitting nearby, but to them, the sound was just another haggard traveler trying to make their way home.

If only that could be true.

As she palmed the towel back into her pocket, careful to hide it from view, she grimaced at her bony hands. Skin ghastly pale in the artificial light, the blues and greens of her bloated veins having nowhere to hide. Despite herself, she had to marvel at the speed of the infection that had transformed her once tanned, squishy body into a skeleton within a matter of weeks. The Host, as she was identified in the files, knew how the sickness was designed: attack the extremities first, then the brain.

A hacking cough escaped her throat again.

The beginning of the end. Soon, her mind would forget how to gulp for air.

A buzz of announcements crackled through the Atlanta International terminal—barely managing to drown out the bustle of the busiest travel day of the summer season—and she stared down at the boarding pass that would soon become the most lethal of weapons. She shifted in her seat, alleviating some of the pain in her back, and heard the crinkle in her pocket. She had memorized the letter already, but she pulled it out anyway, trailing her aching eyes down the typed memo. *Subtlety is key when you approach the agent. Don't let them see you cough.*

The Host glanced over at the woman behind the ticket counter, a colorful scarf tied around a wrinkled neck. A body full of life, she thought. But to those who penned her letter, a shell to be discarded. A tool. Someone undeserving of even a pronoun. Someone with a family. Someone with a name.

From her vantage point, the Host could just make out an E on the agent's silver tag and bile surged into her throat as she averted her eyes, tears brimming uncontrollably at the realization.

The first victim to carry this burden also carried the name of her firstborn. Her sweet sun. Her one of two, precious reasons for accepting this radical duty.

It had only been a medical trial—at least, that's what she had believed in the beginning. The technology company heading the trial had reached out to her directly, bypassing her oncologist, which should have been the first red flag. Back then, though, the doctor had nothing left to offer and her body simply had nothing left.

By the time she realized the tech company was just a front for extremists who had preyed on her unsurvivable prognosis, she knew she was as good as dead.

They saw it differently, of course—deeming her "the lucky one." The first of her cohorts to survive the injection. After that, they stopped calling her by her name, but simply the Host. Patient Zero for their plan to topple the world's governing bodies and start fresh.

Her identity stripped away, they had then quarantined her to a sterile medical suite no bigger than a motel room as the fluid washed through her veins. She didn't need them to tell her what was happening. Unlike the cancer, she could feel this infection spreading underneath her paling skin like a poison. But the letter came sweeping under the door anyway, its words spiking the fever coursing through her body.

Highly contagious. Cannot see your children unless you wish to infect them.

It was the first time she'd ever thanked God for the early death of her husband.

If she didn't do what they asked, the letter clarified, her handlers would infect her children first. But if she agreed, the children would be the first to receive the vaccination. She hated these people more than the cancer, but she had no reason not to trust that they would do either circumstance.

The job would only wipe out her generation—the souls aged 55 and up—the Host reminded herself now, her eyes flicking back to the woman, now holding a speaker to her painted lips.

"Business class flyers for flight UA2235 to London—now boarding."

Her life had been over the day she saw the onslaught of threatening colors overtake the black and white on the PET scan. Her blood was destined to go cold too early, but she still had time to save her legacy.

And so it was, with the treasured images of green eyes and freckled faces flashing through her mind, that the Host stood up, put the crisp boarding pass up to her poisonous lips and suffered through another agonizing cough. Swallowing the lava that longed to erupt from her esophagus, she walked over to the counter, struck up a smile and offered the ticket, looking away quickly as the agent's fingers, still strong and full of color, touched the paper bullet that would send the woman to an early grave in a matter of weeks.

A nod was all she could muster as the agent's face wrinkled with an easy smile, innocently ushering the Host forward to the jetway.

Every limb ached as she shuffled down the tunnel towards the line waiting at the open hatch of the 737. The memo crinkled in her pocket, and a shiver overtook her entire body. The Host had infected their first victim. She had done what they asked, and they had nothing left to threaten. Suddenly she felt incredibly light.

But not light enough.

She wrenched the memo out of her pocket, crumpling it into a tight ball with cold, unfeeling fingers. As she felt the air conditioning blast across her face, she let the note drop through the gap between the open hatch and the jetway—and stepped onto the plane.

ELLE

IT WAS always quiet in Nox. Having a room to one's self tends to suppress all other noise, but this morning seemed to have let in a vapor of eerie silence with the rising sun.

The building was made to keep everything out—or everything in, depending on what side of the walls you were touching—so it was jarring when something, even as benign as a breeze, wafted in.

If she tried hard enough, she could usually cut through the vapid whispers in her own head and pick out traces of conversation that leaked in through the vents from her luckier counterparts not confined to isolation. But this morning, she heard nothing except the familiar internal monologue that questioned how she ended up here.

She padded over to the wailing wall and braced herself against the tiny sink. She could almost feel the mirror daring her to tug her eyes upward. She yanked off the pillowcase she had draped across it for the last three months, the soft material a faithful substitute for her scarred fist.

Eleanor Drake had once looked like her name—soft curves and delicate edges, a frame wrapped in silks from Milan and glimmering with imported moisturizers. Years of effort only to be stripped away by mere weeks spent at Meridian State Prison, leaving a drab pallor that could only come from days spent in the windowless walls of an isolated cell.

Cavalierly known as Nox by those it housed, the jail had been designed to deaden all human senses, and had begun doing so to the slender socialite following her all too public fall from grace two years earlier. At least, that was how the papers had put it. To Elle, it had felt more like an ejection from the society that had built her.

Thrust into an upper class higher than her cheekbones, Elle had been built by Silicon Valley moguls and molded from a life of privilege. She had perfected the art of presentation. From the sculpt of her calves to the use of only her first and middle names, she had learned what impressed people. What intrigued them. What turned the most heads. But on the day she had needed her craft to succeed the most, it had failed. Where once people turned to catch a glimpse of Eleanor Drake, they now shook their heads and averted their eyes as if a glimpse of her would poison their minds with her fear-based propaganda.

Standing now before the dingy reflection, she could still see remnants of herself as the same woman who once commanded a room. The same petite face, once porcelain, now just pale. Her jawline had only been made more defined, accentuating her emaciated cheekbones. Lips joined at the corners with just the slightest lift, while a button nose softened all of the symmetrically sharp edges. The mirror offered one mercy, cutting the reflection off at the bottom of her throat, where diamonds had once swung above curves coveted by many.

Jade green eyes—the only spark left in her lifeless body—lazily trailed up to find a mousy nest of dusky dead ends that she'd hacked off with a bartered, dull razor days earlier. She hadn't seen the outcome of her efforts yet, and curiously, she watched bitten nails trail through the shambles of hair she had once labored over each night. Her new hairstyle had returned a small sense of autonomy, and she smiled into the splintered glass. The jagged reflection allowed only the right corner of her mouth to lift, like the snarl of a rabid dog. She stood there another moment, amused by the metaphor staring back at her. A depiction of what happens when a society molds something to their liking—only to destroy it when they felt threatened by their creation.

Two years she had been within these cold walls, with another twelve to go according to the peers who found her to be a terrorist within her own country. Back then, she had sat in her most flattering pantsuit, sculpted calves tense but hands unflinchingly calm, as only someone innocent and well-intentioned could do. She was sure the very citizens she had been trying to protect, the whole world really, would believe her.

Instead, they had marked her "the beautiful radical" who spewed fake propaganda as a way to infiltrate the government through fear. Deemed a mental threat, she was isolated to her own cell in Nox, which by now, had stripped nearly all feeling.

Some days she yearned for revenge. But most days, she surrendered to the despair. Nox may not have taken her sight, but she could no longer see life as black and white. Mere existence was simply black or more black.

From her crouch in the corner of the cell, she blinked now at the rough walls around her, textured with jagged words carved from a rock and her own bloody hand, and a haggard chuckle rattled the eerie silence of the morning as she thought back to those first months of hope. Back when every etching held the hope for justice, and the belief that someone would walk in, read her declarations of innocence jaggedly etched into the walls, and, for the first time, defend her.

But as the months passed, she had begun to wish for a different kind of justice. The kind that had finally earned Elle her spot in Nox.

Sitting there now, back rigid against the cold wall, she laughed at her naivete written on the walls. She laughed because there was no way she could know that her wish that had just come true.

There was no way of knowing about the thin, wiry woman who had just boarded an international flight, cementing the plan Elle had once tried to warn the world about. The plan that would invoke the first attack of the biomedical weapon destined to decimate the planet and—as Elle had been anxiously waiting two years for—blissfully take her with it.

NOW

ONE

6 August
7:00 a.m.

A SHRIEK pierced the silence like a lightning bolt, sparking every dormant nerve in his body. Inhaling sharply, he felt cold, sterile air snake into his nostrils like a ghost. Sluggish eyes fluttered open, only to reveal a sight he had never seen.

A single room, decorated like a lavish, underground hotel suite. Lush white bedding lay haphazardly across his legs in a king size bed. A fresh hint of lemon clung to the four, stone walls around him. Sleek, marbled shelves stacked full with ceramic dishes filled in a kitchenette to his left, a decadent armoire stood to his right. A single coffee mug perched lazily on a nightstand. Sparks of color hung neatly in frames throughout the room.

Another shriek echoed off the stone walls, and his hands flew to his temples as his eyes snapped shut. When he opened them again, he couldn't deny one, alarming truth.

This room was not his, and yet, it screamed someone lives here.

His eyes continued to move across the space, taking in a sheepskin rug that lay at the foot of his platform bed. He squinted at an emerald green velvet armchair in the corner, willing himself to remember the chrome globe reading light hovering behind it. His gaze tilted upward to find the only window in the room, small and square, heavily textured. As he strained his eyes to get a glimpse of what may be on the other side, he realized the window actually looked splintered—like a mosaic of foggy glass pieced back together. A clunky oak desk backed up against the wall just below it.

Questions surged forward in his mind like a rip tide, the lack of answers threatening to pull him under. The alarm blared off the walls again, fracturing his stream of consciousness.

Nothing looked familiar in this room—but there was something else.

Unease crept up his back like a current.

Something was missing. His heart pulsed through his chest, every nerve in his head reaching out for the answer like fingers wrapping around the trigger of a rifle, eager for the release.

Another shriek, but he didn't hear it amid all the synapses firing in his brain. Dread surged through his body like ice as the final detail locked into place. There was no door.

No way out.

***

EPIPHANY SPLIT through him like shrapnel. A sudden tightness compressed his chest. He sprung off the bed, lost his footing in the slats of the cheap pallet holding up the mattress, and tumbled to the floor. The tips of his fingers burned white as he launched himself back to his feet and towards the nearest wall. He put his hands out and started feeling around the surface, searching for any divot, hole or ridge that offered relief from this ever-growing sense of dread. Finding nothing, he began to crawl over to the next wall before his ears split open again. Only this time, the alarm was chased by a strange, irritated voice.

"Turn the stupid alarm off, Reyes—"

The sound cut off, and he gulped in the sudden quiet as if it was oxygen before spinning on his heels to find the voice.

"A little off there this morning, Cavanaugh? Wakey wakey!" the voice cascaded all around him, lilting with amusement.

No one was here.

Muffled garble drifted in behind the voice, and then there was an audible sigh.

"A little compassion? Really, Reyes, do you know what they've done?"

But he heard no answer—only radio static.

Confusion and fear made his eyes swim as he rounded on his heels and raked a hand through a thick lock of hair falling in his face, searching the room for the speaker or a camera. Some sign that could ease his panic.

"Alright, Cavanaugh, do you happen to remember anything, or rather, anyone—"

The voice broke off, as if distracted. A moment passed, and then it was back, screeching off his stone walls.

"You can't be in here!"

A crackle of static filled the air, replacing the severe voice with more muffled tones. Someone cried out a garbled name and he leaned forward, straining to hear. Then suddenly a voice seemed to be right in his ear.

"Get out of th—!" but it was cut off by the sharpest ring he'd ever heard, as if the sound had manifested into a knife slicing his ear open. His hands flew to his temples once again before everything shut off, the room devoid of noise.

He only had a moment to piece the last three minutes together before he noticed a fine mist of light begin to pour in from the corners of his vision.

He heard something rattle, and without knowing why, he felt his hand shoot to his pocket. But he didn't have time to pull out whatever made the sound before the haze took over, illuminating the inescapable stone walls with a feverish light—and then everything went mercifully dark.

LATER

TWO

"DYLAN."

A waft of a voice tickled his ears, his eyes flickering open from what must have been a comatose sleep. He propped himself up on an elbow and scrubbed his fingers across a smooth scalp, trying to place the voice.

"Hi, Dylan," it spoke again, and he could almost see a smile pulling at unknown lips. Groggily, he tugged at the crisp sheets, assured he would uncover the owner of the voice. But there was no one.

He squinted now, the rest of the room fizzling into clarity before him and he felt the sheets tighten beneath his grip.

He didn't know this room.

Cold gray walls entrenched an otherwise warm interior—a velvet chair in the corner, a slim wardrobe to his right. A small, opaque window let in soft, diffused orange light.

No, he suddenly thought. There was something familiar here, and like a child trying to catch a bubble floating on a breeze, his conscious reached for the memory—but just as he got close, it vanished.

"You're in a safe space," the voice ventured again, their calm tone keeping his anxiety at bay. "Do you know where you are?"

It was a question stated with a twinge of pity, like they already knew the answer. He opened his mouth, only to release a muffled gurgle. He felt his cheeks burn with embarrassment. He coughed a few times to clear the drowsiness from his voice and tried again.

"No. What day is it?"

"It is 7:20 a.m., the sixth of August."

The details landed on apathetic ears. He couldn't even recall what happened yesterday.

"Where are you?"

"I'm speaking to you through a streamlined audio feed," the voice said gently. "Can you remember anything?"

He swept his eyes across the room, the tendrils of his memory sneaking out like greedy fingers aching for the bubble to come back.

"I think so," he said tentatively.

"You can?"

The voice remained unwavering, careful not to reveal alarm nor satisfaction at his answer. Unsure of what it wanted to hear, he tried to explain.

"I do, yes. I— I see a rug," he stammered dumbly. His eyes darted to the white sheepskin, hoping to channel a memory. "I've seen that rug, it's from— it's from—"

"Dylan," the voice interrupted, "There's no reason to be nervous here."

That smile again. His mind painted a picture of lips tugging into a grin with every syllable that seeped through the walls. Realizing they hadn't introduced themselves, he decided to name the voice Smirk until told otherwise.

"I can't explain where I am. But it feels like I should. What's wrong with me?"

"That's totally normal."

He relaxed, letting his eyes float around the room, as the quiet of the voice seemed to urge him to do. Three paper-thin monitor screens hung on stone gray walls like paintings, each displaying a colorful image that juxtaposed the coldness of the cement walls. He kept scanning to find a small kitchenette and to its left, a pocket door leading to a tiled bathroom. The window sat above a walnut desk to his right, muddled light skimming off its surface, pale pinks turning into blue as the day broke outside. His eyes shifted past the white rug in front of his bed, drifting up towards the one plain, unadorned wall. Without warning, his chest began to seize like he was being squeezed through a tube.

As if on cue, Smirk broke their silence.

"Dylan, this is a safe place, but it's okay to not feel okay. You're in a place you've never seen before."

Oxygen seemed to vaporize out of the room with every second he stared at the wall that he suddenly realized should have a door. An exit.

Anxiety and confusion toppled over each other, his mind swimming with questions.

"Seriously, is this some kind of joke? Where am—"

"You're safe, Dylan, I prom—"

"Just—stop talking! This is obviously not a safe place to be if—" Dylan stuttered, breath shallow, "—if I can't leave!"

It came out like a squeak. The more fear that swept into his brain, the more fog it cleared out. He swept his eyes across the room again, looking for another way out.

"Why am I here?" he cried, eyes sweeping to the ceiling as if he could get closer to the disembodied voice. "And who are you?"

Silence on stone echoed back his panicked questions like a boomerang. Annoyed, Dylan wrenched his legs free from the sheets that had entangled his shaky legs.

Finally, a reluctant sigh pulsed through the airwaves of the room. Dylan marveled at how a sound could carry such disappointment.

"You are in a temporary living pod at Modular Enterprises, North American Headquarters," Smirk began to explain, voice soft. Ethereal, even. "For your own safety, you have been quarantined to a room with no exit. During this time, you are being taken care of by the world's most renowned doctors and medical staff. Your window has been textured for privacy—but also," the voice hesitated. "Your own well-being."

His head spun while his fingers began touching all over his body. Preemptively, he winced— but nothing hurt. Nothing seemed amiss except the inescapable room before him.

"Dylan," the voice said, warningly. "I promise I will answer all your questions. But I'm going to need you to trust me before I can move forward."

The words momentarily pulled him back from the cliff of his blind panic, but his suspicion kept his toes curled around the edge.

"I'm having a h-har-hard time breathing," he managed, fingers clutching the sheets into tight balls.

"Here's a trick," Smirk offered, and Dylan willed his irregular heartbeat to sync with each syllable. "Look around you, choose an object to focus on and stare at it until you feel like you need to blink."

The directive made his mind dart into focus, and he noticed his breath begin to normalize. He chose a small coffee cup, branded with a vividly colored insignia in the center, resting on the counter in the kitchenette. He bore his eyes into the ceramic mug until they swam with shallow pools. Blinking the tears away, he said, "Alright, now what?"

"Close your eyes," Smirk instructed gently. "And tell me what you see."

Dylan rested his eye lids and saw blurred edges of the ceramic cup, and then the circular emblem flashed in a glowing yellow-white.

"I see the cup and a really bright circular symbol on its front," he said, without opening his eyes. "The emblem wasn't that bright before I closed my eyes. Is that normal?"

"Yes," Smirk said brightly. "That is called an echo. Your mind recalled an image from memory—short term as it was. The fact that it's so bright tells us your brain must be firing on all cylinders."

He opened his eyes and glanced at the cup one more time. He looked away and shut his eyes again. The image of the coffee mug lit up before him, and he felt calm rush through his veins. He hadn't forgotten it. In time, everything else would start to come back.

"How's your breathing there, champ?" Smirk asked, somehow infusing warmth into the condescending words. A headache began to thrum at his temples.

"Answers, please."

"Very well." The voice took in a measured breath. "In the summer of 2016, an extremist group known as the Scale released a biomedical agent on a variety of nations that targeted very specific generations of human life. The infection attacked the brain and killed sufferers within a matter of weeks." Smirk spoke slowly, methodically—as if Dylan was a bomb wrapped in Christmas paper. "Your generation, however, only suffered minimal side effects."

He stayed quiet, grappling with the information as a clammy hand massaged his eyebrows.

"Throughout our testing, we've noticed a pattern in you and your peers. You all have suffered short term memory loss. While frustrating, we actually deem it a gift," Smirk said, and Dylan felt a muscle twinge underneath his fingers. The voice clocked his surprise, and hurried on. "What I mean is you don't remember the terror that ravaged the world you once knew. These radicals waged a war they couldn't even fight themselves, releasing a disease on three continents that spun out of their control, rapidly morphing into a world-wide pandemic. It sliced Earth's population by 75 percent. The contagion is called Void, but much of the world only refers to the event as The Shift."

Dylan's head began to swell, the words sounding more and more far away. Impossible.

"When the dust cleared, it was determined that your generation, 18 to 34-year-olds—Legacies as we tend to call you—had the best chance of survival. But you needed protection. Enter, Modular Enterprises, an architectural firm that quickly drew up plans for the remarkable facility you sit in now: a safe haven for individuals like you to find purpose on a desolate, compromised planet while medical innovators developed a vaccine. Actually, Dylan, we have been looking for you for months."

His head snapped up out of his hands.

"And you will never understand the relief we felt when you appeared to be in such health," Smirk said proudly.

"Appeared?" he asked.

"Because Void targets the brain, we weren't exactly sure how much damage might've been inflicted. Although Legacies like you have some version of immunity against the disease, the longer someone is exposed to the environment, the faster the brain degenerates under the harsh elements. To have found you, after so many months past Void's release, with such high functioning brain activity..." Smirk broke off, as if in awe. "We were stunned."

Dylan's back dug into the oak slatted headboard, bare feet twitching straight out in front of him. Curious, he glanced down again at the life form the voice seemed to be so impressed with.

A white v-neck hung loosely on his torso, and tan, veiny fingers pulled up the hem where it met with the waistband of black joggers. Clean, unmarked skin stared back. He didn't know what he was expecting, aside from a few bruises at least. A terrorist attack didn't seem like something you walked away from unscathed.

"Are there more of us—you know, out there?"

A silence blanketed the room, and Dylan's heart dropped at the insinuation.

"From what our drones tell us... you were the last one we could have found alive."

Dylan couldn't stop the shaking now. He brought his knees to his chest, surrendering to the realization of the grave reality before him.

"Who exactly is 'we'?" he finally asked after several minutes, scrubbing at his cheeks with dull, bitten nails.

Smirk jumped at the topic, clearly eager to move on. "Modular Enterprises is a global outreach, the helm of the worldwide mission to restore prosperity and equalization to humanity." The voice paused as if waiting for praise. Getting none, they continued. "Your decision to accept our invitation proves your dedication to a new life for all, and in turn, you will be rewarded with unifying our world again."

Dylan's eyes fluttered in confusion. "Back up, I had a choice in this?"

"Of course," Smirk replied, sounding taken aback.

"But you guys rescued me. Said I was the only one left alive—" his head began to ache again. "You mean, I didn't have to come here?"

"Well, ok there wasn't a choice in that particular matter," the voice responded, a soft chuckle leaking through the wall. "We couldn't leave you to die. However, not everyone wants to work with us."

His feet began to drum a beat into the laminate floor, eyes focused on a gnarl in the fake wood.

"And why not?"

The first tinge of annoyance seeped in from the other side of the feed.

"Some souls don't believe in the greater good, and have chosen to believe in their own fear instead," Smirk replied.

"So wait, what exactly are they rejecting?" Dylan asked, accidentally ripping too deeply at a brittle nail. "Or rather, what did I accept?"

Smirk seemed to brighten.

"During a one-year commitment, volunteers of your age group are given the opportunity to serve at Modular Enterprises as we implement a new way of life, communicating with and uniting continents to discover how humanity can survive on this disease-ridden shell of a planet. Upon acceptance of the commitment, the Legacy immediately receives the MW3 vaccine, which ensures immunity to Void after an incubation period of 350 days— hence the time commitment as mentioned earlier."

Dylan froze, and a small trail of blood began to seep down onto his palm.

"Once they are protected against Void," Smirk continued, seemingly unaware. "The final two weeks of a volunteer's tenure is spent giving the vaccine to the Grays— individuals who are either currently infected, have aged out of the Legacy window, or rejected our methods. These souls are being held in separate, quarantined communities here at ME."

The voice spoke so plainly of details that did nothing to calm Dylan's heart rate, and he wondered for the second time that morning how any of this could be real.

"So..." Dylan flailed his hands out towards the walls. "This is all by coercion."

A pregnant pause filled the room, and Dylan pictured more walls thrown up on the other side of the feed.

"We don't stand by that kind of conflict resolution here," Smirk responded. The words were gentle, but Dylan could hear them raking through the teeth of a fake smile. "However, Void has forced our hand. We're chasing the impossible here, and with no precedents, we have to do what we see fit. And we can't let anyone slow us down with their fear."

Dylan felt himself nodding, even as the information still tried to find its place in his memory.

"And I chose to help you?" he asked slowly.

"Yes. We have a licensed psychologist sit down with each Legacy to explain this volunteer program before extending the invitation. Please be assured that you were in your right mind upon your agreement. You may not remember all the details right now because the vaccine you received leaves individuals groggy for the first 24 hours."

Suspicion crawled up his spine.

"Of course, we don't expect you to take our word for this," Smirk said, as if sensing his unease. "So, if you would please find the pen and pad of paper on the nightstand to the right of your bed. I need you to sign your name. This will prove that your dexterity has not been affected by Void, nor the procedure, but it will allow you to compare your signature with the form I will have sent to your pod, proving your consent."

Too overwhelmed to justify resistance, he flopped over in his bed to find the lined notepad.

Without hesitation, his left hand automatically reached for the pen and gripped it between his fingers. Willing them to move, he hovered over the paper in a sudden wave of anxiety.

"I— I don't remember my last name. How can I sign this?"

The voice remained quiet. He felt like he was being tested but was also relieved to be free from instruction. He felt a small wave of independence and tried to turn his mind off. He pressed the pen to the surface and began scrawling a loopy D and before he realized, the lines cascaded into a frenzy of letters, arcing over each other and ending with a squiggled flourish.

Smirk seemed to know when he was done. "Just to verify, can you please read back to me your name?"

He leered at the paper, surprised at how his fingers could operate so efficiently out of sync with his own brain, and read off the name that was slowly becoming more familiar to him the longer his eyes burned into the paper.

"Cavanaugh. Dylan Cavanaugh."

***

SILENCE HAD filled the room again and Dylan sighed as he brought his palm to his forehead and lazily tried to rub life into weary eyes.

Turns out Smirk was actually named Ray and would serve as his facilitator— or FAC—while Dylan grew accustomed to the order of things.

Ray had left on the promise of delivering a copy of Dylan's consent form along with breakfast, both supposedly coming through a large cartridge conspicuously built into his wall.

Now, he slid off the bed, limbs heavy with the weight of information overload. He noticed the oblong, camouflaged sensor that Ray had asked him to find before vanishing back to the vents with a cheery "talk soon!"

Called a Cipher, the machine hung mere inches from the ceiling to the left of his bed, and it would verify the Legacy's reaction to the vaccine, ensuring Void stayed clear of his mind.

The curiously thin device waited for its debut, a small red light blinking on the bottom of the sensor. As instructed earlier, he centered himself underneath the box, planted his feet and waited. Nothing came for several seconds and then there was a robotic voice, distinctly inhuman and unlike Ray.

"Six, August. Cavanaugh, Dylan. Zero."

Everything felt backward here. Ray had explained their new world had chosen to stop recognizing years like the pre-Shift world had. Dylan had balked at this announcement, unease rifling through his edgy limbs at the fact that one of the most fundamentals of life—time—had been rewritten.

"We don't want to acknowledge the horror of the past," the facilitator had explained. "We need a clean slate."

Despite the explanation, Dylan mentally tacked on '2017' to the Cipher's reading as he absently held out his arms and fingers, examining them himself as if to gauge the prognosis— assuming zero to be a good thing. Ray had said this would be a ritual expected of him every morning at wakeup in order to maintain his cleared status while working with Modular.

Or for Modular? He wasn't quite sure yet.

He shrugged off the questions threatening to drown him and walked back to the bed. Without thinking, his arms began pulling at the sheets, grogginess wilting as he let his body react to his surroundings as if he'd always lived there. He pushed the pillows back in place and tucked the sheets in neatly to the sides of the bed frame. He was almost done when his mind seemed to snap awake. There was a crack in one of the pallets at the foot of the bed where the mattress ended. Leaning over, Dylan saw a small hole where something must have splintered through. Staring up at him from the hole was a piece of paper, creased and folded many times.

He wedged two slender fingers through the opening but just as he was about to pull it out from the shadows, he saw bold lettering written in yellow highlighter on the front: **OPEN IN BATHROOM.**

Curiosity burning, he slipped the note into the pocket of the joggers, hiding it from the cameras he now knew must be hidden all around his living space. He finished the bed and then padded across the floor to the bathroom.

Closing the pocket door, he did a cursory glance around the space— a simple vanity with a cupboard adjacent, a subway tiled rain shower and a toilet. Nothing out of the ordinary, until he realized there wasn't a mirror.

Off-putting, but not worth his concern at the moment.

Unfolding the note gently, he found a jagged piece of paper, as if torn from a notepad, filled with a rough scrawl. Dylan turned over to the front and saw a date at the top.

5 August

Dylan, there's no other way to start this but to just jump in. Even if there was, you wouldn't understand half of it. All you really need to know is that it's OK that things feel... off. Actually, I hope it does. They will try to ease you out of it, but that discomfort— your intolerance— is actually your only shot. Our best shot. Don't trust anyone who speaks to you. Only trust what you see.

The letter continued on the back side, but Dylan couldn't focus on the words. The longer he stared, two thoughts prickled at the edges of his mind.

Someone had been in this room to hide that note in such a precarious way, casting immediate doubt on what Ray told him about the pod being isolated. This meant someone had not only found a way in through those walls, but also a way out of them.

Second, and much more confusing, he realized the letter had given him that coveted feeling of familiarity that he'd been searching for since opening his eyes that morning. Clutching the note in a closed fist, he stumbled back over to the nightstand, retrieved the notepad he'd written his name on earlier and brought both back to the bathroom. His eyes darted between the two pieces of paper, trying to find a mistake.

But there wasn't any other explanation. The loopy handwriting on both sets of paper were his own.

THREE

THE WALLS seemed to be getting closer.

It had been nearly one month since Dylan had woken up in a fog at Modular Enterprises, and he was still waiting for it to lift. Through all his years of chasing clarity in pursuit of the truth, he had never found either to be so evasive.

There was one comfort. Slowly, memories of his life before the alleged attack had begun to return in small snapshots. His small cubicle at the newspaper where he could almost smell stale pizza crusts next to mounds of articles waiting to be fact checked. The exposed brick of his small loft where he had lived by himself. The straggly beard of the homeless man on the corner by his favorite coffeeshop.

The details popped in his memory with vivid color, but faces remained in shadows. While at first disconcerting, he soon realized his mind was just coping the only way it knew how. It had always been his tendency to dwell on the reality in front of him, bleak as it may be. This was no different. He'd seen the census records, been told, in the gentlest of tones, how he was the last living representative of his Cavanaugh family. A few cousins remained on the Europe installation, but he'd never been close with them.

Anyone he'd ever cared about was gone, and he would've clung to the harsh reality of that logic— if not for the note.

He had hoped the backside of the crumpled paper would bring more clarity, but it had only been more cryptic.

If you haven't remembered yet, your full name is Dylan James Cavanaugh, born July 31, 1995 in Brooklyn, New York. You'll see the forms, they got those parts right. But that's where the truth stops. By now, your FAC has already told you about Void, the noble effort you signed up for, and how Modular is fixing the world. And sure, those are all technically true. It's how they got you in the first place. It's the lies of omission that you need to be worried about. They say there is no life outside these walls. They say unity is the only way to fix the planet. But it's just a perversion of the truth.

They're not fixing the planet, they're re-creating it. Molding it from ground zero. But you can't create something that still exists.

I can't tell you everything. You're going to have to figure some things out on your own, but I needed to get to you before they did. The echoes are tools. Weapons. Ignore the screens—when you can. Those will overpower any shadows of true memory you still have, and undo all of the work it took us to get to this point. I have to be vague but know that change— real change— is coming. Be patient. Until then, hold on to anything that brings familiarity. Keep making your bed. Keep hold of every dream, and recall its details every night before you fall asleep. I couldn't stop this Turnover, but you have 365 days to stop them forever.

The Artist
P.S. Darkness glows bright when put against the light.

Dylan had committed every word to memory that first day, and then shoved the crumpled note into the top drawer of his nightstand, refusing to bring it out again. He couldn't deny the identical handwriting, but as the month progressed and memories began to return, he still had no recollection of writing those words.

He'd longed to talk about it with someone, but considering the note's warning of his FAC, it was a mystery he had decided to keep to himself for the time being.

He just hoped an answer would come soon.

***

THE POD had a slight chill to the air and he shuffled his bare feet across the cool hardwood floor to the wardrobe, rifling through the collection of gray, navy and beige garments. As he sifted to the back of the rack, he lazily thumbed the sleeve of a checkered red and black flannel. A stark contrast to the rest of the garments, he'd flicked past it every other morning, but suddenly the material looked very comforting. Wiggling into it, however, ignited a trail of goosebumps along the back of his arms. Déjà vu washed over him, but true to form, the sensation withheld any clarity as to why.

Feeling disjointed, Dylan rolled up the oversized sleeves and mentally added the experience to the other unexplainable fragments of thought he kept juggling in his mind. They had become a massive pile of bowling pins, and he was struggling to keep each one in the air without letting even one slip by, forgotten. He slid the armoire closed and began to run through his daily ritual of questions.

Why couldn't he remember writing that note? More so, was he to believe that he had actually written it himself? Perhaps it had been forged by Modular staff. A way to test his brain function and reasoning skills. It had been dated one day prior to the date Ray, and the official paperwork, placed him in the pod, so by refusing to bring it up, he may be making matters worse for himself. Of course there was also the chance it was from someone else entirely. A person close enough to him to know his handwriting, and use it to make him doubt Modular's intentions—

He began to spiral, his thoughts careening in all directions like falling bowling pins. Knowing he couldn't catch any of them, he switched focus onto the one control variable: the echo screens, as Ray liked to refer to them.

Over the last few weeks, he had allowed himself glances at the ultrathin monitors on the walls sidelining his bed. Dylan hadn't given them too much attention, partly in obedience to the note's warning, but more so because the pictures that flashed across them were rather unremarkable. Most seemed to be a version of outreach propaganda, flashing up pictures of happy figures donning rainbow-colored tee shirts and holding up fingers twisted into a W and a backwards E. The mantra of Modular Enterprises was then often draped across the images somewhere: *WE are the legacy.*

The displays changed every few days, all at different times. Once, his peripherals had happened to catch a screen transition. All promises of heeding the note had evaporated into beautiful swirls of orange, blue and purple as he watched a new image take over the screen. He had let himself get closer to the abstract image, pulled in by its disorienting brushstrokes, determined to see the true image.

And then, suddenly, there it was. A bird in flight, colors cascading together to make the creature appear like it had been flying through the frame. Eyes burning, he had turned away, eyes cast towards his bed, but the imprint of the vivid bird suddenly echoed back before him, wings appearing to flap the more he blinked at the stark white sheets.

It was then that he remembered the coffee cup exercise Ray had made him do on his first day. He had been so easily manipulated, and unease crawled up his back like ivy reaching for the light.

He'd avoided the screens ever since.

Instead, he kept his mind sharp by dwelling on the crumbs of memory that continued to pepper in like rain falling in the desert. He let headlines and sidebars of countless articles flick through his mind on repeat, the stories blurring together like a mirage until his head throbbed.

The only detail that never fogged was the date stamped at the top of each paper, which never went farther than the summer months of 2016.

He yearned to know what might have happened to him in those missing months before he was rescued.

"We wish we could tell you," Ray had responded the first time he'd asked. "All we know is where we found you— in a remote section of the Pine Barrens. But that's what is important. *We found you.*"

He could only conjure one memory of those skinny green giants that lined the coast of New Jersey—and it was one he had spent much of his life trying to forget.

"The past is over," Ray had said that day. "Only forward. If you were outside these walls, it was horror. It's best not to dwell on what might have happened."

He still had questions, and while he had found Ray to be a wonderful echo chamber, he struggled to trust the one and only voice that tittered through the walls each morning at 7:20 like clockwork.

The splintered wood still caught his eye every morning as he tucked in the corners of the sheets. He had wondered if Modular had recycled old beds from before the Shift, but when he asked, Ray was adamant.

"While we do pride ourselves on using as many environmentally-friendly resources as are available, Legacies are far too important to be given recycled items. VIP treatment for you guys, twenty-four seven."

Just another question to add to the list, and even though it was growing alarmingly long, he wasn't too concerned. He had always found comfort in finding the answers himself—he'd spent his career on it. Eventually, the truth always came out. Black and white.

Looking around the room now, however, Dylan was suddenly aware of how much gray surrounded him. A restless energy surged up his limbs and he began tidying up the space. Confidence oozed from order, his father had always said. Dylan could use a little more of both.

A burst of static suddenly crackled through his room, making Dylan drop a wrinkled crew neck shirt back onto the chair. His eyes darted around the room, as if expecting someone to walk through some unseen door.

Ray cackled against the walls with a flourish of uncharacteristic peppiness.

"Good afternoon, Dylan! To celebrate your first month here, I have a present for you. I'm patching you through to a fellow compatriot who arrived a few weeks before you did. You both are following the same schedule and making wonderful progress, so I expect you both to have plenty to discuss."

The FAC chirped off suddenly without any means of introduction between the two strangers.

"Roll call, anyone there?" a voice called out.

Dylan flinched. He hadn't realized how dependent he had become on hearing the FAC's voice, and this new voice, with its Southern twang tones twirling among the airwaves, felt like a betrayal.

"Present," Dylan called back stiffly. "Or, you know, whatever smug thing I used to say when I thought I was so funny in middle school."

An approving grunt came back. "Nice one. 'Absent' was mine." A short pause. "The name's Dewey."

Dylan managed a small grin and looked down at his hands he now just noticed were gnarled together and beginning to turn white. He took a breath, untwisted his fingers from each other and rubbed them on his black jeans.

"Dylan. So... some celebration, I guess. Survive one month in isolation and we get new voices in our heads."

Dewey snorted. "Beats talking to the walls. Pro tip, stone walls are the best of friends. Agree with everything I say."

Charm leaked out of the walls like an easy flowing stream, and, disarmed, Dylan leaned back in the chair, content to float away with this fluid voice.

"Dually noted," he offered, smiling through the words. "So what do they have you doing here, Dewey?"

"Translating communications," the Legacy said. "My background is linguistics."

"Jealous. What kind of comms?"

"Mostly just between here and the European installations. I don't actually speak to anyone over there— not yet, at least, they tell me. Just decoding foreign messages and whatnot."

"Why would they need decoding?" Dylan asked, taken aback.

"I assume it's a precaution. I think people are still worried about the terrorist threat."

Dylan tried to think back to Ray's explanation of the Shift. "But who could even be alive, if not within Modular's facilities?"

"I dunno. Maybe it's good ol' fashioned spy stuff they're worried about. Traitors within the walls," Dewey said, voice wavering as if telling a ghost story by candlelight.

Dylan found himself sucked into a vortex of more questions, but his compatriot got there first.

"What about you? What they got you doin'?"

"Coding," Dylan responded, already bored with the topic.

"Alright, Brainiac," Dewey said approvingly. "You one of those dark basement dweller types? You must feel right at home here."

Dylan had to laugh as he stared at the gray stone around him. "No, not at all. I don't actually code. I sift through blocks of it searching for inconsistencies and then report them. I couldn't even tell you what the codes are about."

Dylan felt an overwhelming feeling of inadequacy rise up out of the silence. "I used to be a fact checker for the *Manhattan Herald*," he said, cheeks burning. "I guess they just wanted my detailed eyes."

"Alright now," Dewey responded brightly. "The Herald though, that's no joke. My podunk hometown even gets that one."

Dylan shrugged off the praise. "I enjoyed what I did. I just wish I could do more now. Finding missing slashes and parentheses just doesn't feel super helpful at the moment."

"Hey, our impact will come at the end of our commitment. Our bodies will restore humanity— you get to be a part of that. What could be more helpful than saving the world?"

Dylan had to laugh. "I'm sorry, did Ray click back on?"

A choking noise reverberated off the walls. "You're right. We need a break from Modular talk," Dewey acquiesced. "So what have you found to do when you're not working in the pod?"

Dylan thought back over the last month. There was plenty of online entertainment on Modular's network, but his favorite hobby had been testing the limits of the facility's resource distribution service, DLVRD. It had become something of a game after he had discovered some restrictions, and he listed them off now to his new friend.

"I have a list going of what I haven't been able to get. Cameras, a radio, handheld mirrors, curtains—"

"Hold up," Dewey interrupted. "What kind of feng shui you have going on over there that you need curtains?"

Dylan had to laugh. "Don't judge. I'll do anything to make this room feel more livable, and that distorted light coming in through the window is starting to mess with me."

"Dang, they gave you a window room?" Dewey said, startled.

Dylan bit his lip, feeling awkward. "I mean, you can't see anything. The window is really textured and any light that even comes in is this creepy foggy color."

A soft sigh was all that echoed back.

"For the record, you can't get live seafood either," Dylan said, trying to lighten the mood.

"Shoot. I'd kill for one of those aquariums with all the lobsters," Dewey said, perking up. "You know, like in the grocery stores? Not even to eat. I'd just spend the day watching them prance around."

"My thought exactly."

A soft silence opened up.

"Ok, I lied, I want to eat them."

Dylan snickered. "The food isn't so bad here, though."

"You're not from the south are you?" Dewey asked. "Cause there ain't anyone homecookin' here behind these walls."

"Listen," Dylan said, a grin tugging at his cheeks. It felt good to be so at ease again. "I'm a single male in his 20s who had been living half his life in a one-bedroom loft in Queens, and the other half in a gray padded cubicle with peanuts filling up the drawers. Anything that doesn't arrive in an instant packet is a step up in my book."

Dylan waited for the chirp of laughter, but an awkward silence hung in the stillness. He brought a stubby nail to his lips and waited, the chair squeaking to the beat of his wiggling foot.

"Is that allowed?" Dewey asked tentatively, like a nervous toddler found with their hand in the cookie jar.

"Is what allowed?" Dylan felt a nervous tingle pulse in his fingertips.

"Using gender identifiers."

Dylan felt his forehead scrunch together, fingers tapping on the armrest of the chair. He considered his last words. Had he said something wrong? Dewey raced to fill the silence.

"I'm still getting used to watching my gender usage, but between you and me, I'm just avoiding pronouns altogether. Easier that way," the Legacy tittered.

Dylan recalled the last month, and only now thinking about it, he suddenly realized that neither him nor Ray had ever used gendered pronouns in their conversations. Dylan felt like he'd just stumbled off a circus ride.

"This is so weird. I never realized—I mean, it's been an entire month," Dylan said, unable to connect a coherent thought. He conjured up Ray's voice in his mind. "I question everything, so it's strange that the idea didn't even come up..." he faded away, lost in thought.

"You're talking about Ray, right?" Dewey asked quietly.

"Yeah," Dylan said. "I never asked who...what... they were. I mean, I didn't even care. The idea never entered my mind."

"Eight days in, I was so desperate for human contact, I remember seeing a cute face on one of the echo screens and thinking, 'Wow, which pod are they in?'" Dewey cut off, as if embarrassed. "And it was only then that I suddenly had the thought if they were male or female. Like you said—the idea had just never occurred to me."

A light scratching filled the silence, like nails against a bald scalp. Dylan straightened out his back and eased out of the chair, eager to pace the room and get his blood pumping to keep up with his racing mind.

"Ray is a woman... right?" Dylan said tentatively.

A beat. "Yeah, I think so," Dewey replied, quieter now. "But I think I'm breaking a rule admitting that."

He could still hear the tension in his peer's voice and decided not to push any further questions. That didn't affect his own assumptions though.

"I dunno," Dylan offered. "But I bet some group out there would love to recruit you for their next march."

"I bet," the Legacy huffed. "You know, I honestly miss watching the news. I groaned every time it came on, knowing it would only be bad. But now... I even miss the bad stuff."

Dylan's head snapped upwards, as if it would sharpen his hearing. "What?"

"I mean, I'm not this weird sicko—" Dewey stammered, backpedaling. "I just—I guess I miss conflict."

"And what do you think got us here?" Dylan replied sharply, instantly regretting the sneer that boomeranged off the walls.

"But that was a sudden, apocalyptic event. It's not like there was a fight that brought it on, or some way to prepare ourselves." Dewey sighed. "What I'm saying is that I miss the plain stuff. The normal ups and downs of life. I mean, come on. You've read the books on the shelves. Seen the memories trickle back in." Dylan's eyes glazed over the dusty shelf in the corner he'd been avoiding.

"There's no point in picking fights and sides over how to govern a world in ruin," Dewey said. "The one goal for everyone right now is to just stay alive. And if you ain't a Legacy, you're working day and night to ensure the Legacies stay alive long enough to give you your shot. We have to live, and everyone else knows it," Dewey said with what Dylan imagined was a shrug of the shoulders. "The world has only two sides now. The lucky, and the ones working for them."

Dylan nodded absently, and after a few moments, the fellow Legacy switched topics, regaling their feed with stories of serving in the Middle East. Dylan half-listened, stewing on the implications his compatriot had just shared.

Why hadn't he come to the same inferences earlier? The books and echo screens seemed to have influenced much of his peer's statements, and Dylan guessed that Dewey had never found a note warning about either of the tools.

Despite avoiding those, however, Dylan should have considered the ripple effect on the world. His own selfishness now cruelly apparent, Dylan let his imagination run free. Of course Void had affected everything. Not just his own brain, but class systems, governments and regimes had been surgically ripped apart by a group of terrorists who were most likely all dead now, too. Foreign relations, politics and economies all over the planet had been decimated. What horror had he seen that he couldn't remember?

A snapshot of his mother jerked into his mind, and Dylan clenched his fists. No, he wouldn't go down that trail. He snapped his attention back to the drawling voice still leaking somewhere through the wall.

The two of them chattered on for another twenty minutes, exchanging childhoods and reminiscing on their pre-Void lives. A Southern Alabama kid, Dewey had lived a charmed, fluid kind of life, spending days among the reeds of muddy rivers with a buddy that, reading from Dewey's somber tone, Dylan could only assume hadn't made it.

On his turn, Dylan recalled the concrete jungle of his childhood— regaling Dewey with stories of the high rises, hot dog stands and underground musicians that had colored his days spent as an only child in his parents' Brooklyn apartment.

Conversation started to simmer and Dylan stifled a yawn.

"So, you think they're gonna let us talk to anyone else today?" Dewey asked.

"I'll welcome anything to help me feel more familiar with this place."

"Oh, sure. More voices in our head. That'll keep us sane."

"Hey, it's only for a year, right?" he said, before shifting his voice to sound upbeat and inspiring. "Then we change the world."

Dewey chuckled, but then a familiar voice broke it off.

"Alright Dylan, that's time. I'm afraid I have to let you both get back to work now," Ray said in an airy voice, and like a switch, he was suddenly aware how feminine it sounded—especially after so abruptly following Dewey's deep tones. "There will be a routine questionnaire in your inbox— please complete it before you report back into work. Talk soon!"

A soft click and an eerie silence nestled into every corner of the room as Dylan found himself jarringly alone with his thoughts once again. He picked up the pacing again, shuffling his bare feet along a well-worn path between the kitchenette to the chair, beside his bed, and back again, rehashing the interaction over in his mind. He had enjoyed the social engagement more than he'd have imagined. Talking with Ray had always felt more like a teacher/student relationship, whereas with Dewey, there was camaraderie.

But it hadn't been the conversation with Dewey, enlightening as the Legacy's thoughts on the new social order were, that now prickled at Dylan's thoughts. It was Ray.

He had grown confident in his ability to hear the in and outputs of the FAC's feed, and come to think of it now, he had never heard the soft chirp that signaled Ray's exit after introducing the pair.

The FAC had been there the entire time—lurking somewhere behind the walls, listening.

Tack on personal freedom to the list of things Void had stolen from him.

He neared the kitchenette again, noticing his coffee cup on the counter that had been forgotten in the morning's clean sweep. No, his freedoms weren't completely gone. He could resist anything they asked him to do, evident by his refusal to make echoes or take a single book off the shelf. And he was still here. His free will remained intact.

They were just hindering it.

Small liberties gone unnoticed before the Shift now sparked longing in Dylan. Mediocrities like combing a wild hair back into place had been rendered useless when they shaved his head for "sanitization" purposes. Not to mention the apparent extermination of mirrors. He missed the beauty of closing his eyes as he basked in a natural ray of sunshine, instead of having to watch a distorted sunset filter in through a blurred window. Even tying his shoes—the first notion of independence he'd ever learned in life—was now negated because shoes weren't needed in this sterile, isolated environment. Pieces of himself were slipping away, and not just the part of his memory lost to Void. The disease stole his mind, and it would seem Modular was slowly robbing the rest.

The next eleven months could not go by fast enough.

FOUR

RESIDENT 0018 was quiet. Too quiet.

The Legacy had scored uncommonly high in each of the pre-Void assessments, indicating a strong work ethic and high tolerance of solitary workspaces. A reserved soul, prone to internally processing every struggle.

They had known this. And in the beginning, the resident's reservations had served as a sign rather than a threat. After all, social meekness was a common denominator for all who were granted access into the Elite Candidate wing. Coupled with an elevated white blood cell count, of course.

But no matter how equable a soul might be, waking up to a drastically altered world that they cannot remember should be terrifying.

The success of Modular Enterprises hinged on it.

Fear was the catalyst to it all, opening the door to questions that could quickly be alleviated with gentle answers by a trained facilitator. These navigators walked a delicate wire, bringing their residents into a jarring reality without inciting panic. FACS were designed to be anchors for their Legacies from the very beginning. The bond they shared in that first conversation, as fragile bodies awoke from the drug-induced haze, was one that could not be broken.

When explaining the job to idolizing friends who worked in lower positions at ME, a facilitator spoke fondly of their role, making this connection seem like a sentimental byproduct. But the truth was spoken reverently and only among the FACS themselves: it was a blood bond. A doubting Legacy was a lost Legacy, and like all good navigators, the captain goes down with the ship.

It was simple, really. A world in ruin could not wait for people to fail.

When a Legacy was lost, someone had to pay. While the mind of an uncooperative resident was useless, their bodies were not, so the sacrifice fell on the FACs. The expendable ones.

It's why most of them felt like they deserved a pay raise.

But money wasn't on the mind as the most experienced facilitator at Modular clicked out of Resident 0018's pod feed and headed for the Overseer's office. Seniority allowed the FAC to walk through the inner gates unquestioned. Hooking a white mask around her ears, the compatriot came to the familiar door and hesitated, taking one more glance down at the tablet. Finding solace in the irrefutable numbers.

The backbone of Modular Enterprises snapped to attention as the office door hummed open, gray eyes on green.

"Do come in, Ray," the Overseer said placidly from behind their desk, peering over tortoise shell glasses clinging to the tip of a sharp, alabaster nose.

"Look Easton, I'm sorry to barge in again but I really think you need to see these new numbers."

The Overseer sighed, pulling out a transparent face shield from a drawer before pushing back from the keyboard and swiveling towards the FAC.

"We've already gone over this. The numbers aren't in the dangerous region. You're being too sensitive," Easton said tiredly, crossing their arms for battle anyway. "Given your history—"

"Excuse me?" the FAC blinked accusingly at the Overseer. "This isn't personal. The analysis shows Dylan is regressing—"

"Protocol, please," Easton interjected, glancing furtively over Ray's shoulder towards the open door. "We're preparing for Equinox every day, and the work starts now. You can't let this get personal. No names. No pronouns."

Ray just nodded, a quick shake of the head. She had been slow to conform to the gender theories of ME, her mind still struggling to process the change. She had to fake it better if she wanted to keep her status here.

"Right, sorry." She flipped the tablet around and thrust it onto the desk. "Just look at this. The data shows the resident is not even close to performing how they should be."

The Overseer untucked a hand from the crook of an elbow, holding it out in a lazy invite for the FAC to continue. Ray surged ahead.

"I just received survey answers from the resident's initial engagement session. The disparity between the two compatriots' responses is pretty alarming."

Above the mask, Ray leveled green daggers at the Overseer, imploring the compatriot to share the concern.

"0018 simply does not seem to be cognitive of our ideals here," the FAC continued. "When approached with soul equality, the resident blanched and seemed to have little to no awareness. As mentioned before, the resident rarely asks questions and according to visual cues, the echo screens are not making an impression."

Ray paused to adjust positions, noting Easton's eyes beginning to glaze. She dug tired toes deeper into unforgiving shoes. "I have reason to believe they are refusing to make echoes."

Doughy eyes snapped back to attention.

"Refusing?"

"There have been no long engagements recorded, and in conversation, the resident could barely keep up with the podmate's order of discussion. 0018 seemed baffled by topics that should have been addressed by now, if they were aligning with curriculum, as the other resident has proven to do," Ray replied.

"Who did you pair them with?"

"0017."

Bony fingers grazed across pale lips, Easton remaining quiet a little too long for Ray's patience. The FAC drummed two fingers against the back of the tablet to show it.

"Legacies are people, Ray," Easton finally said. "We can't predict how each one will react to their surroundings. And we can't discount the... trauma... this particular resident endured that first morning, if you remember."

Of course Ray remembered. She had dropped her guard, and it had cost them. They both knew it.

"We have to allow for a learning curve," Easton continued, eyes flitting away graciously. "This is just the first month. The curve always flattens after the next stage."

"Perhaps, but no other resident's numbers have been this disparaging from the curve," the FAC shot back.

Easton held up their hands in mock surrender. "Let's just wait to see how the resident responds to the first memory echo. That's scheduled to transition tomorrow, yes?"

She nodded.

"We also still have the Shriek, which has always proven most effective in theory retention," Easton reminder her, their head tilting down and sideways as if assuaging a small child. "In the meantime, let's keep 0018 out of any further engagement sessions. Can't let them influence the others."

She felt chided, and unsure of what to say, Ray shrugged. She knew Easton could see her doubt but she didn't care to hide it.

The Overseer sighed, rubbing at the lines prematurely creasing their forehead.

"Look, Ray. I treat you differently than the rest of the FACs, let alone the entire team, you know that."

She averted Easton's gaze, knowing what was coming but unable to flee from it.

"I have full trust in you because of what you endured, and Modular is better because of it. But I fear that your past experience has caused you too much—" Easton paused, and Ray could see the gears turning as they searched for the least shame-inciting word. "—delicacy, regarding the Legacies."

"Delicate?" She huffed, a derisive laugh escaping her lips. "My success here should be evidence of the very opposite," Ray said through clenched teeth. "Being a woman doesn't mean I'm a fragile shell, ready to crack at the first cry of a resident."

"I did not say that, nor did I mean it as a weakness," the Overseer replied hastily. "You know I don't see gender like how the old society has defined it." Their eyes flashed. "I'm disappointed that you would even think that about me."

Ray stiffened but said nothing.

"I just don't want—" Easton broke off, voice hitching. Ray met their gaze again. "I don't want you to put yourself in a compromising position. Before is necessary."

Gray eyes seemed to flick from sentiment to steel in the space of the last three words.

The FAC forged on without pausing to analyze the shift. "If oo18 is rejecting, or even just doubting, the process, we can't afford to discredit the threat just because it seems too early. Right now, the part is bigger than the whole, and being that part's facilitator, I am willing to submit to the process," Ray said, eyes flashing more bravery than the rest of her body actually felt.

"Your devotion to this program continues to go unmatched," Easton acknowledged, the flattery of the words clashing with their hardened tone. "But we can't afford to lose the ground we've already made when the stakes are this high. Not when the concern is so premature. You understand, Compatriot Drake?"

The sudden shift to the FAC's proper name was a power move, and trading cold stares, they both knew it. Thrown by the formality, Ray glanced down at the undeniable numbers and data, comfortingly resolute, now blinking rapidly on the screen like a glitch. Realizing the pads of her fingers were deflecting her frustration onto the device, she eased the grip and took a breath as the numbers returned solidly to the screen.

"Protocol is protocol, Compatriot Hill," she volleyed back, returning the atypical vernacular between the two senior level colleagues. Stormy eyes flickered as the name landed, but Easton just squared their shoulders as if to welcome more. "That's what you told me my first day walking into this place, swearing never to pity me over the trauma I had suffered," she said, refusing to blink, knowing that any bit of darkness now would revive the unwelcome memory lying so close to the surface.

"I was a shell when you found me there. My mind was gone, a beating heart the only difference from the rest of those souls in that place. I begged you to leave me," Ray said, boring her eyes into the Overseer's as theirs flitted away. "But you had other plans, as always. You said you needed me, that together— that we— could bring back the light."

Ray squeezed her eyes shut, just for a moment, to reign in the frustration. "I always hated the tag name you gave me. How it reminded me every day of that place. But you said it with such pride. You still do. You revel in the fact that you found a ray of light in Nox."

"You didn't deserve—" Easton's voice came stammering off the floorboards as gray eyes remained focused on the floor. "Nox didn't deserve to keep you."

"Then if you still believe that," Ray paused, wishing she could pull up some kind of emotion, if only to make Easton feel her conviction. "Believe me when I tell you there's a problem here. You can't serve successfully as Overseer if you deny a credible threat in order to maintain forward progress."

Easton looked resigned, a surrender on the horizon. "You realize I can't— I won't— save you again, Elle," they finally replied, quiet words running the path their gaze drilled into the tile floor. Again, she just nodded.

Easton tilted their head back up, eyes softening a fraction.

"Any update from the Infected Wing?"

Ray bit her lip. She didn't want to think about Infected Pod 9B. Her success at her job hinged on her ability to forget about that pod and its inhabitant.

"Nothing new," she said.

"It's such a shame," Easton said, momentarily flicking their gaze over the maze of spines filling up a floor-to-ceiling bookshelf. Ray took advantage of the moment and averted her own eyes, trying to quell the emotion threatening to betray her.

"I'll keep you posted," she offered.

"You always do." And then the Overseer turned back to their desk, sending Ray back to her studio with a silent dismissal.

FIVE

DYLAN LET the lead scratch against the paper as yet another black and white spindly tree came to life before him. In his downtime, he had taken to making sketches of the Modular facility based on the description Ray trickled into their conversations.

Mimicking an evergreen tree, the design included a wide base with "branches" shooting upwards, each man-made limb serving as a hallway with multiple living pods budding on all sides, allowing for easy additions as other Legacies had been found. He glanced up towards his opaque window, a ghostly bluish gray leaking through, and he found himself wondering again what lie on the other side.

"You're not missing much, I'm afraid," Ray had said when he'd asked about the textured glass. "Without anything to keep it in check, smog has taken over so much of Earth's atmosphere that there's nothing to see except streaks of orange gray haze most of the day. We felt it was in our residents' best interest to keep the view ambigous." Ray had seemed to smile then. "Less threatening that way."

He shook his head now, glancing back down at his paper. He didn't mind much. The wonder only made him more eager to finish his commitment—if only for the chance to see this new world for himself, without anything standing inbetween.

He pushed the draft pad aside, massaging his cramping hand as he headed for the bathroom, but he stopped short.

One of his screens had changed. The bird image had been replaced. Sunset swirls of color had morphed into a human profile and without thinking, Dylan found himself walking towards it. A strong jawline and pointed nose of a silhouette made up the shadowy foreground, the profile facing the same direction the bird had been flying. As if the triumphant creature had finally broken free from its frame and the figure was watching it go.

Now less than a foot's distance of the picture, a soft wooded scent clashed against the sterility of his room. His senses seemed to veer off course all at once and he clenched his eyes shut in confusion. Brisk air snuck through his nostrils as a vivid image came to life before him: a wooded clearing, the ground peppered with pine needles and dead leaves. A fire crackled, and Dylan whirled around to find it.

Somewhere in the recesses of his brain, he knew his feet remained rooted to the hardwood floor of his pod, but keeping his eyes shut, Dylan could see this entirely new environment as if he were standing at a mall kiosk testing out VR goggles. Except it wasn't a new environment, Dylan realized. All at once, his senses ignited as the fullness of the memory dawned on him. Lightheaded, Dylan squinted at the silhouetted figure in his mind's eye, the one he'd just seen from the picture, and now, standing in that wooded clearing, he realized there was no question. Heart burning in his chest, his pulse radiated through every artery in his neck and he couldn't stop the word swelling in his throat.

"Dad!"

Backlit with the haze of a dusky, purple sky, his father stood facing out towards the clouds, without a nod of awareness in Dylan's direction. He understood then that his body could not actually be there in that moment, but it didn't mean the memory would play out any differently.

Body and mind warred against each other. He felt the pressure of his eyelids still clamped down tight, while in his mind, he felt the softness of dirt underneath his feet. He wanted to get out. Open his eyes. Be free from the memory he'd shoved away in a box, but his senses had been thrust into overdrive. He could do nothing but remain in the exact same spot and helplessly watch the memory unfold.

Charcoal gray clouds loomed larger, closer. They rolled in black as midnight and all too quickly, the oranges of the fire mixed with the white-purple flash of lightning. His father's face turned then, the weathered smile lines stretching taut as he finally acknowledged his son, yelling to get in the truck.

Dylan knew he stood in the same spot as his eight-year-old self, but unlike fifteen years ago, he couldn't move. He saw, for the first time, the tree sway. He smelled the charred bark and saw the flash of his father's checkered flannel shirt. Then he heard the tree snap.

"Dylan?"

A familiar voice snuck into his conscience and the surprise of it unglued Dylan's lids, the drum of his own heart replacing the sound of the spitting fire. Dazed, he spun on his heels, looking for the owner of the voice, before he suddenly came to. Pale gray walls shrouded him like a cold blanket and he realized where he stood.

Dylan staggered back and sat on the edge of his bed. "Hey, Ray," he said dazedly, sick to his stomach.

"Are you alright?" the facilitator asked, tentative.

Dylan blinked a few times, raking a hand across the baby hairs re-emerging on his scalp. "Yeah. Fine— I'm fine," Dylan stammered, wondering if this was all a game. The minute he'd dropped his guard and engaged with a screen—the one thing she'd urged him to do for more than a month—and now, suddenly she was here. Coincidences didn't happen at Modular Enterprises.

"Why are you here?" he asked cooly, making a show of checking his watch. "It's well past 7:20."

"The Cipher is programmed to sound an alarm to the medical team when the resident's heart rate spikes over a certain number," Ray said, caution to her voice. "I dropped in to check on you."

Dylan peered over his shoulder at the traitorous machine, a small red light blinking in its stoic corner.

"No other reason?"

A slight hesitation hung in the still air.

"I'm your facilitator, Dylan. I care about what happens to you."

Breath normalizing, he arched his back and sat upright. It seemed Ray wanted him to lead this conversation.

"Tell me about these echo screens again," he said, trying to hide the grimace as he offered the olive branch. She wouldn't leave unless he mentioned something about the screen, and he was good at tiptoeing. "Why are they so important?"

A soft creak leaked over the speakers, and he could imagine Ray lounging back in some leather chair, peering out a misty window over a barren landscape.

Or maybe she stared at gray walls, too.

"Through echoes, we reignite imprints of the world that Void stole from us," the facilitator said. "The screens depict images specifically designed for each person—to recover that soul's understanding of what happened, and begin the process of letting go."

"What's wrong with what it used to be? Once we all have the vaccine, why can't we just go back to normal?"

"The world as we once knew it has been erased, Dylan. We cannot just go back. There is no back," Ray responded softly.

When Dylan didn't reply, Ray hastily brought the topic back to the screens, explaining how they were meant to be experienced by each of his senses. This feature strengthened the power of the echo upon the brain, but was not overpowering enough to stimulate the mind at all hours of the day. Dylan peered closer now and noticed three dots the size of pinpricks at the top of the frame.

"Our team of researchers designed the frames to emit mists of air containing highly-concentrated scents that trigger a person's memory," Ray was saying now, and he jolted to attention.

"So, what, I'm just getting Febreezed every few hours?"

Ray snickered. "Not quite. There are motion sensors in the frame that trigger only when a resident is close enough, releasing a scent synonymous with the image you are seeing. We try to stimulate a variety of memories that generally appeal to our Legacies. Having only one generation to work with, we were able to guess what sorts of content would be most influential. Everything from TV shows to notable historical figures to learning styles, we have factored it all in," Ray explained.

Being deprived of physical interaction, Dylan had begun to marvel at how nuanced a voice could be, and Ray's was absolutely beaming now, clearly proud of the organization she worked for.

"In these first weeks of transition, our team ensures that the images aren't too overwhelming, so we like to keep the images broad and, well, soothing. Natural environments, landscapes, animals, etcetera. The kind of images that can reach out to anyone and spark a memory of peace."

A cynical huff simmered just behind his lips and he fought to reign it in. As a rule, most people wouldn't associate the image of a beautiful forest with a traumatic experience. He still had no desire to talk about it with Ray now, but he had to admit the explanation had cut down some of his unease. The memory in the woods had been haunting enough, but he relaxed knowing it wasn't some sick plant by Modular as a way to instill terror.

"Every time you utilize these screens to create an echo," Ray continued, "you are reminding your brain of what the world used to be like. We want to create a version of that world again, but we must also do it through the lens of what we endured. Which is why we cannot just forget the horror, either."

They're not fixing the planet, they're remaking it.

A flash of tension erupted across his spine as the note's words flitted across his mind.

"How do I know that this is what the world was really like?"

"You will, Dylan. Your mind is your fact checker," Ray said, and he could almost hear the smirk playing across those lips again. "All echoes are doing are returning the memories to you."

Ray's voice dripped with persuasion, but glancing over at the nightstand, he knew it would never, fully, work on him.

"Clever technology here. I'm impressed," he said, surprised to find the words to not be a total lie.

"Is there anything else?" Ray said slowly, fishing. He didn't bite.

"I don't think so. I actually have a bit of work to catch up on."

"Ah, very well. Talk soon."

The click sounded and Dylan imagined a painted smile dripping down a disappointed face, like a brand new crayon melting under a hazy orange sun.

He smirked at the thought.

SIX

HER HEAD jerked in her hand, green eyes snapping awake. Elle glanced at the time blinking idly in the corner of her laptop screen, the palm of her hand muffling a startled yelp.

She quickly tidied up the documents scattered on the desk, sorting as she went. Finally, she sat back in the chair, allowing herself a quick breath as she stared at Resident 0017's neat pile in front of her.

It had been two weeks since implementing the Shriek for her group of Legacies, and not all of them were responding well.

Then again, she wasn't responding too well, either. December had rolled in with a wave of new losses in the infected wing and all she'd wanted to do was curl up under the scratchy blanket on her office cot and will the rest of the year away.

She swirled her mug around, the tea bag dancing in the liquid that had long grown cold. Her eyes found the time again, and sighing, she turned to her monitor. No FAC could see a visual of their resident's room until they plugged in and were on-air. In this moment, however, she regretted ever fighting for that rule to be put into the Modular code of conduct.

Elle slid the headphones over her ears and cracked her neck. Moving the mouthpiece down, she took a breath and pressed engage.

Holding the breath captive, she waited a beat, hoping the subtle click of her feed would save her from being the initial shock to the ears. The Alabama native lounged in a desk chair, two fingers at the keyboard navigating a character on one of the Network's popular computer games. Elle silently moved the mouthpiece away from her lips and breathed out. She twisted her neck one more time, set a smile on her face and moved a little closer to her monitor so she could see when the tiny figure on the Legacy's screen was out of harm's way. Knowing when to enter a pod was a game in itself.

"Good morning, Dewey," she said, engaging her FAC voice and shifting into her Ray headspace. To be most effective in her job at ME, she'd learned to split herself into two people.

Dark, bulky shoulders snapped backwards but long fingers recovered quickly, and Ray saw the game pause. Waiting to see how he would respond, she toggled across all available screens, getting a good visual of the whole room. While she saw no anger on the Legacy's face, dark veins rippled just below the surface as if he'd just come out of the gym. Maneuvering over to the back corner of the pod, Ray saw a wrinkled towel lying haphazardly over two large dumbbells.

"Good morning, back," Dewey said pleasantly. "So uh, how are ya?"

The linguist had such an articulate way with words when on the clock, talking to representatives from all over the world on Modular's behalf. Over the last few months, as Dewey had promoted higher within his department, their check-ins had increasingly been interrupted by work calls, and often, Ray had liked to stay on the feed, a silent fly on the wall. She marveled at his ability to sharpen his loping drawl into right angled syllables at the drop of a hat.

But with her, and his pod mates, as she'd observed from previous engagement sessions, Dewey let his native tone fly. She smiled now, the twang wafting over her as she let it disarm her tense body.

Dewey's remained rigid, and she plunged forward, instigating small talk as she used her remote to zoom back on his position. Ray noted that the Legacy looked stronger than when he first arrived. Bursting veins aside, every muscle seemed to be bigger, broader, bulkier. She'd hovered into his pod at random times over the last week and always seemed to catch him in the middle of a set of pushups or bicep curls.

When asked about the new regimen, Dewey had reluctantly explained the exercise helped him feel more productive in isolation. This wasn't a new idea to Ray, who just a few years prior, unwillingly became an expert in regulating one's mental state in isolation. But it was the rate and frequency at which Dewey was exhausting his body over such a short time that worried her.

Dewey was now pouring himself a glass of water and seeing the death grip on the cup, Ray decided it was worth another conversation.

"Your workouts seem to be working. I think in just another week's time, you'll be able to shatter that glass with one squeeze."

Dewey glanced down and seeing the tips of his fingers glowing white, he loosened his grip and gently put it down, offering a halfhearted chuckle.

"Sorry, I just have a big meeting today. New Zealand, ya know. I think I've got a shot though— at finally getting through to them."

Ray peered over at a spreadsheet and saw the nine o' clock time slot blacked out.

"Ah, come on Dewey, you're going to be great. Since when did you start getting nervous about talking to people?"

The Legacy just shrugged, leaning back on the counter and crossing his ankles as if he expected this conversation to be a lot shorter than Ray had planned.

"I bet if they saw you, the Kiwis would sign on real quick," Ray teased, testing the waters. "I mean, have you seen your arms?"

"Actually, it would be a lot easier to have better form with a mirror, ya know," Dewey jabbed back.

"If we let you have a mirror, you'd start thinking too highly of yourself," she joked. "Can't have you Hulking out in these walls."

"Never know until you try," Dewey responded, oddly serious. Picking up on the shift, Ray leaned back in her chair and put her elbows on the arm rests.

"Can I ask you a question, Dewey?"

"Go ahead."

"Is it really the meeting you're so tense about? Your foot hasn't stopped bouncing since you put down that glass of water."

The resident sighed and turned around to rest his elbows on the counter, hands raking across his bare head. "Yeah it is, but not because I'm afraid to talk to them. It's more of a I-can't-fail-at-this kind of thing."

Ray let the admission sit in the quiet.

"You have to know Modular isn't going to banish you if you can't win them over," she replied softly. "We might banish New Zealand," she added with a chuckle. "But not you."

Half a smile escaped his lips, but it quickly vanished.

"It's not Modular I'm afraid of failing."

"Who, then?" Ray asked softly.

Dewey returned his fists to the countertop, a little too forcefully than needed, and spun around in resignation.

"Alex."

Ray dropped her eyes. She knew who Dewey was talking about, the name was all over the files in front of her. But she had to feign ignorance and let him explain it. It might be cathartic.

"My cousin. They were basically a sibling though," he said, trailing off. "We were close."

Ray kept quiet. She hoped the memory would envelop him enough where he forgot where he was and who was listening.

"Grew up in the same neighborhood. When we were twelve, my aunt and uncle passed away in a car accident, so our grandparents took my cousin in until they were forced into an assisted living home. We had both graduated at that point, but no real prospects, so joining up felt like the perfect solution."

"Marines, right?" Ray interjected, feeling safety in offering the information, knowing that that part of his file would've been known by any local doctor office.

"Yeah, I served as an interpreter—always had a thing with languages. Alex became an intelligence officer. Seven years in and we couldn't wait to get out. We'd had enough of traveling and felt like we'd done all that we could do with the military. Both of us were ready to live lives without someone telling us exactly what to do and when to do it."

The guilt-trip was like a punch to the gut. Dewey paused only long enough to ensure she felt it.

"Of course, we'd heard the chatter about some biomedical weapon coming out of the South Pacific, or the Mideast— that was the thing. The rumors changed origins every week, so our commands stopped taking them seriously. Without any real threats on the horizon, Alex and I's last tour was 24 hours from being over."

Ray knew the story but having to hear it from Dewey's mouth made her breath catch in her throat. She pressed her fingers to her lips, forcing them to be patient instead of urging for more.

"It was a routine psychological test. Everyone had to go through it before heading back home. A section of it was firearm safety. Just a test to ensure that we wouldn't come back skittish enough to pull out a gun in a local supermarket and start firing when a sack of potatoes fell off a shelf. It was our last task to check off before boarding the plane back to the States."

Ray remembered the way the Legacy's shoulders had hit the back of the chair only minutes ago. She bit her lip.

"We both were expert shooters, it was as good as done. I'd already booked us tickets for the Blink-182 comeback show," Dewey said, half chuckling but it came out choked. "Al never shut up about them."

The Legacy lingered in the moment, and Ray waited patiently for him to return to the story.

"Alex was just behind me in the schedule, but then I failed the last target, so while I waited in the holding room for the staff to reset everything, they pushed everyone behind me in line to go to the other range. Somehow, they messed up the timelines and sent two people in at the same time. The other officer must have seen Alex first and just spooked. They actually called it friendly fire," Dewey said through a clenched jaw, as if hearing the official statement for the first time.

"Friendly. Fire." Dewey repeated angrily, smacking his palms onto the granite counter, unyielding under the veteran's weight.

"I was the one who brought Alex into the hospital. Alarms were sounding off in every building on base, alerting that gunshots had been fired and all I could do was put my cousin on the stretcher and watch it slide behind a big metal door. And it's that living hell of confusion that I am mercifully pulled out of by the Shriek every single morning. I guess it's the last vivid memory I have before I was exposed, so my brain keeps wanting to recycle it over and over to fill the vacancy. Pretty sucky timing, seeing as I'm waking up to nearly the exact same setting. Sterile air, white washed walls, alarm blaring and Alex is still gone. The last memory I have of regular life is barely even a memory. I'm still living it."

"What happened to the shooter?" she whispered, after a few moments of silence.

Dewey shrugged. "While I was holding Alex's hand, willing the blood to keep pumping, the shooter was just sitting in holding, waiting to be court-martialed—which would never happen. Who cares about giving a rookie boot a trial when people are dropping dead everywhere you look. I never knew their name, but if their mind was already gone enough to fire at anything moving, I hope Void finished the job," Dewey muttered, shaking his head.

"We were the same age. Just a few months apart. But I always felt like I had to protect Alex, like I was the older sibling. And they could have—" Dewey shuddered. "Alex would have been safe here— with me. Just a few more hours, and that kid could be doing so much more for this cause than I am right now. Instead, you get me. This PTSD-ridden, jumpy Marine who is afraid to fall asleep and re-live that day over and over."

Ray took a moment, not wanting to jump in with a quick band-aid.

"I hate cliches," she started, already hating the words. "But it still needs to be said: what happened to your cousin wasn't your fault."

Palms smacked the counter again.

"But it was, Ray! Alex was slated right behind me on the schedule. When I failed, it made everyone behind me move to the alternate range to keep everything on schedule. I caused the confusion, the reason why two people got sent in at the same time. And now if I fail in this job, it's like I'm killing Alex all over again. Actually, there's even more at stake now. Millions of lives are hinging on the work we do here, and if I fail at my part, it could directly affect the outcome. It's—it's getting to be too much," he stammered, fingers starting to shake as he rested his shaking palms against the counter again.

Ray kept her voice low and calm. "Do the workouts help, then?"

The slight change of gears seemed to bring Dewey back to the present.

"Yeah, a little," he answered, rubbing the river of veins on his forearm. "I'm always sore, which makes me feel better ab—" he stopped.

"Feel better about what?" Ray nudged.

"I don't want you to think I'm... like in a bad place or anything," he said quickly.

"Dewey, you can't be of any help here if we don't know how to help you. Only I can make life easier for you, but you have to talk to me."

He remained quiet for half a minute, staring at twitchy fingers.

"I like making myself sore because it makes me feel better about being the one who is alive. Not even because of Alex. I mean, yeah I hate that of the two of us, I'm the only one who made it here. But what about all of the other lives that were lost? I'm just one of the lucky ones? It doesn't seem fair. So I beat myself up with weights to make myself feel better about surviving."

"Like you earned it."

Dewey shut his eyes and hung his head low. "Yeah."

"I'm really sorry you had to—" Ray clipped off, remembering what he'd said about the Shriek each morning. "I'm sorry you can't get rid of that day. I really can't imagine what that must be like."

Her sympathy seemed to do little. He looked dejected but Ray took solace in the fact his hands had stopped shaking as he locked them together and brought them to his lips. Eyes closed, it looked as if he was deep in prayer. As she watched, a heartbreaking thought occurred to her.

As overseas military personnel, she knew Dewey would have been locked down in quarantine immediately after the news broke that a pandemic was rippling throughout the world, which came mere hours after Alex had been shot. Dewey would have remained in that state for months until Modular sent for him. So, the last person to have held those hands, truly grip his fingers, had actually been Alex, desperately trying to hold on to life. She brought her own fingers to her mouth and took a slow breath to steady her voice.

"We all lost people to Void. Children, grandparents, spouses, cousins. Each of them left a huge space for no one to fill. And that's why we are working so hard. To fill that space back up with people who can hear our stories about the ones we lost. We are their legacies. No one else can tell Alex's story but you, and no one will hear the stories without you. Do you see how important you are? Surviving means you get to keep Alex alive."

Ray searched his face on the monitor, his eyes staring at the wall. She knew he saw something else though.

She checked her watch. She hated to disrupt his memory, but Dewey needed time to prep for the meeting. As his facilitator, she had fulfilled her two obligations. Keep the Legacy at baseline—or return them to it—and instill purpose. She felt he had recalibrated, but leaving him in this daze would be unproductive for everyone involved. Especially knowing he had a meeting with New Zealand coming up in mere hours. Modular couldn't afford for Dewey to simply go through the motions that afternoon. The Kiwis already had their doubts about the initiative. Headquarters had to prove it was working, and the way to do that was through their Legacy liaisons. They had to prove the residents were equipped, loyal to the cause and excited for the new future.

She wished she could cover the Legacy's hands with her own, instill human contact again. She let her voice embody the room instead.

"You've been through so much, Dewey, and if working your body to its edge helps, then keep it up. I have nothing negative to say about your hobby as long as you don't hurt yourself outside of a few charley horses. Do what makes you feel justified to be here because we can't afford the alternative. We need you, ok?"

Thinking of the day that lie ahead of him, Ray decided to add, "And hey, even if you don't get the outcome you want at the end of the day, you're not a failure and Modular certainly won't think so either. We're all human."

"Except New Zealand." Dewey said, hinting a smile.

Ray grinned. "True. But if anyone can get through to those robots, I think it's you."

She watched as the Legacy pushed off the counter and, with the slightest of buoyances in his step, sidled across the room to his desk and closed down his paused game.

Job done, Ray started cleaning up her papers and sorted them back in their file.

"Look out for some documents and notes from the Overseer coming your way on the Network, they'll help you in the meeting. Just some recent statistics and projections. Let me know if you need anything else, alright?"

"Will do."

"Have a great day, Dewey."

Ray lingered quietly for a few moments longer, leaning closer to the monitor to see Dewey flipping through some notes. Assuaged, she disengaged the audio feed, and the dark shoulders, straightened and taut with purpose, vanished from her view.

Elle slid off the headphones, as if shedding another skin, and checked her watch. It was 7:15. Dylan would need her.

SEVEN

THIS WAS taking too long. His fingertips pulsed with nervous energy and pulling his knees closer to his chest, Dylan strained to hear the sound of anyone— anything— over the roar of his own heartbeat. He peered down at his swooshed sneakers and dared to slide his foot back and forth. A squeak reverberated throughout the room, but instead of cringing, Dylan held his ear closer to the wall, desperate to hear an answer.

Nothing.

He had lost track of how long he'd been sitting there, but it was so black, his eyes had never adjusted. His skin crawled at the base of his neck, but he didn't dare move, for fear that he would turn and see eyes illuminate the dark.

Suddenly a muffled voice floated up from beneath him.

"Dylan? Come on, seriously, this isn't funny anymore," it called, tinged with annoyance.

Dylan scrambled on all fours and pounded the floorboards, forgetting his concern of what else might hear him. Within seconds, a single door panel shot up, a burst of light surging through the opening like a geyser. A messy bun of chocolate brown hair followed as Dylan covered his eyes and collapsed in relief.

"See, when I said 'no hiding in the guest room', that included the space above it, too," his savior said, amusement quickly replacing annoyance. She leaned forward to get a better look at him. "You're seven. How did your tiny legs even get you up here?"

"I—I used the bookshelves," Dylan hiccuped, still trying to regain control of his breathing. "I thought it would be the best spot ever. I just didn't know how the door worked once I got inside." He brought his eyes up to meet those of the shadowed face, shyness ebbing when the light hit her dimple. Relief washed over him. It only showed when she grinned. She wasn't angry.

"I'm sorry, E."

She rested her forearms on the attic floor. "Well. It was a great spot, Dyl. That, thankfully, you can never use again. I'm on to you now," she said, green eyes slitting in suspicion. "Come on, you had your break—plus some— you little sneak. Back to homework for you."

"Hey," he called as his feet rested solidly on carpet again. E turned. "Have you ever heard anything coming from up there?"

"What? The attic?" She dropped the string and watched as the door fell flush with the ceiling again. When she turned back to him, he felt his cheeks burn. She socked him in the shoulder. "Sure, champ. I hear monsters all the time."

A stifled laugh muffled in her throat and he started after her, indignation pushing his legs to catch up just as the doorbell rang. E jogged ahead, making a leather satchel on the bedroom door handle sway. As her back disappeared around the corner, Dylan felt reality begin to tug at his consciousness. He pushed his legs to move faster, but the longer he fought to stay in the dream, the blare of the doorbell grew more piercing and the hazier the details became.

Light from the end of the hallway effervesced in front of him, burning up bright peach wallpaper as it melted out of his vision. He stumbled towards it, knees buckling as he fell forward, still reaching for the light. Suddenly his eyes quivered open and he found himself sprawled on the floor, breathing in the threads of the white sheepskin rug.

The dream had softened the sound that was now shrieking off his walls like a siren. The bell beat in time with the thrum of his own heart now and amidst the chaos, Dylan felt his muscles take over. Staggering to his feet, he angled towards the Cipher. As soon as his back straightened, the cacophony was silenced, then replaced by the soft moan of the laminate floor panel that had already begun to whine from overuse in the last four months.

"Fifteen, December. Cavanaugh, Dylan." The Cipher seemed to hesitate. "Zero."

Dylan moved his hands to rest on his forehead, wary and dizzy, just like he had every morning since the first of December, when Ray had introduced him to the Shriek.

Right on cue, her voice swept into the room as he flopped back onto the bed.

"Dylan, are you awake?" Ray asked, oddly timid.

Staring idly at the gray walls, a memory suddenly sharpened before him. The same four words quietly dancing with midnight shadows on a bedroom wall. Forehead still throbbing, his mind strained to catch more detail.

"Dylan, are you there?" Ray called again.

The vision dissolved before him.

He raked his hands down his face, letting a scoff erupt in the silence.

"You're kidding, right?"

"I'm sorry, what do you me—"

"Yeah, of course you are. Because where would I go, huh?" Dylan sneered. "There is absolutely no escape. This—" he gestured to the room, "—is a freaking cage!"

The outburst felt cathartic coming off his lips.

For months his life had been defined by a series of reactions. He responded only when spoken to, asked questions only when prodded—but now he was taking control. He was the one who got to spin the conversation. The FAC's silence egged him on.

"This is all one big game to you guys, and guess what, I give up. I give up trying to figure it all out. I'm one of your little pawns and I'll just stay in my one tiny square and wait for you to tell me where to go, what to do and when to do it." Dylan was pacing again and he held his hands up in a show of surrender as he walked.

Ray remained quiet. He imagined her flipping through a binder of emergency responses.

"The Shriek upsets you," Ray finally said, the sudden topic change stopping him in his tracks.

"Of course it upsets me!" he yelled, incredulous. "You threw it at me with no warning!"

"I explained—"

"*The last part of the orientation training*," he mimicked. "Yeah, I remember. Your little alarm clock is designed as a wake up call to drive me to the Ciper and check in. But it's been more than two weeks now, and I still wake in a panic. Like my brain can't acclimate to it."

"But you go to the Cipher the minute you hear it," Ray countered gently. "Your body has proven to be responding. Not all of your compatriots have done the same. One individual broke their arm trying to burst through one of their walls after hearing the alarm for the first time."

Dylan shook off the encouragement, pressing his palms into his eyes. "Maybe my body has, but my mind goes haywire every time."

A still quiet hung in the air.

"What are your first thoughts when you hear it?" Ray finally asked.

"I don't know," he sighed, annoyed he could so quickly be relegated back to an existence of answering questions. "I always think it's a doorbell."

"And what do you do when you hear it?"

"I have a hunch you already know, Ray," he said, numbly moving his fingers to massage the spot on his foot that always launched his body off the bed to get to the Cipher. "When do you ever not know about something going on in this pod?"

Dylan waited for Ray to light up. He actually wished for it. Something to show the facilitator had buttons ripe for the pressing. But a soft sigh came over the airwaves, chased by a white flag.

"You're right," Ray offered. "I know more about you than any other human should know about someone's personal business, and I have the ability to know it on a minute-to-minute basis."

Dylan raised his head. She had never acknowledged that before.

"But that is mandatory for your safety. I know you don't like it, but I'm your eyes and ears outside your pod. A wall stands between us, but you have to believe that I'm on your side. Always."

A cynical huff escaped his lips.

"Look, I'm in this for the long haul," Ray continued. "For the chance to set the world right again. But none of that happens without you. Look, love me or hate me. But keep in mind that it's a luxury to even have that choice. I can't afford to feel emotion. I just have to protect you, whether I like it or not."

He didn't trust the FAC's vulnerability. Instead of sympathy, he just felt manipulated.

"It seems a little unfair that the people most vital to the planet have to live like test mice in a lab," he retorted.

"So, living carefree in a well stocked hotel just because you were born in a really lucky decade?" Ray shot back. "While thousands in our facilities' infected wings are fighting just to stay alive?"

The syllables raked against gritted teeth, proving his words had hit a nerve.

"You know what, if you want to quit— then just say so, alright? I've said my piece. This initiative only works if both parties are willing to do their part and we have plenty of volunteers. Modular needs someone like you, but without your cooperation, the work will become stagnant. We can't afford that loss of time." The emotion began to build in the FAC's voice, and Dylan resisted the urge to hang his head in surrender. He needed to stay alert, to catch every hint, syllable and inflection of a facilitator coming unhinged.

"When you waste time here, you steal time from everyone else who is trying their best to make more of it. Not everyone has the kind of time that you do. You've been so focused on your life, what's not convenient for you anymore, and all the while people are dying. Have you forgotten what our world is now?"

Dylan's tongue twisted and recoiled like a python, and he bit it to maintain composure.

"I don't even know what's on the other side of my walls, Ray. I'm locked in here, told all these things that I can't verify. How can I forget something that I don't remember?" he said, jaw twitching against his clenched teeth.

Unease permeated the room like a gas leak. Neither side wanted to surrender, but given what Ray had just admitted, he was pretty sure the FAC had a lot less time to spend being stubborn than he did.

Time became a smattering of minutes, perhaps hours, measured only by the uptick of Dylan's pride in not speaking. He waited there on the bed long enough to mentally prepare a variety of arguments to any potential rebuttal, but when none came, he took a seat at his desk and began typing his password.

"I don't see everything, you know."

Dylan's finger hovered over the enter key. He was struck not by the realization Ray never cut the feed, but by the way the sentence snapped open with human cracks. Even in anger, Dylan had only heard Ray-the-Facilitator. But this quiet whisper sounded like someone casting loyalties aside in the name of human frailty.

Dylan leaned back in the chair and steepled his fingers together, hoping to keep the upper hand.

"Thought you left."

"Probably should have."

"I'm not going to apologize."

"Neither am I."

Dylan chewed at bitten nails as he felt the playing field level. He rocked in his chair that gave a little too much give after only a few months.

Ray spoke again. "I have the most access out of any compatriot in this outfit, and I've earned it. I won't tolerate judgement from someone who doesn't know the amount of effort exerted on this side of the wall. I also won't tolerate keeping someone in darkness," Ray said, tapering off as if distracted.

Dylan stared at the blinking cursor on the password prompt and felt his resolve melt away.

"Alright, so I'm just going to assume I'm the 'someone' in both of those scenarios," Dylan prodded. "I'm still upset with the way things are handled here so I'm not going to say I'm sorry and beg for a chance to stay here." He paused. "But, I'm never too proud to beg for information that keeps me out of dark places."

Instead of a reply, Dylan felt a buzz began to sizzle in his right ear. Flinching, he stabbed his middle finger into the ear but the sound petered out, quickly as it came.

"Sorry about that," Ray said. "I had to reset all control center modems feeding in and out of your pod for a—uhm," she coughed. "A routine reboot session. A deep clean of the pod, if you will. I am required to tell you that all securities and wire feeds are going to be down for five minutes."

Dylan narrowed his eyes as the words fit together like puzzle pieces. "All securities meaning what?"

"Meaning that I just pulled rank—and the hood over all eyes and ears that daily observe your pod."

"Wait a minute, I'm being watched by—"

"Yes, but do you really want to spend this unsanctioned time talking about all the people who aren't listening to us right now?"

Head spinning but tail tucked between his legs, he relented.

"I wasn't just trying to brag when I said I have the most access out of any employee here. I just do. But I'm not the Overseer, which I can attest, is not an ironic title," Ray said. "I have my limits."

"So, what, just because you aren't the CEO of this whole place, I'm supposed to feel empathy from you? You think you understand how all of this feels?" Dylan retorted defensively, gesturing to the cage around him.

A long, measured breath.

"I'm not asking you to believe me. I'm asking you to trust me. Because despite all that access, here I am, forced to shut off all wiring systems just so that I can explain to you that I'm not all-knowing," the facilitator confessed. "Yeah, a lot of people are silently observing you: from what you eat to what you choose to wear and how often you use the bathroom. But they also observe me. How I react to you, your behaviors and questions." Ray sighed before continuing.

"The longer I'm here, I question why I can't be trusted on my own with my pod of compatriots. When I arrived, I was promised a lot of things that flattered my abilities, tenacity and ambition. I was told I was valuable. Invincible. Irreplaceable, even. I felt empowered." Ray paused, drawing a breath. "Until I realized the flattery, and the position, was only offered because of a situation I was handed, rather than my actual talents. I felt like I had to uphold this unbreakable reputation, but I had to do it while processing some trauma that was still pretty raw."

Dylan held back a flinch as he thought, for the first time, what Ray might have lost to Void.

"My peers began to see the inevitable breaks from this mental dichotomy, and I was put on watch," Ray continued. "I started getting more assessments and less authority. The very thing I was praised for overcoming suddenly became my biggest limitation."

"It sucks to be put in a box, doesn't it?" Dylan commented, quietly.

"Yeah, it does," the FAC acknowledged. "And you're in one because of your invincibility, too. We have told you how important you are— shoved it down your throat really. And look, you're confined to a very limited space because of it. We have our reasons, our safety precautions for it, and I'm sure my counterparts would say the same if I brought up my complaints. I'm not in your exact situation but... I still know the feeling."

The voice petered out, quietly fading into the eerie silence of a pod without its systems on full alert. His monitor had gone dark in the reboot, but Dylan guessed their five minutes of freedom were just about up.

"So many secrets," he said, wary. Ray opening up had torn him down the middle. It had been easy to make her an enemy of sorts. Someone to absorb the frustration of this situation he had been thrust into overnight. But as he stood now, unsteady on his feet, he felt the extra weight of her own burdens now seeping into his own veins, waiting to be absorbed.

"You have to tell me then, while it's still off the record, is Ray even your real name?" he asked, only half teasing.

Shuffling in the dark, he found the edge of the bed and sank down into the pillows as Ray offered a half-hearted chuckle.

"If I told you that, I'd have to kill you."

As if on cue, a buzzing penetrated his ear drums again and, now enlightened, he suddenly felt invisible eyes filtering in from all corners of the room.

"Dylan, are you still there?"

Light enveloped him and he shielded his face with a hand, grateful for a reason to hide his coy satisfaction at being privy to Ray's schemes.

"Yeah, still here," he said, playing along. He screwed his eyebrows together. "What was that?"

The smallest of pauses hung in the air and Dylan could almost see the pair of lips proudly smirking in an office somewhere.

"I'm so sorry about that," Ray replied, a hint of distress lilting at her voice. Dylan felt a surge of camaraderie. Papers shuffled in the background as Ray continued, her words harried, bouncing into one another. "There seems to have been a malfunction and your pod rebooted itself. A systems restart wasn't scheduled for another two months, and even then, it was scheduled to occur while you slept—I know that must have been alarming. Especially after..." Ray trailed off, and Dylan noted the change in her voice. "Well, after what we had been talking about."

She was fishing again. He stood up and idly scratched the back of his neck, considering taking the bite.

"I will say, you guys have a knack for making life in a box quite unpredictable."

"Monotony dulls the senses," Ray replied. "We need you to stay sharp."

"Yeah, I remember," Dylan said, reminded of the FAC's spiel the first morning he had met the Shriek. "I just wish it wouldn't pull me out of such a good dream every time."

"It does?" Ray said, barely masking her curiosity. "How so?"

Dylan bit his lip, stalling. He felt as if he owed Ray a shred of vulnerability after what she'd admitted under cover of radio silence. But he didn't owe anything to the other pairs of invisible ears that he now knew were listening.

"I mean, it's always kind of hazy," he replied, the truth stretching somewhere between black and white. "But there's someone in the dream that I should remember. I call them by a name as if I know them within the dream, but the face is blurry to me. Then every time I get close to finally figuring it out, the doorbell—which is just the Shriek—pulls me out."

He trailed off, refusing to give his audience anything more. Ray was quiet for a moment.

"Do you mind telling me their name?" she finally asked, her tone suddenly high and airy, as if coaxing a scared puppy out of a corner.

He couldn't see the harm in it. Besides, was it even a name?

"E."

A strangled cough dashed off the walls, and he flinched.

"Just the letter?" Ray managed, still trying to clear her throat. "Sorry, down the wrong pipe," she added.

"Yeah, which only adds to the confusion of the dream. But it always feels so familiar and... I don't know, lived in. It's disheartening to wake up from that familiarity."

Finally composed, Ray spoke again, her easy cadence having returned. "I'm sorry the Shriek is doing that—but, you know, that just shows validation in the method we instill here. Albeit slowly, your memories are returning. That's wonderful news. Keep this up and I may be out of a job."

The light-hearted tone nearly lifted the words right over his head. He snatched them back.

"Wait, what do you mean?"

Ray paused, as if realizing she'd said too much. "Well, the goal of a facilitator is to be a temporary guide for Legacies until they reach a level where the FAC can completely remove themselves."

"As in you wouldn't be watching my every move anymore?" Dylan asked, not even trying to shroud his eagerness.

"As in I would relinquish your pod feed to the Graduate Facilitation Division, a sector of Modular that would still be supervising, but functions more as a resource to Legacies for any issues they may encounter."

"Finally, some good news around here," he mused.

"I'm hurt that you don't enjoy my company," Ray bantered. "Keep up this attitude, and I'll just leave right now."

"Don't tease."

A chuckle, and then a sigh of surrender.

"How about we just take it one day at a time. You do your job and I'll stick to mine. Talk soon."

And as always, the FAC clicked off before he could get the last word. Feeling slightly more invigorated by the latest announcement, he stood up, stretched out his limbs and ambled towards the bathroom. He stopped short.

As he passed the echo screen closest to his bed, his eyes refused to ignore the jarring image.

A face glared back, sitting atop a sphere that enveloped a variety of symbols and shapes. His peripherals had seen enough of the screens over the last several weeks to know that this new image would've fit right into the other peppy Modular propaganda, if not for one thing. The current image was blanketed in harsh, negative colors.

Dylan strained to make sense of the image, rearranging colors in his mind. The globe seemed to be Planet Earth, but was surrounded by a spanse of reddish gray fog that threatened to drip right down the wall. A ghostly figure sat atop the gray planet, casually holding a cup in two inky black hands. Looking closer, he realized the figure was actually smiling, but the negative sheen had turned it into a demonic snarl.

Entranced, Dylan zeroed in on the cup in the figure's hands, its harsh swirls of dusky reds and inky blues curling into a shape that reminded him of the peace symbol that once graced the hoods of seventies-era VW buses. But instead of a trident separating the parts of the circle, the symbol was turned sideways in the shape of an E, which was surrounded by murky waves of gray twisting among themselves like metallic ivy.

The base of his neck began to throb and he turned away from the screen, massaging the muscle. Facing the bed, his strained eyes blurred and he blinked quickly to focus.

A breath caught in his throat.

A vivid image suddenly appeared before him as if it had always been painted there on the white sheets.

The more he blinked, the more details he saw in the imprint. Glowing brightly before him was the same picture from the echo screen, transformed into a clear image when illuminated against the stark white of the sheets. Looking at it now, he knew this must have been the true image.

A brilliant sky had replaced the inky red, and the figure, crowned with golden brown hair that cascaded around a petite, angular face, was no longer snarling but flashing a bright white smile. The rotated peace symbol still remained, vivid with white, but now a scrawl of words filled the space in between where the swirls of steel once were.

Eye twitching, he screwed his eyebrows together and, at last, the words came together—a haunting recall of the note that burned in the drawer of his nightstand.

Unity cannot be made where humanity is caged.

He blinked again and saw a smaller line of words, scrawled at the bottom of the symbol. If the first sentence was a metaphor, this one seemed like a pop fly. As if to say, "Hey kid, don't miss it." Dylan sucked in a breath as the words silenced any doubt that someone was poking holes in the story Modular had been telling him.

Life exists outside the walls.

EIGHT

ELLE POISED on the edge of a cold, oak-slatted chair and crossed her legs, willing her thoughts to calm.

She didn't even know why she had done it—exposing that piece of herself. She'd never felt the need to explain herself to the others under her care before. The resident in Pod 0018 shouldn't be any different.

But of course he was. The first week of December had changed everything, and she had spent every day since trying to show her colleagues that it hadn't.

Elle pinched the bridge of her nose, reigning in the panic attack waiting in the wings. Toeing the edge of the third one in just two weeks did not make it any easier to back away from, but at least she knew what it felt like when one was coming. She fingered the rock she'd slipped into her vest pocket before leaving her studio. Pressing her palm into the jagged granite, she refocused her breathing to settle on the pain of its edges. The rock had a very delicate purpose. Looking at it could ground her, bring her back to reality in the middle of chaos. Or it could send her into a tailspin of her past. Teetering between the two somehow balanced the madness of an anxiety attack, and she felt her breathing finally slow.

Confessing her recent attacks with anyone would only allow them to poke more holes into her razor thin façade. They all believed her resolve was weakening. After all this time, Ray was finally bending under the pressure.

People began to filter in to the room. Two of the members—human resource reps— cast furtive looks at her and she smiled smugly, as only a person could do who had scheduled such an abrupt meeting. Seven other Circle members, all facilitators, swept in with an air of superiority, their eyes sharpening above their masks as they each glanced at her. She knew they saw themselves as the iron girders of the whole initiative. She also knew they thought of her as a crumbling support. She fired emerald daggers back at them, daring them to look at her with pity.

Finally the Overseer walked in, scanning the room for the last empty seat. That was the beauty of the Circle. No one was truly in charge.

At least, that was the unspoken idea.

All eyes betrayed that motto, however, as they settled on Easton.

Ray had chosen the seat facing the door with the purpose to stare her jury of peers down, hopefully disarming their suspicion right from the start. She wasn't the weak spot.

"Have all of you read the incident summary that incited this emergency meeting?" the Overseer began without preamble. Curt nods filtered in from around the table. Elle kept her eyes on Easton. "Ray, go ahead."

"As mentioned in my report, I wanted to discuss my recent observations of Resident 0018. Now—"

"First of all, can you please state for the group the resident's identity," interrupted Shawna Blake, one of the veterans to the Circle. A sneer curled the corners of their mouth. "You know, just for the recording's sake."

Aside from a small tick of the jaw, Elle remained resolute. "Dylan Cavanaugh."

Stifled coughs and trapped breaths sliced through the room. Elle fought to keep from rolling her eyes. They'd all read the report, this wasn't news. Saying the soul's name out loud, though, made it real.

"So, Patient Zero," Shawna confirmed.

It was Elle's turn to offer a curt nod.

Postures shifted all around the table as her peers tried to assuage their own nerves. Blake elected to speak aloud all of their fears.

"Are you trying to tell us, again, that you think our lead candidate— our only real hope at this point if you recall— is rejecting?"

They'd doubted her long enough for her to be conditioned to these questions, and the reply came out fluidly.

"What I'm telling you all is that this resident is a human being. An unpredictable soul made out of flesh and bone, not some machine manufactured on an assembly line."

Oak creaked under the shifted weights of several different members, eyes averted. No one wanted to be reminded that their best chance of survival was prone to changing their mind.

"Everything in Pod 0018 is designed to point our lead candidate towards a wariness of the world they once knew. To steer their fear into a compulsion to heal. To be the change. The echo screens, history books, engagement sessions... they all work together to piece a Legacy's memory back together," Elle reminded the Circle calmly. "Each one plays a pivotal role in our mission here, but even when a resident provides hesitation in accepting these methods, the Shriek is the final persuasion. The aggressive tool coaxes a Legacy out of the nightmares of their past. A past filled with memories of a desolate planet ravaged by Void. The Shriek is a savior—"

Elle paused, her pulse quickening as she met several pairs of suspicious eyes. They knew all this. Taking a breath, she brought her palms together and, pointing them in an arrowhead, addressed the group again.

"—when it's successful."

"When?" Shawna parroted, offering a soft chuckle. "Wait. You're about to try and convince us that now the Shriek isn't even working on Patient Zero?"

Elle leaned forward, angling the arrow towards the compatriot's chest. "That's exactly what I'm saying."

"Excuse me," a velvety voice jumped in. Elle swiveled to meet eyes with Landry Tate, another FAC and friend to Shawna, seated so close their shoulders brushed each other. "Aren't these just the same concerns, regurgitated from last month's meeting? Why do we keep wasting time on this?"

"The resident has admitted their aversion to the Shriek," Elle answered, undeterred. "Many, many times."

Landry huffed, leaning back against the chair. "That's completely normal! None of my residents like the sound. They complain all the time."

"Of course they don't like the sound," Elle acknowledged, extending a hand towards the compatriot like an offering. "But they also admit they're just happy it woke them up from the nightmare, right?"

"Well, yeah," Landry said, stealing an uneasy glance at Shawna, as if wary to acknowledge Elle was, indeed, right.

Elle squared her shoulders. "Patient Zero hates the Shriek because it wakes him up."

Nervous eyes flicked from Elle to Easton, waiting for the latter to undo the former's words, but the Overseer kept their steady gaze on Elle. Empowered by her friend's calm, she plunged ahead while the rest of the group still sat dazed.

"This isn't something that I've conjured up in my head, as you all would like to believe. Go back and read the audio transcript of our last conversation. The resident described a recurring dream that seems to be a returning memory from their childhood. Zero says they have been trying to piece it together, but the Shriek always pulls them away before the complete picture comes together. They didn't share much detail with me, but it's clear that the resident is completely unaffected by the Shriek's original purpose." Elle dropped her hands and entangled them behind her back. "This simply cannot be ignored.

A new voice piped up and Elle jolted her neck to the left, meeting a nervous pair of eyes rimmed by red frames. The young FAC had just added their seat to the oval table and had yet to utter any kind of opinion on Elle's concerns. Elle smile behind her mask, hoping the act would soften her eyes. The rest of the Circle had made their loyalties known, but there was still time to win the rookie over.

"So what does this mean?" the compatriot asked, innocence dripping from behind their own mask. "I—I mean, how could this have even happened?"

Elle clasped her hands together, nodding towards the fellow facilitator. "Well, I believe the resident's resistance has effectively shut down the power of the Shriek, which should be igniting the proper memory recalls. This, coupled with the refusal to read any of the books and histories, has curbed any fear or nightmares of what lies outside these walls, which has caused the Shriek to be seen as a hindrance rather than a savior, like it is intended." Elle paused, watching for the fog to clear behind the red glasses. "Liv, I know you're new here to this process. But would you feel comfortable relaying everything you know about Resident 0018's time here?"

A hand shot out, nervously adjusting the red frames on a freckled nose. Blue eyes darted around the table before the FAC spoke.

"Well, to encourage a smoother integration into our isolated pods, each Legacy undergoes a neutralization procedure that aims to remove all Voided cells present in the brain. When 0018 arrived, however, the medical team found that the disease had overtaken the entire temporal lobe of the brain. There were only two options. Painstakingly remove each Voided cell in the attempt to salvage at least some memory retention, or neutralize the entire lobe. As a core team, the Circle chose the full sweep, giving the Legacy the best chance of a full recovery and avoiding any more stress on the body."

Liv glanced to Elle, who nodded in affirmation.

"Yes, exactly. After the procedure, we realized how important it would be for the resident to follow our methods. To reduce the chance of a neutralized memory returning—and inciting confused panic by the resident—our efforts hinged on the success of all other acting parts, most importantly the echo screens and then the Shriek. The protocol we instated at neutralization required a consistent strengthening of the resident's mind to ensure successful repression of their past. Like a muscle needs to be trained, the echoes and Shriek were the tools to do that. But now..." Elle trailed off, glancing down at her knotted hands.

"I voiced my concerns before to do my due diligence as this resident's facilitator," she continued, "but in truth, I never really feared Zero rejecting because I knew they never would. If they had no one on the other side of their walls to catch them, why run? But if their memory is returning in these dreams—and the Shriek isn't deterring them—" Elle leveled her gaze at Shawna now, who had slumped back in their chair, arms crossed. "What else might they remember? We can't ignore this."

Easton stood, curling their long fingers around the beveled edge of the table and met her eyes. The fog had lifted, giving way to storm clouds. Elle felt her fingers dig into damp palms.

"So what are you proposing, Ray? I assume you didn't bring us here just to burden us without any hope of a solution?"

Elle tugged at the bottom of her fleece vest, hoping to obscure her shaking hands. This was the whole reason she'd called this meeting in the first place. She could not hesitate.

"I propose we alleviate the stress on everyone in this outfit and amend the Elect Giver plan. Let there be multiple Givers instead: a diverse group of Legacies that have met our Modular touchstones."

Elle heard audible sighs circulate across the room, and she swiveled to find Liv, who had not been present when Elle had first proposed the plan. The FAC might be her only ally.

"No, these candidates wouldn't tick every single box, but that's the beauty of the idea. They would balance each other to make a single cohesive unit. A stronger force," Elle said, emboldened as blue eyes stared back, wide with curiosity. "This would provide a wider net to cast out in Phase II, encouraging a higher rate of success in securing anti-Void protection among the population that is still left. It just makes more sense to have multiple Givers, instead of relying on one person to save everyone. Plain and simple."

She dared to look at Easton. The Overseer stared down at their hands, now carved into a diamond.

"I hear you, Ray. I do," Easton said, head bobbing up and down, every syllable purposeful. But when their eyes rose to meet hers, the steel was back, a condescending grin to match. "But you know we can't actually do that. Not this late in the game."

Of course she knew. Modular required perfection. Why have a bunch of pretty good Givers when you could have one elite offering? Because that's what that soul would be. A being without any control of their own. As Easton said when they refuted her idea the first time, it's wiser, and easier, to control a single set of marionette strings rather than dozens.

She held their gaze defiantly.

"I don't see how we can let the state of our existence rest on one, fickle, human soul," Elle challenged, feeling her voice rise. "I'm not even talking about 0018! No matter who we end up using, I find it extremely dangerous to hinge our entire plan on one Legacy. I mean, they might as well be toddlers. They're impressionable, prone to throw a fit at any moment, change their minds, you name it. The human soul is uncontrollable!"

Silence blanketed the room, and Elle closed her eyes, realizing her mistake. She knew better than to even breathe a word about the youngest generation that had fallen victim to Void, let alone, mutter a half hearted joke. Even if it was to make a point.

"Alright, alright," Easton interfered. "Maybe not the best metaphor, Ray," they chided softly. The Overseer scanned the room before motioning solemnly for Elle to sit down. She narrowed her eyes in one last attempt of defiance, but then sat down, tucking her quivering hands underneath the table.

"Do any of you wish to support this amendment?"

Aside from a few glances, there was no movement around the table. The hope of Liv, dashed.

"Ray is a dedicated player to our team whose loyalty and trust is unmatched," Easton said. Elle prayed her eyes didn't flicker. "I value this compatriot's opinion and have noted the concerns about Patient Zero's progress. Their rejection, at this stage, would be catastrophic to our progress, so please understand me when I say that I empathize with you all. The fear of having to start all over keeps me at my desk at all hours. But we also cannot let fear drop us into an unproductive pit where we wait to see if the worst is going to happen."

Elle faked a smile and looked down as a few tentative claps peppered in around the table. They came from the newest additions to the table, those naïve enough to believe the Circle was actually a place of equal status, despite the display that had just occurred before their eyes. Elle kept her hands folded in her lap, feeling chastised.

The Overseer turned to her side of the table. Elle looked up, finding that the storm had blown through, gray eyes now placid waters.

"While I do not wish to amend our plans, I do have an idea that may help more than just this resident's progression. For the last month I have been working with the security teams across the international installations to gain more intel on the Scale."

Elle's head snapped back. Easton had promised her the day they walked out of Nox together, never to dive back into what had happened again. Everyone lost someone in the Shift, but Easton knew that Elle had lost more than anyone, and she wanted to forget. Just like everyone.

"Only forward now," Easton had said, chin tilted towards her and she could still remember those eyes of steel, offering such promise.

And her friend had kept theirs, untill now.

"We've worked tirelessly to move forward," Easton was saying now and Elle snapped back to the present, "searching for a way to preserve our race. That took the shape of curating a Remedy. While we are closer than ever before, I feel that something needs to change. What we've been doing clearly has not gotten us far enough. I've employed a coalition to dig up everything they can on the terrorist group. We need to know what they were thinking, analyze their design. Perhaps the only way to move forward is to look back."

Heads nodded around the table, eyes aglow with the hope of something new.

"Patient Zero was the lead fact checker for the *Manhattan Herald*, the lead newspaper that followed the MW3 story up until the Shift. If this resident is already prone to remembering, who knows what else they might have to offer? I propose we take Patient Zero off Coding and add them to the security team."

Murmurs and excited comments peppered off the walls as Elle sat back, hands plunged into her vest, digging her flesh into the rock. Patient Zero was her charge. Elle was the only one that soul communicated with, and if Easton's plan came true, she would hear nothing but details of a past she had believed to have left behind.

She had been in the business of making people forget for so long, she wasn't sure if she was ready to remember.

***

THE DOOR clicked closed as the last Circle member exited the room, Shawna's dark eyes reduced to slits as the FAC reluctantly left the two of them alone.

Elle plucked a wayward cuticle on her thumb, biting her lip as a tiny bubble of blood streaked down into her palm. She shoved the hand into her pocket, letting the rock soak up her blood. Just like it had so many other times.

Easton ambled over and took the chair next to her, twisting it to face her taut body. She shook her head.

"This isn't wise," she said, lips as tight as her calves flexing beneath the chair.

"Come on, Elle. The multiple Giver plan isn't good enough. Let it go."

"Not that," she replied flatly. She stared at a whorl in the table. "Adding Zero to the research team."

Easton let out a sigh and raised their glasses up to crest a wave of sandy blonde hair.

"Do tell. What is it this time," they said, resignation slicing off the question mark.

She twisted in her seat abruptly, finally meeting Easton's eyes. She'd been holding it in for too long, the confession on the edge of her tongue.

"The dreams are about E," she blurted, words tumbling out like racehorses storming out of the gate.

Easton stared at her, unblinking. Thin lips twitched.

"When they mentioned having dreams, I pried," Elle continued, tentative. "And they explained how the same figure appears in this recurring dream. Someone they can't identify, but is called E."

"That's a neutralized memory," Easton muttered, eyes glassy. "We saw the scan. Right there in black and white, you showed it to me," Easton finally said. Tortoiseshell rims returned to their place, but Elle doubted they brought any real clarity. "It was the only way to keep Void from spreading."

"I remember." Elle found solace in the whorl again, keeping her gaze on its intricate swirls as silence encased the room.

"Zero shouldn't." Easton's eyes flashed as they turned to face her. "The Shriek was our backup plan, in the random chance something like this happened. It was designed to keep those memories out."

"I know."

Easton stared at her, tightlipped, but she knew their gaze wasn't really focused on her.

"I have to believe it is a direct result of the resident's unwillingness to participate in the method, and n—not—" she faltered, closing her eyes for a moment. "And not a direct result of... my voice."

Easton's eyes hung on to hers a moment longer before their hand flashed out and slapped the table. Her shoulders hit the back of her chair.

"Damn it, Elle! I knew this would happen," Easton said, shaking their head. "I should have never let you—"

"The whole Circle agreed to it," Elle interrupted, indignant.

"No, they agreed to wipe the lobe," Easton countered sharply. "They never knew about what we did after."

Easton turned away from her, hands wrenching together. "I should have never signed off on it. No other resident gets special treatment. Zero shouldn't have been an exception."

"So you think compassion is an exception?"

Easton flicked an eye back towards her. "Our medical team had made a mistake. In a fight like what we have in front of us, we can't afford to make compromises each time it happens."

Elle pursed her lips together, mind racing to salvage the situation.

"Everything we have done was for the benefit of the Legacy," Elle said calmly, flitting into her facilitator voice. "We did what we thought was in the best interest of our best candidate. For their good. And, thus, for our good." She paused, gauging the silence. "There was no reason for us to predict this fragment of their mind would return. It was a good plan."

Her friend continued to stare at their knotted hands, jaw clenched, and she looked away, shame heating her cheeks. She thought back to Dylan's confession, recalling his exact words. Her foot began to tap against the chair, hope tingling in her toes.

"Easton, this threat isn't even a given, yet. All the resident knows is a single letter from a dream. It doesn't mean—"

"Wait," Easton said, eyes snapping towards hers, halting her babble. "Did you confirm it?"

"No, of couse not. I directed the discussion back to the Shriek and didn't press for any more details."

In Easton's company, silence always fell around her shoulders like a blanket. But now, it began to suffocate her as the moments slipped by. Long enough for a long-banished thought to suddenly rise to the surface. The stillness mocked her, and her resolve crumbled.

"Maybe it doesn't have to be a secret anymore. At least not to Zer—"

"Your existence, Eleanor!" Easton yelled, palms smacking the table again, but Elle didn't flinch this time. She'd expected worse, actually.

Startled by their own outburst, Easton straightened and touched reddened fingers to their temples. "Your existence hinges on the rest of the world not knowing about it," Easton said, quietly now. "We have to remain in control of each piece to your story, outliers and all."

"Then we can't let this resident dig into the past," Elle said softly. She watched the gears suddenly click in Easton's mind, their new plan crumbling before it even began.

A lanky thumb drummed the table, and she knew her compatriot was playing out dozens of scenarios in their mind. She gave them the space.

Suddenly, a smile. The first one since she'd sat down and it tugged at Easton's lips.

"You're right. We have to tell Zero."

Warning bells reverberated across her skull.

"If the Shriek isn't working, we need to give Zero a reason to keep going. Incite some kind of motivation, right?" Easton asked, clearly a rhetorical questions as they plodded on. "We control the narrative. Tell the resident who and where E is—"

Elle's breath hitched.

"—with discretion, of course," Easton added quickly. "Just enough to stabilize the resident's curiosity so they don't ask questions that tie you down. Explain the relation, and just..." Easton grasped for the words. "Just say they are in the building."

Elle turned the idea over in her mind, hearing them with naïve ears like Dylan would. "Clever," she acknowledged, despite the rock forming in her gut. "And when Zero asks why they haven't been able to remember them?"

Easton shrugged. "You'll tell the truth."

Elle's mouth hung open.

"Zero is going to unravel."

Suspicion flashed across Easton's eyes. "Which is why, of all the competent FACs in this building, we decided you needed to be their handler. Is this still something you can handle?"

Elle could not afford hesitation. And frankly, neither could Dylan. If he was given to anyone else... she didn't know how she could remain on the installation.

She squared her shoulders and nodded. "I don't like it, but yes, I know how to do it."

"Good," Easton said, standing up and ambling towards the walls dotted with thumbtacks holding up maps and charts. "Reinstate trust. Convince the resident that our number one priority is them." A long index finger shot out and drilled into a North America covered in red pins. "Void. Is. The. Enemy. Just explain the omission of information was solely to protect them. You know as well as I do if we told Patient Zero the whole truth right up front, they would have spiraled and we would've lost before we had even started."

Elle glanced down at her own knotted hands. Easton was right. She had known all of that, but they had made those decisions before she knew Dylan's reluctance to assimilate into Modular culture. She wondered if the lies had even been worth it.

As she brought her eyes back up, she met Easton's, now turned away from the maps and intently focused on her. A sad smile played on their pale lips. She couldn't tell if it was compassion or pity.

"We have to do it this way, Elle. We need to get this candidate back on track. Like you said: for their own good. For all of our good."

The smile curled upwards now and their eyes seemed to focus on something past her. Something shiny and elusive.

"This is actually perfect timing—" Easton flicked their gaze back to Elle, before they drummed their palms on the desk.

"What?" she asked, caution prickling her neck.

Easton flitted a hand, ignoring the question. "You're going to need to act fast on this." Easton glanced at their watch. Elle guessed it was past midnight by this point. "Tell the resident today, gently of course, and watch them like a hawk. There can be no sign of regression at this point. Only. Forward."

"Frankly, I don't think the resident can regress any further. They have shown suspicion at every turn, and still continue to cooperate. They are even putting in more work than any of my other residents."

Easton threw a cockeyed glance at her. "Really, Elle? You've been here too long to be that naïve. You know better than anyone in this entire facility what people can hide in plain sight."

"We've increased surveillance, added precautions, vetted the residents much more closely," she said, indignant. "There's nothing that goes on in those pods that can be hidden, or at least not for long enough to become a threat."

"Right," Easton said absently, turning back to the maps.

Something was off. Elle remembered the flash in her friend's eyes earlier.

"What is it?" Elle prodded

"Hm?"

"You. There's something you're not telling me," she said to Easton's back.

They were quiet for a few moments, fiddling with some tacks. A soft sigh.

"We've had a breakthrough."

Elle snapped her head back, startled. "The Remedy? It's ready?"

Easton let their head fall and rubbed the back of their neck, finally turning back to meet her gaze. "Medical still estimates another few months, so I wanted to keep it quiet as we continued to monitor our selection for Patient Zero. But now, with this new plan in place to restore the resident's trajectory, I think this just might be the God-forsaken universe telling us the time is now."

She could almost feel her eyes bulging in their sockets. "You think Dyl—the resident could be ready that soon?"

Easton's eyes narrowed. "Why so concerned? Out of anyone here, you should be the most tired of lying to our Legacies."

"Of course I am, but that's not a reason to rush something like this. I mean we're only four months into this..." she stopped, incredulity cutting her thoughts off. "Ok wait, please just let me lay it out for you: you think we're ready to extract the resources needed from a resident who has been wary and extremely cautious of us for months now— and use those very cells to create an injection that will inoculate every living person?"

Elle searched the Overseer's face for any trace or flicker of revelation, but it remained stoic. Offended, even.

"I was there when these walls first came up, Elle. I was there to welcome the first wave of people who swarmed our doors. I saw the suffering... the terror... etched on their faces. I have thrown every last penny to my name at this project because I know it's necessary." Easton pulled back a little. "I know what this takes, Elle. And yes, I also know you work with the resident every day. But you don't see everything. I know more angles to all of this than even you do." Easton paused, sweeping their tongue over a row of teeth, rippling against closed lips. "And I'd appreciate it if you didn't question me again."

Elle bit her lip, shoving her hands into her pockets.

"You know, I went back to the audio feed of the day Zero had a sudden Pod Reboot," Easton said, the abrupt change of topic injecting an eerie calm into the office. "Well, I've been reviewing a lot of the information stored in Pod 0018 actually, but something in particular stood out to me on that day."

Elle drove her thumbnail deep into her palm.

"Why did you tell the resident about the Graduate Program?"

She felt like a rabbit stepping into a snare. The question itself wasn't odd, only the timing of it.

"I thought it would give them encouragement to keep up their work," she replied passively. "Use the resident's own complaints to our advantage. They complain about us hovering, we tell them to work harder and we'll back off. It's a direct cause and effect."

"Even though, as Patient Zero, they will never make it to the Graduate Program."

Elle shrugged. "The resident doesn't need to know that." She was surprised by the lack of emotion in her voice. She was also exhausted.

Easton studied her for a moment and the crescent moon imprint sunk deeper into her skin.

"You have this need to promise Patient Zero more than any other of the residents under your facilitation, and yet they never ask for any of it. It's like you're trying to protect them from something."

The Overseer continued to look at her quizzically. An anxiety attack here would be the end of the line. She pushed her toes into the front of her shoes so hard, she waited to hear the leather snap. She welcomed anything to deviate her nerves from splintering right through her skin.

"Are you still sure that you can remain impartial as this Legacy's facilitator? After all you— both— have been through?"

She narrowed her eyes back at him. "As I said before, yes." Any extra words might poke holes in her own belief of the answer. Easton let the affirmation hang in the air as if they could analyze the word for truth right from their chair.

"Good," Easton finally said, and then their eyes drooped slightly. "I know I've let myself see Patient Zero as the means to a very desired and necessary end, but—" Easton stammered off, turning back to the walls. "I forget the candidate is a soul just as much as all of the souls they will be saving."

"You make that sound like the Elect Giver has to die," Elle said thickly.

Easton paused, their shoulders sagging. "So many have already. It's time to change that."

The somber atmosphere threw Elle a life preserver and she scrambled up out of the chair before any of the tension from earlier returned.

"Very true," she said, and pushed back from the chair, her back creaking along with the oak slats. "Well, I need to get some sleep. I'll report back to you after I talk to the resident."

Easton simply nodded, words echoing over their shoulder as she opened the door.

"You always do."

NINE

COLD COFFEE grounds clung to the bottom of the mug as Dylan idly swirled it in circles with one hand, the other scrolling through emails. But his mind was elsewhere, recalling every line of the note that was burning a hole in the back of his drawer. The warnings minced with the words he'd read from the screen's message, and together, they had singed and simmered at the forefront of his mind all night.

They're not fixing the planet, they're remaking it.
Unity cannot be made where humanity is caged.
They say there is no life outside these walls.
Life exists outside the walls.

It was like remembering the missing lyrics to a favorite song. The evidence was there, it could no longer be a figment of his imagination. An unmistakable link, confirmation that the Artist was real.

He had spent the better half of the night replaying the note in his memory for any more links. As black had surrendered to the pale streaks of gray dawn filtering in through the window, Dylan had suddenly remembered the postscript, familiarity having made him forget the final comment.

PS: Darkness glows bright when put against the light.

The darkest of images, washed in gloom, only to be illuminated with flashes of vibrant color when put against a white surface.

That couldn't be a coincidence.

He knew the screens were heavily monitored, and while he couldn't understand how one of their own tools could be working against them, he had to be cautious. He hadn't let himself stare at the image again, fearing it would draw Ray's attention to its wrongness, and then the screen would be scrubbed clean.

But he needed more time with the image. Time that couldn't be recorded in a facilitator's notebook.

His patience had waned with the hazy orange of sunrise, and his eyes were just beginning to droop when the hiss of a chute sliced through the quiet pod.

Opportunity coursed through his fingertips, but he willed himself to lazily move towards the chute, as if he hadn't wasted hours of sleep imagining the next few minutes. He slid open the hatch and ran his fingers along the cool shine of a gray, dull razor waiting behind the plexiglass. Clutching it like a prize, he shuffled to the bathroom, keeping his eyes averted from the screen pulling his attention like gravity.

As soon as the door slid closed, he shook the balled up coffee filter he'd hid in his sleeve that morning and laid it on the vanity, gently smoothing out the creases against the smooth porcelain. He flicked on the shower before turning back towards the door and crouching down with the blunt blade. He glimpsed the small print in the bottom corner that he'd discovered the night before.

This door was created from eco-friendly recycled materials.

Heart pumping, he gripped the razor and lifted it to the corner of the door, applying curt movements up and down. Shavings immediately fell in a haze of dust and a smile crept over his lips. With quicker movements now, he began to shave a small square into the bottommost left corner of the pocket door, where it would remain hidden inside the wall the majority of every day. He didn't need the hole to be very large, just enough for a single pupil to peer through. A crude square of hatch marks appeared before him within minutes and he shimmied to his stomach to test the view. It was like looking through a piece of Chex cereal.

It would be enough.

As the water pounded the tile behind him, Dylan scrambled back to his feet. He picked up the coffee filter and gingerly tore it down the middle with two fingers. As one side floated to the floor, he crouched back down and lightly pressed the other side to the makeshift window with his forefinger and thumb. The material shook a little as Dylan tried to calm his heart rate.

A wave of familiarity washed through him as his eye fell on the jarring picture that strangely had begun to feel like the only piece of comfort in this place.

He tried not to imagine a recording wheel spinning somewhere deep in that screen's mechanisms, but he would have an excuse ready if it came to that. His eye took a second to adjust through the haze of the filter, and after studying the screen for an entire minute, Dylan pulled back to sit on his heels, the pocket door sitting like an open canvas before him.

He blinked to clear his watery eyes and the door lit up in a torrent of color. Shades of green and blue effervesced before him, the sky surrounding planet earth like a guardian while the same words he'd been chanting that morning danced in the space around the twisted peace sign.

The more he blinked, the clearer the imprint became, and suddenly he realized the peace symbol was actually the Modular logo, only rotated ninety degrees to take on the E shape. He searched the picture for anything else he might have missed, looking inbetween pockets and curls of color until his eye lids grew heavy. As the echo imprint dissolved, Dylan massaged his strained fingers and forearm. He would scavenge for a piece of tape next time. There was no way of knowing how long this image would stay, but he had to believe this was just the beginning of these secret messages. The next transition could come at any hour, and he had to be prepared to study it for as long as he needed.

Dylan took the razor and washed the debris down the shower drain before turning it onto his own skin, trimming up the short dark hairs tickling his neck and ears. Ask for a razor, you need to show the evidence of its use.

He hadn't missed mirrors, until a sting of red dripped down from his ear onto his collarbone. He shut off the tool and was just turning the taps back on to wash up when a dim voice filtered in through the door. He stopped short and glanced at his watch. 7:25. He'd completely lost track of the morning.

"You there, Dylan?"

An urgency tinted the words, lifting Ray's calm cadence up an octave. Uneasy, Dylan quickly dried his hands and toweled his face dry. He stashed the razor in a drawer and slid the door open, pasting on a dry smile.

"Hey, good morning," he answered.

"He is alive," Ray replied, a trite attempt at banter, but Dylan thought it sounded stifled. "I've been calling out to you for almost five minutes."

"Geez, give a man some space."

A nervous hand unconsciously darted to his head, suddenly aware of his shoddy haircut. Pulling his fingers back, they came away tinged with red.

"Oh, shoot." Dylan ducked back into the bathroom and snatching the towel, he stole a glance down at the door to make sure his peephole was hidden in the pocket of the wall. "It's been a minute since I've used a razor," he called out, sheepishly blotting the wound.

"Well, you will have the chance to get a haircut from our in-house barber at the end of your commitment, if you don't want to try it again."

"The same in-house barber who shaved my head when I got here? Yeah I don't think so."

"Ok. Whatever you like."

Dylan sidled over and fell into the armchair, feeling awkward in the stale air. The FAC seemed preoccupied, and he tried not to think about the rudimentary hole just out of view a few feet behind him. His fingers began to fidget as he filtered through excuses for his erratic echo behavior.

"I'm not here for a check-in," Ray blurted.

Dylan's pulse quickened. He was confident that Modular hadn't sent him those secret messages on the echo screen, and he wasn't about to hand that knowledge over to them wrapped in a bow. But he also hadn't come up with any alternative reasons for why he had decided to start looking at the screen.

Ray continued in his silence.

"Yesterday, something came up and I believe it to be in both of our interests to address it, sooner than later."

Dylan shifted in his chair, planting both feet on the floor in a show of defiance.

"I don't think I need to expl—"

"I'm sorry, Dylan, but yes we really do need to talk about it," Ray interjected, catching him off guard. The FAC had always been intentional with letting him have the space to talk. "And I'm going to implore you like I did that very first day to please remain quiet until I can finish. This is a sensitive matter that will incite a lot of tough questions, and I don't want to open up any chance of miscommunication."

Dylan pushed himself forward, elbows tattooing divets into his thighs. This wasn't about the echoes. A nervous cough blanched against the walls before Ray tried speaking again.

"As you know, at Modular, we are a team of innovators and peacemakers working together for a common good, to restore health and unification to a compromised planet. Some days, we work together like a well-oiled machine. And some days, we are clearly a team of humans. We make mistakes."

Ray paused hauntingly. Dylan already wanted this conversation to be over.

"Not all souls come to us the way you did. Your mind was still your own with minimal effects of degradation from Void. Individuals approaching the higher end of the age gap are more at risk of full contamination, as our minds are built to degenerate at a faster rate the older we get." Ray paused as if to ask permission to continue.

"Upon arrival, we put these individuals under immediate care just like everyone else. However, our medical advances, as you know, do not cure Void infection immediately. When a soul retains heightened levels of degradation, they are not allowed to receive the inoculation, as there can be no signs of Void infection for the remedy to incubate successfully. Instead, they are put into a community pod with other Grays of the same circumstance. These pods are the priority groups to receive the inoculation by Legacies upon their own completion of incubation." A breath. "Are you still following?"

Dylan only had energy to nod, unease curling around his throat like a noose. Dylan had never felt the limitation of the walls more than in this moment when he wished to shake the facilitator madly until the rest of the story spilled out.

"When you arrived at Modular, there was a piece of your temporal lobe— the section that harbors facial retention— that had been completely exposed to the disease. We had two choices: methodically remove each Voided cell in the attempt to salvage at least some memory retention or neutralize the entire lobe. As a core team, we opted for the latter, giving you the best chance of a full recovery and avoiding any more stress on your body."

Dylan's head spun with this new information, but that didn't sound like the end of it. A buzz began to sizzle in the soles of his feet as he waited for the final shoe to drop.

"When you awoke, we tested your long-term memory and you checked every box on our list. Except for one," Ray said, hesitation threatening to burst any patience Dylan had left. "You failed to retain any recollection of your sibling."

The floor fell out from underneath his bare feet, the buzzing replaced by numbness. Every limb turned to air as he dropped, his pounding heart struggling to catch up. His eyes stung from the freefall and he blinked, only to find his head between his knees, hard wooden planks staring back at him. More words dared to keep bouncing off the walls instead of leaving him alone.

"The core team made the decision to keep this information from you when you came out of the recovery because your sibling had to be put in one of the infected pods," Ray explained softly. The hits just kept coming.

"Your body had already been under so much stress from the disease. Sharing the specifics of your memory loss on top of having to explain the threatened status of your sibling... we thought it would be too overwhelming for you."

"A brother or sister?" he said, voice hissing through clenched teeth.

The facilitator seemed taken aback by the interjection.

"Brother or sister?!" he screamed.

Ray's breath caught and Dylan knew why. But his fury wasn't about to tiptoe around their gender rules right now.

"You stole a piece of my family from me. I deserve to know the answer to this simple question."

Reluctance danced off the walls.

"Your sibling arrived to headquarters in—" the FAC finally said, fumbling for words, "—in a delicate state. I cannot share the specifics, as the individual is not in my jurisdiction or care. But you are. You are my priority. I will do anything in my reach to help you through this situation. You have to know we kept this from you for your good."

Ray's sympathy sickened him, and he ignored it along with the bile threatening to clog his throat.

"So she's in this building? I need to see her."

"Your sibling is a Gray, Dylan. In one of the infected sectors. Visits are prohibited. And it is not in your best interest to—"

"I don't care about saving the world right now. All I want is the one piece of my world I still have left."

Ray's voice trickled out of the ceiling, laced with resignation and, he hoped, hurt.

"Infected residents can be compromised at any time. We can't make promises of anyone's future here." The floor dropped again. This time, Ray gave him the room to spiral, hovering quietly in the wings.

"I need to see her," he finally said.

"Dylan—"

"I don't care about protocols. If I really am your biggest concern, as you say, then you had better figure out a way to connect us. Otherwise I refuse to stay here. At least Void can't lie to me."

"There can be no connection to any other human until your incubation period is done, Compatriot Cavanaugh." Ray said it gently, but the formal vernacular made him feel scolded and he lit up again.

Before he could fire back, his facilitator jutted in.

"I had asked you to please wait to hear all of the information before interjecting. I know you're upset. And until last night, I had felt guilty every day since you arrived, knowing that you didn't know all of the truth. I comforted myself knowing it was better for you to be ignorant of it all. But then, you told me about your dream. I have reason to believe you're recalling your sister's lost memory. This is a huge breakthrough in the anti-Void stimulants from your incubation process. It's working, Dylan. You have to stay."

He wouldn't be emotionally responsible for a liar's guilt, but he didn't have the energy to tell the voice to shut up. He also wanted to believe what it said. He kept quiet.

"Please just listen. Before you make any decisions, I would like to remind you that the infected pods are the first groups to receive the inoculation from a Legacy's hands. However, we have to choose receivers wisely. The vaccine has the best chance of success in compromised individuals who have a similar body composition as the giver. So, while an infected soul, who might only have days left, may be on the list to receive a vaccine first, they will have to wait until a Legacy with the closest matching genetic makeup is available. And the closer the resemblance, the higher the survival rate."

Ray said this slowly. Too slowly. As the manipulation dawned on him, the facilitator nailed the coffin shut.

"If you leave, Dylan... you're taking the best chance of survival away from your sibling."

Unable to feel anything at this point, Dylan nearly let out a laugh at the absurdity of the situation.

"First you lie to me, and then you manipulate me when I get upset about it."

"It's not a manipulation," Ray shot back. "We did all of this for you! This omission of truth was never meant to be some willful weapon of our own making." She took a deep breath. "I'm just telling you your options at this point," Ray said, concern dripping off the syllables. "I want to give you all the information for your consideration."

"So kind of you to do that. Four months and a sister later," he seethed.

"I get it, ok. We messed up. But the incubation process still has months left. You leave now, you won't have any protection. There's nowhere else to go," Ray said calmly, as if coaxing a cornered puppy back into the kennel. "Please. Your sibling is not the only one who needs you here. You're doing so much good here. I think you know it's the only option."

Dylan looked around the room. The walls hadn't moved any closer, but he'd never felt more trapped. He was too exhausted to work out any other alternatives. He felt comfort knowing he still had months to figure one out, but then fear rose up just as quickly. He had months, but did his sister?

Ducking his head in resignation, he scrubbed the back of his neck with aching fingers. A sting answered him, and he realized he must have cut himself a few times that morning. It felt like he'd lived a year since then.

"The minute my incubation is complete, you will personally escort me to my sister's pod and then we're gone."

Tension dripped through the air waves. He wished he could see the strain and anxiety wrinkling the FAC's face. Just the slightest infliction of suffering would be aloe to the searing pain in his chest.

"I see," the FAC replied flatly.

"And I'm going to want a daily update on her."

A trapped breath. "I would not advise—"

"No!" He screamed at the wall. "You don't get to advise me anymore. You were willing to let her be completely wiped from existence!"

"It was never like that, Dylan! I—" Ray's voice shook. "I wanted to tell you. But this situation is complicated—for everyone. We believed it was for your own good."

Dylan was up and pacing now, palms scrubbing his face. "You know what, I'm sick of people deciding what's good for me. I want you out. Now."

"I'm sorry, Dylan," Ray said, hesitating, waiting for another interruption. "Talk soo—"

"No, we won't."

The click seemed to vibrate off the walls. Dylan realized it was the first time he'd ever had the last word. It wasn't a comfort.

They had lied to him. They absolved themselves in their own eyes by deeming it one of omission, but it had been a flat out lie.

First, they'd taken his memory. They said it was just the short term, but if they could keep the existence of his sibling from him, they were definitely capable of fibbing about every part of their methods here.

A strand of blurred sunlight caught a glint of chrome on his wardrobe. They'd taken his daily freedoms next. And now they were keeping him from his own flesh and blood.

Three strikes.

***

HE STARED at the white door of the bathroom and leaned his forehead against it. Pod 0018 had been radio silent for a full week.

Stockholm Syndrome had settled in with the loneliness, and by the end of the fourth day, Dylan had begun talking back to the Cipher.

When he'd told Ray to get out, he didn't even know what he was demanding in the moment. But it seemed she had taken it as a firing, as her voice had not returned to his cage. The Shriek had become his only company.

Dylan had paced circles around his room immediately following Ray's exit that day, spending the hours stewing in his anger that his protectors could have deceived him like this. He'd been so blindsided from the announcement that it wasn't until that night before realizing the E from his dreams must have been his sister all along.

He played back every detail he could remember from his dreams over the last months, his mind flicking through snippets as if they were Polaroids. A leather satchel slung over a freckled shoulder, peeling peach wallpaper, bunkbeds and midnight shadows. Sitting at a chipped kitchen table, alone, his gaze transfixed across the table on the steam rising out of a ceramic mug, imprinted with a red, cursive 'E' in the center, encircled by green ivy.

They felt like memories, and yet he couldn't actually remember living them. As if they were memories from someone else.

Questions he hadn't had the composure to think of at the time now boiled in his stomach. What is her full name? Does she know about him? Had they come in together?

He couldn't bring himself to invite Ray back in to his airwaves, so he'd spent his newfound alone time trying to resurrect the buried memories of a sister. But it had been days now, with nothing to show for his time and he'd grown restless with the constant silence.

He switched on the computer and numbly began to reorganize the desk as a barrage of new message alerts chirped for his attention. He didn't bat an eye. After the first three days had gone by without an update on his sister as he'd requested, he'd boycotted the inbox.

He took hold of the mouse and navigated to the Orientation folder on the desktop, picked a file at random and double clicked. It didn't matter what the topic was, he just needed the background noise.

A soft crackle sounded throughout the room as the recording loaded. He realized he had jumped into the middle of a lesson that had been spliced into two files. Dylan tossed another wayward pen into the drawer and shoved it closed as Ray's voice suddenly broke the silence. The words sounded vaguely familiar as the FAC began to describe the future of the ModPods.

"...It will be called Equinox. Each ModPod is a prototype, if you will, of the grander complexity of the ModCommunities to come. Now, you live in isolation, but when souls are safe to coexist again, these communities will be larger scales of the pod you see around you. Condensed bubbles of life, pieced together like an atom to ensure safety precautions—"

Dylan's voice on the recording cut in.

"But I thought the vaccine would make us immune to whatever is out there?"

"Yes, however we're being cautious because we have yet to know the state of the environment outside these walls. Our data shows that nothing living remains. So while we may be safe from the virus, the air itself is likely not hospitable for our existence."

Dylan felt his eyes start to glaze over now just like the first time he had heard all of this. He kept the audio playing as ambient noise while he flitted around the room tossing discarded clothes into a basket, making the bed and drying the dishes. He'd worked himself into a slight sweat and padded to the bathroom, turned on the taps and let the cold flood his body. His nerves lit up from the shock, limbs feeling taut and refreshed. If only his brain could do the same.

He hadn't forgotten about the screen, but the image washed in negatives had not changed, despite the other two screens in his pod still transitioning every two weeks or so. He felt forgotten.

As much as he had wished it, Dylan refused to believe Ray's absence meant no one was watching, so he had continued to avoid staring at the eerie screen without the use of his peephole. But when it had refused to change, he had quickly lost interest in staring at it.

Turning the dial hard to the left, he let the warmth relax his chilled limbs as Dylan stared at the white tiles until the water wrinkled the pads of his fingers. He'd long since memorized the image that still haunted the side of his wall with its inky swirls and grisly smiles. He flitted through the details now in his mind as if he was flicking through pages in a photo album. The hidden inscriptions, a clear sky, twisted logos, a brown-haired figure sitting—

Dylan's pulse shot up, interrupting his conditioned flow. He stared at a chipped tile, not seeing it but rather a flash of chocolate hair wrapped in a bun shooting up and out of an attic door. *I'm sorry, E.*

The inscriptions from the screen had never been the most important message. It was the figure. The savior from his attic vision—his sister.

He'd never seen a clear picture of the person in those hazy dreams, but the visions never seemed like his anyway and he'd written them off as convoluted images from things he'd read. But that was all before he'd known he'd had a sibling.

The water cut off as Dylan lunged for his towel, his brain flicking through the Polaroids again but inserting the figure from the echo screen into each fragment.

Slender fingers wrapped around the mug as golden brown hair tickled the edge of a tea bag, the face from the screen leaning forward into the steam. That same smile brightening the darkness of an attic, uncovering a dimple that let him know he wasn't really in trouble. Green eyes chastised him as she punched him in the shoulder after ridiculing him about monsters. Wavy brown hair, framing a heart shaped face, falling over the railing of a bunkbed as a voice whispered in the dark, "Dylan, are you awake?"

His skin pimpled, déjà vu washing over him like another douse of cold water and the towel dropped to the floor. Her voice was seeping in now from under the door, soothing and ethereal, curling around the steam from the shower.

"This atom design then," Ray was saying on the recording still playing in the other room, "will act as a living organism that connects hundreds of ModCommunities, offering the ability to control a potential outbreak. If one ModComm becomes infected, we will be able to cut off connection efficiently so that the entire installation won't be compromised..."

Dylan's head spun and he pressed it against the sliding door, closing his eyes to focus on the tone of the words. The cadence of every syllable. His mind continued to play the images before him, wide green eyes on a freckled face embodying the ethereal voice, and it was like a chain reaction. Gaps closed, pieces moved into place, the picture was complete. Epiphany struck like a match as Dylan took a mental step back to look at it altogether, and he realized he knew the voice not from a few dreams.

It was the only voice he'd known since waking up in this pod.

He'd never based anything on emotion. And yet, here he was about to take a really big risk on a feeling. Because perhaps all the lies he had uncovered were based on a truly hopeful fact: his facilitator, his only tether to life on the outside of this pod, was actually his sister. Why they didn't want him to know the connection would be a question for later, but right now, he couldn't deny that when Ray's voice mixed with the memories he knew now to be his sister, the walls of his pod fell away and the world made sense again.

He kept his eyes closed a little longer to savor the moment until the audio playback automatically shut off.

His limbs felt heavy, like he was emerging from an out of body experience. Returned to his cynical self, he now felt hope evaporate into the white walls. Just because the memory felt real didn't mean they were the same person. If a single voice is the only one you hear for so long, it's easy to make it look like anybody you want.

Or was that just another lie?

TEN

FROM: Overseer <EHill@modularenterprises.com>
TO: Dylan Cavanaugh <DCav0018@modularenterprises.com>
Re: Promotion—effective immediately

22 December
Dear Compatriot,

It has come to my attention that you have ignored all incoming messages from our staff in the last seven days, and I understand it is with good reason.

I know Ray has said their piece, however I must confess with my own words how sorry I am for the circumstances. After seeing Void's grip on such an important part of the brain, we reacted on behalf of your best interest. But with hindsight revealing that you still have remnants hiding away in that temporal lobe, I admit that perhaps it was a knee-jerk reaction.

Our mantra here at ME is forward progress. Everything we do here is with our future in mind. However, now seeing the strength of your mind, and its refusal to forget, has made me question if we should take a look back.

Upon your receipt of this memo, you are no longer working in the coding department, but will report to me directly as we work backwards, researching everything we can find to learn more about Void and its design so we can best fight against it. The strength of your memory combined with the unique perspective you had while employed with the *Manhattan Herald* gives me great encouragement that we are on the cusp of something great.

I look forward to connecting with you.

In harmony,
Easton Hill
Overseer, Modular Enterprises

ELEVEN

THE KETTLE whined as he adjusted a sheer filter over the opening of the coffeepot, yawning as he watched an apocalyptic sky drift in through the window, smoggy sunshine melding with the glass decanter like a fog. His body tensed seconds before the Shriek resounded through his ear drums.

"Cavanaugh, Dylan. 23 February. Zero."

Retreating from the Cipher, he fell back into bed, his shoulder driving into something hard. He pulled at the twisted sheets and uncovered the spine of a book. *Understanding the Shift: Aligning Past and Future.* He winced and rubbed his shoulder, checked that the corner of his page was dog-eared and then dropped it into the top drawer of his bedside table. As it fell, the book jostled the only other thing in the space; the objects a metaphor for the twist in his gut. One of them, a book that revealed a world that he had forgotten. The other, a crumpled piece of paper that inferred he had never forgotten at all.

And he could only be loyal to one.

Joining forces with the Overseer had given a new purpose to his days, his eyes poring over pages of text, cross-referencing the books on his shelf with the *Manhattan Herald* articles he'd once helped bring to life. Political uprisings, ancient ships discovered in the Indian Ocean, another celebrity overdose. The details were all there in his memory, returned like an echo as soon as his eyes hit the pages. But a swerve of the mouse—a single click on the archives folder dated after Void, small as it was—and his mind went blank. The last story he could remember every single detail from was a fatal military exercise gone wrong in Kuwait.

He can see his name written under the Staff section in those later editions, right there in black and white. He would have read and re-read every fact within those pages. And yet the fact was, he'd forgotten entire periods of not just his life, but the world around him.

He'd always thought void to be a synonym of nothing. Zero. Black. But he'd been wrong.

Void was chaos. Not black, not white. Just gray. The color of haze. Mist. Gone before you can put your finger on it.

He had hoped the more he uncovered the past, the quicker his mind would unravel the memories of a sister. The ones before he entered Modular's walls, that is.

When Dylan had finally opened up his message inbox, he had been welcomed by an onslaught of emails he'd missed from Cipher Baseline Management, announcing some slight alteration of the phrase: *The individual you requested medical updates on is stable, under review.*

As he had read the messages, he couldn't help but smile at the cheeky fib. Of course Ray was stable. And he doubted there was anyone who walked among Modular's walls without being "under review."

He had spent the last several weeks trying to align the visions of his past with what he knew from his time with his facilitator. Whispers of visions peppered his nights, but the faded details of wallpaper, Converse shoes and smirks were all too quickly snatched by the Shriek each morning. His latest notion had him awake at all hours, trying to beat the Shriek and fan the flame of returning memories. But it had been two months now, without any revelations on either side. He was tempted to invite Ray back, but principle had proven to be more convincing. He couldn't reward their lies. The truth would come out one way or another, he just had to wait.

He poured a cup of coffee and tucked himself into the armchair, body weary from his sleep deprivation techniques. Scrunching his eyes closed, he willed memories to bubble up to the surface and the milestones surged forward.

Mom and Dad in the audience at his school play. His tanned face streaked with black paint as he clutched a gold trophy from a high school baseball tournament. Charred wood in a burned forest.

People live for the milestones, but he yearned for the inbetween. The small moments, the mundane. That's where his sister must live.

His eye lids began to droop, and his arm jolted, nearly spilling the coffee. He willed his mind to focus and it grasped for something to cling to. The echo screen suddenly flitted into his mind, and annoyed, he swept it aside like an application taking up too much space on a phone. There had been no change, no more secret messages, and he had all but decided the image had just been a psychological game that he'd fallen for, hook, line and sinker.

He recalled images of his old house, desperate to trigger another memory of a soul he must have shared at least a part of his life with. He squeezed his eyes shut and faded wallpaper wrinkled into the edges of his mind. A worn gray sofa, jade green ottoman and Moroccan rug danced into his vision while chestnut cabinets adorned with antique knobs filled in the gaps. He then inserted the faces he knew.

Dylan's mother, olive skinned, dressed in her favorite cardigan and holding a copper watering can, bent over a small potted plant while his dad leaned back in a rust-colored recliner, newspaper shrouding his face. Dylan willed another face into existence, but only a fizzle of gray appeared. Like a mirage at the end of a desert road.

Frustrated, he surrendered and let the mental image play out.

His mom straightened, arching her shoulders back before letting her bare feet take her back to the kitchen to refill the pot. As she retraced her steps, her hands idly flitted to a corner of the wall where the hallway started.

"We really need to get someone in here to re-line this," she said to no one in particular. "This heat is just melting the paper right off."

Dylan's father peered over a corner of his paper. "Huh. Maybe these hot summers aren't so bad, after all."

"James Cavanaugh! You backstabber, you were with me when I picked this out."

"Darling, that was seventeen years ago. Back then, I didn't know you could say no when your wife asks 'do you like this color?'"

Turning away from the wall, she shot him with emerald eyes. "You've lied about liking it this whole time?"

His father shrugged and flipped the paper back in front of his face.

She hesitated a moment and then paced back to her succulents, huffing over her shoulder, "Then you can peel it off yourself."

The exchange felt so familiar—so lived in—Dylan didn't dare turn away from the memory. His eyes found one of the drooping pieces of wallpaper and he let his mind sit there.

Suddenly the sound of footsteps echoed off the wall. He rounded to see his mom and dad in their same spots, unchanged in his memory. The footsteps then retreated just as quickly as they came, as if jogging ahead of him, and he registered the faint ding of a bell pinging off the walls.

The scene was familiar, and yet just out of reach. The nerves in his brain reached out like greedy fingers, desperate to take hold of the memory. He could feel his forehead tightening under the weight of concentration and as the bell grew louder and more shrill, he felt the memory slip farther and farther away. Exhausted from the effort, his eye lids surrendered open.

The blare of the Shriek reverberated off the walls as he pulled his neck out of the crook of the chair. It was already another day? He must have fallen asleep.

He felt the pang of loss. He'd wasted so much time sleeping— time that could have been spent researching. Remembering.

Dylan rubbed at his eyes, trying to blink the memory of home back into focus but a strange voice swept it aside.

"Cavanaugh! It's time to get up, let's go!"

The sound bit through the room like an icy wind, blowing Dylan back against the chair. The Shriek erupted again, pounding his ears and he put his fingers to his temples in an effort he knew was futile.

"Who is this?!" Dylan yelled over the din, stumbling to the Cipher.

The Shriek silenced as his feet found their place.

"Cavanaugh, Dylan. 24 February. Zero."

The cold voice returned.

"Medical. You were late."

Without preamble, Dylan then heard a soft click as the voice retreated to wherever it called home. Still reeling from the jarring wake up, Dylan padded to the restroom and splashed cold water on his face before hunching over the counter on his elbows to let his head hang down.

Blood rushed to his brain, but he ignored it. Taking a breath, he opened his eyes and, just under his left armpit, he caught a glimpse of the ragged hole in the door behind him. He was pretty sure his peripherals would have caught any changes, but with the state of his mind lately, he suddenly wasn't sure.

He crouched down and made himself comfortable before snagging a quick peek through the lens. Nothing had changed, but he stayed in his position, reacquainting himself with the swirls and haunting scowl. He was just about to pull away when he caught a flicker on the screen—a glitch.

Cemented to the floor, he watched in awe as cold blues dripped down the screen like a trail of rain melting down a windowpane, blending at the bottom into a pool of silvery orbs and inky pixels.

The effect was so immersive that Dylan's eye began to ache at being pressed so tightly against the door.

After everything had morphed together, the colors began to walk back up the screen, rearranging themselves into a new blurry image, daring to be decoded.

When Dylan was sure the transition was complete, he blinked a few times to clear any dust before training his left eye onto a small triangle near the center of the image. Then he began to count.

At thirty, he sat back up on his knees and backed away from the door. As if his dry pupil was a projector, a bright image blinked into existence, and he waited for the irregular shapes to make sense.

Compared to the previous image, this new picture was far simpler. A single pair of pale pink lips, unadorned and cracked as if from a harsh winter, appeared in a hypnotic, three-dimensional perspective. Four capital letters took center stage as they wove in-between chapped lines of the lips in a deep red, skeletal font. *LIAR.*

Rather than a face, the mouth was attached to three thin strings as if it was a marionette, and Dylan's eyes trailed up the pocket door to see what controlled the lips. His breath caught as he saw the familiar M of the Modular logo, oriented this time back to its regular state, as it sat at the helm of the strings. The letter's three lines trailed right through the circle surrounding it and continued down to attach to the pair of lips.

Two of the strings were stretched taut, but the string on the far right of the lips was slack, as if trying to contort the grin as it proclaimed the one word message. Clearly, the Artist had wanted to convey that Modular was at the helm of lies, and Dylan sat back on his heels, dejected. That message had been instilled in him on day one, thanks to the note.

What was surprising, however, and a little unnerving, was the image of the lips themselves.

He had never met Ray. Never seen her lips. Yet, he couldn't shake the feeling that he was looking at an image of them now because staring at the fading image, there was no denying it.

The lips were clearly manipulated into a smirk.

TWELVE

THE NUMBING drone of an alarm made her arm jerk. Wide green eyes blinked idly at the numbers. 7:20.

They dared to come every morning, the monotony of her alarm a tease at her failure. Her guilt. Her loss. She'd crossed the line between facilitator and resident. She'd allowed herself the treachery of finding a friend behind the wall, and now they were gone.

It had been two months of barely sleeping. She was tired of waking up to a void of responsibility, and instead, spent her newfound time burning her sun-deprived skin under the shower until it turned pink. The relationship between a FAC and Legacy was one built to endure just about anything. They were linked for life, as many of her fellow facilitators proudly liked to say. But the longer a Legacy went without their facilitator, the more that tether frayed. Elle was sure Dylan didn't miss Ray. How could you miss someone you didn't even know. Dylan had never seen the scars on her hands, or witnessed how his easy laugh made her entire face light up, age lines pushing out from the corners of her eyes like bolts of electricity. And he hadn't watched her fingers anxiously pick at pink skin every time she had to explain Void to a memory-swept Legacy.

Nox had robbed her ability to shed tears. It was just another way the prison had continued to torture her. She needed an outlet, a way to let her body get rid of the anger, the exhaustion. And yet, the burden of a facilitator was to bear the fears and anxieties of those in her charge.

She wasn't sure how much longer she could stand.

Elle zipped up her vest and shook her hair free from the shower cap before settling down in her chair. Thank goodness for Pod 0023. Sawyer Hayes was one of the easiest Legacies in her charge, always quick to please and adoring of anything Ray offered to share. Knowing there was a curtain, sheer as it may be, between herself and the person she became when the headphones came on, Elle had humbly come to enjoy the praise. Besides, today of all days, she could use some encouragement.

The FAC clicked on and smiled as a rosy cheeked face snapped its attention away from a notepad filled with scratchy handwriting.

"Ray, is that you?" the cheery voice asked. "You won't believe what I just remembered!"

Ray felt the corners of her eyes crinkle. Relaying these re-discovered memories had become a weekly tradition. Ray savored the moment, knowing all to well that a resident's acceptance of echoes was not a given.

"Please, do tell."

"I was re-reading that book from orientation—there's so much in there that I don't know how I'm ever going to retain it all—and got to the part about the soul who knew what was coming, like two years before it happened. I must have glossed over it the first time," Sawyer said without much breath between syllables.

Ray's heart rate picked up. She knew her place in the book, and she knew it was required reading, but most residents never brought it up in conversation.

"And the name sounded so familiar, but nothing was clicking, ya know? So I took a break, splashed water on my face, just to refocus." Ray quietly nodded, loathe to hear more. "And on my way back, I realized one of my screens had changed to a new picture. It showed this veranda porch with a gorgeous rocking chair, and when I got closer, it was like a breeze blew in this smell of wood and corn. I hadn't realized I'd missed it so much." Sawyer paused, momentarily lost in the memory.

"It was my mom's chair. And then the name hit me. That porch was where I'd been sitting the day I heard Eleanor Drake had been charged with treason. The trial had been the only news for like a year, and so even us Indiana hillbillies were following the story."

Sawyer continued to rehash Elle's personal history, no way of knowing the truth.

"Obviously, I couldn't be on their side back then. I mean, people that pretty usually have an evil streak. But I was still so stunned when the decision came back," Sawyer recalled. "And then to realize now that Eleanor was right all along. Tragic what must have happened to them, being left there in that prison... knowing you were innocent, knowing the danger that was lurking and there was nothing you could do about it."

"It must have been awful," Ray said, unsure of what her mourner expected her to say.

"And that's not even the saddest part," the Legacy continued, somber. "The book said that Overseer Hill's rescue team happened upon a pile of rubble in Mississippi—they only figured out that it was Nox after finding pieces of wall with all these markings on them, information warning about Void..." Sawyer trailed off, gold-ringed fingers clutching at her heart. "Like Eleanor had etched their innocence with the hopes someone would find them."

Ray looked down at her hands, remembering how the rough surface had carved into her knuckles as she had chiseled into the wall.

The writing had been her way of coping with the situation, at least in the beginning. While everyone believed her to be guilty, she refused to forget her innocence. So she had scratched, etched and scraped everything she knew into that rock—facts she'd told the court and some she hadn't—until her hands bled. She was still waiting for the scars to fade.

"The things they must have known," Sawyer was saying sadly. "What they could have told us. I still don't understand how the Scale could have found Elle any faster than our teams..."

Ray bit her lip, remembering that first conversation as she had sat inside a suffocating quarantine tent. Struggling to breathe through a mask, staring at her bandaged hands. Easton had held them softly, warmth emanating through their own gloved fingers, as they tried to explain why the narrative needed to be controlled. Elle's damning information had been splayed out on that wall for anyone to find, to the detriment of the enemy that had just set off the Shift. Everything had been put on display on that wall, and finally, the evidence to back Eleanor Drake's accusations was now out in the open, killing millions.

If the enemy found out Eleanor was still alive, Easton had warned, life would be even more dangerous for her than it already was. So, still in shock, Elle had nodded along to Easton's plan and watched numbly from the small window of a plane as Nox was blown to bits—and Eleanor Drake, as the world had known her, wiped from existence.

"Gosh it's just so sad," Sawyer trailed off quietly now, finishing her version of a eulogy. "Maybe Void took Eleanor's mind before the terrorists found her."

Ray just nodded, exhausted from having the darkest point of her life echoed back to her by this bubbly individual who thought she understood everything.

"Yeah, maybe."

"Anyway," Sawyer's attention snapped back into present day. "I had an idea after all that came rushing back to me. It would be so cool to insert hidden messages into the echo screens, kind of like psychological innuendos that go unnoticed at first. But then the more a person looks at them, the echo sharpening in their mind, they start seeing the true meaning. It's my own little way of honoring Eleanor."

Feeling touched, Ray's irritation faded.

"And preserve a little bit of patriotism. Really give the Legacies some pride in the cause."

"That sounds like it could be very beneficial, Sawyer. Well done."

Ray didn't have to look up at the video screen to know the Legacy was beaming.

"Yeah, Sal thought so, too. We've been brainstorming some innovative ideas into screen production recently, and I can't wait to add this to the mix." Sawyer's face fell. "But we can't actually move forward until we hear back from Coding," she said, idly scratching at one of her many pins adorning a denim jacket.

"I mean we both know where the holdup is though, am I right? Have you talked to Ellis recently?" the Legacy asked, annoyance tinging her words as she pointedly flicked off a piece of dust on the button, as if Ellis was the dirty speck that needed to be ridden.

Ray kept her trained composure. It wasn't that hard mediating between two Legacies who were unable to communicate aside from a facilitator and one shared professional thread on the Network.

"Compatriot Ellis is doing their part, just like all the rest of us, okay? Rest assured there are no dropped balls on either side of these walls. If one of my team members starts to slack, I will ensure something is done," Ray soothed. "You are doing a magnificent job, Compatriot. These ideas are brilliant and we simply couldn't do any of this without you. I'll be checking in with your cohort on this project shortly, and I'm excited to hear more about it."

Sawyer groaned. "Leaving already? Can't you stay longer?"

"Tomorrow, ok?" Ray promised, smiling through the words as she closed down the feed.

Elle took off the headsets, rubbed her temples and braced for the last call of the day.

***

A HUNCH-BACKED Ellis hovered over a keyboard, barely acknowledging her hello as Ray began their daily check-in ritual. If not for the Legacy's unrivaled intelligence of the coding world, the team at Modular might have deemed the resident unfit for elite status based solely on their apathy. 'Gets along well with others' was not a requirement for those taken into the project, but those that did garnered a much higher projection of success at the end of Phase I. And it was a facilitator's job to get each of their pod residents to a level fit for integration into Equinox—the end goal.

Even though Ellis was withdrawn, the resident was still engaging daily with the echo screens. Remembering that surprising detail now, Ray devised a new tactic.

"Compatriot Harper, I know you're busy, so I just wanted to do a quick check-in with your wall screens. I have here that you sent in a complaint about a defective image?"

At this point, she was already a liar. What was one more in the name of forward progress?

Narrowed eyes swung to find the space that must have seemed closest to her voice.

"Uh no, I didn't," Ellis mumbled. "The screens are all fine."

Comforted that the resident was alert and responsive, Ray pretended to hmm and haw.

"That's weird. I must have jumbled up inquiries from another pod. So sorry about that."

Nothing came in response.

"How's that arm?" Ray offered, and she watched as Ellis glanced at the white cast. A shrug. "Hurts."

A Legacy of few words was a different kind of hurdle to jump. With Sawyer, Elle often struggled to stay on topic, but at least the resident was always in want for more information. And what was a FAC without providing necessary information.

But with residents like Dylan or Ellis, the lack of questions or, frankly, any cares at all, made her job much more difficult.

"Again, I'm sorry about that, Ellis. We are working on improving our methods to ensure that reaction to the Shriek doesn't happen to anyone else."

She toggled over to another view and zeroed in on the resident's face. She noticed a twitch of the coder's lips but other than that, the Legacy was subdued and likely just wanted to work.

"Okay, thank you for letting me know about the screen issue, glad to hear everything is in proper order. Let me know if you need anything else," Ray said, cheerily signing off, happy to shed the FAC skin for a few hours.

Elle pulled off the mouthpiece and drained the dregs from her stale coffee. She checked her watch, feeling the energy seep from her body with every flick of the tiny hand. One more task and then she could fall into her bed and sleep the rest of her day away.

Elle ran her fingers through her short, matted hair and swerved the mouse to find the facilitator database. She typed in various passwords and jumped through encrypted hoops until she got to the Echo Management files from each of the eight residents under her facilitation. It had been a few days since checking the numbers, and she opened up a few of the files to check the line graphs on the residents' echo retentions.

She finally got to the bottom of her list, scrunching her eyes at the file size, trying to determine if it had changed since the last time she'd looked. Dylan's file still measured in kilobytes as opposed to his counterparts' gigabytes of information, but she was pretty sure the number had changed.

Curious, she double clicked the file to open the detailed charts. She let the eraser end of her pencil trail across the screen, streaking behind the uptick of the graph's line like a comet as her pulse skyrocketed.

She hadn't realized it from just the file size, but the clear picture before her showed that the echo rebel in 0018 had had a shift in priorities, small as it may be. Looking closer at the data, she suddenly realized why the file size hadn't seem to change much.

Each elevation in the graph recorded only partial engagements with the echo screens—which wouldn't have registered as even a byte of information—signaling that the resident was essentially peeking at them. Full facial recognition had not been documented. Almost like the resident was afraid to look at it.

She knew the screens could only document engagements lasting longer than a glance, which she felt was only fair. No use trying to analyze a resident's erratic engagements when it was truly just a result of someone looking around the room for a missing shirt.

Elle chewed on the eraser as her mind wandered, trying to connect the dots in front of her. FACs had their place on the Modular totem pole. Just as she'd foolishly told Dylan, they couldn't see everything. When it came to echoes, Elle could see the total amount of engagements, when they happened, and for how long, but she did not have the clearance to actually see the echo screen image itself. A balance of powers, as Easton had justified it.

Frankly, she had never cared. Her job was to ensure her pod company of residents simply used the screens, and once she saw the data flood in with engagements, she could tick off that part of the checklist. Up until now, she had lacked any curiosity of what her residents could see on the other side of those walls. Created by Modular employees and compatriots, the images would have likely resembled the same themes as the images adorning the rest of the walls in the ME North American compound. Besides, most of the time she heard feedback from the Legacies themselves about what they saw and how it made them remember things about the Shift.

But now she stared at the unyielding evidence on the line graph, showing that Patient Zero had increased echo engagement by 45 percent over the course of two months. There had to have been an instigator to suddenly propel Dylan into motion.

She would just have to work backwards.

Elle slid her chair a foot to the left and played with the dials on a sleek gray box. She watched the scrubber rewind far enough and then pressed play. A low hum filled the room for several seconds, followed by a click.

"Good evening, Dylan."

As her own voice resounded through her office, Elle fixed her eyes on the computer screen showing the echo data charts. She noticed a faded gray streak intersecting with the first black plot point on the chart, signaling one of the screens had changed images around the same time as Dylan's first engagement in months.

Which might have made any other Legacy stop and stare... but for Dylan, the screens had been changing all along, and still, zero engagements.

The conversation drawled as the recording played on, and she scrubbed forward to the timestamp matching up with the resident's first echo engagement since orientation.

"Do you mind telling me their name?" she was saying. Elle flicked her eyes back at the graph, taking note of the faded gray line.

"E," Dylan replied.

Elle's finger jammed the spacebar, pausing the audio playback, pulse pumping again. The screen appeared to have changed as soon as Dylan mentioned—

No, it was too convenient.

Elle swerved the mouse again, changing the date input of the graph to see a broader overview of Dylan's echo data over time. Sitting back in her chair, she crossed her arms, taking in the picture. The graph looked like a medical miracle. A flatlined patient, suddenly brought to life.

There was no denying it. Dylan had ignored the screens—requiring quite a bit of effort considering the size and proximity of the three tools in the room—until this one moment in time. A moment when a screen happened to transition at the mention of a forgotten sister. A moment that, according to the data before her, altered Dylan's priorities.

Elle knew better than to believe in coincidences. Those were a thing of the past. Before Modular Enterprises.

She felt the familiar tug in her chest. Like a dusty storage bin destined to remain unopened for years in an attic, Elle had been tiptoeing around it since the day Dylan said "E." She had hoped to dodge his memory. It was easier for everyone that way.

The life she had led before the Shift felt so far away, sometimes she believed it had never actually existed. But then the cold rushed in, sending shockwaves of weakness and dependence through her body, making sure she remembered that it had.

She shuddered at the thought of another conversation with Dylan. Not because she feared his questions.

She was afraid of the answers.

THIRTEEN

A RAINBOW of colors circulated the Modular logo on the half-loaded page, taunting Elle's patience as she hovered in the shadows of the hallway. The facility had shoddy service in the basement of the building, but she needed the evidence. She needed confidence.

She'd never lingered long enough outside this door before to realize the effect it had on a visitor, but standing here now, she felt herself sway. She took a breath and watched the exhale form a misty cloud against the shine of the chrome. As it cleared, her distorted reflection took its place, lifting the right corner of her mouth ever so slightly. All too familiar. Too much like the snarl of a rabid dog.

A glare of white snatched her attention as the database finally loaded and she stared down at the graphs. The facts, unable to be regarded as "too sensitive." Letting the tablet fall to her side, she rapped on the door.

The door flung open and she stepped back in alarm as Easton stood there, slim torso filling in a narrow gap, obscuring the rest of the office. Their eyes flicked past her for a moment, face taut but flushed.

"Compatriot," Easton offered a curt nod, the formality making her step back an inch.

She clutched the tablet now to her chest and returned the nod. "Easton." An uneasy pause as she waited for them to realize her intentions and shift out of the gap. They didn't. "Uh—I'm just here for our weekly summary about the Elects..." she trailed off, unsure of what else to say.

A blank stare remained frozen on Easton's face, and then suddenly they nodded hastily, eyebrows unwrinkling, shoulders loosening.

"Sure, of course. Sorry, I just thought you were going to be—" Easton furtively looked over her shoulder again as they stepped aside. When she turned back to them, their expression was the same one she'd always received in this room. "Well, someone else," Easton said, easy smile playing at their lips.

Elle felt her fingers tighten around the tablet. "Oh. I'll make it quick then," she said quickly, boots clacking against the hardwood as she found the nearest chair and perched on the arm rest.

Easton sidled around her and leaned against the front of their desk, ankles crossed. They clearly were not expecting this conversation to last long, and she decided to test the waters to figure out how to approach the subject.

"Patient Zero had asked for updates about their sibling—what have you told them?" she asked tentatively.

Easton shrugged. "Medical has been sending them updates about their stability."

A pang shot across her chest

"And the resident has just... accepted it?"

Easton looked at her quizzically, but then lightly hopped off the desk.

"It would seem," they replied, rounding the corner of their desk, picking up a yellow folder and tapping it against the hollow wood before dropping into the chair with a sigh. "So you got anything for me?"

Elle looked down, finding solace in the black and white on the screen. "Yes, actually." She took a breath, meeting Easton's expectant eyes. "Nothing out of the normal with my current residents," she began. A hitch caught in her throat, trapped between those last two words. Eight residents. Now, seven. "But as I reviewed their echo behaviors from the last week, I noticed that 0018's had elevated."

Easton leaned back in their chair but said nothing.

"Granted, the graphs show only partial engagements, but the sudden elevation in these engagements is rather interesting solely based on their previous behavior of rejecting the screens."

"Of course they are looking at them," Easton said plainly.

Elle blinked, the lack of their alarm disarming her as her weapon fell to her side, the screen having gone dormant. Unnecessary. "Excuse me," Elle said, incredulous. "You knew about this?"

A slender hand curled around the silence of the room, as if conjuring the answer. "I just mean, that's not a surprise. The echo screens are background music. They are designed to capture every resident—even the most rebellious."

Elle dropped the tablet onto the chair beside her, eyes returning to size up her friend. This should be a bigger deal, but Easton just clasped their hands together and rested them on the desk. "Ok, clearly this is not the reaction you were wanting. Let's restart." Easton sat upright, took a deep breath, drummed the desk and leaned back again. "Echoes? But Zero has never engaged with the screens. Are you sure?"

"Don't patronize me," Elle snapped.

"Ok, ok," Easton held up their hands in mock surrender. "Serious question. When did the elevation of engagements start?"

Elle retrieved the tablet, despite knowing it by heart.

"Back in December. The fifteenth actually."

An eyebrow perked, the left corner of Easton's mouth lifting with it. "When we decided to task them with the new research."

She'd never seen Easton more smug. She wanted to slap it off their face.

"Also the exact same day that the resident told me about the dream about E."

Easton's face fell for a moment, and then their eyes flicked to the wall behind her. She could almost see their mind turning.

"And there has been an uptick of engagements ever since?"

She nodded.

A sudden clap made her jerk.

"The plan has worked! The more Zero has researched—and rediscovered truth—the more accepting of this life. Hence, using the tools we've given them."

Elle faltered at Easton's wide smile.

"You don't think it's... too convenient?"

"What's too convenient?" Easton asked, eyebrows scrunching together.

"The same day we find out Zero's neutralized memory is possibly returning, they start making echoes. An act that they had repeatedly been resisting for months."

Easton sighed, twisting to sit upright in the chair. Resting their elbows on the desk, Easton stared right at her. "What if it was your words, Elle?"

"What?"

"You're the most talented FAC we have. What if everything you've said to Zero actually made an impact?"

Elle hadn't thought of that. So many had questioned her abilities for so long that she had grown used to the idea she wasn't doing much of any good. Her shoulders sagged as she stared down at her shoes.

Easton relaxed, easing back into their chair.

"Listen, we'll never know what made them loath to use our tools in the first place—I mean, we have our doubts—but what matters is that they are using them now. This is great news, Elle."

She closed her eyes, willing the doubt to go away. She pressed her palms into them, but the questions still hung on. She shook her head, embarassed that she couldn't surrender to Easton's confidence.

"That's the problem, Easton," Elle said, slowly bringing her eyes back to theirs. "Why now? What if it's some kind of manipulation?"

Easton's face wrinkled together for a moment, and she saw the frustration begin to pull at their lips. But then, all at once, it went slack.

"You don't want to let them go."

"What?" she gaped.

"It's okay, Elle. This has always been the goal," Easton said, syllables so gentle they could be stolen by the breeze of the air conditioner. "To guide a soul into preservation. You got Patient Zero to this critical stage. You can relax now." She glanced down, suddenly interested in the freckles dotting her arms that were now crossed over her midsection.

"Eleanor. You are not irrelevant," Easton continued. But all she saw was a flash of blood splattered concrete and etched walls. Those words echoing from behind a yellow hazmat suit.

"I want to go back in," she said.

Easton pursed their lips together, eyes questioning. "You have seven other elect residents to tend to. It's not like you have nothing to do." Their eyes were almost pleading. "You've done your part. Your tenacity, your will... it's what has gotten them—us—this far."

"Are we really that far? You told me months ago that we were close to having the Remedy!"

"Yes," Easton replied curtly, "but then our best FAC alerted us that our elect resident was being triggered by something we never thought would be a problem... so I thought it best to have a little cushion of time before pushing forward."

"But you haven't even told the Circle. You're not one to hide your achievements."

"I'm hiding you."

Her lips grew taut. They might have freed her from Nox, but she'd built herself right up with Modular's walls. She alone had weathered that first month's tormented nights when she would awake to the stone walls of her quarantined sector, and she'd be halfway to the wall before she realized the rock in her hand was a stress ball stamped with the ME logo. Easton may have gifted her life away from Nox, but she alone had had to figure out how to survive leaving it.

"Just consider it. Please," she said through gritted teeth, cheeks heated.

"Ok," Easton offered.

She rose to her feet, smoothing out her vest.

"Hey—you know," Easton said abruptly as she snatched the tablet from behind the seat cushion. "I have Research and Development coming here in an hour to go over some of Phase II's blueprints. I need to look over the latest reports coming in from Recon to get the best idea of what we're working with out there. I don't want that Kiwi loyalist on R&D to throw me any more curveballs." Easton grimaced, never one to see the benefit of dissonance. "Now, obviously you can't be here for the meeting, but I could really use your eyes to help me look over the data. I got lunch?" Easton offered.

Gratitude ballooned in her chest, the urge to feel needed pulling her away from her self-righteous anger just moments before.

Elle shrugged and then nodded absently, returning to her spot. This time, however, she lounged properly in the chair, as she'd done countless times before. She turned to look at her friend as they swiveled to the computer, typing in a DLVRD order.

Her rescuer. A soul who had given her the opportunity to change the world as she'd always wanted to. They had given her a platform. And although no one outside of the leadership sector would ever know who she truly was, or realize the full circle of her journey, she felt honored to be in the place Easton had put her. But given their earlier comment, maybe that place was just a trophy spot on their shelf.

Over the course of her tenure at Modular Enterprises, she had believed Easton's and her relationship to have evolved from mentor and apprentice to equal confidants. The Circle had been designed as a way to keep powers equal among the highest leadership of Modular, but everyone knew who reigned. And they all knew who their number two was.

It had never been about romance. They were both too aspirational to be distracted by emotions. Besides, Void had stolen the luxury of getting attached to people. They all knew better.

The two of them just had a way of flying on the same wavelength. Easton gave her the coveted prize of feeling truly known. Sure, the Circle knew that Eleanor Drake was in their midst, and while they were sworn to secrecy, she felt no loyalty from them. In fact, she thought they all harbored some level of distrust, even now after so much time had passed.

With Easton and Elle, trust had always been a two-way street. But as they neared the end of this road they had been building for so long— a bridge to a beginning, rather— she felt more worry than she did encouragement by the Overseer's leadership going into the homestretch.

Something had felt off the last few months, and reflecting on it now, Elle let her mind travel back to that first week. The Overseer had been isolated, holed up in their office and, as everyone assumed, anxiously at work. This had always been normal, it was how the Overseer coped with the stress of waiting for the initial data pulls to come in. So, when Elle had barged into their office for the first time that week, fingers clutching her tablet full of data she had hoped was wrong, she had expected to find her compatriot poring over the same information, head in their hands. Instead, she had opened the door to find her friend reading a book.

It was one of Modular's of course, as pleasure reading wasn't really sanctioned in the headquarters. Easton had said it had been a while since they had brushed up on what the world was like before the Shift, and that it had felt like 'a good time to remember the good times.'

She must have looked bewildered because Easton just laughed and put the book down, imploring her to have a seat and share what was on her mind. It had been the first time she'd ever seen them smile so early on.

Easton had told her then to calm down, just as they would say the next three times she came in panicked. They reminded her that the team couldn't make any rash decisions when it was still so early in the cycle. It was like they knew something she didn't. And that was when the edginess first crept in.

Where she once had run to find solace and camaraderie, she now encountered unpredictability and apprehension.

It had started to make her feel incredibly lonely. Nothing seemed to faze Easton anymore. She remembered when a meeting with R&D used to send the Overseer into a tailspin of disorganized chaos. She would walk in to see them slumped over, hands twitching against a desk in shambles, peppered with data sheets, pens and Advil capsules.

Sitting across from Easton now, Elle watched curiously as they finished the food order and checked emails before pulling open a wide desk drawer with dozens of neatly rolled up papers.

Easton Hill was different, and she realized now it was because they really must have known something that she hadn't that first week. A breakthrough in the Remedy couldn't have happened overnight, as they seemingly wanted her to believe. For months, Easton must have known this was going to be the last cycle. And they had kept it from her.

A soft breeze wafted across her skin as the air conditioning kicked on, bringing a sense of betrayal with it.

Walking out of Nox was like emerging from her own coffin. Her trust in people may have been shattered, but she could still offer loyalty, and she had clung to it tighter than the clothes hanging from her lifeless body. She had vowed to follow her savior out of that cell, to the ends of the Earth.

She used to view Easton Hill as a mirror, a reflection that looked so much like herself, just a little brighter. But the closer success came to Easton, the dingier the reflection became. Where she once saw herself in them, she now saw the jaded version that had appeared before her in Nox.

But she couldn't drape a sheet over this one and pretend it didn't exist.

She remembered their countenance the morning she had had to report Dylan's memory loss. Easton had sat there, waiting with a wide grin plastered across their face, chin resting on one fist like a cocky child. Her heart had sunk then because she knew they had expected her to waltz in and proclaim that their prize resident had officially passed all the medical team's checks. Chances had been good, the elite candidate had been on the highest spectrum for everything else.

But Elle had had to be the one to deflate the balloon, and she had watched nervously as the confident smile vanished, fist loosening to cover a thin mouth in astonishment. Then, concern. The Overseer had crumpled in their seat, shoulders sagging as they silently listened to Elle read the medical team's post-op summary. At first, she thought Easton was just mourning the piece of imperfection of their prized resident; a failure, as Easton would see it.

But then they muttered into their hand, "It's one thing for Void to take our loved ones. It's another thing to make us forget them."

She had looked down, feeling like an intruder on an intimate moment until her friend caught her eye and, barely audible, said, "I'm sorry."

To this day, she still didn't know for sure if the apology was for her, but it had felt pointed. Like they knew what Dylan's memory loss really meant for Elle. It was that sensitivity towards the human psyche that had made her confident in the decision to follow Easton into any venture.

The Overseer was a force, and the subject of Void used to enrage them into action. It's what had motivated them to transform a mid-size architectural company into a global movement. She didn't know what they had looked like before the Shift, but in the first month of being at headquarters, she had watched Easton grow thinner and bonier. There wasn't time to eat, they would say.

And when they used to talk about Void, it was always with snarled lips and slitted eyes, as if it was a real entity standing before them that they didn't dare acknowledge.

The thought of failure had kept them humble and kind. A human being. But now, as success grew imminent, Easton seemed to be losing their humanity.

No one else seemed to see it. No one appeared to realize that Easton was isolating themselves, canceling meetings and pushing the team away in the name of diligence, and Elle was growing tired of hearing praises of it rattling off the walls of the rec suite. She knew better than anyone what it looked like to lose all sense of emotion, and Compatriot Hill was quickly becoming desensitized. When they dared to exude any emotion, it was usually exhibited in sarcasm or a joke. After emailing them the report on Ellis's injury from the start of the Shriek trial, all she had gotten back was: "And to think we almost chose them to be the Giver. Dodged a bullet."

She quickly averted her gaze down to her tablet now as Easton swiveled to face her again. They opened another desk drawer, and pushing past a sealed bottle of Advil, Easton pulled out a pen and some thumbtacks and quickly went to work unrolling the charts and attaching them to a bulletin board that had never looked like it fit in this sleek, modern office.

They began presenting the latest data coming in from the recon drones, and Elle leaned back in her chair, barely able to concentrate past the disquieting gleam flashing in those gray eyes while Easton spoke of the 'incredibly smart' bacteria still inflicting degeneration on the planet. They used to address the disease only as *the problem* and even then, they only discussed it when context had forced them to. Watching the wonder flicker across their face as they looked at the live data, she wondered what Easton really thought about Void now.

On paper, it had been the ignition to their success. The reason to mold their company into something that could provide a safe haven for survival until a vaccine would give future generations a fighting chance. Easton Hill's role in preserving life itself had elevated them to be somewhat of a god.

Maybe their praise of Void was because they were on the edge of beating it. Like a sailor who lauds the sea, demanding people to respect it, only because they had made it home alive to tell them to. It's easy to scoff at something dangerous when you know you've already conquered it.

Now that Easton was on the verge of unleashing a remedy, maybe they were just proud of the impending victory against the disease. But then Elle thought of an alternative.

Maybe they were glad it had happened.

FOURTEEN

FROM: Overseer <EHill@modularenterprises.com>
TO: All Facilitator Team
Re: Your Attention Is Urgently Requested

28 March
Dear Compatriots,

I am delighted to finally share with you all that a remedy has been completed.

This is such a great tribute to all of you who have dedicated your lives to our project to unify this great planet once again. This achievement is one to be shared by all because it is for all. Allow me to congratulate you first and foremost on this milestone.

With that being said, I apologize for the lack of fanfare – I would have loved to announce this in person, followed by a full celebration, but I didn't want to wait a moment longer to tell you all that Phase I is complete. And the first steps of Phase II are to begin immediately.

Pod 0018's facilitator will return as they prepare our Patient Zero for retraction. Testing will take place over the next quarter as we analyze our elect candidate for proper adoption of our ideals and standards for life in Equinox. We will ensure they exude a willingness to subvert to the new rite of equality and the standards of the new race. At the culmination of testing, the Circle will convene to make the final decision on whether our Patient Zero is ready to become the Elect Giver.

Congratulations, again. This is a victory for all of us.

In Harmony,
Easton Hill
Overseer, Modular Enterprises

FIFTEEN

DYLAN LOUNGED against the pillows, a Rubik's cube idly twisting in his hands. The methodical movements, the sound of tiny cubes clacking against each other, helped him arrange the various shards of his life flying about his brain as if they were his own mental puzzle that simply needed to be sorted into place.

As he let his mind unwind, a pair of pale, chapped lips fluttered up from the surface.

Of all ways to animate a pair of lips, the Artist had chosen a smirk. A flick of the thumb and a column of green slid into place. Smirk. The name he'd given the voice that first day. The nickname of a sister refusing to admit who she was. Ray had to be the Liar with the smirking lips.

Believing this to be true, however, meant that whoever was trying to reach him wasn't just sneaking into echo screens on the walls. They had found a way to not just warn him, but persuade Dylan that they were watching, too. If they knew about Smirk— middle fingers swished a block of red together— they were in the walls, listening, watching, maybe even protecting. Comfort fell across his shoulders, enveloping him like when he used to fall asleep on the couch and someone covered him up with a blanket. The flick of his thumb and the yellow twisted into place with a satisfying snap.

Operating on the assumption that the lips represented Ray, what then was the Artist trying to convey? The fact she's lying about her relation? Two index fingers impatiently spun the cube, waiting for columns of blue and green to link up. Or was the idea that she's Modular's puppet, doing the lying for them? A FAC had the sole responsibility of being the one allowed to speak to the Legacies, so the lies had nowhere else to come from except through them.

A white row emerged out of the chaos. Dylan was suddenly reminded of vulnerable words bouncing off the walls of a room void of any sound.

"I don't see everything, you know... they also observe me. I'm not in your exact situation but I know the feeling, okay? You've got to trust me."

Brows furrowing together, he used both hands to contort the cube into what he needed. Ray had always seemed so in control. Gentle, but resolute. But they were just a toy. Just like him. Ring finger twisted the last rebellious row into a column of solid white and Dylan took a minute in the quiet to enjoy the perfect arrangement. Had he solved the cube two seconds later, he would've been too focused and missed it.

A soft click rippled through his ear canal like a bullet. Until that moment, he hadn't realized he'd been on edge for the last three months, wondering, anxiously hoping he wouldn't hear it. But once he did, a feeling of inevitability shook through him. Like waiting in the unsettling quiet to see if the aftershock would be worse than the earthquake.

"Hey Dylan," her silky, ethereal voice said. "Is it alright if we talk?"

***

DARK BROWN hair fell across shoulders, dimples shining as pale lips asked him if he was listening.

He opened his eyes and found his own fingers gripping the completed Rubik's cube, his shoulder blades taut and driving into the headboard. This voice sent shockwaves through his body, confusion and anger colliding with the memory of comfort.

"Dylan, please. Can you hear me?" the voice was pleading now.

His eyes shot to the screen, a ghastly smirk playing at black lips, and he could almost feel warning eyes, hidden somewhere in the walls, watching him.

Siblings lied to each other all the time. She was a part of Modular, and they had forced her to lie, for whatever reason. He didn't have to trust her. What mattered in this moment is he had her, a tether to the life he once had.

"Yeah, I'm here," he finally replied, apathy clipping off his sentences. As far as they knew, he should be livid that Ray was back. He would have to play their game if he wanted answers.

A long breath. Relief.

"Listen, I need you to know that I heard you. You told me to leave, and I did," Ray said, pleading still rising in her voice. "And if it wasn't necessary, I wouldn't have dishonored your request."

Dylan kept his eyes on the cube, restless fingers spinning it back into chaos.

"You have entered into the final quarter of your incubation period, and, as such, it's important to begin preparing you for transition. As your facilitator, I'm afraid I'm the only one qualified to handle this task."

Ray trailed off, and Dylan realized she was waiting for him to give her something. Any kind of reaction to gauge her next words on.

"Alright, do what you have to do then," he said, a little more callously than he intended.

The next ten minutes flashed by in a smattering of questions that resembled an exit interview from a job, and frankly, it was becoming an effort to keep his attention. As the voice bounced off the walls, he marveled at how the sound unlocked the vault of all those in-between moments he'd been searching for. Visions sprung to life before him and it took every ounce of brainpower to hear the questions, but he wasn't ready to sweep the memories away.

"How well do you maintain a clean living space?"

The two of them sitting at the kitchen table, jokes spilled over Oreos and mugs of tea as his mom pittered around the kitchen with a towel.

"How many hours of sleep do you normally get?"

Shushes whispering down from a top bunk as night danced shadows on a wall.

"What physical activities do you most look forward to?"

A ping pong ball rallying off their paddles as the hours pass in a cold garage.

"Hey so I have a question," Dylan suddenly found himself saying, coming back to full consciousness with his four gray walls.

"Well, I don't thin—" Ray stopped herself. When she spoke again, her tone had shifted, a register higher. "I suppose that's only fair," she revised.

"You ever had a nickname?" he said, launching his subtle attack.

"A nickname?"

"Yeah. Is Ray the only one you've had?"

The FAC considered the question long enough to chip away at his hopes.

"No, I've had a few in my life," Ray replied, and then more softly, "... Another life."

Dylan's pulse quickened underneath his skin, prickling his fingers as they began to work the cube again.

"You took awhile to introduce yourself that first day," he recalled. "It was kind of like you were waiting for me to figure out who you were on my own."

"Well, it can be alarming when a stranger suddenly starts speaking to you."

"Yeah, a stranger," Dylan muttered. "So what were some of your nicknames? Or perhaps if you told me, you'd have to kill me, right?"

"What? Of course not!" Ray exclaimed, alarmed.

His snicker died echoing off the walls. "No—Ray, it was just a joke," he said cautiously. "From what you told me all those months ago."

"Oh right, right," Ray said, a stilted giggle dribbling out of the audio feed. "So did you?"

"Did I what?"

"Ever have a nickname."

Dylan paused for a moment, attic walls seeming to form around him.

"I think I did for a little while," he shrugged, shaking the vision clear. "My sister called me Dyl. Boring. Too easy."

A scoff shuddered through the room.

"I guess creativity didn't really run in the family, did it?" Ray said, chuckling.

His hands began to sweat, and Dylan was grateful for the cube as it hid the tremor of his hands. She'd taken the bait with the first question. The FAC never even faltered at the insinuation that he knew Ray was a nickname.

Time to push a little further.

"Did you know her?" he asked flatly, feigning apathy. As if every hope didn't reside on Ray confessing this truth.

"No."

He hadn't truly expected her to admit it, but the cold reply tore at his resolve.

Ray seemed to realize her tone and spoke again quickly. "As my charge, you are my only priority. On paper, I knew you to have had a relation within the facility, but I did not inquire further as I did not see how it would be in your best interest."

Dylan took a breath. One last shot in the dark. "So you don't even know their name."

"All I knew was 'E'," Ray said. Then as if epiphany had struck, "Huh. Same as you, I guess."

Her tone was gentle, but the subtext seemed to sneer at him through the walls. He was suddenly reminded of the fact that had he never mentioned the dream, Ray would have never admitted what Modular had done to him when he arrived.

He stared at the wall of blue in his hands, but saw only red. His lips curled but he stayed silent.

"You know what? I think you've given me enough answers for today," Ray said tentatively. He was sure she was watching him. Gauging his every move and twitch. "I would like to return tomorrow to continue the evaluation. Would that be alright?"

He hated their relationship. How it had been built on lies. She was hiding who she was, and he was forced to hide that he knew it. But to keep him grounded in that truth, he'd devised a sort of game, looking for clues in every nook and cranny of her voice. He paid attention to every word and syllable, but more importantly, the pauses between. And with those puppet strings still burning in his mind, he believed that every catch of breath meant Ray hated what she was being forced to do, too.

The only way to figure out if that was true was to keep her talking.

"That's fine," he replied cooly, as if he was doing her a favor.

"Tomorrow, then," Ray said brightly, and it was as if a window had opened up before him. Those lips curling into a grin, exposing a tanned dimple.

So familiar, and he almost started to smile if not for a fraction of discomfort. Something felt wrong.

The click softly echoed through the room and he was alone again. Twisting in his sheets, he cracked his back and shook off the feeling.

He turned out the lights and slid under the covers, letting the memories unlocked by Ray's voice flick before him like slides on a projector.

He was content in these moments, reliving the past, and felt like he could let the days slip by in this routine until his commitment was over. But then what? Would Ray follow him into the new, hospitable ModCommunities? Or stay on the workforce here at headquarters? He certainly didn't want to work for Modular, but it seemed worse to leave the only family he had left with those snakes.

The questions continued to burn in his mind over the next weeks, subsiding only when Ray's voice returned to his airwaves. The banter was back, and as much calm as she brought to his soul, he still went to bed restless. He'd tried every manipulation possible to get his facilitator to admit the truth, and after weeks of getting nothing, he realized the only way to confirm it was to see it in black and white.

He took a cursory sideways glance at the echo screen. He already knew the best hacker in town, he just needed to figure out how they did it.

SIXTEEN

EASTON WAS right. She wasn't irrelevant.

But there was a fine line between peripheral and replaceable and Easton seemed to regard her as somewhere between the two. Still needed, if only for the fact the Overseer couldn't stand to let her go.

It was one thing to be an essential asset to a mission. It was another thing to be the prize of an egomaniac.

At best, Elle had always seen her friendship with the Overseer as just that. Two friends, which, in this world, was as close to a kinship as you could get.

At worst, two coworkers passionate about the same thing, communicating in the same ways. Kindred spirits.

But now she had come to realize that it had been neither. The signs had lain dormant until just the right catalyst could bring them forward, and Dylan's memory had churned up the perfect storm. Zero's setbacks had caused a chasm between them, reflecting Elle's missteps like a mirrorball, casting unwanted doubts on the Overseer's leadership.

She'd seen the disappointment in Easton's face. Had Dylan's memory never been triggered, the Remedy might already be in place, and Phase II would be well on its way. They blamed her for letting this setback happen.

She could live with others' disappointment. She'd co-existed with it for years now. But her failure was different this time. It had built a new boundary to their relationship. She, the misfit teenager prone to error, Easton the distrustful parent afraid of what else she might do.

Just like an unwanted baby found on a doorstep, she could still picture herself, curled up in the fetal position, found lying in a corner of a cell, unwanted.

She belonged to Easton. As such, Easton would remain loyal to her forever, love her in everything; even if they didn't approve of everything she did.

But in this, she'd lost all power.

Or perhaps she'd never had it at all.

SEVENTEEN

DYLAN STOOD rooted to the floor, the board creaking softly beneath him as he absently shifted his weight, his mind calculating.

"15 May. Cavanaugh, Dylan. Zero."

It had been nearly three months since the echo screen had morphed into those smirking lips, and he'd grown so used to the image blending into his surroundings that he couldn't even guess when it must have changed.

But standing there under the Cipher that morning, his peripherals had registered a shift, and anxious curiosity now coursed through his body. Like slowing down to watch a traffic accident, he wondered what sight would be waiting for him on the other side of the bathroom door, all too well knowing it would only add to his confusion.

More questions he couldn't answer. More reasons to question the people he worked for.

Or perhaps this new picture would finally be the answer.

He switched on the shower, his knees hitting the floor before the first drops of water touched the drain. His eyes burned as he centered the left one in between the peephole and tried to stare, unblinking, at a tiny circle in the middle of the abstract image soaked in awkwardly bright yellows, aqua greens and midnight blacks.

Dylan waited as long as he could before taking a breath and easing back onto his heels. The picture came alive before him.

Immediately, he locked onto the tiny circle he'd used as the focal point. Lit up before him was the peace shape seen in the other two imprints, each one resembling the Modular logo, but with the bisecting lines twisted in a different manner. Their sequence seemed to be working like a clock. This one was now twisted into a 3, and the entire symbol was poised at the center of a tee shirt striped with red, white and navy blue in the shape of the Union Jack. Dylan narrowed his eyes and realized the contorted logo was actually a part of a short phrase tattooed across the middle stripe: *find th3 Link.*

A slender, flesh-colored neck stretched through the top of the screen, but quickly began to dissolve away as the imprint faded on the door. The shower continued to run and Dylan got back down on his knees, pressing his eye against the thin filter, taking in the rest of the picture. Only then did he notice a smattering of eight numbers, two each placed inside of four red stars shaped in a diamond at the bottom of the shirt. It took him another try at the peephole before he had memorized the eight numbers: 06, 18, 19, 90.

None of the numbers, nor their sequence, jostled any importance to him, but he kept them running through his head to cement them for the day they would.

***

"SO WHAT exactly do you do here?"

"Excuse me?" Ray replied, seemingly taken aback after the last twenty minutes of chitchat.

"Oh, I know you're my caretaker or handler or whatever, but truly, what do you do when you're not talking to me?"

Dylan had grown tired of the game they played every day; each one trying to manipulate the other with subtle questions. Of course, only one of them knew they were playing. Ray seemed to act as if she was just carrying on conversation amid her own forced agenda of questions.

Ray let the laugh die on her lips. "I think you forget we're all trapped here until you Legacies can set us free."

Dylan perked up, happy to have found a segue.

"Well then, by all means, it would be in your best interest to do me a favor then, right? Help me help you?"

Ray went quiet for a few moments, which he found odd. She once had jumped at every chance to help him. Lately, it seemed like everything he asked was analyzed carefully.

"In theory, yes," the FAC replied slowly. "I'd love to know what you have in mind."

"I waste so much time during work hours sifting through thousands of articles and documents. I think I would be of more help if I had a program installed on my computer that created a shortcut—some kind of advanced filter—that narrows down the computer's field of vision for specific queries. It would make my search processes go faster."

"Have you asked the Overseer about this?"

"No, honestly the idea just came to me so I thought I'd run it by you." Dylan replied. "You are my facilitator though, specifically in place to give me anything I may need or desire, right?" he mocked.

"Well, I think I know of a compatriot who would actually be the best person for the job," Ray said, ignoring his tease. "I'll run it by Compatriot Hill, and if they give a go-ahead, you'll receive a direct message board invite from a coder in the Pod Systems department, Ellis Harper. It will be a private thread where the two of you can talk details of whatever you may need."

The next day, Dylan heard a ping and rushed over to find a calendar invite asking him to join a chat room, and he clicked to accept. A message was already waiting for him.

> So you're the one doing the confidential research with the Head Honcho. Must be something special. Dewey said you seemed cool enough during orientation, but then never heard from you again. Typical elitist.
> Listen, you obviously have enough power here so maybe you can figure out how to make your life easier all by yourself. I can't help you.
>
> In harmony,
> Link

Dylan's cheeks burned as he read back through the message again, bewildered at its hostility. His fingers were hovering over the keyboard, anxious to return an attack, when he suddenly stopped, only now seeing the signature.

Red, white and blue flicked into his mind. *find th3 Link.*

The Artist had promoted the idea that finding 'Link' would lead to help, however, the incendiary message alluded to the opposite.

Dylan's fingers drummed the table in time with the blinking cursor waiting to type a reply. Had Ray put him in touch with the wrong person? The FAC had said Dylan would be connected with an 'Ellis'.

Dylan swiveled the cursor around, exiting the private message, and then released his fingers to fly across the keyboard, anger pouring out onto the keys as Dylan imagined his group of peers talking about him behind his back.

Without pausing to review the email, he pressed send.

Ray responded within five minutes.

Dylan, I'm so sorry your request was met with such negativity. Before the Shift, Ellis had a very successful gaming presence and it's been really hard for them to let that life go. Despite our best efforts, they still prefer to be called by that username online.

We've been working with Ellis on their socialization skills. They have required more interaction and engagement sessions in the program, so we've allowed them more opportunities to talk to other Legacies. They were actually the one who injured themselves when attempting to break out of their pod, so you can understand their delicate state.

I'm sorry again, please allow me a few hours to find someone else in the department who may assist you.

In harmony,
Ray

The response answered Dylan's questions in the vaguest way possible, and while it was too logical to refute, an itch burned at his fingertips.

If there was even the slightest chance that someone else in this building was working against Modular, he needed to find them.

Dylan returned to Link's message, scrolled past the words aching to punch him through the screen, and began to type a reply, peppering in cryptic lines along the way.

Link,

I'm really sorry you feel that way. I'm not better than any of you and never thought so. We're all in the same cage, and the longer I'm here, the less human I feel. I'm like an imprint of what I used to be. A shadow. I've started to think the walls are speaking to me.

I don't even remember what kind of life used to exist outside these walls, but if pictures are any indication, it was all pretty negative. I just wanted one chance to do something the way I used to do it... before all this.
Thanks anyway.

In harmony,
Dylan

He figured more than just one pair of eyes would read it, so he triple-checked his words to ensure innocence. Then he pressed send.

A reply came back shortly.

Look, mate. Sounds like there's something wrong with your walls. Tell your FAC. Just leave me alone.

Dylan read over the message a few times, analyzing the words and everything in-between, but it was clear. This Link was a dead end.

Shoulders slumped, he leaned back in the chair, dejected.

Emptying his mind, he filled it back up with every word from the note, recalling the warnings. He called up every harsh swirl, nook and cranny of the Artist's pictures, scouring his memory for the various clues. The finer details of the first two images had been lost to the foggy gray of his mind, but the essentials remained.

His sister, brown waves cascading down slender shoulders as she sat atop a planet of cascading words, their warnings perpetuating the haunting image of the next transition with the amorphous, smirking lips. And now, a headless figure imploring him for the first time, to take action. To find the link.

And he'd done it. He had found Link. Just not the right one.

His eyes landed on the Orientation folder on his desktop, and before he knew it, his fingers had found the mouse and were clicking to open the folder. He picked a file at random and let it play.

This had worked the last time he needed answers, perhaps it would work again.

Like the first time, he wasn't listening for content. He tuned his ears to every gap between phrases, the wary pauses, the silk of her voice. He leaned back in the chair, twirling a pencil around his fingers as he shut his eyes and let his mind open like a book, willing the voice to bring him answers.

The exchange droned on as he increased the volume and got ready for bed. He scraped at his memory as he paced the room, the bristles of his toothbrush idly gnawing at his gums.

Ray seemed to be a common factor in each screen. The figure from his dreams, holding a mug with the ME logo turned into the shape of an E. Lips contorted into a smirk, the word '*liar*' front and center. A tee shirt with no head. Unidentifiable.

Just like his facilitator.

"Okay Dylan, that's enough information for one day," Ray was saying warmly on the recording. The toothbrush hung limply from his mouth as he moved to shut down the window.

"Talk soon."

His finger froze.

Toothpaste foamed in his mouth, but that wasn't what made him feel like he was suffocating. He'd known something was off when Ray had returned from the long hiatus, but he'd never been able to put a finger on what.

Since the day he had woken up in this room, Ray had ended their conversations the same way; with her getting the last word, and it was always with *talk soon.*

Until the day the facilitator had returned to Pod 0018.

Realization dawned, blooming ever brighter as pieces continued to fall.

The questions she hadn't understood, the jokes she couldn't remember. Her voice like a melody—only a tad off key.

But voices could be faked. Inflection, trained.

Dylan had been studying the spaces inbetween syllables for so long that he'd stopped hearing the words, and only now did he realize what it had cost him.

Because if he had truly been listening, he would've realized that for the last three months, he'd been talking to a stranger.

EIGHTEEN

THE CIRCLE had never been more on edge.

Ten pairs of eyes, holding fierce stares of frustration, dread and *what nows?* bounced off each other only to land on the one pair of eyes that was staring at the table, face unreadable.

Of course, Elle thought, no one could really know what Easton was ever thinking. She had once believed to be on the inside track—holding a direct line to their thoughts. But now she knew better.

Finally, pulling their gaze from the abysmal charts spread before them, the Overseer eased down into their chair, letting their cloudy gray eyes sweep over the room of stormy ones.

"As we all can clearly see," Easton began, gesturing to the papers, "this was not our ideal outcome at the culmination of this quarter."

The stillness of the room bit off the plain and underwhelming statement in an awkward silence. When it was clear the Overseer wouldn't elaborate, voices began to jump over each other in an unusual show of dominance.

"How are we supposed to move forw—"

"Is this really the candidate we chose?"

"Ray should never have been let back in there—"

Elle felt several pairs of eyes on her, and ignoring them, cast her own towards Shawna Blake, who remained rooted to the chair, eyes downcast, lips tightening into a silent thin line.

"Clearly there has been no forward progress in this individual. Why did we not alter the direction of their program sooner?" Landry Blake said, turning to glare at Elle menacingly before flicking their eyes back to the Overseer. "We could have changed the trajectory weeks ago, but instead, we waited to evaluate them until the last available moment!"

Truly curious of their answer, Elle watched Easton intently from the opposite side of the table. They flicked their gaze to her for a moment, and despite fingers jittering in her lap, she squared her shoulders and braced for the blame. She'd carried it for years now, she barely noticed the weight of it anymore.

"I had plenty of reason to believe there was nothing wrong before," Easton said, eyes returning to Landry. Easton rested their elbows on the table, steepling their fingers and staring at the space inbetween. "And I stand by that."

Landry fell back into the wooden slats of the chair. Elle watched the room come unglued while simultaneously trying to piece together what the Overseer could possibly have planned for the rest of this meeting. She had gone over a dozen different versions of how this discussion would go in the safety of her quiet sector earlier that morning, and none of them were playing out now.

Another facilitator piped up. "Zero has showed no change whatsoever. The echoes still are not working, the dreams getting more vivid... and their vernacular seems completely unaffected by our binary method. How can you not be upset by that?" they cried, pushing back a piece of black stringy hair coming loose behind their ear.

"Perhaps they are resistant to Modular's theory of knowledge," Easton acknowledged, casting their eyes on the papers before them. An index finger traced a black line up and down. "But they have been looking at the screens."

"Not enough, if their dreams keep returning," Landry mumbled back.

"Maybe. But I have reason to believe our research project has been rather successful," Easton said. At the response of several eyerolls, the Overseer rushed on. "Although we have not found more detailed information on the Scale's design, I believe the resident's research has led them to be more..." Easton trailed off, eyes cast up and away as if searching for the words on the ceiling. "Content with our world as it is today."

"But we need them to be prepared for the world we've built for tomorrow!" another voice cried out. Elle turned to see Michal York up out of the chair next to her.

"Frankly, Overseer, I find it more than surprising that you, who provided the most scrutiny out of all of us in picking this candidate, would make any kind of allowances simply because a resident is apathetic, at best!" Michal said, adjusting their white mask, striking against their dark skin, as it slipped under their flaring nostrils.

"And what about the conversations? We all read the transcripts. At the base level, I'm most concerned with the resident's rejection of gender fluidity, which will clearly affect our plans for controlled race reproduction.

We won't be able to manage population if gender normative roles return to what they used to be. We've worked so hard to reset biological instincts—"

Someone else jumped in, cutting Michal off, but instead of finding the voice, Elle turned to look at Shawna again. Elle couldn't remember the last time a Circle meeting went by without a word uttered from the abrasive facilitator.

Frustrated voices tittered around the room but Elle let it fade as she studied Shawna. A long, oval face framed by coal black hair falling in shallow waves onto rounded shoulders. Their blue eyes the only feature winning the battle against stress and a life spent indoors.

Apart from their sallow skin, the two facilitators were vastly different. And yet, one had so easily replaced the other.

"Plus there is clearly no aptitude for conflict resolution management, and frankly no reason to believe this resident would subvert to peace in any situation," one of the Circle members was saying, and Elle returned her attention to Easton.

Despite the attacks from all sides, they seemed unfazed, and Elle's curiosity continued to burn. If not to cast Elle out of the Circle officially, what was the point of this meeeting?

"Dire situations call out the best... and the worst in all of us," Easton said, ever in control. "Patient Zero has been put through the ringer— perhaps you all have forgotten—so of course they are not reacting perfectly. But they will," Easton nodded down at their hands, as if trying to convince themself of the statement. "When surrounded with the right environment," they added.

Landry had regained composure in their chair, but incredulity oozed out of them like a dragon spitting fire. "So you still want to go through with it?"

When the Overseer didn't respond, they lit up again.

"All this effort—the sacrifices we all have made—just to let the most resistant Legacy we've ever had become the foundation we build everything on?" Landry erupted. Suddenly they swiveled to find Elle. "Wait." A haunting sneer slowly passed over their lips as Landry turned back to Easton. "Don't tell me this is all because of them," they said, pointing a finger back at Elle.

Easton stood up now, shoulders squared in hostility, but hands clasped together at their chest like a politician begging for world peace.

"You have forgotten we live in a world that cannot handle ideals. And that is precisely why we're doing all this— don't you see, everything we've done is to create an ideal future. A world where what happened to us can never happen again."

Easton's smoky eyes had turned a little wild, fanning into an ashy blaze, as they loped to the cork board, adorned with overlapping posters of the world and the decimated countries that once created it. Keeping eye contact with the group, Easton jammed a finger into one of the global maps. "This is for them. For all of us!"

No one moved. It was uncharacteristic for the Overseer to raise their voice in a Circle gathering, in passion or in agitation, and Easton suddenly seemed to come back to themself. Or, Elle thought, whatever version of themselves stood before them all now.

"Listen, I understand each of your concerns, and I hear them. I really do. I have had plenty of misgivings in the last several weeks," Easton admitted, and eyes all over the room shifted back up from the table, encouraged to return to their object of affection.

"We cannot create life. We always knew this. But we can train it, hone it. We have a chance here to reset the human existence, but we cannot forget that humans are a force. As a race, we do not lie down for anything, and it was that sudden realization that made me look at this seemingly unsurmountable obstacle, as you all have pointed out, as an advantage."

Landry spoke up again. "Please, Compatriot," they said, derision leaking off their lips. "Do tell us how you've come to this realization."

Easton turned to Elle's side of the circle. Her pulse shot up.

"It was actually Ray who said something that completely altered my perspective."

Elle winced as a few groans filled the air.

"And since I think I've talked way too much this morning, Ray," Easton said, holding out their palms as if offering her a gift. "If you would please share with the Circle what you told me about your own fears with Patient Zero?"

Elle faltered. She'd come to this meeting under the premise she would be an ornament. Just for show, not to speak.

Her mind spun in the anxious quiet, trying to remember what Easton was referring to.

"Ah, I forgot," Easton said after a few moments, saving her. "Ray has had so many concerns regarding this resident that it must be difficult for them to remember which of them I'm talking about."

A few snickers across the table. Elle reddened.

"Ray had told me early on that perhaps we had made a mistake in choosing this elect candidate. Zero exuded a concerning resistance to the environment, seemingly internalized everything as a way to encourage their own feeling of independence and lacked any real motivation to learn our new social processes. However, the longer they engaged with Patient Zero, Ray identified a will that went unmatched. Every other resident we had pooled together as potential elect candidates had intellect, discipline and an aptitude for change, but none portrayed such strong determination as 0018."

Easton glanced back towards Elle. "When Ray explained this to me, I began to see that, if molded correctly, this would be the strongest attribute to the human race. It would bring a strength that our researchers had been lacking in the remedy formula."

Easton had returned to their seat and now leaned forward on bony elbows. "You see, all of these obstacles we have been trying to overcome with our Elect Giver are actually going to be the Remedy's biggest strength."

A soft voice emerged from across the table.

"Overseer, please forgive me for interrupting, I don't mean to question your decisions—" Elle rolled her eyes as she waited for Liv to get to the point. "I understand their personality traits are admirable, but do they even like us? If they haven't conformed to our practices here, how will they ever move forward with us?"

Elle raised her eyebrows, annoyance ebbing with the surprisingly logical question.

"It's a good question. And prior to this week, I would not have known how to answer it. But watching Zero interact with their facilitator these last few months, an individual they seemed to have hated the last time they had both spoken, their relationship has turned a full 180. Dare I say, the pair even appear to be friends."

Elle's knee jerked under the table. Her eyes narrowed as she searched Easton's face, but they kept their eyes on the rest of the Circle members. As if they were pointedly avoiding hers.

"Even if Zero doesn't talk exactly like we want them to, or prioritize our non-binary theory tendencies, the foundations are there. But most importantly, Patient Zero has processed and accepted the," Easton threw up air quotes, "sibling snag, as we like to have called that detour. Questions about the sibling seem to have evaporated, and all anger has dissipated."

A match struck in Elle's gut. That couldn't be true. She'd heard Dylan's voice the day he found out, vitriol seeping out of every syllable as his face contorted in anger.

No one could have turned a 180 from those emotions. Not truly.

Her fingers began to fidget and she clamped them together as her foot twitched under the table.

Suddenly she found herself standing up.

"Excuse me but I have to interject," she said, feeling cheeks burn the shade of Liv's glasses. "I'm not sure if we can write off the resident's agreeability as a sign to move forward."

Easton tilted their chin up. She was supposed to be decoration. Silent.

"Why am I not surprised," they said plainly.

"Yes, Zero is talking and seemingly open to cooperating with our program, but what if it's just a façade? A way to ingratiate us until their time is up and— as they believe—walk away from us. We can't stake our entire future on someone we can't trust."

Even though her eyes were trained on Easton's, Elle saw a few tentative head nods around the table.

Easton unflinchingly returned the stare, letting an awkward pause reverberate around the room before speaking.

"This coming from a person who is supposed to be dead."

Behind the clear face shield, an arrogant grin wrinkled the left side of Easton's cheek as a few snickers rippled around the table.

"Ray, you're at the center of this movement, alive and well, while the rest of the world thinks you don't exist. You hide behind the biggest façade in this whole complex."

The knife in her back fogged her vision, and she brought her hands behind her, digging one nail into the palm of her hand to stay present. Flexed calves were the only reason she didn't fall back into the chair.

"I've wondered for a few months now whether we could still count on you— trust you with Patient Zero. You've done so much for us, but now with the Remedy complete and ready for induction, I think it would be too risky to let you continue with the facilitation. So while I—" Easton shook their head, sweeping their hand across the table, "While we all have appreciated your efforts, I think this issue is now put to rest."

The few eyes that had looked at Elle with camaraderie quickly shifted back down to the table.

"Any more questions?"

More silence.

"Alright, let's move on."

As Easton's voice faded to the background, she fought to focus on the room around her. She was somewhat aware that she remained standing, but she couldn't feel the chair behind her.

It had always been a floating doubt in her mind— if her peers cared for her at all. Or were the cordial relationships, the shallow greetings prior to Circle gatherings just a result of their intimidations of her friendship with Easton? As she sat down, dazed and embarrassed among a silent room of people unwilling to come to her defense, she felt the weight of obsoletion return with a quiet vengeance. She'd felt it flood her veins that day in the courtroom as her lawyers sat awkwardly next to her. An ornament then, too, unable to speak, poised for decoration. Delicate in the jury's hands.

And she had sat there, helpless and silent, as her peers—a sample size of the very same society who had welcomed her with praise and adoration— opened their hands and let her fall.

Shattered.

Then she'd met Easton. Welcomed, again, with open palms, the only difference this time being that they were sheathed in yellow plastic.

And just when she had finally begun to feel put back together—two pale, bony hands had opened and let her fall.

There were too many pieces this time.

Exhausted, Elle swayed in the chair but managed to tune her ears back to the conversation.

"I have heard your concerns," Easton was saying, tapping their fingers anxiously atop a yellow folder lying in front of them. "But I have one more reason why we simply cannot exchange our Patient Zero at this time."

Easton stood up, the yellow folder clutched in their hands, as suspicious eyes trailed the Overseer's path to the bulletin boards.

"The Drone Recon Team infiltrated Atlanta International three months ago, which as you all may recall, was identified as the origin of infection." A few nods around the table, along with several bewildered stares. "The airport had been under lock and key by the Global Health Alliance, but after some leadership breakdown, the board finally granted Modular access. And our technology was able to pick up a crucial piece of evidence. A typed memo, addressed only to someone known as 'the Host.'"

The numb fog was clearing and Elle sat up straighter in her chair, toes prickling with anxiety. Whatever this was about, it was big. And she hadn't been told about it.

Elle glanced at Shawna, curiosity fanning into anger as she saw the apathy pulling at Shawna's blank eyes. There was no shock or tension building in those eyes like the rest of them. But of course there wasn't.

They knew already.

Elle felt the obsoletion fall over her shoulders like dirt upon a grave.

"We had reason to believe it was instructions for the individual who first carried the disease. So, I ordered Medical to try and identify the recipient. It took weeks to handle the delicate piece of paper and run the tests needed, but finally—" Easton waved the folder in their hand. "The data came back. And there was only one individual who returned as a match."

Every eye trained on Easton as they elongated the moment, walked back to their seat and slapped the folder onto the table.

"Jane Cavanaugh."

A hush resounded through the room as dawning blanketed the room.

The Circle never used names, but that didn't shield a single soul at that table from realizing the momentous irony before them.

The son would restore what the mother had destroyed.

NINETEEN

DYLAN WRIGGLED under his sheets, mind refusing to bow to sleep.

Thirty-one days remained before his commitment was over, and he felt as lost as the day he woke up in this cold, gray room that had, worryingly, begun to feel like home.

He'd been put under care of the Graduate Facilitation Division, his own facilitator having been transferred for a reason untold to him. He hadn't pressed.

He didn't feel the loss of anything. He wasn't sure how the two voices could sound so alike, but the real Ray—his sister—had left him months ago.

Without their catalyst, however, the memories and visions had begun to dissipate. Overseer Hill had also called off the research, saying they'd found what they needed. With nothing productive left for him to do, his last month in this echo chamber loomed ominously before him.

He shot an eye towards the echo screen, the vibrant awkwardness of the mixed up colors sending a tingle up his back. Not only was his time in this pod limited, but the clock was also ticking on the Artist's words. *I couldn't stop this Turnover, but you have 365 days to stop them forever.*

Dylan's fingers began to fidget and he gnawed at them nervously. 335 days in, and what did he have to show for it? A million little fragments floating around in his head, but no real answers.

He thought of Link. A dead end, but not useless. Their words had sparked an idea that Dylan had tried to ignore for weeks—its risk factor too great.

But time was running out, and Dylan was tired of reacting.

It was time to take matters into his own hands.

At this point, it would be too risky not to.

***

"I THINK there's something wrong with one of my echo screens," Dylan told the unfamiliar voice, not trying to hide his nerves.

A long pause. Dylan imagined the facilitator on call looking over his abysmal echo engagement data.

"How— how would you know?" they asked dumbly.

"Don't get excited, ok. I just saw it in my peripherals, but it looks nothing like the other two on the walls, and I just wondered if it was supposed to look that way."

"Uhm, what—" the voice responded, sounding out of sorts. "What way? What seems to be the problem with it?"

"Surely you've seen it. It just doesn't match anything else," he replied vaguely.

"I can't see any of the images that are projected onto the pods. I— I just know when you're looking at them—"

Thrown by this new information, Dylan tried to cut in, but the voice had already interrupted their own sentence. "Listen I'm just about to go into a meeting, but I'll forward this along to IT and have them take a look. Thank you for the heads up, Dylan."

The click of the feed felt like a nail in a coffin. There was no going back now, and Dylan dug his toes into the soft rug, convincing himself not to pace. He had to look normal, in control, to anyone who was watching.

Whoever was behind those secret messages in the screens, it was time to draw them out. He needed to know who they were and why they were doing it. He didn't have time to wait for another transition.

By telling Modular staff, he had just given the most advanced technology experts a reason to analyze and potentially rip apart that screen for a 'problem' that had been Dylan's only comfort for months.

He had ratted out his only friend. He dropped helplessly onto his bed, and stared at the ceiling.

The silence had never been louder.

***

AS DYLAN waited for something— anything— to happen, he mulled over the implication that FACs couldn't see the images displayed on their precious Legacies' walls.

Ray's words echoed back to him. *I don't see everything.*

He'd never questioned why Ray had never said anything about the mismatched image screen; he'd simply been too preoccupied with ensuring Ray didn't find out his use of it.

But to know that Ray never even knew any of the pictures that they nagged him to memorize, it solidified his belief that Ray had always been a helpless puppet.

A flash of light suddenly stole his attention and he swiveled in his desk chair to see all three screens light up in a blaze of white. An M appeared at the center of every screen, encircled by a flashing rainbow of colors while the screens seemed to reset.

Pushing down the blazing curiosity and putting on a face of apathy, he returned his focus to the email thread with a coder in another Pod Community—one who didn't seem to think Dylan was too good for them.

While he threw together a response, Dylan saw a pop-up notification of a new email, sent from IT, letting him know his screens had been restored and to please let them know of any further glitches. Dylan thanked them, stifled his burning curiosity and kept his focus on the message thread for another twenty minutes.

Finally, he slid the pocket door closed and fell to his knees.

Vibrant blues and yellows filled a perfect sky, while a circle of silhouettes held hands and danced in a field of flowers that looked anything but sinister.

The deed was done. Now all he could do was wait.

TWENTY

ELLE SAT on her worn couch and maneuvered the piece of rock in her hands, analyzing its ridges and bumps. She watched shallow depressions appear on her palm as she rolled the jagged rock around her hand, refusing to look at the binder that someone had shoved underneath her door earlier that morning without a word—a jailer offering her a last meal.

She wondered if Shawna had been exiled, too.

The Circle wouldn't have known why, of course, but both facilitators were at fault for the same thing.

Failure to succeed. Of course, only one of them could be blamed for it.

She'd spent the last two weeks wallowing without purpose. Quickly following Easton's revelation about Jane, the Circle had voted to proceed forward with Resident 0018 as the Elect Giver, citing that the resident would inherently offer the most effective antidote by sharing the same DNA as the origin patient.

With nothing left to test, Dylan had been released to the Graduation Facilitation Division after all while the Remedy was prepared for induction. Elle had been released of all other elect candidates in her charge, who were now redundant and as common as the rest of the Legacies in the compound.

The winner had been chosen. Now they all just had to wait.

She put the rock back delicately on the desk and finally picked up the binder, touching the corners as if it might burn her before reading the title: MW3 Vaccine Components & Procedures.

Data analyses from hundreds of experiments and trials filled the pages and made her dizzy. She was too tired to soak in the information, so she kept flipping until she found a page describing the innoculation's composition.

Elle ran her fingers down the list of ingredients in the shot that would cure the world, but the medical jargon made her eyes cross. A few pie charts followed the bulleted items and then she noticed a paragraph at the bottom, typed in very small print, but written in laymen's terms. She eagerly jumped to it.

> Once injected into the nervous system, this vaccine will serve to provide not just safety and immunity against Void but to effectively eliminate the human body's violent inclination to conflict and resistance to consequence. By removing the sense of will, the MW3 Vaccine will promote peace, harmony and subversion among all members of the new Evergreen Race.

The panic attack was on her before she could ward it off.

The words scrambled together as her eyes swam. She fought for breath, the implications from what she had just read burst in her brain like flying debris, splintering everything in their path.

Promote subversion, eliminate resistance, establish harmony—Easton's plan hinged on creating absolute perfection through the elimination of conflict and violence. The innate characteristic of the human will had been the biggest obstacle to Easton's ideal world. If the vaccine eliminated it, an individual could be molded into any belief system. The body would still be there, but their personhood would be gone.

Easton must have come to the realization that to make Dylan the Elect Giver, their will could not just be trained. It would have to be destroyed.

And Elle had helped Easton realize it.

It didn't matter that Dylan had been asking weird questions or refusing to conform. In the end, none of it mattered. All Easton needed at this point was the Legacy blood, and the relationship to the origin patient.

The terrifying epiphany ironically made her breath catch, and her pulse began to settle back into a normal rhythm.

Anger made it race again.

While all of them had been grinding their nose to the sterile floor, ensuring safety and preserving quality of life among all the residents, Easton had been off whispering amendments to the Remedy in the doctors' ears, unsanctioned and unapproved by the Circle.

Shaky fingers found the pages again, and flicking ahead in desperation, she found a calendar of scheduled procedures. Her heart in her throat, Elle saw that the first Remedy Induction was to take place by the sixth of August. How poetic.

A thought had been niggling at her ever since she'd been dismissed at the table, pride bruised and beaten by her closest friend and confidant.

When she had agreed to fake her own death, she did so clinging to the fact that two people remained alive to remember the person she once was.

But one of them was so clouded by tunnel vision that they had refused to let anything stop them from their perverted idea of saving the world. And the other one, trapped in a stone enforced room, was completely unaware that their soul would die because of it.

She had to tell Dylan everything. She would be risking everything with the flick of a switch, but then again, she had already died a long time ago.

She booted up the computer and as a shaking cursor hovered over the Engage button, Elle tried to steady her pulse. As soon as she was in that feed, there would be no going back, and she wouldn't be able to call it a necessary precaution this time. She pressed enter, glanced at the yellow switch, but refused to touch it. It was time for the veil to come down.

"Hi Dylan," she began, her fingers already moving to find the Pod Reset button that would let her confess everything without disturbance. "There's something you need to know."

But nothing came back, not even the hum or whir of the pod, and as she opened her eyes, her heart dropped to the pit of her stomach.

Everything was black. The pod was completely offline.

TWENTY ONE

SOMEONE WAS here.

Dylan didn't even have time to massage his ear from the sizzling buzz before all of the systems in the pod went dark, joining the kind of silence he'd only heard once before in the middle of an argument with Ray.

Fear began to creep up his spine, and his ears seemed to scream from the strain of listening for anyone— anything— in the darkness. Then the laptop screen in front of him lit up and began whirring as normal.

Dylan cautiously leaned forward and brushed a finger across the trackpad. The cursor didn't move. He brought his sweaty hands back to his lap and perched on the edge of the seat.

Suddenly the cursor swept across the screen.

Dylan jerked and blinked a few times. It wasn't a trick. His hands white knuckling the edge of the desk, he watched the cursor navigate itself to a tab called *Headquarters Index* on the startup menu that he'd never seen before. Or maybe it had been grayed out? He couldn't remember now.

Then the cursor stopped, resting on the tab with a dropdown menu hovering idly on the screen. When it didn't keep moving, Dylan reached a tentative finger to the trackpad again. The cursor responded.

Looking through the menu items now available to him, his eyes were drawn to *Echo Systems Data*. He moved the cursor to land on it and tried to click, but the screen didn't respond. He tried moving the pointer to settle on a different spot and realized the cursor wasn't under his control again.

Feeling chastised, Dylan watched the cursor slide down to a different menu item called *Legacy Census*.

Taking the hint, Dylan slid a finger again and, seeing it respond, clicked on the words. A password window flew onto the screen, blurring everything in the background of the desktop, and without hesitation, a sequence of 11 characters, shrouded in asterisks, blinked onto the screen. Just as quickly as it appeared, the panel dissolved, and a PDF document opened onto the screen, entitled **Legacy Census: Modular Headquarters, North America.**

A bar at the bottom showed a timeline of blinking boxes, alerting three minutes left to load 345 pages.

The cursor blinking innocently back at him, Dylan tried to rein in his wild thoughts. This was where he had been led. He had to believe the Artist had caught his hail mary. And perhaps this was theirs: resetting his pod so that he could find something in this unauthorized document.

His fingers shook as he scanned the desktop, waiting for the list to finish populating, and happened to notice the timestamp. **31 July | 10:28 p.m.**

The importance of the day hadn't registered when he had heard the Ciper that morning.

Taking it as a positive sign, a new vigor surged through him as the final pages loaded. Rows and columns of black and white appeared before him, an unending list of names filling the space. The sheer amount of data was disorienting, the only differentiating mark at first glance was a strange symbol that appeared in the margin after some of the names.

Then the cursor was out of his control again. Pages shuffled past him until they landed on surnames starting with C. Dylan touched the trackpad, and the cursor was his again.

Remembering the instructions his colleague had given him about refined searches, Dylan pressed three keys at the same time. Shift-3-Enter.

A query box appeared with a search window and with jittery fingers, he typed *E. Cavanaugh* and pressed Enter again.

An error code appeared, explaining there was no such entry matching the query. Trying not to worry, he veered directions and typed *Ray Cavanaugh*.

The same box appeared.

Now annoyed, and aware of the ticking clock of the Pod Reset luxury, Dylan sat back and waited for the cursor to do the work for him.

But the cursor didn't move. He was going to have to find his sister by himself.

Helplessnenss threatened his sanity. Rubbing his palms over his face, he thought through everything that had gotten him to this point.

Memorized phrases floated up into the darkness and he snatched them as they came, trying to plug them into the problem before him. He rehashed all the echoes, but none of the words clicked.

Then he remembered the numbers.

After repeating them like a chant for so long, they came back to him quickly.

He attacked the keyboard, typing in *06181990* into the refined search window. A text box announced: *1 of 1 entries loading.*

A name suddenly appeared before him.

MAGGIE R. CAVANAUGH

One of the little symbols appeared after it in the margin.

Saying the name in his head, a warmth surged through him. E had been short for Maggie. Of course, as simple as *Dyl.*

He clicked on the hyperlinked name and a single document opened up on the screen. He ran his eyes down the page in awe as the words painted a picture of his sister, just as he'd been imagining from the echo screen.

DOB: 18 June 1990
Hair color: brown
Eye color: green
Place of origin: Brooklyn, NY
Relations: DYLAN J. CAVANAUGH

He kept scanning, trying to find any indication of where in the complex she must be. He wondered if employees had offices. He saw a tab titled *Location* and more information underneath.

Infected Pod 9B
Arrival: 20 February 2018

His gut dropped to the floor. She really had been in an infected pod? The information began to dance before him as the words swirled into a maze of dizzying dots. Then he saw the next line.

Last Cipher Login: 4 December 2023
Expired: 5 December 2023

He saw the words, but nothing past *expired* registered in his brain. Dylan's head pounded but his fingers refused to keep moving. He scrolled for any other comments—anything redemptive—but nothing changed the information in front of him. He clicked on the back arrow and the list of C names continued below Maggie's listing.

Something wasn't right, it couldn't be.

He needed all the facts. A way to check if the words in front of him meant what he was terrified they meant.

Suddenly Dylan remembered something Dewey had said in their one conversation, and scrunching his forehead together, the words came back to him.

"*Alex went through those doors and then everything was just over, just like that. I can't remember anything else. Void sucks, man.*"

Dylan screwed his eyes shut and tried to remember Dewey's last name, racing the cursor down the page to the Ps when the gear finally clicked. Finding Dewey's name, he scrolled to see what was listed under *Relations*.

ALEX C. PERKINS € PreV
Expired: 6 August 2016

A firework exploded in his mind, coherence disintegrating into sparks. He might not be able to trust a Modular system, but he could trust Dewey's grief. That wasn't a lie.

The unyielding facts stared back at him in black and white, but unable to face the truth any longer, he pushed back in the chair and fumbled in the darkness to the bathroom. When the lights came back on, he didn't want to be seen.

Sliding the door closed, Dylan allowed himself to crumple onto the floor as facts whizzed through his mind like bullets ricocheting off every nerve, the truth slicing through his gut like a knife.

She was gone.

Ear to the tile floor, Dylan could see only black through the hatch marks of the door, and he wondered how much longer the pod would be in darkness.

He glanced at the peephole, and the coded images came racing back, their awful truth punching him in the gut. Never had he been so angry to learn the truth, and suddenly he hated the Artist for making him find it.

He stopped short. There had been a date of expiration, but he couldn't remember anything past the word *expired*.

He slung the door aside and hovering above the desk, Dylan found Maggie's listing again and read the alleged date of death.

5 December 2023

A wave of hope washed over him. If his sister was truly gone, then she had expired in the future. There had been a glitch in the system.

Right?

He had woken up months ago to a new world in shambles.

That's what he had been told.

And, perhaps, foolishly taken to be fact.

Dylan's hand shook as he scrolled back up to find his own name under Maggie's *Relations* tab and clicked on the hyperlink.

His own file popped up and the sweaty pads of his fingers traced across the touchpad to find *Location*.

Pod 0018

Arrival: 20 February 2018

Last Cipher Login: 31 July 2024

Words and numbers swam together as his eyes strained to make sense of the information on the screen. His body wanted to thrash and pound the walls but the confusion swarming his brain cinched his limbs to the chair like a straitjacket. He sat motionless, the information staring back at him, refusing to change.

Glitches didn't happen at Modular Enterprises. His sister had never been his facilitator. She wasn't even sick.

She was dead.

And if the numbers were right, she had been for more than six months. They had let him sit here in this pod, all the while watching him, taking notes and lying to him every day.

But that wasn't news, of course. He'd known they were liars from day one.

What he hadn't known was that day one started six years ago.

TWENTY TWO

BLACK BOOTS clacked against silent halls, the late hour making the noise deafening. She cringed on every step but didn't let it slow her down. She couldn't waste a moment.

Everything was unfamiliar and yet exactly as she knew it should be. The walls, corners and stairwells she'd studied in one dimension now unfolded in dizzying right angles before her. She'd never seen the exterior of the facility, as she'd been snuck in under the cover of darkness upon arrival all those years ago, but she had pored over the blueprints of her new home during those first few weeks while she waited for work. She'd marveled at the design that emulated a giant oak tree. The base housing and offices made up the 'trunk' of the tree, with offshoots of ModPods branching in all directions. High, low, right, left—she'd found it all fascinating.

Probably because she had assumed she would never get to see any of it. She had been ordered not to leave the eighth sector in the chance someone recognized the face that was supposed to be dead.

Like a ghost, she now found herself gliding up to the double doors that led into Sector Zero, the section of the facility housed underground that made up the roots of the design. Before pushing the doors open, she tilted her head to catch a refracted look of herself in the chrome reflection. Tawny roots had finally overtaken the platinum blonde that the world had always known, but she'd covered her bob with a company-issued ball cap anyway. On her stumble out of her office, she'd had the wherewithal to flick past the clear face shield, snatching the white cloth mask instead. There was little to no chance that the few people she might pass would even have reason to wonder. The problem would be the personnel at the entrance to the pod hall, whose job it was to scrutinize anyone who came close.

Aside from a bunch of dark and dotted lines on the blueprints, she had never seen the details of the entrance to the Elect Candidate Wing, and she clenched her jaw to keep it from unhinging as she took a cursory glance of the hall that looked like the front reception area of a cold dentist office.

Dark leather chairs splayed on mid-century legs waited for visitors who would never come, as books stamped with ME collected dust on the side tables. Elle couldn't fathom who this reception area was for, but she didn't have time to figure it out.

She kept her feet moving forward, pointed toward the heavy steel double doors ahead of her and the cagey side window next to it. Hard brown eyes peered through two layers of plexiglass at Elle as she confidently stepped forward and wordlessly offered her ID card, pushing it through a thin slot. Authority didn't require explanation, and she didn't plan to talk unless it kept her from getting through that gate. A gloved hand snapped the card back through the opening.

"Eleanor Stryck," the guard read amusedly, adding unnecessary enunciation to the surname like a child learning to read. Thin lips drew an unimpressed line behind the clear face shield. Despite butchering the pronunciation, the guard's recital of the name made her jawline twitch. She hadn't heard those names together since her eighteenth birthday.

Elle had given Easton the go ahead to change the name on her identification papers, but she'd never stepped outside the leadership sector to have to use it in person. She cracked her neck and rubbed it dramatically, feigning impatience while trying to counterbalance the twitches, in case the guard had seen them.

"Officially. But most people around here know me as Ray."

Bushy eyebrows bounced upwards as the guard's neck snapped straight.

"Oh, Compatriot, I didn't realize. I'm—I'm so sorr—"

"That's alright, Compatriot," Elle interrupted, unable to wait through the flushed apologies. "It's quite late and I need to get this done. If you would please..."

The guard nodded quickly and slid the card back through the opening. A soft click echoed through the hollow hallway and Elle clacked through the opening as steel slid open. At the first turn, out of sight from the blushing guard, she broke into a run. She knew there would be eyes on her, but they were at least seven floors up and she'd get to Dylan before they could.

Racing down the corridor, she hurried past the labels as they got lower and lower. 0024, 0023, 0022 ... finally, her hands wrapped around a slim oblong handle next to the panel inscribed with 0018. She slid her ID from the vest pocket and brought it up close towards the screen.

A waft of a voice tried to penetrate the din of her heart hammering in her chest, and she flung her ear to the wall.

Dylan?

She couldn't make out what the voice was saying and her fingers trembled as she tried to stabilize the sensor on the ID in front of the code reader, desperate to get inside. The voice cut through again, but much louder this time. Closer.

"Ray!"

A gloved hand slapped the card out of her stunned hands. A flash of sandy hair flew into her peripherals and she wheeled around to find Easton gripping her wrist as they glared at her.

"What are you thinking?" Easton yelled out, suddenly looking over their shoulder and lowering their voice to a curt whisper. "Why are you out of your sector? What if someone sees you?"

Anxiety coursed through her body, cementing her right hand tight on the door handle. It was anger, however, that made her eyes flare.

"Why does it matter?" she demanded, wrenching her left hand free and nearly spitting in Easton's face as she returned the harsh whisper. "An hour ago, you essentially banished me from the Circle. I don't have a job here anymore, which was the last tether to any form of an existence I could ever have, and you knew it."

The Overseer's eyes crinkled at the ends as eyelids slitted. If it weren't for the hand unable to let go of the door, she'd use it to slap the feigned confusion right off their face. She really didn't have time to endure their act tonight, not when Dylan was on the other side of these walls, blind to the imminent danger.

"You don't care about either one of us, not truly. If you did, you'd allow a FAC access to stabilize a volatile Legacy who is likely panicking right now in total darkness."

"Darkness?" Easton's voice bounced off the corridor, surprise mixed with concern. "The feed is off?"

"Off, as in completely severed. I can't even plug in, it's totally offline," Elle said resolutely, hand still clasped on the handle. "I need to get to him. This is the only way."

Gray eyes flicked to the reflective chrome wall, as if they could see right through it. Maybe they could, because an air of steadiness seemed to wash over them.

"It's probably just a malfunction, it's been about sixty days since the last Reboot, right?" Easton said, and she considered the math. In her haste to get to Dylan, she hadn't thought to consider any other alternative to why the pod would be offline except that he was in immediate danger. The Overseer must have seen the fear and suspicion etched on her face.

"When the pod returns online, we will have someone from the Graduate Facilitation Division check on them," Easton said patiently. She nodded, even as fingers still wrapped around the door handle.

"Elle, you really shouldn't be here," Easton offered slowly. "You aren't their FAC anymore."

Standing now in the hallway, heart rate slowing as steel eyes studied her, Elle saw the situation as if she was one of the cameras hovering in the corner above them.

Not only had she defied orders by leaving her sector, but she'd done so in order to break into the sealed pod of a Legacy who was no longer under her facilitation. And all she could say to defend her rash decision was that she'd happened to notice the pod feed had been separated.

Surrendering, her fingers loosened around the handle and she turned to lean against the cool metal, sliding down to rest her knees against her chest. She could feel the camera follow her, the sense of being watched all too familiar.

She snapped her head back up, realization dawning. She locked daring eyes with her compatriot who'd tentatively walked a little closer, their long arms hanging limply at their side, unsure of what to do.

"If you didn't know the pod was dark, why are you here, then?"

Easton's eyes darted away, briefly.

"You weren't in your office. I wanted to see you, so that I could explain—"

"How did you know I came here?"

Easton hesitated but held her gaze. They stood there, hovering with their head tilted down like a mourner at a gravesite, hands clasped together near their midsection.

Finally Easton spoke slowly, keeping their eyes trained on hers.

"Eleanor, you have to already know."

"You're tracking me." She'd meant it as a question, but feigning surprise was more work for both of them. Elle raked her fingers through oily hair, closing her eyes in resignation.

"I've always been an experiment to you. A dog on a leash with a lot of clearance, but no ability to actually leave your sight."

"Come on, Elle. That's not why I did it. You need protection."

Elle scoffed, and Easton hurried on. "Protection from Void, those that weaponized it and—" they paused, unclasping their hands to rub the back of their neck. She returned her eyes to theirs, daring them to say it. "And the Legacies you've trained."

"You think I need protection from them? I'm just a part of the problem." She gestured to the hallway. "They need protection from us."

"You can't truly believe that," Easton snapped back. "You can't see the bigger picture. You're too nearsighted."

Elle's fingers burned white against her knees as she stood up to meet Easton's eyes.

"I read the binder, Easton." They took a half step back. "I read what your precious Remedy is going to do, and that's not what I signed up for. It's not what any of them signed up for," she said, jabbing a finger against the wall.

Easton followed her finger, and she saw the gears linking up in their mind. Easton stepped backward suddenly, head bobbing up and down.

"That's why you're here. To tell them. Warn them, I suppose," Easton said to the walls, averting her eyes. A chuckle dared to leave their lips as a gloved palm floated out towards the door. "So what, you thought you would just waltz in there? Infect the entire atmosphere? You're a Gray now, in case you don't remember. You have been for some years now."

"I don't have to go all the way in," Elle challenged. "Just the quarantine chamber. You know, the one-way screen you had custom made for Pod 0018, so that Maggie could see their brother."

Easton's eyes flickered.

"Yeah, I knew about that," Elle continued. "Before they— well, back when you had a heart. When you thought of the residents as souls and not just ingredients to your success."

Easton tucked their hand back in the crook of their arm and leaned back against the wall, staring up at the ceiling. "That's really how you see me."

Elle stormed in front of them, jabbing a finger into the Overseer's chest.

"You've erased me, do you realize that? I don't have a purpose here anymore, and they all know it. What am I going to do here now, Easton?"

They opened their mouth to speak but she cut them off. "That's not even the point. I thought we were friends. I deserved to know what you were planning, this— this complete manipulation of humankind." She felt the heat searing her cheeks as her voice became a shriek against the hollow walls. "You can't just eliminate the human will! That's not life, Easton!"

They took the onslaught without expression, shoulders braced against chrome, eyes on her black boots.

"How long have we been at this, Elle?"

She drew back her hand but trained jade daggers on steel gray eyes, unwilling to relent.

"What? Finding a remedy?"

Easton just nodded.

"Seven years."

"More than seven years. 2,610 days, actually. 62,640 hours spent by the world's most intelligent innovators and researchers all collaborating to find a way to exist on our planet. If we couldn't create a solution to live with this disease in this long, we were never going to figure it out. I used to think it was possible. We just needed time. But time kept taking more and more of our doctors. Analysts. FACs. Void was stripping us of options and resources, so—" Easton's thumbs drummed against their white shirt sleeves. "It was time to be drastic."

Elle remained rooted in front of them, letting Easton speak because the longer she kept them here, the more time Dylan had. Even if it was being spent in the total dark, he was locked in there and that was the safest he could be right now.

"We've had the science ready to face Void for a few years now," Easton spoke again. "The problem lied with how to assimilate the Legacies with the rest of the world they would be saving, the former having been living in an isolated world without conflict, violence or sickness for so many years."

"I thought that was what Phase II was for," Elle clapped back, defensive of the plan she'd thought was going to happen all along. "Training citizens for the Equinox installations."

"It was. For a while. But that was never going to work. It might have been Eden for a month. Humans finally let free in the world again. Surely, they would remember not to take life for granted. They might have even been model citizens, offering kindness to one another, enjoying the good company of others, extending generosity. But come on, human nature can't stay grateful for that long before the selfishness slithers in."

Elle stared into her friend's eyes, clouds of gray swirling around the black hole of their pupils, as if they were waiting to be swallowed up by the inevitable. Easton looked beaten.

"Void forced a shutdown. So we have to force a restart. The only way to have harmony on this Earth is to eliminate the choice not to have it."

"What's wrong with trusting in humans?" Elle argued. "We can't let history define decisions we make in unprecedented times. You don't know how people can adapt to this. It could make us stronger."

Easton leveled their gaze at her, sympathy laced with condescension.

"Really, Elle? Of all people, you want to trust in humans? The same people you gave your entire life up for, only to have them cast you aside and send you to prison for it?"

Elle looked down at the white scars. "That was before they all knew better. I can't hate them for being ignorant." She brought her eyes back up to Easton's. "But I can hate you for letting me think I could trust you. You cast me aside like I was some pawn in the way of your checkmate. And you don't have the luxury of ignorance. You know everything, Easton. Everything."

They suddenly kicked off the wall, reaching for her wrists but she shrugged away, defiance surging through her body.

They backed off but searched her eyes for any pool of empathy she might have left. It was down to a trickle. "Elle, that's not what happened. Please, that's why I came to find you. I wanted to explain my actions."

Crossing her arms, she lazily held out a hand, mocking him to continue.

"I was losing the Circle," Easton said, voice pleading. "You saw it. I know you did. Frankly, ever since that unsanctioned Reboot stunt you pulled, they've been on edge about you."

Elle raised her eyebrows. No one had said anything about it being a stunt. She rubbed at her arms, tracing the freckles, suddenly feeling exposed.

"They didn't want you to be leading the Elect Candidate group anymore."

Her pulse quickened. They didn't like her, but they'd always veiled it with some level of respect towards how she fulfilled her role.

Or so she had always thought.

Her eyes narrowed.

"And you thought Shawna could do better."

Easton scrubbed a hand across their face.

"You're still mad."

Elle's eyes went wild, voice echoing off the walls. "Just because I stayed quiet didn't mean I was okay with it! You erased me from that pod!"

"The mistake with Zero's neutralization involved all of us, but you were the one who had taken the brunt of it," Easton countered. "I thought it was best to finally let you off the hook."

"Don't even," Elle snapped. "You blamed me the entire time for what happened. It was me who suggested the voice alteration. Me who invited Maggie to speak to their brother. Me who worried too much. Hovered too much. And when Zero started remembering—you took me out." Her finger shot out towards Easton's chest again. "Don't act like you did this for me. You just needed a scapegoat."

Easton shoved their hands in their pockets, their shoulders sagging.

"You're right," they said, voice resigned. "I didn't do this for you."

Elle took a step back, their admission like finding a snake in the grass.

"We were so close to the next step that I couldn't afford a step back. I wanted to send you back in there, for Zero's sake. But you hadn't made any progress. I didn't want to risk it." Easton kept their eyes on hers, matter of fact. "Then I remembered your switch. I realized we could do both."

"And what a success that was," Elle sneered.

"Come on, Elle. You can't blame them."

"Why not? No one else does. They all blame me for Shawna's failure."

"We couldn't tell the others. You know that."

Elle sighed and rubbed her palms down her face. Of course she knew that. The little yellow switch had been their dirty little secret. The riskiest decision, and they'd done it without Circle approval.

Just eleven months ago, but it felt like a lifetime. Back when Easton shared her compassion. Back when the only danger was that they cared too much. Back when Easton didn't have the Remedy.

They had come too far. Too far for anyone—Elle was quickly realizing—to stand in Easton's way.

"I kept quiet for you. To save your reputation," Elle said. She turned back to Easton, nearly whispering now. "But what about mine?"

Easton held her gaze, biting their lip, but remained quiet for a long time. Somewhere, a clock ticked the minutes by. Easton's eyes dropped and then crept back up. Their hands reached for hers, and it was like the first day again. She was sitting in a briefing room, surrounded by gray walls, as Easton held her tender, bandaged hands and explained how she could start over here. She had felt such hope.

"Give me the Turnover."

She snapped to the present, hands pulling back from Easton's.

"What?" Elle asked.

"The Turnover sequence. Inject it into me."

She shook her head in confusion.

"What will that do? Are you insane?"

Easton took a step forward, grasping her fingers. "You don't think I trust you, or at the least, you don't trust me. This is the only way I can show it. Give me the injection. A restart."

"But then— then you'll forget everyth—"

"Yes. I will. Someone will have to fill my spot in leadership of this place," Easton said, slowly, eyes turning the color of concrete as the implication cemented in both of their minds. "You deserve it."

Questions surged through her mind. Easton was relinquishing command of Modular Enterprises to her, just like that? Let alone, to someone who had just argued against their intended plan. Why give her the opportunity to alter the direction of the Remedy?

Or had Easton already set the plan in motion, and everything was on autopilot no matter who was in control?

"I know what you're thinking, but I still trust you."

She knew her face wasn't that transparent. Easton just knew her too well. Elle analyzed their face now, taut and drawn as if ready for battle, but gray eyes pled for a truce. Easton Hill may know her well, but the recent months had made her doubt she could say the same for them. Did she still back everything this company stood for? Because if she didn't, she couldn't bring herself to lead it.

Remedy aside, she'd given everything to this movement, and she'd fought to make it what it was now. Their ultimate goal wasn't just about making life livable again—it was about changing the world into one where its inhabitants could thrive. Yes, Void had destroyed everything. It was an unfathomable catastrophe that she'd fought tooth and nail to stop before it had even started.

But it had happened anyway, making those left standing with no choice but to accept it. With that acceptance came realization for opportunity, and now it was here at their feet.

At her feet.

Power surged through her veins.

Perhaps Easton was right. Humanity couldn't afford to go back to life as it was. If history had proven anything, human nature has always been drawn to the status quo like a magnet, and look where they'd ended up.

No, they had to fight fire with fire, and this remedy might be the perfect incendiary. Drastic measures had gotten them into this mess—only drastic measures could bring them back out.

The choice blurred the lines of ethics, but in a world where humanity teetered on the edge of extinction, morality was bound to get muddy.

"You're an extension of me, Eleanor," Easton said, interjecting her thoughts. "This just makes it official. We went into this with the same mindset, we will finish this as one."

She looked past their shoulder to the reflective chrome wall and saw her lips moving but barely heard the words.

"Ok. I'll do it."

TWENTY THREE

THE CHIME made them both jump.

Easton recovered quickly and shifted under the blankets to get comfortable while Elle stood up and lifted the plexiglass of the DLVRD chute. Pulling out the single tube, she ogled at the dark green liquid barely filling the vial, incandescent as two gloved fingers gingerly held it up to the light.

She brought the tube back down to eye level and caught a flash of trepidation cross over Easton's face.

"Maybe we should go to one of the labs to do this," she said reluctantly, looking around the office that, albeit organized, was nowhere near hygienic standards. Easton sighed and scooted back against the pillow.

"What is there to prevent? More infection?" They shook their head with a small smile. "Just do it here, keep the lab areas sterile for the Legacies."

Elle hesitated. "And you're still comfortable with the plan?" she asked, sitting down on the armrest of the black leather pleated couch, suddenly aware of how much it looked like the chairs in Sector Zero's waiting area.

"Considering the Circle-wide memo has already been sent, I don't think I have a choice at this point."

"I mean, all they know is that you'll be operating solely out of your office from here on out, all mandates and orders to come by encrypted key. No one knows it'll actually be me."

"In true Eleanor Drake fashion." Easton said, a wink pulling at their lips. "You'll have sole access to everything now with my cipher keys and logins, so you'll have to grant me access as a guest to see the Echo Database when I wake up."

"You're sure that'll be enough?"

"Just let the process do what it's supposed to do. I've always believed in the method. Frankly, it's overdue that I practice what I preach. The bigger question, though, is if I'm going to believe you when I wake up," they said, tapping the white binder resting on their lap.

"And you want me to tell you everything, right off the bat? Cause you know that's not usually how we do things. How will you trust I'm telling the truth? Anyone can make a binder full of crazy information and say it's true."

Easton shrugged. "Everyone has a trigger. Just tell me your real name. It'll bring it back."

Elle smiled. It was a comforting thought. She'd spent so long running and hiding from that name, and soon it would be used to bring solace and calm back to a soul.

"Okay, now remember," she said, fussing over the blanket and tucking it around Easton's waist. "After I give you the Turnover, it'll be like you're waking up on the last day before the Shift. You won't know me, so I don't think I should be in the room at first. I'll pipe into your office and help walk you through it."

"It only took seven years, but I'm finally going to get to see what Ray can do, firsthand," Easton said, but the joke landed a little more nervously than she thought Easton intended.

Holding the vial between her fingers again, her own nerves crept up her arm like tangled vines. She knew it showed on her face but there was no use trying to hide anything from Easton now.

"Elle, this is a good thing," Easton said gently, letting a hand rest against hers, as it tried to keep the tube steady. "You're meant to do this, meant for this. And if it gets to be too much, I'll be back to operating standards again in just a few weeks, I'll be here to help you. The Turnover is the biggest reason why we don't have everyone's trust. Doing it to myself? That'll shut them up," Easton said, grinning.

Easton's confidence tapered her anxiety, and the green liquid grew still as she looked down at her hands.

Easton let the grin slide away and suddenly turned their chin towards her, meeting her eyes with a warning glance. "You do know that this—" Easton tapped their fingers against the binder. "This is the best chance to give these residents freedom? I've been over every other alternative, five times over," Easton said tiredly.

They looked back over her shoulder now, eyes glazing over. Elle lightly squeezed their shoulder, and their eyes snapped back to hers. "There's no other way to do this. To help everyone. Please, you understand?"

She sat there holding the syringe like a harmless pencil in her fingers as Easton drilled passionate eyes into her own.

It was their last method of persuasion, she realized. They needed her to say it, to be sure that she would take hold of the fire that one push of her thumb was about to extinguish from them.

"I'll make it happen." She bit her lip and then twisted it into a soft grin. "And then I'll report back to you."

Easton chuckled softly and turned away as she hovered the needle over her friend's bicep.

"You always do."

TWENTY FOUR

DELIRIUM FLICKED on with the lights.

His head felt like a boulder as he heaved it out from the crook of his arm. He'd lost sense of time as he'd slumped there over the desk and his eyes adjusted, narrowing onto the screen still blazing its unescapable truth before him. His cheeks felt both cracked and damp, and he realized the tears were still falling.

His eyes flitted around the room as the fog began to clear in his mind, and landed on the vibrant echo screen close to his bed.

Like a switch, the anger shot him out of the chair.

"Ray! Come on out, you lying little puppet! Come in here and tell me to my face what you did to her!"

He staggered to the wall and pounded his fists against it, the physical pain like aloe to the grief ripping through his body.

No response.

"Come on, Ray. I know one of you can hear me. I don't care which one of you shows up, but you can't hide in the walls this time. I know everything!" he yelled, pacing the floor. His teeth clenched as he found a new wall and began pounding again, rattling the echo screen.

"You can't ignore me forever. I don't know what I'll do," he said, a strangled laugh stumbling out of his lips. "It might be dangerous to my health."

He felt a wildness surging through his veins as he circled the room, and he didn't try to rein it in. Strangled words and bitter cries came out uncontrollably, and before long, he lost track of how much time had passed.

The anger hadn't dulled, but his limbs ached. Words no longer made it past his exhausted throat.

Suddenly, an unexplainable calm began to rise up from his toes, confusion rooting him to the floor. Apathy tingled his fingertips as he stared at them, wondering why his knuckles were bleeding.

His knees crumbled beneath him as he melted onto the rug, eyes tilting up towards the ceiling. The last thing that he saw was a fine mist trickling out of the Cipher.

Then it all went black.

TWENTY FIVE

THE OVERSEER'S body lie motionless underneath the blankets, and with one more glance at the chrome walls, Elle cut off the feed. Back in her own office, the weight of the matter pressed in on her from all sides. Easton was thoroughly under now, and it was time for her to step into their shoes. She arched her back against her chair, set her shoulders and, peering at the scrap of paper Easton had hastily written their passwords on, signed into the Network as the Overseer.

As icons loaded onto the screen, she was blindsided by a popup window, outlined and blinking in red, alerting that Pod 0018 was sending out a distress signal. The message included a hyperlink and she swerved to click on it. Immediately, a new window popped up and she flinched as a live picture of Pod 0018 appeared before her.

A navy tee shirt hung haphazardly on Dylan's torso, wrinkled and riding up his waist, as he pounded the wall underneath the Cipher. She was struck by the sudden awareness that Easton could observe residents at all times of the day, without engaging with them. She felt lightheaded with the implication, but had no time to dwell on it, as her Legacy was veering closer and closer to insanity. Elle moved her mouse to see if there was audio available, and a timeline scrubber appeared. Her fingers moved before she could question the action.

The Legacy jumped and paced backwards, arms flailing about in rewind as Elle played back the last several minutes of life in Pod 0018. When she pressed play, Dylan's voice blared through her speakers.

"...but you can't hide in the walls this time. I know everything!"

His fists burned red as he kept banging the walls as if she was a rat that he could spook out.

A simple Pod Reboot could not have made Dylan act like this. He'd gone through one before, he knew what it sounded like in his ears. The sudden darkness shouldn't have set him off.

She needed to know what had brought him to this, and she needed to do it fast. The timeline hovered in front of her, tantalizing. Glancing at the time on the computer, she bit her lip and pushed the scrubber back harshly, until she saw the monitor go black. Peering closely at the screen, she then pressed play. Radio silence and total blackness filled the space as the timecode ran, proving all systems in the pod had been squelched.

Suddenly, lights flooded the room, illuminating a figure hunched over at the desk. A thick layer of brown covered his scalp where the hair was in a hurry to grow back. Elle watched closely, waiting for the breakdown to start.

Shoulders began to flinch, then bounce. Short breaths reverberated throughout the quiet room, and he tried to stifle them as he dug his face deeper into the crook of his elbow resting on the desk. Elle caught the timecode and, tracing back the last few hours in her mind, she estimated it would have been while Elle and Easton were trading vocal blows right outside Dylan's sound proof walls.

A pang shot across her chest as she realized he was sobbing, and she could have been right there with him, helping him through whatever had caused this meltdown.

She pulled her eyes back to the figure on her monitor and finally, his head lifted. He looked up, a blotchy, tear stained jawline coming into view as he appeared to suddenly notice the lights. As he turned, she got a full view of Dylan's face, and she recoiled as if she wasn't eight floors up and looking through a video feed.

Once, on a family safari, she'd watched a lion finish a full meal right in front of her when a wayward zebra crossed the road in front of their Jeep. Elle had watched with white knuckles on the locked door handle as the lion charged the smaller animal. She saw the wild glint in the beast's eyes. The animal didn't need more food. It just wanted blood.

White knuckles gripped the mousepad now as she saw the same wild expression in Dylan. He wheeled around in circles like a caged animal, looking for some embodiment of her voice. Then the yelling started.

Elle closed her eyes, letting her face fall into her hands. He could only be referring to one 'her', which meant he knew. Somehow, he'd found out, and she didn't have the time to figure out how.

Heart racing, she skipped ahead on the timeline and saw it scrub over the course of two hours. Frantic now, Elle tried to think of how to get in. Ray wasn't allowed back into Patient Zero's pod, according to what the team of overseeing FACs knew at the moment. And even if she could get in, what would she say? Anything she said would just make matters worse.

But she couldn't leave him like this. Another warning pop-up blinked onto the screen.

Your direction is urgently requested, Overseer. Respond ASAP.

In the chaos, she'd forgotten her new role. No one knew that she was Acting Overseer, nor would anyone know who sent directives as long as it came from Easton's credentials. Closing her eyes, she tried to get the tone right and then began typing:

Send Ray in. At all costs, Patient Zero must be stabilized.
In harmony,
EH

As she waited, she reached for the rock, tumbling it over her fingers, every muscle in her body twitching with adrenaline. A muffled buzz echoed through her office and she jumped. She yanked the desk drawer open and glanced at the small screen. *Incoming Call: Graduate Facilitation Division*. She swiped to accept and a rushed, desperate voice slid through the other line.

"It's Reyes. Zero is going berserk. The Overseer has ordered you to stabilize the resident."

Ray tried to inject confusion into her voice. "But I'm n—not their FAC anymore," she stuttered. "I was ordered not to—"

"Guess the rules changed, Ray. We don't have time to argue, we've already had to sedate the resident once. They are in total hysterics and they're only asking for you."

"Alright, alright, I'm activating the feed now," she replied, the fluster no longer an act. She hadn't stopped to consider what she would say once she was in.

"Oh, and Ray," Reyes added hesitantly. "The resident knows everything. How long they've been here, Maggie's death... we have no idea how. We had to explain the Turnover just to give them a chance to breathe. Just thought you should know."

"Thanks."

Elle ended the call and returned her eyes to the screen. She looked around the monitor, secret avenues and limitless possibilities waiting to be unlocked before her eyes. But that would all have to wait.

She signed out of the Overseer's account and logged back in with her own, fingers moving on autopilot to find Patient Zero's pod inputs. Heavy fingers brushed over the small yellow switch, leaving it alone. While she dreaded the next few minutes, it felt like a weight was already sliding off her shoulders. She couldn't hide from Dylan Cavanaugh any longer.

Taking a deep breath, she pressed to engage. As the screen came to life, she saw Dylan's head snap up as two clenched, red fists came to rest against the wall below the Cipher.

"Ahh, there you are," he said, baring his teeth in a sinister grin. He backed away from the wall and stared up at the ceiling, trying to find her. Fear now crept along her neck as she willed herself to speak. There would be no going back after she did.

Déjà vu momentarily stunned her, as she remembered having the exact same thought mere hours earlier. Back when the environment would've have been controlled, where she could have been on the offensive and set the pace. Now she leaned close to the monitor and caught the clench of his jaw, the incensed flare of brown as his eyes dared her to speak.

"Hi Dylan."

The shaky voice bouncing off the walls of Pod 0018 made them both flinch. The Legacy's wry smile vanished.

"Who the hell are you?"

"My name is Eleanor Stryck." She paused, eyes searing into Dylan's face to mark the moment her final lie landed on his ears.

Only eyebrows flickered, uncomprehending.

"You once asked me if I had a nickname," she continued. "Ray is mine."

Pixelated brown eyes widened in a muddled mass of anger, confusion and disbelief. "But your voice isn't—" he started, but it was no use to keep him in the dark any longer.

"Technology allowed Maggie's voice to be imposed over mine. That is how I spoke to you these last months." Well, most of them, anyway. She didn't need to make things any more confusing for him right now.

"This is your actual voice?" Dylan cried out. "Why would you do that? You used her this entire time to manipulate me? Offering hope— all the while, you knew full well that she was dead?"

Elle felt the tears prickling her eyes like needles. "It was her suggestion, Dylan," she said urgently, desperation edging out the softness this kind of conversation needed.

A wicked snicker seethed from Dylan's lips, a fist resting between the wall and his shaking head. "No, no. That's not the truth. It never is the first time you tell me something. Come on, try again."

Elle pried her hands apart, not caring to see the blood her brittle nails had likely drawn, and cupped both hands around the headset. It was as intimate as she could get to Dylan right now, and she could only hope the closeness would draw out the authenticity of her words, because at this point, she didn't even know how to speak truth anymore.

"I understand you have been told about the Turnover." Elle paused, waiting for any recourse. Dylan didn't move.

"As such, we measure years here in cycles. At the end of the most recent cycle, or August 2023 as you would think of it, your sister Maggie believed their health was quickly deteriorating. They were aware you didn't remember them but asked the Overseer for permission to allow them to act as your facilitator for the first day of the next cycle. It was sort of a last wish—" a crack clipped off the sentence as Elle tried to push past the emotion trying to clog her throat. The memory surged forward anyway.

Pleading hazel eyes behind plexiglass, begging to have just one conversation with a brother who might never remember their sister.

"I think E hoped that if they could just speak to you, your memory of them would return."

Elle looked up now at the monitor in front of her to find Dylan sitting on the edge of the bed, fingers drumming the pallet frame as his head hung low.

"The Overseer was reluctant to allow it, as the first moments of a Legacy waking up on the first day of a new cycle are delicate and require an experienced facilitator to guide them out of the fog. But Maggie—"

"Stop saying her name like you care about her," Dylan said abruptly, head still low.

Elle changed directions, knowing a rebuttal would do nothing to help him understand.

"The Overseer had their concerns that the voice would stir up confusing questions for you, potentially derailing every ounce of progress we had made up to that point. But there was also the chance that the voice would return memories we believed to be lost to Void, and thus show an opportunity for medical advancement and a chance for others in your position to get their lost memories back. So, Easton allowed it. I stepped aside and watched as your sister tapped into your feed and spoke to you like a natural," she said stiffly, suffocating a sob. "She would have made a wonderful facilitator."

Dylan still rested on the side of the bed, feet arched and bouncing, calves rippling loose gray gym shorts.

"That was her that day? I yelled at her. I had to ask who she was. I didn't even know her voice."

"Yes," Elle said carefully. "You also called her Smirk, which made her laugh for a long time once she got off the mic. Said it was just like you to make up your own name."

Seemingly unaffected by the nostalgic memory, his eyebrows furrowed as wiry fingers massaged them.

"So that entire first day, I was talking to her?"

"No," Elle said quickly, anxious to make Dylan understand. "Although E did a wonderful job, we had to ensure that you remained on track with normal orientation protocols, which only I knew. However, we realized your sister's voice had quite an effect on you. You didn't seem to recognize it, but it was the quickest you'd ever calmed down after a Turnover Sequence..." Elle drifted off, allowing him space. "Something in the voice resonated with you."

"So what, you just found a way to clone her voice and pipe it in over yours?"

Elle had actually never known the technology that allowed it, she just knew that she'd been kicked out of her office for an hour and when she came back, there was a new yellow switch on her input board.

"Essentially, yes."

"And she knew about it."

"Yes. After every Legacy Turnover, Maggie didn't let one cycle go by without asking about you. I shared the files with her and, every cycle, E watched you have the same confusion, ask the same questions. It took you a long time to adjust, every time, and your sister hated to see you that way. But then we watched how you came out of this last Turnover... your reaction to waking up was nothing like the previous years'. We knew it was because of E. Because of their voice."

Elle smiled as the memory played out in her mind, unafraid of remembering this time. She couldn't let herself forget.

"Your sister begged to be trained as a FAC then and there, but with their condition... we just couldn't..." Elle trailed off, knowing Dylan wouldn't want to hear more. "So instead we gave your sister their own kind of legacy. Through their voice."

Dylan was up and pacing now, hands fidgeting through his hair as he walked. "So Maggie— she knew about everything, the Turnover, the lies, how long you've kept us here?" Anger coursed through the syllables.

"The value of the Turnover is to lessen the emotional effects of being kept in safe isolation while we searched for a vaccine. Those in the Infected wing do not require complete, sterile isolation so it was inefficient, and illogical, to use that resource on the souls who could forget things on a minute-by-minute basis."

"So, you all just let them lose their minds, without any intervention?"

"Our sole purpose was— is— to save them, Dylan. We are utilizing every depleted resource we have to bring them the Remedy. We are already spread too thin, if we tried to ease the Grays' minds, we would never have the opportunity to save any of them. The only way was to keep moving forward."

Elle grimaced as she realized how much she sounded like Easton, using the same argument they had used only weeks ago.

"You don't have it."

Elle was suddenly brought back to attention as Dylan's soft words gaped in the silence.

"Have what?" she asked.

"A remedy. You've never had it. That's why you've kept us here all this time, restarting our memories so we didn't realize that you haven't made any progress."

The Legacy had stopped walking, lines vanishing from his forehead as if two roads in his mind had finally intersected.

Elle dropped her head and let the silence affirm what he already knew.

"So she died, believing in your lies."

"She died with hope!" Elle cried out, aching for the soul in front of her to understand why they had done everything they'd done to him, to his family. "Hope was the best case we could give anyone. If the world didn't have hope, then what did that leave us? Despondence, misery... that's not life, Dylan. It's death."

Dylan tilted his head up, eyes narrowing towards the ceiling.

"Maybe. But you didn't even let us choose which one we wanted."

When the FAC said nothing in return, Dylan flung a flat palm back into the wall, rattling an echo screen.

"Damn it, Ray!"

She flinched. His head hung beneath his shoulder blades, and she wondered if this was it. The end of everything the last six years had been working towards.

"I want out. Now. Today," Dylan said, confirming her fear.

"Whoever you are, you obviously have power here. Get me out."

"Dylan, it's not that easy."

"Yes, I think it is. You can't hold me here. Not with everything I know. And, thanks to you, I'm well aware you and I are not the only ones participating in this conversation," Dylan raised his head now, extending a hand as if he was addressing an audience. "Now a whole lot of other people know that I know. And I'm thinking that's not a good look for you, Ray," the Legacy seethed.

"Please," Elle said, the plea shaking her voice. "Don't let Maggie's faith be in vain. Don't walk away from this. We have it, ok?"

She surprised even herself, admitting it. She hadn't planned on telling Dylan, but at this point, all the cards were already on the table.

"Oh, don't tell me," he said, derision leaking through a snide grin. "The Remedy? You're telling me now— just when I'm threatening to walk away— that you've found the cure? Well great, give it to the others. I don't want it."

Elle barely felt the tear trickling down her face. "Maggie wanted you to have it."

"Don't talk to me about what she did or didn't want!" he screamed, veins surging and popping like bloated purple rivers up his neck.

"My sister spent years hoping and believing that a group of manipulators would save her! And you just let her die, manipulated, with no one by her side. You didn't give either of us a choice," he said before his knees buckled. He collapsed to the floor, choked sobs cascading against the walls alongside the sound of pounding fists on hardwood.

Limbs numb from heartache, Elle felt her mind lift out of her body, disconnecting from the heart as she took in the situation before her.

For seven years, she'd watched individuals have to be reminded over and over again that they had lost so many people dear to them. She justified that, to them, it felt like only remembering once. But even just having to remember what Void stole once was excruciating, and she'd never been able to do anything to stop it.

Now, watching Dylan writhe on the ground, she saw the pain radiating through this soul's entire body and it dwarfed every other experience she'd had to witness.

But this time, she could actually do something about it.

Dylan was right. He knew too much. Everything he ever cared about had been stripped from him.

There was really only one option, and while it would appear heartless, it was rooted in the utmost compassion. As the decision cemented in her mind, Elle looked down at her hands and saw thin white scars shaking—but she felt nothing.

This would be her final act as Patient Zero's facilitator. She'd always promised them safety, guidance and preservation of life. This was the only way she could assuredly carry it out. The procedure would make Dylan the ultimate hero in future generations' histories. Maggie would be a casualty, wiped from existence. But perhaps it was better that way, Elle justified, turning her head away from the resident still cradling himself on the floor of Pod 0018.

If she could neutralize Dylan now, she would. But for the Remedy to work, they needed to retract the resources and tools that Patient Zero had gathered over the last few integral months. Sedation was the only gift she could give right now.

Elle reached for the phone again, and she spoke curtly to interrupt the angry barrage of questions when they answered.

"Reyes, I don't want to hear it. I'm afraid there's nothing left for us to do at this point. The Overseer is, I'm sure, aware of the situation at hand so let them decide how to proceed. Just keep me posted on anything else that is required of me," she said, promptly hanging up.

She took one last look at the monitor, and the trembling soul before closing it all down and signing back in with Easton's credentials. A buzz vibrated her vest and she reached for Easton's phone that she'd grabbed at the last second before leaving their office. Without urgency, she pulled it out, slid the *decline* button on and tapped out, "Can't talk, orders for 0018 forthcoming."

Another vibration rattled her hand but quieted after just two rings. Satisfied that her message must have gone through, Elle turned her focus to Easton's unlimited screen once again. She found the inbox and began typing.

FROM: Overseer <EHill@modularenterprises.com>
TO: Graduate Facilitation Division
Cc: All FAC Personnel
Re: Immediate Evacuation Orders for Pod 0018

Compatriots,

It's been a long road as we have all watched Resident 0018's journey here at Modular Enterprises. After viewing the situation at hand, I believe it is in everyone's best interest to begin the Retraction process as soon as possible. Therefore, I'm ordering the resident to be sedated and prepped for transport to Sector 01 Labs, with accompaniment only by their facilitator, Eleanor Stryck (Ray).

When the resident is thoroughly stabilized, prepare the Remedy for transition. Our Elect Giver is ready.

Congratulations, all.

In harmony,
Easton Hill
Overseer, Modular Enterprises

TWENTY SIX

A SHOCK of white enveloped Dylan as his eyes tried to open. A beige blanket laid across his midsection and his fingers twitched against a white sheet. Reclined against a bulk of pillows, he could just make out a bright linoleum floor that met up with walls the same disorienting shade. His eyes struggled to look around the unfamiliar room without inflicting a searing headache, and as they did, he caught a flash of color. A thin tube of deep red ran from somewhere behind him up to a sleek pole which held a clear bag of the same color.

As the scene groggily emerged before him, his mind told him to be afraid, but his body couldn't muster the energy. In some ways, it felt like nothing was different from waking up any other day— the agonizing quiet, sterile air, cold walls. Then again, there was nothing that said someone lives here.

But there was someone.

The blankets jolted as his whole body tensed upon noticing the slim figure shrouded behind a face mask sitting in the corner of the room, surrounded by a glass cubicle. The way they sat, calves taut, profile jutting out indignantly, made him squint in scrutiny. Did he know them? Was that how people sit?

It'd been so long since he had seen a human in the flesh, the simple questions made him feel off-kilter. He'd forgotten all rules for interpersonal interactions, and suddenly his hands buzzed with an electricity, but they were too heavy to move. A groan escaped his lips and the face turned abruptly.

"Who are you?" Dylan mumbled.

The figure turned in the chair to face him, resting a tablet on a flimsy side table before crossing their hands gently at the knee.

"An assistant," the figure said simply, full of warmth. They must have realized Dylan was in no place to spare extra words, and they rocked a black ankle boot back and forth patiently before continuing again.

"After the... events of last night—" green eyes flicked to search his face, as if asking if he could remember. He mustered a nod as he strained to sit up against a mound of white pillows. "You were showing signs of potential danger to yourself, and leadership was very concerned about how to ensure your safety within your isolated pod. You were sedated and brought to the lab wing of Modular, a private sector where you can be kept isolated— but still within quick reach if an emergency should call for that— while they make a decision on what comes next."

"They," Dylan huffed, pulling a sneer. "You mean, Ray?"

The assistant didn't break eye contact. "No. I'm afraid they have been released from their duties."

Dylan averted his eyes down to the scrunched blankets at his lap.

"Good," he said, perhaps too roughly. Or maybe not roughly enough. The assistant still had their eyes trained on him and he nervously tried to come up with conversation.

"And you're here because..."

"They still deem you a threat to yourself, so I'm here to—" the assistant waved a hand out as if it was fishing for the right word. "Oversee your care."

Dylan puffed out a lip, and then offered a slight nod. The assistant causally sat back and idly continued to wiggle their foot, no sense of urgency to have conversation, opting to just sit in silence. He looked down at his hands and then back up again, surveying the individual now as they tilted their head away from him.

He didn't remember many details from the night before, the anger and whatever sedation they must have given him had dulled most of it. He still felt incredibly unbalanced, and he wasn't sure if it was because there was another human in the room or if it was because they looked oddly familiar. Wisps of brown hair sprouted beneath a gray baseball cap and while the mask obscured much of the face, high cheekbones peeked out with just a whisper of shine. In the dull light, however, it looked anything but natural.

He squinted again. Despite the shadows of the hat, he felt like he knew the face... but distantly. As if they'd appeared in a dream.

A buzz rattled the silence around them, and with the most urgency he'd seen so far, the assistant snapped their head to the tablet resting on the table. Eyes grazed over the device and they quickly snatched it up, fingertips dancing above the screen in a flurry of hollow taps as only dull nails can do.

A whoosh resounded through the quiet room, as Dylan sat hypnotized by the scene. It was so beautifully simple, watching another human being live their life. To observe the unique way in which a person chooses to tell their body to do this or that, opening a window to the mind in the simplest and most nuanced of ways, was to know them, if only for a moment in time.

The assistant was now watching him, and he was snapped from his thoughts. They stood up and tucked the tablet under their arm.

"Something has come up, I'm afraid."

The assistant pushed the door open, but then turned back slightly, a soft smile at their lips.

"Talk s—" the assistant began to say, but bit their lip quickly, smile still intact. "I'll be back in just a bit. Get some sleep."

Dylan watched the figure grow smaller and more distorted through the haze of the textured door leading out from the cubicle. Now without any distraction to the pounding between his ears, Dylan massaged his forehead and fell back against the pillows. Fog clouded his mind, pulling his heavy limbs down into the soft mattress and without energy to fight it, he let sleep takeover.

***

PULLING THE cap lower, Elle stared down at the tablet, not even pretending to be lost in focus. A few pairs of white sneakered feet shuffled passed her, but she didn't dare look up to acknowledge any of them.

She ducked into the nearest elevator but refused to open up the feed until she stepped into her office seven floors later and locked the door. Safe from eavesdropping eyes, Elle switched on her monitor and pulled on the headset. As the screen powered on, she brought her attention to the tablet again and maximized the picture in picture, which showed a very clumsy figure shuffling, or more like flailing, objects, papers and maps across a desk. Her foot rattled against the metal desk until finally the monitor came to life and she logged in with Easton's passwords. She found the feed that connected into the Overseer's office and then flicked the switch to turn on audio. Pressing onto her elbows, she leaned in close to the monitor and let her habits take over.

"Easton, you're okay," she began, trying to insert herself into the room like she had wished she could do every time she had to watch a soul in this disillusioned state.

"Wh—what is happening to me?" Easton cried out, looking for a body to the voice.

"Easton, I can explain everything, but I'm going to need you to steady your breathing first. This is crucial, ok?"

As her friend paced, she launched into the script they had hastily written together in that same office just eight hours earlier, jumping between the scrawl of notes and instinct.

When she'd finished, her friend stopped dead in their tracks.

"And who are you?"

She looked down at her notes, saw the multiple asterisks as if she thought she'd forget this part.

She wondered if her mouth could even say the words she'd vowed to never say out loud within these walls. She trained her eyes on her friend as they tucked a slightly trembling hand into a pocket and waited for her to answer. This would be a test of faith in Easton, but then again, they had put the utmost trust in her, hadn't they? She owed Easton this much.

"Well I have a nickname people around here like to call me," she answered finally, taking in a breath. "But you might remember me best as Eleanor Drake."

Easton was emotionless, but the shaking had stopped. They returned to the couch and sat now, hands raking through a head of hair, a treasure that no other soul who had undergone a Turnover had ever gotten to keep. She noticed how their eyes kept flicking to the binder that had been discarded on the floor in what she assumed was a very abrupt wake-up.

"The binder is confirmation of everything I've said to you," she said gently, watching as Easton moved to pick it up gingerly, as if it might burn to the touch. Ironic, Elle thought, remembering her own hesitation with the pages.

Easton began to flick through it with reluctance, but with a look she'd seen plenty of times before with people in this state. Too shocked to be scared... instead, just curious. She could work with that.

A harsh bang made her jump in her seat, jostling her headphones.

Startled, she toggled views of the Overseer's pod to try and find the source. Any unnerving noise could set off an individual in Easton's delicate state, but they hadn't even flinched. When the banging erupted again, she realized the sound was coming from behind her.

She steadied her voice.

"Easton, I'm going to let you be for a little bit as you get used to everything around you. Know that I'm just a call button away if you need anything, alright? I'll be back shortly to check in with you."

She waited a beat and saw their head shift in the slightest nod.

Pushing off the headsets, Elle stood up, the smile warping into an anxious line as she switched off all the monitors before padding towards the door. Elle touched a finger to the keypad next to the door and saw a fish-eye view of the hallway.

A manicured hand poised above the door, preparing to send another barrage of knocks. It belonged to Shawna Blake.

Nerves lit up Elle's arms. There was no reason for the compatriot to be here unless on suspicion. Elle bit her lip, weighing her options.

Elle wasn't allowed to be anywhere else, now without any responsibilities having delivered Patient Zero to their lab room hours ago. The longer she took to answer, the worse her situation looked.

Elle buzzed the door and then calmly swung it open.

Arms folded, Shawna offered a curt hello, but their quick eyes glancing over Elle's shoulder betrayed the fact they were only there to scout for information.

"Have you heard anything from Overseer Hill?" the veteran FAC said patronizingly, but their eyes were wild. On the edge of panic. "No one can get a hold of them and Europe and Asia representatives are freaking out. They found out about our plans to push forward and are livid that we didn't seek panel approval."

A few stars appeared in front of Elle's eyes, but she closed a fist behind her back, sinking brittle nails into her palm. Her vision cleared.

Elle frowned and shook her head slightly. "Wait a minute, I thought the resident was just being held for monitoring?"

Shawna eyed her quizzically. "You didn't get the email," they said, stating it incredulously rather than as a question.

Elle feigned hurt. "What email?"

Blue eyes flitted around the room behind Elle, and she flinched, knowing the mess that Shawna was taking in. A blanket tossed onto the pull-out sofa, sheets scattered across it, the face shield teetering on the back of the bathroom door by a single strap from her rush out the door the night before.

"So what have you been doing?" Shawna asked, ignoring Elle's question.

Elle shrugged. "I don't know. I've never been without a job here. Thanks for asking though, feels great," Elle said, biting her lip and pushing the creases of her forehead deeper. "So, what, you're telling me Patient Zero is about to receive the Remedy? They can't be ready."

"Well, the Overseer has ordered it," Shawna said, shedding some of the armor as they stepped half a step back and rubbed their face. "I'm a little wary of it myself, mainly just for the fact that it seems to be such a big decision to make without telling the other headquarters. But I also just want this to be over, you know?"

Elle remained on guard, but leaned against the door frame, mirroring her compatriot's loosened demeanor. "Look, I haven't seen Easton and frankly, I don't think they want me to. You were at the meeting."

Blue eyes darted away as Shawna bobbled their head like a desk toy. Elle held her breath, wondering if the apology would actually come. Or, at the least, some acknowledgement of the blame.

"Yeah, it was a long shot coming here," Shawna said instead, and Elle bit her tongue. The battle wasn't worth it.

"The Circle just—" Shawna continued, bringing their gaze back to Elle. "Well, we thought maybe that meeting was just a show. You two have always been a little different from the rest of us."

It was her turn to bob and weave. Elle looked down, grim. "Things are different now," she said truthfully.

White sneakers shuffled nervously as Shawna coughed. "I'll let you get back to—" the facilitator trailed off, pitying eyes cast over Elle's shoulder once more.

"Thanks, good luck," Elle replied, already moving to close the door. She watched through a crack until Shawna's back disappeared around the corner.

She snapped the lock and hurried back to the desk, allowing her heart rate to pulse unfettered through her fingertips as they trembled against the mouse. Her and Easton had agreed to not alert the Global Leadership Panel until Zero was under neutralization, where there would be no going back. It was a manipulation, but they would all see the wisdom later.

But if the other headquarters all knew now, something had leaked. And what exactly did they all know?

Logging in to Easton's network, her own questions surged forward along with every new ping that came through Easton's inbox. She didn't open any of them. The memo titles were ominous enough.

Re: Who Authorized This Decision?
Re: Leadership Panel Gathering Required ASAP
Re: Unacceptable Trespass of Authority
Re: China Will Not Move Ahead

The stress elevated with every scroll Elle made down the list.

Everything was derailing in front of her, and she was tied to the middle of the tracks, unable to do anything but wait for the train to come.

TWENTY SEVEN

"ORDER, ORDER in the court, please," the judge called out, white tufts of hair careening off a balding head in the icy air conditioning.

Cameras continued to click but the shuffling of notepads, excited feet and whispered murmurs halted as the defendant sat down, the wooden chair screeching against the marble floor.

She recoiled slightly but quickly recovered, calves flexing from pointed toes underneath the chair. Blonde shoulder length hair was wrapped up in an elegant twist at the nape of her neck that elongated her impossibly long neck. She jutted out a fair chin towards the jurors, quietly acknowledging them. From his angle in the audience, he could see their glares and a wave of righteous anger surged through him. He glanced around the courtroom, saw a few security guards stationed near the doors, but doubted if they would really do anything for her if emergency called for intervention.

Amidst the reporters, city officials and out-for-blood onlookers, Dylan caught sight of a dark-skinned woman, dressed in casual clothes but without any notepad, phone or camera. Even Dylan, who wished not to remember anything from this awful day, had brought all the right tools to blend in with the crowd. But aside from hiding towards the back, the spectator seemed not to care about looking out of the norm.

Turning his head away, Dylan made a mental note to watch for her after the hearing. He flinched when his eyes came back around to the front.

A lock of blonde-flecked hair flinched, too, as a man averted his eyes so quickly, he had to adjust his glasses back up onto the bridge of his nose. The judge launched into a barrage of lofty prose as he began the proceedings, but Dylan kept his eyes trained on the back of the man's head, unease rippling across his back for reasons he couldn't make sense of.

The sudden creak of a door snapped him awake. The assistant was back, and Dylan couldn't hide his alarm.

It was her.

TWENTY EIGHT

ELLE SQUEEZED through the opening on tiptoes, trying to edge into the cubicle without waking the still form on the bed. She slipped into the chair and adjusted herself before setting down the tablet gently, but it clamored against the table when his voice startled her.

"I know you."

Her neck snapped up to find Dylan staring at her, not quite as wildly as the other night but with the type of aggression that made the hairs on her neck stick up. Anxiety and regret washed through her. She should have masked her voice earlier that morning. Foolishly she had assumed he would be too sedated to recall minute details like that.

She began to open her mouth, but he spoke again, looking off past her shoulder into empty space.

"The woman in the courtroom."

Elle tried to keep her jaw from locking. He couldn't be remembering... not after all this time.

She raised incredulous eyes to meet his squint. She'd seen those eyes search for something familiar for so long, and now as they stared back, she saw it.

He remembered her. The tiniest of smiles crept out of her lips, twitching her mask, but just as quickly, she felt it wipe away as the implication threw an unwanted memory on her like a wet blanket. After pushing it down for so many years, Elle had a flash of what it felt like to live in that moment in the courtroom. The tense calves, her hands balled tight. She'd never thought about anyone else even being in the room, let alone watching on television, but now that she tried, she realized she couldn't recall the details. Things had grown harder to remember from back then. Suddenly she needed to know about that haunted day.

"How did you—" she stammered, trying to form a question but her mouth gaped. Her cheeks flared. "I mean, what do you remember?"

Deep brown eyes sized her up as if to see right into her mind, but his eyes flashed in confusion.

"There's nothing to remember. It was just this dream I had before you came in. I was in a courtroom, the scene as classic as if I was living out a movie. The wooden chairs, cameras clicking, an annoyed judge and a bunch of jurors glaring at the defendant as they walked in. And it was you. You were the woman they glared at, and in the dream, I knew you. I actually felt this weird surge of protection every time I caught a glance of your face. It felt so real until I opened my eyes, and then you were just there, sitting right across from me as if I'd never woken up."

The story lit her nerves to embers, seizing the muscles, and she clasped her hands together tightly, trying to hide it. The details matched, at least, from what she could remember now that his recall had cleared some of the fog. But that meant he had been at her trial, in the flesh.

He was never supposed to be there. Alarm coursed through her body, but all too quickly it melded with something else. Something softer. The feeling felt foreign as it shuddered through her body and as the grip loosened between her interlocking fingers, she realized what it was.

Comfort.

It seemed that Dylan didn't know the dream had been an actual memory, and a choice warred within her now.

She had spent that first year out of Nox poring over the data coming in from the Drone Reconnaissance Team, hoping to find his face in the pixelated images. She knew he could make it a long time, he was only twenty-two, and a resourceful one at that. It's why she'd chosen him as her informant years prior.

But the more days and months that passed, the bigger the radius of distance. The closer he might be towards whoever had set off Void. After an entire year had passed, she knew he could have been anywhere, and she had to focus all of her energy on the Legacies they did have in the safe haven. So she had given up the search.

And then out of the blue, his face appeared on Easton's "New Acquisitions" memo to all FAC leadership. Taken aback, Elle had gawked at the grim face blankly staring back at the camera, daring it to confirm if her hopes had really come true. Dull, sepia eyes, ringed by sleep-deprived shadows, peered back above tanned cheekbones smeared with muck and grime, or whatever lied outside the Modular walls. She'd seen the face in better conditions, but it was still Dylan.

The Overseer boasted about the new opportunities that this new group might offer, and Easton had sung the praises of the rescue team, made up of courageous Grays, who found them in some makeshift fortress in the outskirts of New Jersey.

Elle had been relieved to know that Dylan had been found and finally in a place that would provide a barrier between him and the enemy they had once worked so hard to find, together. She had longed to speak with him; to trade stories, reminisce, before he was put under the neutralization procedure that always carried a threat to wipe more than just Void from memory.

But any connection between the two of them might instigate questions, and it was better not to reveal any link between her old life and whatever existence she was hiding behind now. Not even to Easton.

So, she kept to her business for the first two days, refusing to even think about him. That is, until the new Elect Candidate for the 2018 Cycle was chosen.

As the facilitator tasked with leading this elite group, which at the time, comprised only of a single resident, Elle fought between excitement and dread as the Circle voted Dylan Cavanaugh to be the newest addition.

In order for a FAC to succeed, they had to bond in a very detached way with their Legacies, and she doubted if she could pull that off with someone who shared a past like the two of them did. But what choice did she have? The decision had been made, Dylan was the newest Elect Candidate and that put them under her charge. Any protest on her part would throw up red flags.

She didn't remember much from that first day as Dylan's FAC except the pounding of her heart in her chest as she spoke for the first time. She begged the quiet air around her, pleading the words not to come. She didn't want to lie to this soul if they asked the question.

And Dylan didn't.

While she shouldn't have been surprised— they had only ever communicated through encrypted messaging back then— it had stung more than she cared to admit. She had dared to hope in some spiritual level of connection, that he would feel her presence.

If he had, he'd never said it.

So without the reminders of their past, she had plunged ahead, the years passing by without the sabotaging tendency to care too much for a friend who didn't remember her. She had even managed to convince herself that they had never known each other. It was just easier that way.

But now, if he was remembering...

Perhaps it was just the sedation. The traumatic realizations of the last six years. Or maybe it was just seeing Elle's face, despite her best efforts to conceal it.

Whatever the reason, Dylan knew exactly who she was, even if he couldn't formulate why. And sitting there before him, a thin layer of glass separating them, she could dismiss the dream right then and there. Eliminate any chance of hurt that would surely come from the confession.

Or, Elle could drop the truth at his blanketed feet.

It wasn't really a question, of course. She knew her answer the moment she'd chosen to walk into that glass cubicle, masked or not. She'd thought about it for six years. She'd just hoped he would remember.

"That wasn't a dream, Dylan."

The words left her mouth with such assuredness, she felt like she'd left her body again. A quick fist, nails digging painfully into flesh, proved she had not.

Dylan's veiny hand rubbed tired eyes, as if the assistant had just told a lame joke. She squared her shoulders and drilled her jade eyes into him.

"What you saw in that dream, it really happened. Ten years ago. I didn't know you were there, you were never supposed to be, but everything you described... it's all true."

His eyes grew like brown orbs, big enough for her to see flecks of yellow emerging like rays of sun trying to rise over a desert.

"I knew you?" Dylan said, awe striking at the same time as dawning, and he spoke again, this time into the blankets spread on his lap. "I knew you," he repeated, without question this time.

His entire face went slack as he continued to stare down the sheets, and she could almost see gears turning, unlocking a vault in his memory. Dylan tilted his chin back up and as he did, she unhooked the mask from behind her ears. She let it fall as it slithered to the ground like a discarded snakeskin.

Dark lashes blinked wildly as she watched Dylan grasp for the bubble before it could disintegrate.

"Eleanor Drake."

Elation, satisfaction and relief rippled through her and she couldn't avoid the smile at the sound of someone speaking that name without hostility or trepidation.

"You were my source," the Legacy said. His forehead wrinkled in confusion. "You're— you're alive?"

Elle averted his narrowed gaze, coyly shrugging her shoulders as his fingers drummed the bed sheets. She remained quiet, waiting for the memories to return to him unbridled now. She had a feeling they had always been there. Dormant, just waiting for the right catalyst.

"You were in Nox," he said suddenly. Warily. "I checked on you, tried to visit, but they told me you were in isolation."

She flicked her head up in alarm. "You tried to see me? Did you use your name?"

"Yeah— I mean, no, I think I remember being careful." Catching her look of concern, he grew defensive. "I couldn't just leave you out to dry, Elle."

Dylan cast his eyes blankly onto the ceiling, but turned back again, the wild returning.

"You died," Dylan said, and his eyes scrunched close together as the lens of his memory sharpened before him. "It was a whole story... I checked the facts myself. A relief team went looking for you at Nox but the whole place had exploded or something."

He looked up at her now, confusion and relief wetting his eyes like muddy pools.

"Modular found me first," she answered, and it sounded robotic. "I'd written everything we knew on those walls. Easton said it would put me in danger if the wrong people found out I was still alive with that information, so we faked my death. Then they blew up the place."

Dylan was still, absently staring down at his fingers knotted together.

"I didn't forget you, you know," he said softly.

"I see that now."

"I just— when I thought of anyone I cared about—I remembered they were all gone." Dylan's voice was hitching. "It was just easier to—"

"It's okay, Dylan, I understand," Elle said gently, her limbs aching to propel her body through the glass if only to hold her friend's hand.

"And we've been here, together in this facility, this entire time? Have you always known I was here?"

She looked back down at her fingers, picking at inflamed cuticles now, as the silence affirmed his guess. She didn't want to see the sting of betrayal flash across his face. His voice recovered quickly.

"Well," he said, almost jaded. She felt her guard go up. She deserved whatever was about to come, but it didn't mean it wouldn't be hard to hear.

"It's nice to meet you."

Her breath stalled in her throat and she glanced up at him, checking that it wasn't a bitter joke.

Dylan Cavanaugh simply smiled back at her. The same genuine grin she had seen hundreds of times on the monitor in her office as they used to banter as FAC and Legacy over the years.

She let out the breath and it came out as a full-blown laugh. She hadn't heard it in so long, she nearly flinched as it echoed off the walls.

"I guess that's kind of true, isn't it?" Elle tittered, suddenly bored with her fingers and tucking them into the pockets of her vest.

How unjust it had been that she and Dylan never had the chance to have any real semblance of a friendship before Void. When she'd inadvertently been caught in a tangled net of shell companies, she knew she couldn't untie the knots on her own. But they had never actually met; Eleanor Drake and the anonymous fact-checking wizard she'd employed to chase paper trails.

No one knew that part. They all assumed she was the frontwoman. But Eleanor had always been the middleman. Just, too public of one.

She had needed someone to scout for intel. A person with access but without eyes on them at all times. Dylan was a part of the biggest media outlet available at the time, but young enough to still care more about truth than whatever version of truth sold the most paper.

They'd agreed to never speak in person, clandestine meetings out of the question. They introduced themselves with screen names, but she also knew he was good at what he did. He'd do his research and figure out who exactly was the anonymous whistleblower needling for information via his resources. If he didn't, she wouldn't have chosen him.

But he was never supposed to follow her once things went south.

"When did you find out it was me?" Elle asked him now.

He shrugged, no longer straining to recall the memories. They seemed to come to him naturally, without effort.

"Honestly, you were hard to track. I never knew for sure until our information leaked and the media caught hold of it— which I saw before the general public ever did, so at least I could prepare myself— and then I just had to put two and two together. No one else had been talking about it, so I knew it had to be you."

Dylan was staring back up at the ceiling again, as relaxed as she'd seen him in days.

"I laid low there for awhile, but then I stopped hearing from you and that's when I began to panic a little bit. I had always been a cynic, but after what the public did to you... I couldn't leave my apartment." He was gazing at her now, protectively but also with pools of sympathy. "Their fear was immediate. They all panicked. They were afraid you were manipulating them into something. They didn't even let you explain your side."

She nodded absently. Void and time had diluted some of the worst memories, but she could still see the scorns, the lines of fear gripping stranger's faces when they used to pass her in the street. Dylan must have seen her unease and coughed.

"So apparently everyone around here has nicknames," he said, trying to change the subject but the flick of his jawline showed residual pain. "What's yours?"

"Oh, tags are just for the FACs," she said, trying to shrug off the question. She wanted to go back to the past, the place where she had never had to lie to him.

"Come on, you need one." He drummed the air, fishing for the right words. "What about Elly?"

One eye squinted closed, amused. "Okay, sure, Dilly."

He pursed his lips together. "You know, Elle's not so bad."

She smiled down at her hands as they both nestled into a comfortable silence. Then she remembered something.

"Hey, earlier, you said you had a dream about me in the courtroom. I don't remember much of anything from that day. What do you remember?"

Dylan shifted under the blankets, which tugged gently on the red bag. She hoped he didn't notice. She didn't want to address that part yet.

"It was your conviction hearing." Elle must have raised her eyebrows because he chased his words quickly. "Look I know it was dangerous, but I had to be there. I couldn't let you do that alone."

Elle just nodded, showing her appreciation and also encouraging him to continue.

"I don't know, it seemed like a typical hearing I guess that you'd see on television. A tired jury, bored judge and bloodthirsty spectators. Most of the people I saw had some twisted expression of excitement, jostling each other just to get a glimpse of the event. It was sick," Dylan said, disgust oozing from his lips. He quieted and seemed to lose himself in the details of the day.

"You had blonde hair then, coiled up all nicely against the back of your neck."

Without thinking, Elle reached up to feel the brown strands fluttering about her face, grimacing at their brittle ends.

"Your lawyers were pretty resigned—nothing left for them to do I guess but be there for the punch to the gut. Nothing else really stood out in the dream." Dylan recalled, eyes veering back to her as the words fell away, and Elle offered a gracious smile.

A wrinkle suddenly appeared on his forehead.

"Oh, except one more thing. I caught a weird glance from some guy a few rows in front of me— probably two rows behind you, and close to the wall."

She tried to create the setting in her mind, curating images from all the fuzzy details that desperately clung to her own version of the memory.

"Tall guy— sitting, he was still half a head taller than everyone around him— with fancy designer type of glasses. I'd caught him staring at me, but as soon as I did, he turned away. If the dream truly is a memory, apparently the guy was important enough for me to remember."

"Weird," Elle mused. "You didn't know them?"

"No, at least, it didn't occur to me that I did. It would've been one thing if he had just been looking around the room like I was, and we accidentally caught each other. But he was so far away and to the side that it couldn't have been coincidence. The way it happened just gave me the creeps."

"Tall with glasses," she repeated. "Anything else you remember? Maybe I'd know them," Elle tried, feeling anything but confident.

Dylan shuffled again under the sheets, appearing to strain for the details. "Maybe blonde hair? With flecks of brown through it. Like sand. Reddish brown glasses, bony shoulders... eh, that's all I really got—"

But Elle had stopped listening. A drum thumped in her ears as she tried to fight off the unwanted questions flinging themselves at her defenseless mind. No, they'd never known each other until the day her hero had shown up in a Hazmat suit, offering her a gloved hand, extending the safety net. Elle had never even heard their name until after Void had happened.

But there was no doubt as to who Dylan was describing. She had grown to memorize that hair as it fell like sheared wheat in front of gray eyes while the two of them leaned heads together over charts, graphs and stale cups of coffee. She remembered how those bony shoulders had bounced and jittered every time a compatriot had expired. And she would never forget the height that towered over the Circle in their unwavering formidability that seemed to promise hope and success.

But if Dylan was right, if they had been there all that time ago... then all that she'd seen— and promised to follow to the ends of the earth— had been a façade.

Elle could hear words trying to penetrate through the glass, dark eyes drilling into her, but it all felt too distant. Too far away.

Instead, she kept her gaze on trembling fingers as they manipulated the tablet to call up the home page of Modular's website, searching for a photo. The face of the company was easy to find and turning it to be flush against the glass paneling, she finally gave her attention back to Dylan.

"Is this the person from your dream?" Elle asked, voice so shaky she would've thought it had come from someone else.

Dylan was staring at her, and as she waited breathless for his reply, all her senses seemed to elevate and she noticed a flash of concern on the Legacy's face.

"Huh, yeah," Dylan finally said, squinting through the glass. "Just take away a few wrinkles and crow's feet there around the eyes, and that's the guy."

The tablet clattered to the ground.

TWENTY NINE

IN HER periphery, she could see Dylan's mouth moving frantically, but her head was pounding too hard to hear the words. Seeing his face shadowed with concern, she felt a pull in her chest. Like a tide pulling her out to sea.

She wished she could let it take her away.

Instead, she made a quick escape, barely calling out an apology before darting through the glass door without a look back.

Back in her office, she keeled over onto the bed, hands over her face as if to peel the wool that had been cast over them. Hearing Dylan's words had sparked a flame within her, and she refused to bow to the gender ideals any further.

Elle had been relegated to a fairy tale. Rescued by a man who had put her up on a pedestal for his own trophy case.

She didn't even care that he was a man. It was the fact that he'd used his anti-gender theology as a way to manipulate an impressionable, and vulnerable, world—all in the name of compassion—and she'd been his first victim.

I'm hiding you.

Easton's smirk seared through her memory, and she shuddered.

She'd been his first prize.

Elle had never questioned why Easton refused to refer to themselves as a man or woman. Even when her mind had struggled to conform to the non-binary theory, it was easy to see Easton for who they were. A being unto themselves, a force to be reckoned with.

She had always seen Easton as she had that first day in Nox. A soul bent on saving the world. They had hinged their movement on equality, prostrating themselves at the feet of inclusion. Harmony for all.

But she was quickly realizing that the notion served a different purpose. It leveled the playing field. When everyone is on the same level, people let their guard down when, perhaps, they never should.

If Easton Hill had been at her trial, she had allowed her entire life to be altered by a conniving liar. Her existence, manipulated by an artist.

Her mind spun with the agonizing possibilities that all tried to answer one simple question: *why?*

If what Dylan had dreamt was true, Easton had wrangled a front row seat to her conviction, which meant he'd been close to her case. Why keep that a secret? Why pretend that the first time they'd ever seen each other was within the stone walls of Nox?

She shut her eyes tightly now, trying to remember the first time she ever remembered seeing his face. Surrounded by cement— etched, chiseled and sparkling with her blood— he had looked pitifully at her, like she was a wounded animal, spooked and clinging to the shadows.

"What's your name?" Easton had asked gently. Innocently.

No one had asked her that in two years and, yet, she felt so wrought with anxiety that she couldn't allow herself to admit it. What would her rescuers think when they realized who she was? Likely, they would simply turn around and leave.

Perhaps it was better that way anyway.

But she'd forgotten about the writing on the wall. When she had stayed silent, the carvings had spoken for her. She had watched in quiet terror as she watched five pairs of eyes, shielded by yellow hoods, look behind her at rows and rows of evidence that had made America think Eleanor Drake was plotting genocide. She had sunk to the musky tile floor, eyes closed, waiting for the sound of clunky boots to retreat. Instead, one pair eased closer, and then those cloudy gray eyes were suddenly there in front of her, and like a fast-approaching storm, she couldn't look away.

"It's you," Easton had said, mystified as he took in her wiry, mousy frame. "We didn't expect to find any survivors here."

He'd trailed off as he reached down to help her up and led her to one of his colleagues, his head turned back to take in the four walls again.

Days later, as she sat marveling over blueprints and drafts of the first Modular HQ, she reflected on her and Easton's introduction. Someone with his economic intellect would have kept up with the news, so she had been surprised to remember how shocked Overseer Hill had been when the team had found her in Nox.

Everyone and their uncle knew where she'd been sent.

The shard of black rock sitting on her desk now seemed to dance in front of her strained eyes: mocking her, laughing that she had never thought to question the surprise in Easton's eyes that day. Had her hero been truly dumbfounded when he came across her decrepit existence that day? A total life-saving coincidence?

Elle sneered back at the rock, returning the silent laugh. No, there were no coincidences at Modular Enterprises.

Perhaps he had found exactly what he was looking for that day.

***

EVERYTHING HURT as Elle paced the room, and even though all she wanted to do was lie on the couch until Void stripped her mind, she knew the world, once again, rested on her shoulders. And once again, no one living in it even knew it.

She rubbed her neck, soothing nothing, and turned to the computer.

Elle logged into Easton's account and opened up the Modular network's search engine. She typed all keywords including, and related to, everything about the name Easton Carter Hill. Hundreds of hits came up, the first dozen headlines featuring some version of *"Head of Modular Enterprises Champions World Rescue."*

She scrolled past the first several pages that had clearly been doctored by the social outreach team, and found the outsourced information document serving as a biography to the entrepreneur, hidden thirteen web pages deep. Hundreds of people had added to the document over the years, but, unsurprisingly, the latest footnote was dated August 2016, the month everything changed.

She scrolled past the introductory information, as she knew that would tell her nothing she didn't already know. Then a phrase jumped out at her as she read beneath the Early Professional Life tab. According to the page, which had three separate footnotes to confirm the fact, Easton had first named his business Cutless Technologies.

A twinge pulled in her chest as she read the words, which were hyperlinked and as she clicked, she was taken immediately to the homepage of Modular Enterprises.

She returned to the socially resourced page and saw the name again. Her mind pulled at the loose thread, her eyes straining as she stared at the screen. Just as the words began to blur in front of her, the knot pulled loose.

A memory sharpened before her, from probably twelve years back. She sat in a basement, fingers bitten to the nubs, fear overtaking her motivation to keep going. In spite of all the painstaking research, all the risks taken, she had finally gathered the courage to pull the plug on their months of work.

Her fingers hovered over the keyboard, prepared to type the words to her colleagues when a ping echoed off the hollow walls.

Sent from a business contact she didn't recognize, the message had cryptically offered to fund Elle, and her team, in any *world-relief endeavors you may find yourself in*, as the email had read. There had been no personal sign off except the business name, Cutless Tech. After a quick Internet search, she had found a rudimentary webpage for the vague start-up company.

She had never told her colleagues about the offer, as it felt too mysterious and having not gone public yet, she couldn't trust anyone. But the fact that someone believed them had been enough to reignite her fire. Hope had been renewed.

Elle rubbed her temples methodically now, trying to make sense of it. Had Easton been their believer? She quivered now with the thought of having given so much time, respect and awe-filled gazes at the individual who had known the truth from the beginning... and refused to come forward.

She thought back now to quiet silences between them, coffee and mind-numbing data abandoned as Easton prodded gently about her history; the time in Nox, the trials. It had been an international affair. Elle knew how visible her situation was. But she also wasn't so vain to think that everyone in the world had followed it, so when Easton asked, Elle felt oddly comforted. Not so much by the questions themselves, and the memories they uncomfortably dug up, but because there had been someone who hadn't cared to know everything about her back then. For that, she had let him in.

But now, it seemed to have all been a manipulation. All those details she had long forgotten by now—the suits, the juries—he had seen them for himself. So, why the prodding questions? To force her to be more vulnerable? Was it his way of trying to offer therapy that he thought she needed? Or rather, was it some way to elevate his own sense of superiority, and it had nothing to do with her?

A spark sizzled in her mind. Something Dylan had said— she wheeled around, hoping the sudden movement would jolt her memory to bring back the words.

I'd caught him staring at me but as soon as I did, he turned away.

What if it never was about her, she thought now, heart sinking to the floor with a quiet, eerie thud. When Easton had gone to her trial, perhaps he had only gone because he knew someone else would.

Which meant Easton likely knew more than just a few courthouse details. The only question left now was how much.

THIRTY

THE ROOM looked the exact same as when she'd left it, save for the thick white binder resting on the cotton blanket, shifting and then stabilizing again at every rise and fall of Easton's chest.

Despite all the lies and haunting questions begging to be answered, she looked at the sleeping figure now and could see nothing but the truth. A man who had lorded power over her for years, all the while trying to make her think they were equals the entire time.

She yearned to yank him out of whatever peace he was in right now, barrage him with her questions. But waking him would only add confusion, and right now, that was the last thing she wanted. Elle needed Easton to have as clear of a head as possible before she could ask him about the past.

The Turnover was proving to be quite a handy little tool. Erasing everything from Void and on meant it had eliminated every lie about their history he'd used to manipulate her, leaving only the parts that she desperately needed to know now.

Unsure of when Easton would wake, and wanting to check on Dylan's feed, she started to minimize the screen but moving the mouse illuminated an icon with two backward arrows.

She'd forgotten the unlimited resources that Easton had provided for himself as Overseer. Curious now, she clicked on the rewind icon. The screen went black for a moment, loading the images, and then the same view of the Overseer's office appeared, nothing different except for the timestamp, which had jumped back four hours.

Wonder washed up with a wave of guilt as she realized the cameras at Modular were always recording.

She'd known she could check in on a feed at any time. She had done so during Easton's first twenty-four hours, waiting to see movement on the screen which would alert her that he was awake. But Elle had assumed the camera feed only showed the live pictures.

Guilt ebbing, power surged through her fingers as she clicked again, and now an image of the office appeared, but with a figure mindlessly flipping through pages of the binder on the couch. She clicked backward again and saw Easton sitting on the edge, head in his hands, binder back on the floor.

Curious to see how far back she could go, she continued to flash through scenes but then stopped short when she caught a view of herself, perched on the armrest of the couch, a thin syringe balanced between two fingers.

She had never been present during the initial injection of a Turnover sequence; her job started when the residents woke up. Although she'd been the one to plunge the syringe into Easton's arm, she'd left in a hurry, suddenly feeling like a criminal hiding a body.

Elle estimated that it had taken at least half an hour from when she closed that heavy chrome door to when she saw it again on the screen in her office. By the time the feed had connected, Easton had looked just as she'd left him, cotton blanket stretched taut across his body like a straitjacket, highlighting the slow rise and fall of his chest as he slept through the resetting of his mind.

The play button teased her, casting a hint of doubt at what those walls might have seen in the short time she wasn't monitoring. It's never safe to assume things, Elle thought. She swerved the mouse and clicked.

The video played in real time, and knowing the dialogue firsthand, she kept the playback on mute, not wanting anything to distract her as her eyes surveyed the whole room. She watched Easton flinch, again, as green fluid raced to mix with his bloodstream, and she watched the two friends smile at each other as if saying goodbye. She turned away, feeling like an intruder on a tender moment.

When she turned back, she just caught a glimpse of her boot leaving the screen. Elle toggled to a view of the door and as it closed, she switched back to an overview of the couch. Easton's body was still, refusing to spasm as she'd read some residents' limbs were prone to do post-injection.

Even so, the lines and creases of his face hadn't ebbed as they should have under rest. She toggled in closer, examining the way his face remained taut, almost straining. His chest continued to rise and fall steadily, just barely in the frame of the zoomed shot, eerily juxtaposing the tension still evident on his face. Elle rested her chin in her hands as she stared into the screen, daring the lines to dissolve away.

Gray eyes suddenly flashed open. Elle jolted, goosebumps erupting across her arms. Easton blinked a few times, grimacing as long fingers combed through his hair. Entranced, Elle followed him with the cursor, toggling among the screen views to keep him in her sights.

Like witnessing a miracle, she watched with bated breath as the body rose from the blankets, wavered for a moment and staggered to the desk a few feet over. He pulled out a sealed bottle of Advil that had grown to be a staple in the Overseer's drawer. His fingers fumbled to pour out the contents, but instead of tiny white pills, two large purple capsules tinkered out and Easton deftly slogged them into his mouth.

Elle felt her jaw go slack, eyes squinting with incomprehension as she watched the mystery pills' immediate effects, smoothing the wrinkles and crows feet into a contented glow as Easton's legs teetered back to the couch. He cinched the blanket back under his body, tight as when she'd done it herself, and his eyes floated closed. The breath finally left her lips, and she realized the entire scene must have lasted thirty seconds. A blip in the system. If the sequence had been erased, the only difference between the scenes would have been the appearance of wrinkles one minute, and the contentment of a face at rest the next.

Elle felt a new knot twist inside of her gut. Medications were not simply handed out within these walls. Even doses of Advil were heavily monitored.

The mysterious purple pills had been important enough to hide, and had clearly been a set piece of Easton's plan.

A plan obviously separate from the one she had helped him make.

She'd thought his manipulations had been silenced when she had plunged that needle into his vein, sending him into blissful ignorance.

But that wasn't true. She was still his toy. And she'd played right into his hand, blissfully unaware.

***

It was only a matter of time before she was found out.

Emails had continued to flood the Overseer's inbox, and barricading herself behind office doors, she had spent all her time coming up with ways to circumvent the other countries' fears. Just as Easton had done with her, she had tried to convince them that this was the only way.

And with every heated reply, she began to see Easton's plan for what it truly was. Easton had removed himself from the situation that he'd created, in the name of loyalty, only to thrust Elle into the public eye to be used as the scapegoat.

Again.

Through narrowed eyes, she watched him now on the screen. He paced the room confidently, ghastly pale fingers reaching out to trail along the spines of the books he had ordered to be written, removing a few from their perch on metallic shelves only to return them again.

As if he knew she was watching. With elongated fingers, he dramatically manipulated the pages to his will, just as he had done to her own invisible strings for eight years.

Her chest was on fire.

She fell to the floor, knees and palms hitting hardwood, as her chin strived to get higher, searching for air. But all too quickly, the enormity of the situation—the gravity—shoved her back down, breathless.

All threats subsided before her except for the one requiring oxygen. She flung a numb hand above her and it flopped onto the desk. Fumbling around, her fingers finally landed on the sharp rock and she gripped it tightly, the edges digging into her skin. Blinking through tears, Elle watched as three thin streams of red dripped down her wrist, merging into one pool as they fell onto the floor.

The pain of the rock subsided as she stared at the trickle, mesmerized by the flow of blood that meant she was still alive.

She was surviving.

And the only way to keep doing it was to keep moving, keep thinking. One threat at a time.

Her eyes blurred, but her mind sharpened to identify the first priority: Easton was not under the influence of the Turnover. She'd performed the injection. She had wiped away the drops of blood herself.

Her mind began to pulse with the implications.

The purple pills were some kind of an antidote, or failsafe, to the Turnover technology, which means there would have been test trials, data, evidence.

Gingerly, she pulled herself back up into the chair, setting the rock down and wrapping a nearby face mask around her left hand. Small rivers of crimson bled into the white fabric like a toxic red tide.

Waking the monitor back up, she flinched as the screen opened back up to Easton's office. Elle took one last look and then pressed the red x icon, feeling a flourish of relief as the screen blipped away.

She had grown weary of looking at people through a camera lens. It had never shed any extra light on people, anyway. She had learned over and over again in this facility that human nature rarely let their guard down. Everyone kept their secrets, even from cameras.

Elle manipulated the mouse to open up the file search and began typing in keywords: Turnover, restart failure, antidote, failsafe, purple.

A dozen document files appeared in chronological order, all named in chaotic ways using jumbles of numbers and letters. She double clicked on the first one and was met with walls of untitled text.

Urgency flung her fingers back across the keyboard as she plugged in a shortcut and searched the same terms. The document lit up in yellow.

She continued this method through all eleven other documents, jotting notes on the back of the charts and spreadsheets still scattered across her desk. Her fingers darted between the pen and the mouse, her mind rapidly processing the key points as she went.

Evidently, the Turnover Sequence had failed multiple beta tests until a safety net was created, called Analepsis. The failsafe served as an undo button, and was taken orally, so as to avoid any more invasive trauma to the resident.

The purple capsules reversed the memory-wiping effects of the Turnover, causing the resident to live their lives in a rewind, starting with the most recent experience and returning memories in reverse chronological order.

Not only was it a mercy save in the chance the Turnover backfired, Elle realized, but it also seemed to be a way to undo Void's effects on the brain. She looked back over all the notes and wondered why this medicine had never been revealed to the Circle, let alone the Panel. It seemed like the perfect way to appease the other countries' worries about their methods. By creating Analepsis, Easton could have defended the Turnover because, according to the data, the purple capsules could only activate by mixing with the Turnover serum. If you had never received the injection, you couldn't get your memories back.

A double-edged sword that Easton had apparently deemed too sharp to fall onto.

But he was no longer in charge.

Her head pulsed, her hand still bled and her eyes strained in the dim light, but she refused to stop. The more she read, the more her shoulders buckled under the responsibility.

An idea had been simmering since she saw Easton slide those pills into his mouth. She had swept it aside for its absurdity, and as it bobbed back up to the surface now, a chuckle seeped out of her lips. Recoiling off the walls, it sounded maniacal in her ears.

The risk was simple, black and white. Life or death.

And there was only one choice. Elle didn't know who else, if anyone, knew what she did, but she was the only one in a position to do something about it. To change the storyline. To pull the strings.

And if she knew Easton like she thought she did, she wouldn't have this chance much longer.

***

"YOUR ORDER is being prepared."

The subject line pinged onto the top right of her screen and she quickly cleared the notification. She took one last glance at the feed showing the lab room, and caught a white coat leaning over Dylan's IV. Satisfied, she whipped her hat, satchel and a black mask from the door handle and swung it open.

Tired feet moved quickly; the ankle boots subbed out for the silence of the company-approved white lab sneakers. Elle knew the DLVRD order would take longer to arrive to Easton's office pod than it would take her, so she took her time, clinging to the wall like a shadow.

She arrived at the all too familiar door, and with one quick glance over her shoulder, she swiped Easton's keycard and slipped inside. Elle had hoped to catch him off guard, but the immediate darkness of the room blanketed over her shoulders like a net, the dim glow from his computer the only light as it cast dull blue shadows upon the walls.

"Who's there?"

The gritty voice slowed her advance into the office, and she grew still, analyzing Easton's motives. Given the darkness, it was reasonable to believe he truly did not know who had just entered his quarantined pod.

Or he could be playing his game true to character.

It was safer to assume the latter and, true to her own character, she followed his lead.

"I'm sorry to barge in like this, Easton," she began, feigning apologies and grateful for the shadows hiding her face. "It's Elle, your facilitator... your friend. I wanted to meet with you face-to-face, just to see for myself that your recovery process is moving along as it should."

The more she talked, the more she could convince herself to believe it. Clarity blossomed before her as her eyes adjusted in the gray.

"And to make sure you're still eating," she added, flourishing a hand towards his rail thin frame. Easton let out a grunt as he stood up from the couch, his face twisting into a painful wince as it illuminated in the blue of the screen. She watched him closely, trying to remember her notes about the potential side effects. His movements were shaky but that could have been from either the Turnover or Analepsis.

"Wh—what time is it?" Easton asked, eyes squinting.

"8:00 in the evening. Have you been sleeping alright?"

"Yes, yes, probably too much, honestly. Must be why I feel so groggy."

"Here, let me," Elle shuffled across the room and fidgeted with a device on the bookshelf. Rays of manufactured dusky light suddenly began to rise up the walls and she turned around to see Easton take a good look at her now. Any other day, those eyes would have disarmed her, allowing her to relax.

Now she only armored herself.

"So, you're— you're the one who has been speaking to me?" Easton asked tentatively. It was strange to see him shy. She resisted every urge to roll her eyes.

"Yes, you should remember me as—"

"Eleanor Drake."

She plastered on a smile under the mask, hoping her voice would follow its lead.

"Very good, I'm relieved to hear you remember our first conversation together. Sometimes that first day is a massive jumble of information that many souls tend to forget. But you know," Elle changed her tone as if speaking to a child. "You're doing a great job, Easton."

Condescension leaked out of her words, and she dared him to call her out on it.

He didn't, nodding idly instead, unimpressed with her praises. She changed topics as she leaned her back against the bookshelves.

"I did just want to ask, Compatriot... how are the echoes going?"

She nodded towards the computer screen that was now in her line of sight. She snuck a glance. "Were you able to find the correct file folders alright?"

Easton glanced at it, too. A colorful image burst forth with an array of colors, filling the entire screen. Elle wasn't shocked, but she was disappointed. Easton had covered his tracks.

"Indeed," he replied brightly. "The science behind these devices and the images are truly mind-bending. I've learned— or, I suppose, re-learned— so much," he said with a wink.

Her gag was drowned out by the sudden chime of DLVRD. Easton jumped as if he'd never heard the sound before. It almost looked believable, she thought. Painting on a smile, she walked towards the door, calling over her shoulder.

"I ordered you something that has always been our favorite. Thought it might help you remember," she added with a wink of her own.

She heard the shuffling of his feet as she allowed herself to turn her back to open the hatch. A steaming box waited as she retrieved an opaque bottle the size of a test tube, and shoved it up her sleeve. Then she grasped the food firmly with two hands and walked back to Easton, setting the food down on a side table before dragging it in front of him.

"Listen," she instructed, coy tone oozing through the mask. "I'll be back in a little while to make sure this is all gone, understand?"

He offered a thin smile. "Yes, Compatriot."

"Good. See you in a bit," she said, the words slithering off her tongue towards the serpent lounging on the sofa.

THIRTY ONE

THE DOOR latched with a click and all the breath left her lungs in a single gust. The indiscriminate bottle had burned a hole in her pocket the whole way back to her office, and she'd spent the entire jog back waiting to hear Easton's steps behind her or for the medical team to pop out from behind every corner.

Once safely back in her sector, her brain swiveled like a Rolodex, searching for the next immediate threat.

Dylan.

With Easton at the helm, everything Modular had ever stood for had been compromised. Elle had been Easton's most trusted ally. Shawna's words had proved it.

If he was complacent to manipulate Elle from the beginning, it was safe to say everyone under his leadership had had their strings pulled. And whoever was chosen as the Giver was about to bear the brunt of that manipulation.

Before she could help her friend, however, she needed to know exactly what he knew. Or better yet, how he had come to know it.

Dylan would be safe for as long as his blood continued to neutralize, which by her calculations, would be another 24 hours. He was probably wondering where the assistant had gone, but if all went according to her incredibly risky plan—she would explain everything soon, without fear of who was watching.

If it didn't, he wouldn't remember a single thing anyway.

Elle drummed the mouse with her fingers, thinking back to the events of Dylan's outburst in his pod. From her angle, the only odd event to be the catalyst was the pod reboot, which still didn't make any sense.

Dylan had already experienced what that ritual had sounded and felt like, she had walked him through it.

Her fingers stopped.

She had walked him through it. Her feed had never been cut off during a reboot.

Elle recalled the way she had scrubbed backwards on the timeline of the recorded pod feed— the inky, silent blackness of nothingness, and then suddenly light.

Whatever had shut down Pod 0018 was not an ordinary maintenance procedure. It had shut down every input and output in that pod, which went against every protocol Modular Enterprises had ever put in place.

The shutdown had been organized and carried out deliberately, and Elle needed to figure out why.

***

IT HAD been years now since her staff training, and she felt her mind reach like tentacles for the information: the coding symbols, shortcuts and methods that comprised Modular's online palace. Given the level of technology and possession of such invaluable commodities that the enterprise owned, their securities were created to be impenetrable. Navigating them was like trying to find a single bathroom in a castle.

Elle suddenly understood why the securities department took up two entire floors.

A migraine began to pulse at the base of her skull as the hours crept by. The screen taunted her lack of expertise as she maneuvered among countless files, often getting lost in the chaos of folders breeding twenty more, and then having to close out of the entire system to restart all over again.

Switching gears, she opened up the Command Line on the computer's operating system and began typing in keywords and phrases that she remembered. Her stomach began to ache with hunger, eating having become a luxury for those with time. Elle ignored the emptiness, fingers impatiently tapping the keys, pleading that they would know the right strokes that would unlock what she needed.

Suddenly a system automatic reply blinked onto the screen, the green letters setting her hopes, and nerves, alight.

[User Password:

Elle glanced down at Easton's scrap of paper again, typing gingerly with one pointed index finger, afraid that the system would be unforgivable after one chance. She pressed enter and a new window maximized onto the screen before her, seemingly identical to the Command Center window, but filled with walls of white letters, numbers and characters. Leaning closer to the monitor, she picked out a line of mostly English.

[outputs-Pod_0018]

Her eyes swam in the dizzying mass of white lines after it, and she put up a finger to the monitor to steady her focus. Finally, she found the words *Pod_Override* and, eyes swimming, she trailed her finger across the screen to find the initiator.

It was a simple username, and her jaw came unhinged with a painful click. Elle felt her back hit the forgiving cushion of her chair, but then it seemed to dissolve as the sensation of falling sucked her into a vortex of memory. Spit out onto a creaky plastic chair, she felt humidity seep into her pores as she looked around at the towers of cardboard boxes on either side of her. The vision rushed back with a surge, flashing before her as starkly as the three white words that had blinked hauntingly against a black screen: *It's all true.*

The three words from the anonymous screenname had been the catalyst to everything. Before, it had only been a hunch, born from a simple inconsistency she'd happened to find when managing benefit donations from all of her sponsors. A large check had bounced, and when she tried to find the donor, it led her to what appeared to be a shell company, which then bred more shell companies. The paper trail kept going and soon it wasn't about the money anymore but satiating her curiosity. That is, until her little hobby led her right into the throes of a darkweb group who had radicalized the theory of checks and balances, its members believing themselves to be worthy of holding the gavel.

Elle had known she was in too deep, and yet she couldn't stop. Soon she had found herself at all hours of the day, holed up in her dank basement, hunched over an old desktop computer scouring pages on darknets. For weeks, she had kept the concerns to herself. The information had scared her, and she wasn't willing to share anything with anyone she cared about until she had all the pieces.

She had thought she was being careful, but she was in over her head, and within a month she had been interrupted one evening by an unknown username taking over her computer, messaging her through the system's command center.

Privacy violated, she had nearly smashed the computer right then and there, preparing to throw it in the Potomac. But then the user had begun asking questions that she, herself, had been pursuing for weeks. She had dared to admit to the hacker what she'd been chasing, and waiting with fingers tied in knots, she had actually hoped they would laugh her theory off. But then those three words came.

After hours of trick questions and cryptic tests, the two of them had curated enough trust in each other to share names and basic information. With Eleanor being in the public eye and her new friend under the government's jurisdiction, they both had quickly realized the need for a third private collaborator. Dylan had joined the team seamlessly, despite being kept in the dark regarding either of their identities. It was just safer. The lesser he knew, the better for all three of them.

Then all hell broke loose, information leaked before they were fully ready to go public and before she knew it, every piece of her own evidence was used to put her away.

When Elle went to Nox, she could only hope that her team had gone dark, too.

Until Dylan had arrived at Modular, Elle had believed no news was good news.

She hadn't been able to do the same for her other colleague. Within the first week of arriving to Modular, she'd let herself scroll through dozens of pages, stalling for time, hoping not to see it. As she had run her finger down the list of P's in the database, she had seen the € first. The name had blurred before her and she had dropped her head into twitchy hands.

Now, Elle blinked away shallow pools and felt a stabbing pain in her skull, the headache growing more and more intolerable. She realized her head was in shaky hands yet again, as if the memory had never been one at all. She looked up and saw the light of the computer screen.

No, it was different this time. There was still a wall of black and white text, but instead of it confirming the death of her colleague, the numbers and letters before her appeared to have just blinked her friend right back into existence.

***

CONFUSION, RELIEF and urgency battled for dominance in her gut. Most compatriots used screen names here, but none like the one she saw now in the source code for Pod 0018. It was too nuanced a name for

Elle not to have noticed if they had been here working for Modular all this time.

Which meant, not only were they alive, but they had hacked into Dylan's ModPod feed, desperate to communicate with their old comrade.

As the pieces locked together, Elle felt a momentary surge of resentment that her friend would try to connect with Dylan instead of her.

Until she remembered that everyone thought she had been long dead, too.

As Elle gnawed at her fingernails, logic bit at her heels. She counted on her fingers, unwilling to trust her sleep-deprived mind to perform basic mental math.

It couldn't be true, her source would be at least 35 years old now. Even if Modular's census count had documented them wrong, they would have expired by now, especially without Modular's interventions.

They should have.

Tho words pinged off Elle's mind. Everything she knew of the new world had been based on the knowledge she had gleaned in the confines of this complex. What had she actually tested— seen— for herself? Maps. Books. Census data.

Everything had been curated through Easton, and she'd never had a reason to doubt it.

The Overseer said Void destroyed everything not contained by steel and metal, so she said let's build a fortress. He said they needed to develop a vaccine, she agreed to the testing. Her savior stripped her of her identity, she watched it burn to the ground.

Her closest confidant said she should take over as Overseer, she said when can I start?

She had never questioned him, and because of her ignorance, she'd been blind to the possibility that there could be a different truth waiting outside those walls.

She'd never had the Turnover, nor been forced to make echoes, but she'd been brainwashed all the same.

In her mind, she laid out the rest of her plan like a blueprint, its absurdity quickly forming into reasonable necessity. With one last look at the username floating there in the middle of nonsensical jargon like a beacon, she closed out of the Command Center, patted her pocket and slipped out the door.

She clung to the shadows despite the wee morning hours. No one had a reason to be hovering around the lab sector while the residents slept, the majority of them being heavily medicated. But Elle was still jumpy as she eased the door open into the glass partition of the dim room, and she caught a glimpse of the door panel: oo18 D. CAVANAUGH, ELECT GIVER, status: stabilizing.

Elle pushed through the rest of the space quickly, urgency propelling her forward. Dylan didn't have time for her to hesitate.

She pulled out the thin bottle of capsules and a pen from her vest pocket. She looked back up at the unmoving figure lying on the white sheets, seemingly at peace from the extra sedation she had ordered through Easton's credentials just hours earlier.

Peace. It was all she had ever wanted for her friend. She'd lied, manipulated and deceived him for so many years, and did so with what she thought were pure motives. She looked back down at the bottle and with a steadiness she didn't feel, her fingers scribbled a brief note on the white label of the bottle. Then she popped open the cap, carefully poured out two purple capsules and slid them into her pocket. As the cap clicked closed again, she shook the tube and heard the two remaining pills rattle.

She drew a breath, tucked the precious gift into the sleeve of her sweater and reached out her hand to press a small silver button. A deafening click sliced through the silence and Elle cringed, shooting another glance at the bed.

Dylan didn't react, nor did any alarms, and she eased forward.

Goosebumps pimpled across the backs of her arms as she entered the same airspace as a Legacy for the first time in this post-Void world.

She kept her eyes on the still form, unsure of what to say if Dylan woke, but refusing to go any slower. She made it to the side of the Legacy's bed, keeping her back positioned to face the wide-angle camera resting in the corner of the ceiling.

Trembling fingers grazed an olive-toned knuckle. Seeing no repercussions, Elle lightly shook her hand and the bottle slid down into a glistening palm. She tucked the treasure into his own hand quickly, but it was just enough time to feel the warmth of his body... the will to survive, still coursing through his veins. A sudden jolt of anger course through her own, and she pulled away quickly, afraid of what subconscious noise might pour out of her exhausted soul in the silence.

As she backed into the shadows, her aching body yearned to sink into the floor. To return to oblivion.

As she slid out into the sterile hall, she wondered if, perhaps, her wish would come true all too soon.

***

IN THE back of her mind, Elle knew this would be the last time she made this walk. The burden of it weighted her steps, but her mind was made up.

She'd crept out of Dylan's lab like a wolf hunting in midnight shadows, feet stalking a well-worn trail, eyes slitted in unwavering focus, her mind calm. The kind of peace only brought on by the inevitable.

The elevator continued to shudder upwards as a red € lit up on the panel, signaling she was passing Level 3, the infected wing. Elle tried not to wince as a slew of faces passed through her mind.

Then an idea jostled through the grief, and Elle slung her satchel around, whipping out her tablet. The sound of swipes and taps echoed throughout the chrome box as she swept through her email archives. She attached the file, hastily typed out an explanation and pressed send.

The elevator continued to ding, approaching level 8, and her fingers flung themselves madly across the screen. For the final time, she accessed the account for the Overseer of Modular Enterprises, swept a finger to find the email settings and made a quick addition. The elevator door slid open as she cinched her satchel closed. Still no soul in sight, she pulled the hat down reflexively. This floor had felt like her home for so long, but that was before the veil had come down. Where once the shiny grays reflecting off the hallways effervesced with excitement and opportunity, Elle now saw the walls for what they were: a disorienting illusion to distract its inhabitants from the way they actually boxed them in.

She saw the door at the end of the hallway, looming larger than ever, but she refused to slow down. Knowing it would be locked from when she'd left, she pulled out the keycard and without preamble, just as their relationship had always allowed, she swept in without a knock.

Faux sunlight lit the room in bronze fluorescence, a clear perversion of the actual time of day, and she hardened her eyes to find him amidst the eerie glow.

Easton stood preternaturally still, a blue pushpin wedged between two fingers, vignetted by a backdrop of more maps than she remembered ever seeing on that wall before.

Finding his face, she saw it all. The wheels of his mind spinning, the locking of gears as it realizes the sudden emergence of a cog, and then a fast rewind to determine the best choice of action to remove the cog.

Which was fine. She was betting on his problem-solving skills.

"Ray."

The compatriot spoke the name she'd never told him since the injection like a disappointed father, and it cracked the façade that had been lingering in the air since she had sunk the needle into his arm.

"Compatriot Hill," she countered, tilting a smug head. "How are you feeling?"

A crooked grin loped across his mouth as he looked down at the pin, idly spinning between a thumb and forefinger. His head lightly bobbed up and down, eyes trained on his fingers, calculating.

"You're not even going to try and fake it? Keep pretending you're under the influence of the Turnover? C'mon it was fun," she sneered.

"What's the point? You seem to already have made up your mind, and we both know there's no changing it once you've come to a decision."

"So, you'll admit it, then. You never intended on having your mind wiped, nor did you ever really believe I could be trusted as Overseer. Three days of outright lies," she felt her eyes narrow to slits. "But we both know it goes farther back than that, don't we?"

Silence nestled into the corners of this office that knew it well. Any other time, she would have accepted the absence of noise, giving her the chance to formulate the right words. But today, time wasn't on her side.

"I just want to know why."

"You just accused me of a myriad of things..." Easton said slowly. "I'm going to need you to elaborate."

She rolled her eyes. "Why would you even let me think I could have this role? Did you just want someone to put the noose around when there was inevitable backlash? Are you so cowardly that you don't even believe in your plan enough to stand behind it?"

Easton held her gaze. She held her ground.

Suddenly he spun away from her and jabbed the tip of the pin into a South American city, poking as benign of a hole in the corkboard as the one residing under the white bandage on his arm.

"Have you ever heard of the placebo effect, Eleanor?"

"Yes," she said curtly, not caring to hear a psychology lesson.

Undeterred, Easton flashed a smile as he turned to face her again.

"Well, I always found the idea fascinating. So much so that I implemented the theory into our global mission here. Without a treatment, souls were lost, despondent and weak. As soon as people believed they had it, there was joy, compliance, unity and hope. It was a 180."

"I remember the lies, Easton."

"A little petty of you to say that about something you so easily agreed to be a part of." A tsk sound slid out of his lips and she wondered how an empty stomach could actually boil.

"I agreed to a lot of things. But then again, it never really mattered what I thought anyway. You were always in control of everything, regardless of how I, the Circle or the Leadership Panel ever felt."

"Ah, but that's where you're wrong," Easton said, shaking his head and wagging a finger at her. "You always mattered the most to me. You knew better than anyone what was out there. When you started to turn from me... when you nearly blew everything that day outside Zero's door..." he trailed off, his forehead creasing as he stared at her. "I had to give you a placebo. It was the only way to keep your loyalty."

The twitch of a jaw was all she offered him.

"And look how you responded." He gestured both hands towards her stiff body. "You've gained the confidence to barge in here, stand by your principles." He grabbed the white binder, punching a finger into the cover. "You've instigated the process against all odds! Adversity knocking on your door—" Easton broke off to glance back at her, a pang of sympathy crossing his face. "Ah, yes, I'm sorry about leaking the details to the group, but it was better they found out sooner than later."

Her mouth fell open with the revelation, and he seemed to gain momentum.

"But you've pushed it all aside! Knowing that what's best for humanity will win in the end, regardless of what other people think. I knew you could hold your own, I just needed you to believe it. And that wouldn't have happened if you believed I was still in command."

Elle cocked her head towards him. "And you know how I would react in any given situation?"

"I've known you a long time, Elle. Come on," he snickered. "Give me a little credit."

"Hm, almost eight years now that we've known each other, isn't it?" She said, challenging. He just shrugged.

"Sounds about right."

"Yeah? I still remember that first day. The cold stone walls of Nox, the confusion—you seemed to loom larger than life in that safety suit. Just like a real hero."

Easton squinted an eye, her sudden acclamations confusing him momentarily, but praise was too tantalizing to him to avert for long.

"You remember? My helpless body just lying there on the grungy floor, desperately waiting for anyone to help." She stole a glance at him. He looked down at his shoes like a meek child unsure of how to take a compliment, but the smirk playing at his lips spoke otherwise.

"Of course, that wasn't the first time you'd watched a soul in need, pitiful and yet, receiving no mercy. This was just the first time you did something about it."

The smirk evaporated.

"A woman sitting in a courtroom, innocent, just hoping for anyone to have the courage to stand up and defend her. I never imagined that an entire room full of Americans could be so solidified in the same opinion, but hey, my back was to all of them so what do I know? Maybe you can tell me what it felt like to sit in that courtroom, knowing an innocent soul was going to suffer, and not do anything to help."

A new cog. He didn't look away in guilt, but she saw the gears retract again in the stale quiet, sent into overdrive yet again to absolve this surprising new threat.

Finally, his lips quivered at the corners, a plan having formed. She waited patiently, with both curiosity and dread. He sat down on the couch, leaning forward with his elbows resting on his knees casually as if in an attempt to disarm the tension. She felt every muscle as she stood paces from the doorway, taut as a whip

"I wondered when you would find out," he conceded, staring at the ground. He let out a long breath, laced with resignation. "I was building something for a client, back when the company was— well you know. Barely staying afloat. Anyway, this client refused to offer their name, but had very specific needs. Things like, the space had to have enough power hookups for multiple devices but also had to be incredibly mobile. The kind of flexible that allowed the resident to pack up and move it on a dime. Back then, I took on every client. But this request felt... wrong. So, I had a private firm dig into the client." Easton looked up at her for the first time. He must have caught her alarm. "We were small. We needed protection, too. We couldn't afford to do business with criminals, and this felt like something I might not want to be affiliated with."

Easton ran a hand through his hair, a subtle sign of nerves.

"They came back with a name. Dylan James Cavanaugh."

She'd been expecting it, but she still jerked. Easton's hands rubbed together as he stared down at them.

"They also came across some online transmittals between Dylan and an IP address linking to an Eleanor Drake. Both entities appeared clean as a whistle, according to the experts, so I thanked the firm and sent them on their way. But I'm a curious soul. I kept the printouts of the conversations. Was it wrong? Absolutely. But hey, I like a good conspiracy story as much as the next person— so I started doing my own research. Some days I even felt like I was a secret collaborator with you two."

Elle wasn't flattered. "Then what?"

Gray eyes fell a bit. "Well, the more I found, the more concern I had. You guys were onto something, but I had no clout. At best, I was the grass that the Forbes totem pole stood on. I couldn't offer anything more than a few dollars here and there if you needed it. I didn't use my name, but I wrote to you—"

"Cutless Tech."

Easton twitched. "You remember my email, then."

Elle folded her arms and leaned against the bookshelf. "I remember being filled with hope that someone believed in us. Only to be left hung out to dry. Imagine my surprise then when I did a little research of my own recently, only to find out it was you behind Cutless all that time ago."

Easton's eyebrows shifted. "I don't remember you responding."

"I didn't trust anyone back then. Seeing where we are now, looks like I made the right decision."

Easton looked at her, amused. He sauntered over to his desk and lightly hopped up on top of the wood, reclaiming the position he'd always held over her. Her eyes flickered to a wrinkle in the pocket of his gray joggers as they stretched over his hip. Anxiety threatened to bubble up, but she kept it at bay. That kind of fog could derail everything. She had to stay sharp.

"So, you knew. That's what it comes down to. You knew I was right all along, and still, you let it all happen."

Easton drummed the sides of the desk. "What really could I do, Elle? I said it earlier. I wasn't anywhere close to who I am now. The influence I had on any part of the business world was flimsy back then, let alone the political side. When everything happened, I— I just wanted to see you. I know it sounds silly, but I felt like maybe you would be able to feel my support."

Her eyes flickered, threatening to soften.

"I also wanted to see them."

Elle lifted her eyes back to him in surprise, and Easton continued, softly.

"Dylan, I mean. I wondered if they'd show up at your hearing. All this time, they had been in the shadows, never coming out to defend you either. And you say I'm the coward? You both had equal parts in this, and they let you take all the blame."

Elle shot off the bookshelf, thrusting a finger in the air towards his chest. "You don't get to call anyone a coward, Easton. Why didn't you tell me, huh? You had plenty of time to tell me all this. It was a long flight from Meridian."

"I had grown protective of you. I didn't want to rehash old trauma."

"I'm a big girl. You don't get to decide how I can or can't cope with things."

"Well, I also wanted to make Dylan pay for what they let happen to you."

"By throwing them into a safety net? You were the one who fought for Dylan to be an elect candidate. That promised the highest level of care!"

Easton clicked a tongue. "I can see how you would think that. It also meant the highest level of monitoring. I saw everything."

Elle felt herself retreat half a step as stony eyes trained on her face like a sniper.

"Here was this individual who'd left you out to dry, and yet you clung to them like they were your savior. I saw your search records. I knew you had tried to find them for months. But I did, Elle. I was the one who found Dylan. I did it for you."

Easton's eyes were boring into hers now and she wavered on her feet, the confessions derailing from the track she had expected this conversation to take.

"After they arrived, I thought you'd be happy. Finally, content. But things got worse! Anything that put the resident in harm's way, you tried to fix or change. Even if it meant halting the entire process, or sacrificing yourself. It was you who persuaded me to allow that Gray to be the resident's facilitator for a day. You constantly tried to make allowances for Dylan, regardless of how it would affect our ultimate plans."

Elle matched his gaze, despite the unease numbing her toes stuffed into the front of her sneakers. His eyes danced with equal parts satisfaction and challenge.

"That was all hard to swallow, but I looked past it. The actions of a committed facilitator. But then you started keeping secrets from me, in order to help them. I was your hero, Eleanor! Me. I went after you... while that *friend* of yours cowered in some sinkhole in New Jersey."

Any argument would be futile when Easton had his pride hurt this much, and Elle was too exhausted to try. She stayed silent, on guard.

"Yeah, I knew about your fake emergency Pod Reboot. You thought every feed had been disconnected, didn't you? Guess you know better now that your Overseer eyes have been opened, even if only temporarily," he said, a sneer plastered across his face. "You sat there, dispelling all your fears and limitations onto Zero, searching for an entity to hold your crutches. What did you expect them to do? Hear the frailty in your voice? Demand your rescue?" His eyes mocked her. "Then you just outright lied about it. I get why you didn't confess to the Circle... but me? Honestly Eleanor, it felt like a betrayal."

His hands clasped together now as if they were trying to contain his anger. He never liked to show a loss of control, but he did like to hold a grudge. The question was how harsh he was willing to carry it out.

Getting no apology, Easton plodded on. "As soon as Dylan stopped responding to the Shriek, I realized I would need a backup plan. I'd secretly always wanted 0017 to be our choice. They took to the echoes, had the smoothest assimilation and reacted with the highest fear tendencies to the Shriek. The data was all there."

"But the mother—"

Easton clicked his tongue. "Ah, yes. That would have been poetic. But that was the nail in the coffin actually. When we found that out, Dylan was scratched. Their DNA was too close to that of Void's patient zero. Too risky."

Elle's mind was on overdrive, trying to connect the pieces she knew to make sense.

"Then why persuade the Circle to keep Dylan on?"

"You saw them. They were already panicked. I had to make it sound like a benefit. Plus, I needed there to be some urgency—and who doesn't love a good full-circle story?"

So many lies.

"I wanted to tell you, truly," Easton said, seeing what he believed to be hurt flash across her face. "But how could I when you'd kept so many things from me? Our trust was gone."

Shawna's blank face, unaffected by the revelations in that final meeting, suddenly came to her mind—and Elle felt the pang of betrayal again.

"You have performed rather beautifully," Easton continued, interrupting her thoughts. "Exceeded my expectations there, getting 0018 out quicker than I'd assumed you would. All honesty, I thought you were playing me outside their pod door those few nights ago. But then you instigated the Retraction process, just like I'd asked. I almost thought I got you all wrong... till you showed up here today."

Easton suddenly hopped off the table and Elle jolted. He just laughed as he strode to the table and grabbed the binder, flicking through its pages.

"It's fine that you came to visit a little early. Just forcing my hand a little sooner than I intended, but everything is still going to plan," he said.

Elle glanced around the room that had once held such safety; the promise of something better to come. Now all she could see was an end.

She steeled herself as she tried to speak at last, but anxiety rested like boils on her throat and suffocated the words. Gurgles seeped out instead as her cheeks burned.

"Why did you ever come for me then?" she managed to say. "That day in Nox."

Easton looked almost sad as he placed the binder back down. "I had to keep you close."

"For what? Your moral code? Be the hero who saved the soul who tried to warn everyone? It was never personal, or about me at all. You just wanted to show everyone your moral compass still pointed north."

"That's not true. It was as personal as it could ever get." He walked towards her now, casually flicking out a hand and then he sighed. "You wouldn't understand."

"Oh, I think I understand completely," she said, hardening her eyes, refusing to retreat.

They were both quiet. She wondered where the needle was. The desk drawer? That pocket? She knew he had to have been prepared for this moment. She wanted an answer, but she also wanted this to be over.

"Even if the Shift had never happened..." she ventured quietly to the floor, unsure exactly how to give voice to the thought that had been niggling in the back of her mind for months. She lifted her eyes, daring him to answer honestly, for once. "We would still be exactly where we are right now, wouldn't we, Easton?"

"What does that even mean?"

She steeled her gaze in one last dare to get him to admit it right in front of her, knowing full well he wouldn't budge.

"Your Remedy. A cure to eliminate the human will. It was inevitable. You've had this end planned for years. You just needed a means."

"What?" Easton said, a sneer pulling at his lips in that grin he had used to earn her friendship, and she knew. "You can't hate an opportunist."

"Then what was the point of me? You knew what you were always going to do."

"Oh, Eleanor. Isn't it obvious? You were born to be a scapegoat."

Suddenly the flash of green appeared out of nowhere. Even if she'd wanted to, she couldn't have acted quick enough to block it. She felt the needle and then the fog laid on her like a heavy blanket.

THIRTY TWO

FROM: Overseer <EHill@modularenterprises.com>
TO: All Modular Enterprises Worldwide Personnel
Re: Emergency Lockdown Protocols - Activated

5 August
Dear Compatriots,

It has come to my understanding that a great manipulation has occurred under my watch. Many of you have been concerned for the well-being of our choice of Elect Giver, Resident 0018, Dylan James Cavanaugh.

Late in the evening of 4 August, the facilitator for our priority resident revealed themselves not only to be highly unstable but actually someone altogether different than any of us at this outfit ever realized. After an intensive investigation over the course of the last eight hours, it is our belief that Eleanor Drake, a prisoner serving twelve years in retribution for threatening the United States with the creation of a biomedical weapon, had escaped from their holding facility when Void was released. They found refuge within our walls with an obscured identity, and proceeded to infiltrate my trust, along with the Circle's. With full transparency in mind, I have attached an audio recording of the individual confirming their identity.

It would seem that as our efforts were finally coming to a head, Drake tried to derail the entire process by first attacking me with a sedative before stealing all of my passwords in order to take over my position, acting as Overseer without anyone's knowledge. In this short time, the individual made unsanctioned approvals to send the Elect Giver into Labs where they ordered the early processes of Retraction. Drake then snuck into the resident's lab as they slept and, we fear, injected a strain of Void into the resident, who as you know, would have been the source of life for every human being remaining on the planet. The Evergreen Race would have been compromised from the start.

For obvious reasons, Compatriot Cavanaugh needs to be quarantined and cared for properly, so they will be returned to their ModPod effective immediately. Thus, we will be unable to carry on with 0018 as our choice of Giver.

Given this horrendous affair, I worry what other entities may lie in wait to destroy our future, so with haste, we must continue with the plan— which is outlined briefly for you all in the following attachment. We will be implementing the Remedy Transition for our backup Elect Candidate: Resident 0017, Dewey John Perkins. While they are a backup, this is in no way to say that they are not an exemplary choice for this task. Compatriot Perkins was the first to be added to the Elect Candidate Program and shows great strength and mental aptitude to take on this act of duty to the world. We have run out of time, I'm afraid, and this is our only option left. If we wait any longer, we may never get the chance to try.

See below for an attachment of the IP address that Drake used to access my information. Please crosscheck your email back codes and if you have received anything with the same address, immediately delete.

Thank you all for your great patience, and your care and concern for myself as well as our Legacies. We can't wait for the next steps to finally be taken.

In harmony,
Easton Hill
Overseer, Modular Enterprises

THIRTY THREE

THE TINNY ping of an email resounded through the hollow room, and Dylan jerked awake, relief swelling through his limbs.

He couldn't remember being moved out of the white, sterile cube that had perpetually looked a little fuzzy around the edges, but watching the mundane drip of his blood for hours on end had begun to threaten his sanity, and looking around his pod now, he had never felt so happy to be in a box.

At least he knew this box.

But all too quickly, a sharp pang hit him in the chest as his last memory sprung forward.

A black hat. Long, alabaster fingers brushing his knuckle.

It had taken everything in him not to flinch at Elle's touch. When the glass door had creaked open, it was as if every hair on his body twitched, his dormant senses back on high alert, despite the grogginess of his limbs.

Cracking an eye, he had seen brown wisps peeking out from a familiar black hat. He had burned with questions, but her trepidatious walk kept him silent. He wasn't supposed to know she was there, and he trusted her enough to give her that.

In turn, she had given him the first skin-to-skin contact in six years. His eyes closed in the darkness, Dylan had marveled how the subtlest of touches could warm an entire body. He treasured the minutes, the slight heaviness of her touch in his palm offering comfort, until the grogginess returned with a vengeance.

He had wanted to say something before he surrendered to sleep again, but as he opened his eyes to speak, the room was empty.

The slight weight in his palm hadn't been her hand after all, but a small object that his fuzzy vision couldn't quite make out. He had fumbled for his pocket and slipped it in just before sleep had taken over.

Snapping to the present, he rocketed up in his bed, nerves alight as he frantically dug into the tangle of sheets, blindly searching for his pockets.

A soft rattle answered, and he took a long, measured breath.

He untangled himself and got out of bed, letting unsteady feet take him to the protective covering of the bathroom before shooting a hand into the pocket and pulling out a small bottle.

Confusion fogged his mind until he saw a note on the front, and a small grin played at his lips.

Take both if you see the mist.
-Elly

Eleanor had never come back, and he grieved for their brief reunion. She had been a bridge, connecting his past, an evasive thing, and his future, which was unpredictable and terrifying.

She had been a breath of fresh air. She had made him remember what it felt like to have purpose. She had made him forget about Maggie.

But now he was back in the place where questions only suffocated him, and he was running out of air.

A second ping launched off the walls and Dylan slid back the door. Gauging by the misty light refracting through the window, he guessed it should be mid-morning, which meant his handlers had turned off the Shriek.

A creature of habit, he ambled over to the Cipher anyway.

"5 August. Cavanaugh, Dylan. Processing."

All of his hairs stood on end. For as long as he could remember, the machine had never reported anything different other than the date.

Unnerved, his fingers began to pulse and he drummed them against his thigh, shaking the small bottle still hiding there. At the sound, a small wave of peace wafted over him, Elle's friendship a silent presence.

...hold on to anything that brings familiarity.

The line from the note dropped into his mind like a gift, and his heart raced at the implication.

After all this time, could she be the link?

He dropped into the desk chair and typed out his password, twitchy fingers still on edge from the Cipher's reading. Dylan opened up his email, but before he could begin searching her name, his attention shot to the new messages emboldened at the top of his inbox.

All three had come from Overseer Easton Hill, who had stopped contacting him since their research ended.

He went to click on the most recent one without thinking, but caught the subject line of the oldest—sent around midnight. **PLEASE READ FIRST**.

He clicked, and a small wall of text filled the space. His eyes were immediately pulled to an icon of a small video camera at the bottom of the email. The attachment was labeled: *From E.*

Adrenaline surging, Dylan forced his eyes back up to the text.

Dilly,

I'm sorry for every lie. None are worse than the others, but I hope one day you can believe me when I say that I believed all of them were to serve you in the best way possible. Throughout the entirety of our friendship, my loyalty to you has never wavered, only my name. The world once knew me as Eleanor Drake, but you know me best as Ray.

It has been an honor to watch over you these last six years, but I've come to the end of the road. My eyes have been opened, just a little too late. I can only hope you still have time.

If my plan has worked, you'll be getting another email, perhaps a few, from this address. Read every single one, but don't respond.

I'm on your side, Dylan. I always have been. Those pills in your pocket are proof, but I know you need more. So I'm going to let someone else try and persuade you.

Just watch the video, please. Before you do anything else.

-Elly

He fingered the lump in his pocket, his head spinning, and yet his eyes could only focus on the file. He double clicked.

A small wooden stool blinked onto the screen amid a room so full of color, Dylan had to squint. His heart pounded as he waited for something to happen and he flinched when the video image jolted.

A thin torso suddenly appeared in the frame, emerging from their spot behind the camera.

Lanky fingers reached towards him, straightening the lens before backing up towards the stool. Almond skinned legs scampered onto the seat as cropped, chestnut hair veiled the figure's face in shaggy, unkempt chunks. Finally braced on the chair, the person swept a hand across their forehead and looked up at the camera.

Dylan's breath caught in his throat.

Dimples erupted across a gaunt, heart shaped face, dotted with freckles. The figure from the echo screen, come alive.

His sister, resurrected.

A hand shot out in a shy little wave, and then retreated into the nest of hair as if embarrassed.

"Hey Dyl, it's E. I don't know if you know who I am—this is a really weird thing to be doing. I just feel like time is slipping away so fast and if I don't do this now, I'm not going to remember."

Dylan's eyes stung, but he kept them trained on the screen, afraid that if he blinked, the only memento of his sister's existence would be blotted out forever.

"I've asked your facilitator to keep this for me, in the chance..." Maggie looked down, raking her hands through her hair, and Dylan took in every feature, committing every detail to memory.

"Well, in case there comes a time when you need to trust in something again. I know you, Dyl. You're slow to come around to people, and after everything we've— everything you have been through— I don't fault you for it. But I trust your facilitator to know when the time is right to let you see this, and if I don't make it through all this—"

Maggie suddenly made a gagging noise, and Dylan snapped back in his chair.

"Gross. Am I literally in some angsty TV movie right now? Dad would be so proud."

Dylan felt a strangled laugh begin to form in his throat as he sat entranced with this person before him, a stranger to his eyes but a familiar warm blanket to his heart. His eyes filled with tears as he tried to stuff the emotion down but the strain was overwhelming. A full bodied laugh erupted out of him, breaking the dam.

Half sobs echoed off the walls, melding with the fullness of his laughter and on the screen, Maggie leaned forward to rest her elbows on knobby knees, her smile returning, as if in response.

"I just wonder sometimes... if I'm not here, then I want to know someone is still watching out for you. Someone to put that warm blanket over your shoulders when you fall asleep on the couch. It's selfish because I know you don't know who I am. You think you're an only child. But I can't live with that. I need to be sure you're alright, and your FAC is the only one I trust to do that."

Dylan knew he was being manipulated again, but this time, he didn't care.

"Do you remember what Mom always called me? Her *ray of sunshine*." A sad smile lifted her gaunt cheekbones as Maggie swiveled to look at the vibrant walls around her. "I made this room for her. For us." Maggie glanced down at black Converse shoes, biting her lip. "I hate that I didn't try to see her at that clinic. They said she had been doing so well—so I took the time for granted..." she said, trailing off.

Dylan felt his chest tighten, his body unwilling to let his mind wander to lost moments.

Maggie suddenly shook her head as if clearing away spider webs.

"When I found out who was taking care of you, I knew it was a sign. Please, Dyl. Trust Ray, ok?" Maggie pierced him with green eyes that had once danced before him in the darkness of an attic. "Ya got that, champ?"

The video cut to black. Dylan blinked and when she didn't come back, he drew back on the mouse, rewinding the file, and hit enter. The words no longer a surprise, he sat enamored with the girl on the screen. He watched the contortions of the lips as Maggie spoke, the twitch of her hands as she twisted them together in her lap and the way her laugh peeled back the drooping lines surrounding her dimples. This was the girl from his memories. Almond tanned legs jogging past yellow wallpaper, wavy hair flung over the side of a top bunk, dimples peeking through hot steam rising out of a ceramic mug.

He let the video play over and over, swerving the scrubber back to the start as soon as the blackness dared to take her away. This human before him, awkwardly perched on a stool in the most vulnerable form, was no figment of a disease-ridden imagination, nor were they some perversion of yet another lie. Her awkward gangly legs and shy smile were too pure to be wrong.

No, nothing could be more real than the human on the screen before him and realizing it, a swell of grief crashed into him. He finally had proof that she had been alive, but he had only gotten it after she was already gone.

***

HIS HAND had gone numb, idly scrubbing a finger across the trackpad back and forth for as long as it took him to lose all sense of time. A small black dialogue window popped up in the upper right corner of the screen, obscuring half of Maggie's face.

Offended, Dylan swerved to close out of it immediately, nestled back in his chair and pressed play again.

As long as he kept her talking, he could convince himself she was with him. He began filling the silences in the video with his own responses, turning the one-sided viewing into a conversation between two people existing at different times.

She asked for his cooperation, he cited multiple reasons for his refusal. She implored him to trust Ray, he begged her to see how he couldn't. The dampness on his cheeks had grown stale, hardening with his own twisted desire to change her words, but with every new time he played it back, a little part of him gave in to her sincerity; the purity still trying to burst through the murky, disparaged parts of her infected body.

Her words never changed, but his rebuttals grew weaker and weaker until jittery fingers launched him from his seat. A soft rattle interrupted one of E's monologues and he paused the video, fingering the bottle in his pocket again.

The question danced in his mind like a puppet pulled by taut strings.

After everything, could he trust a liar?

A pair of cracked lips formed in his mind, and he could almost hear the mocking laugh. Because, of course, he had to.

He had no one left.

***

DYLAN RETURNED to his inbox to find the next email in line. Paragraphs of text appeared before him, but he was more taken aback by the recipients list at the top of the memo. *Modular Enterprises Worldwide Personnel.*

He had never been referred to as personnel while serving at Modular, nor had he ever received a group email before. Dylan nearly clicked back out of it, not wanting to waste his time with basic company emails, when he suddenly caught sight of his name within the text of the email. His eyes raced back to the beginning as he began to read, fear quickly turning into confusion and then dawning. His heart hammered in his chest as the gravity of the lies from the last year began to pull him into a tailspin.

Eleanor had deceived the team at Modular, but for what? All the details couldn't be true, as she hadn't injected anything into him when she had visited that night.

However, she clearly had betrayed the Overseer's trust in some way and Dylan knew enough about Modular leadership to know that that behavior wouldn't be handled lightly. Despite his qualms with her, a fear crept up his spine on her behalf.

When he reached the bottom of the page, another small dialogue box appeared in the corner of his screen and he deftly closed out of it, anxious to read the attached file titled *Remedy Dispersal.*

Dylan tore his eyes across the brief document, greedy for any information that would explain Easton's message, which clearly was never meant for Dylan to see.

Just as quickly, Dylan wished he'd never seen any of it. The image of bright white walls dotted his vision as he continued to read. A constant drip of red splattering into an opaque misty bag. He wanted to throw up.

Shaking fingers scrolled down the page to see if there was anything else, begging for a second page to declare it was all one elaborate prank, but the scroller didn't give. He flitted back up to the top. Stomach in knots, Dylan read it again, knowing nothing would change, but hoping his mind could justify the words.

RETRACTION:

Take stabilized blood from chosen Giver to test for neutralization and proper induction into all blood types. Once deemed fit, Medical personnel will siphon cells from Giver's hippocampus in order to harvest all trained procedures, social understandings and proper cohabitation behaviors necessary for life on Equinox Installations.

REMEDY:

The resulting composite of Legacy blood and the retracted impulse synapses from Giver will be mixed with the serum that will target, and attack, the brain's aversion to social and ethical compliance, thereby instigating the subversion of innate tendencies towards conflict and superiority.

IMPLEMENTATION:

All three components will be comprised into a single vaccine, which will be copied for wide spread immunizations for all surviving citizens within Modular Enterprises installations across the globe, to create the Evergreen race, a people equipped to withstand Void and the threat of it ever happening again.

All the schemes, lies and omissions had driven Dylan to grief and madness over the last few months. And, finally, he had the reason for them all.

It was explained in frilly language but Dylan saw right through it.

For years, Modular staff had worked to engineer a vaccine that would restart an entire race. Through sensory-adept technological devices, all-seeing cameras, and expert psychological games, they had been training bodies and minds to adhere to a new world, and wiping the slate clean when it failed.

They had manipulated time, and now Easton was prepared to use it as blackmail.

The human race simply couldn't last much longer.

When Elle had snuck into his lab that night, he'd been saved from becoming the person responsible for eliminating the human right of free will.

But for what? He was still as trapped as ever.

Every nerve in his body felt tense, like a match just waiting to be struck. The black dialogue window box slid back onto his screen again. He dragged his eyes over the message, already hovering the cursor over the red x.

[Link182] We have noticed irregular activity in Pod 0018. For further assistance, please respond. This is our final notice.

His fingers burned like a tiny flame at the end of a matchstick. He clicked within the window and a response box appeared. With nothing to lose, Dylan quickly tapped out a reply.

[ModPod_0018] Who is this?

Dylan lightly drummed the keyboard, feeling idiotic that he was likely talking to an autobot from the help desk division. Words blinked onto the screen in a matter of seconds.

[Link182] Assistance. Please confirm, is this Patient Zero?

[ModPod_0018] Not anymore.

No answer came back for nearly a minute. Dylan was about to exit out of the window when a reply appeared before him.

[Link182] Is this Dylan Cavanaugh?

[ModPod_0018] Yes.

[Link182] It has been noted that you have been removed and suddenly returned back to your inhabitance. Do you need assistance?

It felt like a trap. He'd learned early on that coincidence was always manufactured within these walls, and it was awfully convenient that this query would come right at the time of an internal crisis. He wasn't stupid, he knew he had been reading and reacting to the alarming emails in plain sight of cameras, but he didn't think they cared enough about him anymore to observe and analyze everything he did. No longer their Giver, he was useless to them.

He went to re-read the initial message that he must have ignored twice before, wondering if there was something he missed that would clarify the reason for the dialogue window even appearing in the first place. Alarmed, he suddenly realized the previous messages from the thread had already deleted themselves.

Uneasy, he quickly tapped out a reply.

[ModPod_0018] I'm not sure I need it from someone who won't even tell me their name.

[Link182] We don't really have a name, but I think you would know us best as the Artist.

THIRTY FOUR

A CACOPHANY of taps resounded in his ears. He saw words appear before him in his own response box. But he couldn't feel his fingers. Everything was numb.

Instead of a name, the Artist had offered an encrypted link to talk away from the Modular network and without the need for auto-deleting messages. Both parties were aware that cameras could see anything on Dylan's screen and neither knew how much time they had.

The urgency emanating from the other user's rapid replies seemed to seep up through the keyboard underneath Dylan's fingers, making them even more jittery.

In a daze, Dylan fired questions at the Artist, testing their identity, verifying minute details of the echo imprints he could still recall so vividly.

[Link182] Yes, 'Link' was a connection to this username and part of our plan, but there were multiple variables at play. Ideally, Ellis would have resisted all Modular propaganda this cycle and reached out to you himself, using his own screen name, which was also Link. But it appears he fell to their control after the recent Turnover, and we've been unable to contact him. Our backup plan was for me to hack into your computer and talk through this platform. Thought the warning from the echo imprint might offer you a sense of safety if you'd already seen the name.

Ellis. The pod mate who had chewed him out over email, refusing to help— had always been on his side? The realization bred dozens of follow up questions that Dylan knew they didn't have time for now.

[ModPod_0018] Before we go any further, I need your name.

[Link182] Sorry, not safe enough here.

[ModPod_0018] We're in an encrypted chatroom where you've already divulged plenty of secrets, why won't you tell me?

[Link182] Man, I forgot how annoying you are. You were so high and mighty the last time, too. You didn't get my name back then, and you're not about to get it this time. Just call me Link.

[ModPod_0018] Back then?

[Link182] Yeah. Back when you, Elle and I were renegades saving the world.

Both of his cohorts, resurrected from the dead—from his perspective— within a span of three days.

Dylan had grown so accustomed to having news knock the wind out of him that this latest blow almost felt natural.

Almost.

He made it to the bathroom just in time, and as his head hung over the bowl, he screwed his eyes shut, trying to remember the days that he once thought to be so dark.

Link was right. He'd never been told either of their names— too risky, in their words. Until, that is, a leak sprung and Elle had been forced into the limelight.

She went to Nox, Dylan hid in plain sight and never heard from the anonymous third member of their party. Having never known any personal details, Dylan couldn't get in touch.

And the longer Elle sat in Nox, the harder the slap in the face when he heard nothing from the person he'd always called Anon. It was easier for him to think they had died, especially after the Shift.

Dylan stalked back to the computer.

[ModPod_0018] What's wrong with you? I thought you were dead! Where have you been?

[Link182] You think you've been the only one in danger since that day? You never knew what I did for a living, but my position became... dicey. Too visible, too close. Contacting you would've only made it worse for the both of us, but I still kept tabs on you. Once Void hit, I'd tracked you as far as New Jersey, but by the time I got a hold of someone close enough, they said you'd been picked up. I figured you were safer with them.

[ModPod_0018] Safer from what? Void?

[Link182] That... whoever started it. Somehow, someone must have figured out what I—we—knew and it suddenly became clear to me that they weren't happy about it. There was no way of knowing if they knew about you, too, but the longer you stayed alive, I figured you were in the clear.

[ModPod_0018] If you thought Modular was so safe, why didn't you try to get in?

[Link182] I was within a year of aging out. They wouldn't have wanted me. Besides, the entire world was ogling Modular at that point. Whoever weaponized the pandemic, their eyes had to be on the one place that was trying to undo all their work. I wasn't about to willingly expose myself like that. Plus, I had too many others with me at that point, I wasn't just going to leave them, and they weren't going to be allowed into Modular's walls.

Others.

The coded, swirling words from the first screen echoed back to him. *Life exists outside the walls.*

It was all true.

Dylan glanced at the bottom of the screen and was shocked to see a half hour had already passed. The ticking clock forced him to start rattling off bullet point questions, desperate to know everything he'd forgotten.

His old colleague responded in time, explaining how international affairs had been decimated as countries, big and small, were left to the unqualified hands of unwitting twenty-somethings. Those in political power edging the danger window did what they could to prepare the younger generation, but too quickly, Void took them.

The world was in mourning, Link said, and yet had no time to feel it. Every time someone came up with a reasonable plan of avoiding extinction, there weren't enough qualified people alive to carry it out.

Link explained how they couldn't even bury the dead; not knowing the intricacies of Void, people were afraid the contagion could spread simply by proximity to an Infected.

[Link182] It was chaos, man. I mean, that's what you get when you leave the entire world to panicked people whose only life experience with international catastrophe was reading about it from a textbook. Survivors isolated themselves, hid in their own homes, tornado shelters... and woods in New Jersey, apparently.

No one wanted to be out in the open air. But once the death toll seemed to plateau, people began to come back out, and honestly, it was kind of beautiful. After the first three months, everyone—all nations—just united. No one knew how to lead, but since there were no leaders left, we all tried to be one together. Medical students from all over the world collaborated in desperation to research and create an immunization as trust fund teenagers threw their money at them. Anyone who felt like they had any talent or resource tried to find someone who could use it to beat whatever this was that had overtaken the world.

Dylan's eyes burned from staring so intently at the screen. Throughout all his research for the Overseer, he couldn't remember any of this information. If anything, the words he'd read contradicted what Link was saying now.

But before he could interject, another paragraph appeared.

[Link182] Then people started dropping again; those who had edged out of the 18-34 window. That's when the hazmat suits came out and Modular Enterprises came onto the scene. Somehow in just six months, they had built a structure large enough to house isolated living cells which were connected to one mainframe. I still don't know how they got that headquarters built so fast—someone must have had a lot of money to throw around—but desperate times can make people achieve great things, can't they?

Dylan stared around his room ogling the progressive features: the DLVRD chute, Cipher, echo screens. Technological advancement at its finest, and it was staggering to realize how quickly it had come together.

[Link182] As soon as the facility was complete, people swarmed their doors. When other countries saw the footage, they started pooling their own money together, bought the blueprints and soon every continent had a Modular installation. And somehow, they took in everyone. That was the beauty of the Modular design: the framework could bend, elevate and widen in conjunction with the amount of people that continued to come knocking. It yielded to constant change— like some massive tree built of chrome. They just kept adding more branches.

It seemed like a dream come true—but not everyone was willing to believe it. Over the course of that first year after Modular had set up camp, I had unwittingly formed a kind of resistance group. I was still underground, chasing the threads we'd pulled at just a few years prior, trying to find whoever could have started all of this. Through my online connections, I found loners who were too afraid to come out of hiding places of their own, but wanted to do something. Many were young, obvious priorities for Modular, who didn't want to be forced into isolation. They wanted to choose it for themselves.

A thread pulled in Dylan's chest. There had been Legacies just like him outside these walls, choosing how to live their lives, for years.

Relief and jealousy surged towards each other, sending shockwaves of anger throughout his body. Had he willingly gone with Modular all along? Or had he tried to resist? When his memory refused to answer, he got up and started to pace as more walls of text came through.

Most were Grays who were too afraid to go to Modular, but still wanted to use whatever time they had left to do something more worthwhile than wait for their minds to go. Even after all this time, they are still the hardest workers out of everyone on the team.

Dylan stopped short, leaning forward on the desk to stare at the word Link had just used. Dylan raced his fingers across the keyboard, hoping to beat his colleague before a new wave of information hit.

[ModPod_0018] There are Grays still surviving outside of Modular walls? Without Legacy blood?

[Link182] Of course.

[ModPod_0018] How is that possible?

[Link182] It's still not proven, but it seems that any individual who had been in some semblance of isolation throughout the first month of Void's release was able, and continues, to withstand the worst effects, regardless of their age window. One friend of mine was working on a four-man submarine crew when

Void hit. Didn't surface for five weeks post-Void, and I just talked to him yesterday. He's 43.

[ModPod_0018] So people who had limited physical contact with others at the time the pandemic released are also immune like Legacies?

[Link182] No one is actually immune, we all come out of the age window at one point. I think that's why Modular wanted to stash away every Legacy they could find. Build an arsenal of blood that kept Void at bay. But that isn't the only way. Ironically, while isolation was the key to protecting many Grays from Void's strongest effects there in the beginning, close contact with people— namely, Legacies—is what saves them now.

[ModPod_0018] Close contact... as in, humans interacting with other humans without any barriers?

[Link182] That's correct. Modular wouldn't know, as they are too afraid to ever consider putting a Gray in the same room as a Legacy, but there's some kind of ripple effect. Whatever protects Legacies from Void radiates from the body and onto whatever living organism is close by, like an anti-bacteria. It's not a cure, of course. Degradation does occur the further people push out of the Legacy age window, but it's slow moving. Life sustainability is much longer for Grays who live in close contact to those with Legacy blood than those who completely isolate themselves.

The truth felt like shrapnel splitting his entire body apart. He had never liked life here, but he had found solace in knowing at least he wasn't suffering out there. And all this time, he could have been living on his own terms, doing what he could for people who couldn't.

He could have saved Maggie when she expired out of the window.

He clamped his eyes shut and dimples flashed before him. Had she known what lied outside? Ray— or Elle, he realized with a jolt— had said Maggie knew all the truths about Modular, and still supported them. He could still hear Maggie's calm words from her video, imploring him to trust.

Brother and sister. So alike, both deceived into cooperation; into thinking there was only one way out. Their only difference now was that he was still alive to know that there wasn't.

[Link182] You've been quiet. You're thinking how all of this is going against what they wrote in those books?

[ModPod_0018] I flicked through a few of them, yeah.

[Link182] Not sure how much of it you read, but all reading material stamped by Modular was their way of rewriting history. Or at least, the history that happened in between Void's release and well, to present day. Considering their readers lived the same year over and over made it pretty easy to fill in the gaps. The echoes were backup sensory models to enhance the "memories" that the books explained. I know you didn't look at those much, but if you had, you would've seen a bunch of fear-inducing stuff. Modular wanted you all to believe that life within their hedge of protection was the only way to preserve the human race and that anything outside was a land run by terror. The echo screens presented made-up images of life after the Shift: wars, conflict, strife, the like.

[ModPod_0018] Wait, I did see an echo early on. But it wasn't anything bad, or at least, to anyone else it would've looked perfectly serene. It was a beautiful picture that looked exactly like— well, just a bad time of my life.

[Link182] When your dad died.

[ModPod_0018] How do you know that?

[Link182] We know a lot of things. But yes, that image wouldn't have looked scary to any other Legacy in that building, but remember how pods are tailored to each individual? Well, that echo image was chosen just for you. Fear is malleable and Modular got really good at molding it for their benefit.

Anger boiled his bloodstream, every limb at its breaking point, aching to burst through the wall. Make his own door.
The image spurred a sudden memory.

[ModPod_0018] Ellis. You said they're with you?

[Link182] Yes, they've been a pretty integral piece to our work here.

[ModPod_0018] Who else is on the inside then?

[Link182] Oh, we aren't on the inside.

[ModPod_0018] What about Ellis? I thought he was your undercover spy or something?

[Link182] Oh no, he was actually a pretty late arrival to the team. That's a whole separate story.

[ModPod_0018] Then how do you know all this internal stuff about Modular and what they've been feeding us all this time?

Link didn't respond for a minute and Dylan pressed his fingers to exhausted eyes. The reply ripped them back to the keyboard.

[Link182] From you.

[ModPod_0018] What? You think I'm faking here? I didn't even know any of this an hour ago.

[Link182] Dylan. This is the fifth time we've had this conversation.

THIRTY FIVE

WORDS DARED to keep appearing before him, but Dylan ignored them, spinning in his chair to get away from the onslaught of revelations.

His eyes landed on the nightstand and he thought about all of the signs he'd stashed away there... the notes, doubts, secret echo messages he had willed himself to believe were from someone on the outside. Now that he knew it was real, Dylan felt like he was in a dream.

Five years, they had been trying to reach him. That is, according to what the messages still pinging in behind him said. Dylan spun back around and scrolled up to find where he'd left off.

[ModPod_0018] Yeah, still here.

[Link182] I know it's a lot, but if it makes you feel better, this is the least amount of questions you've ever asked by this point.

[ModPod_0018] Just keep talking.

[Link182] So 2019 was the first time we actually tried to connect with you—your second cycle. We knew you were there in '18, but it took us several months to build up a hub strong enough to get in. Bandwidth and WiFi are hot commodities out here. Anyway, they had some security, but it was little to nothing. They were saving the world, who would go against them? We hacked in to the database and found some quick easy details about where you were in the facility. It was so simple—too simple, in hindsight.

Dylan couldn't scroll any further and realized it had been five minutes since Link's last message. Heavy fingers slogged across the keyboard, just managing to eke out a question before letting them retreat back to his throbbing forehead.

[ModPod_0018] What'd you do?

[Link182] I sent you an encrypted email, easy as that. I explained who I was—
or rather, how you knew me—and why I needed you. Again, at that point, all
we were trying to do was to see what resources you might have there to help
us finish what we started back then with Elle.

You remembered that part of your life, a few details more hazy than they
should have been, but not too alarming. What worried me was how you
refused to believe I was talking to you outside Modular walls. When I finally
convinced you, you asked me what it was like out there; if there was war,
famine, disease, etc. I was so taken aback that all I could do was to ask why
you thought that. I'll never forget what you wrote: "But the books say it's
desolate out there. Nothing lives. I remember... mass graves, looting, sick
people everywhere. And the smell. Every time I walk past a screen, I smell the
rot."

His gut twisted and although he knew it wouldn't help, he clamped his
eyes shut, trying to find the memory of when he had thought that. The
pictures he had painted to his old colleague were too jarring. How could he
have forgotten what that fear felt like?

[Link182] We learned almost everything from that first conversation with you.
You told me what you knew, or what you thought you remembered, and I
debunked it. Every time. Over the course of three hours, we began to piece
together the lies and fake history they had been feeding you over there.

[ModPod_0018] What made me trust you? If all I knew was what Modular
told me, I can't imagine how I would've believed anything different.

[Link182] You sure you want to ask this question?

Every hair stood up on the back of his neck, anxiety prowling across his
skin like a lion creeping through underbrush. Sweaty palms smoothed them
back down.

[ModPod_0018] We're not doing this again a sixth time. Just tell me
everything.

[Link182] You were pretty doubtful at the start, no surprise there. I knew I would need a catalyst for you to distrust Modular; something that would get you to think they weren't quite as honest about things. Telling you about Maggie was the best option to do that.

Just seeing her name split Dylan's head into a myriad of numb fragments.

[ModPod_0018] You knew I'd forgotten her?

[Link182] Not exactly, but I knew how close you both had been before Void. Every time you, Elle and I would talk about the future, somehow Maggie always came into the discussion. You wanted to make sure she'd be taken care of if things went south for us. So, I thought it was weird when that first time we spoke in '19, you never even mentioned Maggie. You asked about your mom, a few friends... you hoped that I had come across them underground. When you didn't ask about E, I figured something was seriously off. When I had looked for you in the database, I'd seen her name, too. I knew she was alive.

But when I told you about her, that was our first mistake. All you wanted was to get out and see her, and it drove you mad. You lost it, telling me you were going to make them get you out. I tried to calm you down, but was suddenly kicked off the network. I'll never know what you did, but I imagine it involved enough outrage for Modular to swoop in with meds. We learned quickly that subtlety was going to be key moving forward.

[ModPod_0018] What do you mean, meds?

[Link182] Well it's just a hunch, but after I was suddenly whisked off the chat, I was able to get back in a few days later. I asked how you were and you had zero recollection of anything I'd said. Over the years, we've gathered some intel and we think they call it 'instigative transient global amnesia.' Basically makes you forget short term memory for a 48-72 hour window.

Dylan thought back to an image of red fists pounding against a white wall. The next image in sequence was him waking up to a white room, linen sheets and a full body ache.

[Link182] Anyway, after that first encounter, we knew there was something wrong with Modular. My biggest pursuit was still aimed at finding anyone still out there related to the Scale, but I needed you to help me finish it, and if you were locked away in some mind-altering prison, my goal would never come to fruition.

[ModPod_0018] A little selfish but ok.

[Link182] We kept trying the email thing that first year, and even though they had upped their encryptions and firewalls, we managed to still fire off an email to you. I didn't waste time and explained as much as I could in the single email. We got a confused reply back from you, which was expected, but then I saw my original email within the thread and realized keywords had been blacked out, redacted. The words must have tripped security sensors and we backed out immediately, going back to the drawing board.

Words had started to run together on the screen and Dylan began jotting notes down on a nearby scrap of paper to try and keep it all straight. Link continued to hammer out a chronology of how those early years went, explaining that when Modular came on the scene, all the world nations agreed to follow Easton and his movement to the end of the earth. All, that is, except New Zealand, which was the final country that had been ordained to have an installation.

The country knew from the beginning about the Turnover idea, it was a foundational part of the program, and hated it. They didn't believe in altering minds, even if it was for the individual's benefit, as Modular claimed, and demanded that their own citizens be retrieved from the North America HQ. When ME had refused, citing that they needed as much diversity in Legacy blood as they could find, New Zealand ceased cooperation.

Meanwhile, Link had been galavanting the black market of internet trolls to find any way in to Modular, and came across a thread from someone in New Zealand threatening to invade the headquarters.

The two of them shared what they knew, trading information on the Turnover, propaganda and false memories, the latter being news to the Kiwis since they had backed out of the plan so quickly. They never knew the rest of the inner workings of the pod installations. According to Link, once they found out the level of deception, it made the country distance themselves even more.

[Link182] They didn't join up with us or anything, but it was reassuring to know we weren't the only ones worried about life on the installations. Now that we knew about the Turnover, it gave us a second wind. More fuel to get you out of there. Over the course of the next four years, we came up with a slew of ideas, some crazy enough that didn't make it off the ground, and others that actually worked. We hacked into DLVRD once, sent a letter rolled up in some coffee filters. We just didn't think to warn you not to read it in a place where all camera angles could catch you reading it. You likely read it immediately, reacted badly and they intervened. We believe that each time this happened, which was at least once a cycle since 2019, Modular gave you transient global amnesia and then when the memory of whatever you'd read or seen from us returned, your FAC talked you out of it, likely even citing the confusion as effects from Void.

Dylan thought back to the first few days of orientation, when he'd nearly blurted out how he'd found a note under his bed. He had almost ruined everything right from the start.

[ModPod_0018] Why wouldn't they have given me the Turnover again?

[Link182] Well for one, they had a calendar to stand by. Each elect candidate turned over on the same date each year, it was easier to monitor that way. But more importantly, they never knew which year was going to be the winning one, when they found a cure. They needed you to have the right mindset to go out into their new world, to inoculate the infected. They spent so much time every cycle ingraining their propaganda into you and a Turnover would've undid all their work of that year.

[ModPod_0018] So every time you told me the truth, I was then immediately brainwashed?

[Link182] Essentially. It was much more frustrating on our end, to know how close we were and then strike out yet again, back to square one. While each failure gave us new insight on how best to connect with you the next time without setting off Modular alarms, each failure also made the place even stricter on security protocols. We were religious about our own safety measures, so it seems they have never figured out who we are, but that didn't change the fact that Modular's inter webs became a jungle gym of complex securities, VPNs and firewalls. By 2023, last year, we were at our wits end. And then finally, they slipped up. They made a Kiwi mad.

His hand was cramping but he knew time wasn't going to wait for the pain to subside. He kept his eyes glued to the screen, anxious to hear the end of his own story.

[Link182] Ellis Harper is one of the New Zealand natives the country had tried to get back in 2018. Modular decided to add him to the Elect Giver program towards the end of the cycle in '23. A privilege for Legacies is that you guys get the Shriek. From my understanding of how you both explained it— the bell was designed to inflict disorientation as you came out of fear-driven dreams that the echo screens had been programmed to incur. They start this at the end of orientation as a way to test that the echo screens are producing enough sensory engagement and fear-driven mentality, even when residents are unconscious. To a trained Legacy, the Shriek seems to be their savior because it pulls them out of the fear. But, it's actually a way to propel the fear into reality, to keep the dream living on.

The pencil clattered to the floor as Dylan jumped back to the keyboard, excited to finally offer insight.

[ModPod_0018] I hated the Shriek, but that was because it always pulled me from good dreams about my childhood, or Maggie... even though I didn't know who she was at the time.

[Link182] Yes, that was all by our design actually. It used to not be like that, but I'm getting there. The first time Ellis heard it, he didn't react well. He was drawn from a very frightening memory and in the chaos, thought he could burst his way out of the room.

[ModPod_0018] Yeah, he broke his arm and everything. My FAC told me that happened.

[Link182] Well the hit must have jarred something in his mind because up to that point, he'd been told—and believed— to be American. When it clicked that he was from another country, he was pissed. The dude is a coder, you know that? After the arm drama, he figured out a way to get around Modular's radar and sent a message to his home country. Next thing I know, I'm getting coded messages from the Kiwis again, and they want in. We each had our own motivations— I needed you back, they wanted to save Ellis—but it didn't matter. We each had resources the other needed.

Once our team had expanded, we had more heads reeling together and the process sped up quickly. We knew this time to start off slow, to not make your observers see any reactions. Knowing Ellis was already angry at Modular, we fed off that and went for him first. He latched on immediately, and still avoiding alarms, we then set our sights on you. We deliberated about the plan for days and finally landed on sending you a book we knew was required reading. We had Ellis write instructions and a hyperlink on the inside of the cover. The idea was that you wouldn't act suspicious when you got the book, nor would it look odd to any watching eyes. Then we just prayed you'd read the inscription without much reaction. After four years of failures, you performed wonderfully. You followed the link, which connected us on a chatroom like what we're doing now. Everything was finally going exactly to plan and, together, we were formulating a plan for you two to get us inside the walls.

The only problem was that there were only 40 days until each of your next Cycles started. You and Ellis started making contingency plans for if you weren't able to get us inside the facility before the next Turnover. You both needed a way that would remind you of the truth, but without alerting Modular staff. It was actually your idea to use the screens.

Dylan's mind was reeling. The entire story that Link had just put before him felt like someone else's life. To be thrust into the narrative without any memory of it ever happening was overwhelming.

[ModPod_0018] The secret messages from the imprints? That was all my idea?

[Link182] Yeah. I think the idea came from your own rollercoaster experience with the screens. As soon as we told you the truth in early '23, you immediately stopped looking at them. You told us about a dream that you had every night, the one that the Shriek always rescued you from. Something about being in an attic... claustrophobic, hearing noises you couldn't make sense of, a shadow popping out of the hatch. It terrified you.

After a week of avoiding echoes, you had the dream again, but the details were clearer. I managed to find a photo from years back on our old chatroom feed, and when you saw it, you said it was the same face as the one in the dream. Once you knew how the Shriek and echoes performed in conjunction, you realized the only way to work around Modular's radar was to manipulate their own tools. So in 40 days, Ellis worked his magic, hacking into your network of echo screens. We couldn't make things obvious, so he devised a way to schedule out transitions over the course of several months, starting whenever you mentioned the name 'E'. It signaled our belief that you were beginning to remember, which showed you were ready for a nudge in our direction.

[ModPod_0018] They were pre-scheduled? You mean, you weren't watching me and then creating the images from whatever you saw? All those clues, the smirking lips—"

[Link182] Oh, we've been listening this whole time, but even if we'd wanted to, we couldn't have changed them. Once you designed them, Ellis scheduled them out and that was that.

[ModPod_0018] I designed them?

[Link182] Dylan, you're the Artist. You wrote that note, and you came up with every single one of those pictures—the negative and the imprint—in advance.

Head spinning, Dylan stuffed the revelation into yet another box and, gritting his teeth, read on.

[Link182] Well, our plan failed. ME leadership got wind of us again, and panicked. They instigated the Turnover six hours early and we had no choice but to bail. You and Ellis were wiped, and all we could do was hope the contingency plans worked. But Ellis went MIA, communication-wise. We just had to hope the echo screens would work for you.

You had scheduled a flannel shirt to be delivered to your pod the day before the Turnover... you didn't explain, and I didn't press. But I wondered if that had helped soften the chaos of the beginning days. Plus, the note to yourself must have been effective. That one was my idea. With Ellis's help in the previous cycle, we'd been able to access old archives of your camera feeds. We saw how you reacted the first time you heard the Shriek, and oddly, it was the same every year. You would spring out of bed in a panic, right off the end of the bed. Over the years, it seemed like there was even a little dent or hole in the bed frame from where you leapt off it every year. I thought it would be the perfect spot to hide a letter of caution to yourself. I made sure to remind you that it needed to be just cryptic enough to cause a seed of doubt, but also without information that would give away ourselves in the case someone found it before you did.

[ModPod_0018] Alright so let's fast forward... you haven't heard from Ellis, you know that I'm getting the echo messages, you takeover my pod to show me Maggie's name... why did you wait until now to finally reveal yourself?

[Link182] Because you left the room.

[ModPod_0018] You knew that happened?

[Link182] The pods have activity monitors built into the system, and we managed to add ourselves to the notifications list. We couldn't see live feeds or anything, but when we failed to receive any movement notifications for three whole days, we started to worry. When the activity spiked again today, we knew we had to connect, no matter how blatant it might look to any observers.

[ModPod_0018] Well I don't think they're watching me anymore. I got an email that I wasn't supposed to see, and it's not good, Link. The vaccine—or remedy, or whatever they're calling it—is ready. And it's going to change everything.

[Link182] Don't be dramatic. Whatever it is can't actually fight Void. Nothing can beat it. Whatever they came up with is just going to be another stalling tactic.

[ModPod_0018] I'm serious, I'll send you the attachment. They've made some kind of serum that drastically changes the human brain. I don't think they know I know... Eleanor must have secretly added me on the recipients list or something, but I got the email straight from the Overseer's account. It's bad, and it's happening soon.

[Link182] Eleanor?

[ModPod_0018] I'm still processing what she did to me all those years, but she's the only reason I'm not strapped to a chair with blood dripping out of my body.

[Link182] What are you talking about?

[ModPod_0018] When they moved me, they had hooked me up—

[Link182] No, I mean Eleanor—who is that?

[ModPod_0018] Eleanor Drake—you know, the third member of our little renegade trio?

Link didn't respond for a long time, and Dylan felt his fingers start to fidget uncontrollably. Now that he knew so much, he felt even more helpless, powerless to do anything within these walls. A ping broke the silence.

[Link182] That's not possible. Her name was nowhere in the database. She died.

[ModPod_0018] She went by Ray or... Eleanor Stryck. She was my facilitator— what, I thought you knew?

A surge of camaraderie rippled through his chest. He knew all too well the crippling sensation of realizing something you had thought to be fact— had only been an illusion.

[ModPod_0018] Listen, I honestly know how you're feeling but you have to push it into a box and deal with it later. I've read the emails. I don't know what you're waiting for but the Overseer has already put stuff in motion. I'm out of commission, and they've already taken the next Legacy in line.

Link snapped back to attention, responding immediately.

[Link182] A new patient zero? Did they say the name?

[ModPod_0018] Dewey Perkins, 0017.

When no response came back, Dylan worried Link had left. Fingers tapped anxiously on the armrest, and his eyes trailed up to the misty window. He wondered how many others were out there.

The cursor blinked at him mockingly in the text box. Finally a message came through.

[Link182] You're sure?

[ModPod_0018] I'll forward you the email right now if you want. But come on, we're wasting time, you gotta get moving. Dewey's a good guy.

[Link182] I know, ok. We're coming.

Dylan's foot rattled against the desk, helplessness seeping in from all sides of the limiting walls that barred him from being a part of the fight. Without thinking more about it, his fingers whipped across the keyboard and hit enter. He prayed his cohort hadn't left yet. The message blipped in front of him.

[ModPod_0018] You hacked computers. Can you get into DLVRD?

A pencil dropped to the floor and Dylan tried to still his leg. He didn't want to steal any of Link's time away from helping Dewey, but he also couldn't sit idle. A soft ping made his leg jerk.

[Link182] What do you need?

He glanced up at the opaque window one more time, and then tapped out his reply.

[ModPod_0018] Get me a gun.

THIRTY SIX

SHADES OF gray danced before her as Elle focused on the back of her eye lids. It had taken all of her strength those first few minutes to remain motionless, as she knew Easton stood guard over her, analyzing every hair on her body for movement.

But then his footsteps receded from her, and she realized that the effort had left her with no energy to resist the overwhelming desire to sleep.

She forced her mind to replay every detail of the last several minutes, resisting the temptation to surrender to the black.

As soon as the needle had slipped into her arm, she fell limply into Easton's arms, and she'd let her eyes close, allowing her mind to focus on her bearings. She felt him lift her incredibly heavy limbs, and she tried not to shudder.

As he bent to drop her onto the cold leather couch, she leaned ever so slightly away from him and into the back cushions—just fleetingly enough for her tongue to dart out behind her mask, find the two purple capsules tucked into the inside fold, and guide them down the back of her throat. She had swallowed before his arms had even retreated from underneath her back.

Now all she could do was wait for the purple pills to do whatever they were designed to do, and hope she didn't fall asleep before then.

Easton hadn't cared enough to cover her with a blanket and vulnerability wrapped around her in its place. Anxious fingers ached to bite into her own skin, if only to relieve the pulsing tension ripping through her entire body. Elle felt her mind break apart in fragments, trying to keep every nerve from shaking.

Then all at once, it stilled. Aching limbs numbed, the soft buzzing within the pod went silent. Everything was suddenly, simply void.

***

ONE SECOND she'd been fighting, and the next it was like she'd been splintered into a million little atoms, no single part of her feeling anything. Was this proof the Analepsis had worked, or evidence that it had not? Either question brought her nothing but indifference.

She was vaguely aware that the blackness appearing before her was the back of her own eyelids, but the less she felt of her body, the lighter the darkness became.

Then she realized that the black around her was igniting into a silvery, blurry haze, like a projector being manipulated into focus. While the rest of her body seemed to float, Elle remained oddly aware of the heaviness of her eye lids still weighing down upon her cheeks.

Suddenly the walls of Easton's office pod appeared upon the silvery white canvas of her closed eye lids, the image sharpening before her. The UV simulator radiated dusky colors against the bookshelf, dim light bathing the spines of Easton's manifestos and lies. The maps and charts tacked onto the bulletin board lit up with a clarity she'd never seen before, but just as she tried to get a closer look, her point of view rotated to show Easton standing just off to the side, spinning a thumbtack and boring steel eyes into her. She heard his voice, dim in her ears like it was through a wall but before she could move her own mouth to talk back, Elle heard the soft echo of her own.

"I just want to know why."

The movie playing before her was her own memory's echo: uncontrollable and unchangeable. Numbly, she relaxed her lifeless limbs and succumbed to the flashback.

The two voices bantered in rewind as she watched Easton unabashedly play coy to her sudden entrance. Everything felt the exact same as it had minutes— hours, perhaps—earlier, except that everything was in more vivid detail and sped up, and she tried valiantly to store away fragments of information she hadn't been able to see the first time she had lived it.

Her mind jumped from memory to memory, scenes of her life playing back in reverse chronological order. Sterile hallways dimmed as the quiet blackness of Dylan's pod encircled her, the slight touch of his hand filling her, once again, with a warmth that felt powerful enough to unclench her eye lids. And then just as quickly, her hand drew back, anxiously clenched around a cold, plastic tube as she waited in the viewing room.

The visions flickered as she lost all construct of time, and the longer the movie played, her attention grew more and more rapt. She realized she had forgotten so many experiences that, with the knowledge she now had, were alarmingly obvious. Easton eyeing her over the table as she defended her countless arguments, smirking like he knew exactly what she was hiding behind. Why she was so protective.

And now she knew, that had been exactly right. He had always known.

More scenes flew by and she was suddenly looking through a single glass panel into a room lit up by the colors of the outside world. Shades of sea foam white crashed into ocean blues, splattered haphazardly onto walls surrounding a quaint wardrobe painted the color of the sun, a small chrome desk—shiny as a road just after it rained— and a single wooden stool, propped up by three legs of solid oak.

Amidst all of the color rested the soul that had put it there, now just a freckled face with a limp dimple, cruelly devoid of life. The sight of Maggie was the worst of the flashbacks and it felt as if it lingered longer than all of them to that point. Elle tried to look anywhere else, but she was powerless to alter her gaze, just as she was the first time she'd lived the scene. The loss had stung deeply, not so much because she'd had a personal relationship to Maggie but rather, because of the one she'd built with the only living soul Maggie had left. The soul that couldn't remember his sister.

The vision mercifully swept by, replaced by images of her days spent bonding with her elite Legacy residents. Conversations that had once built such anxiety in her before suddenly seemed so meaningless now.

The images faded into grainy blacks as a new memory flashed before her. Elle felt the corners of her eyes pull faintly as she squinted, already knowing her present body wouldn't help bring any clarity to the past memory. A flash of white startled her before her eyes could adjust, and she suddenly realized the scene. The first night of Cycle 7, mere months ago. Elle had dared to tap into Dylan's pod feed that night, hoping that his ears wouldn't yet be accustomed to any particular sounds. Even though that first night of a new cycle was always restless, she had never invaded her residents' privacy that early.

She had also never let anyone but herself be the voice who pulled a Legacy out of the Turnover's haze. So, keeping the headset and mic resting on the desk, she had flicked to engage, telling herself there were too many potential ripple effects for her not to make sure he was still okay.

Her breath caught now, just as it had the first time, as she watched the whites of his eyes flick around the room before retreating behind lidded eyes. The memory allowed her to watch him rest peacefully for another few seconds, and she relished the calm. The first day of the cycle then rewound before her and even though she knew it was coming, she didn't have time to prepare herself before see was seeing Maggie again.

Eyes poured out hazel light as long olive fingers clutched a mouthpiece for dear life, pale lips twisting and moving with squelched excitement. Elle had never seen a dimple so prominent as when she watched Maggie have a conversation with her brother for the first time in six years.

Then Maggie's favorite two words were reverberating in her ears again, all too quickly. The dimple faded as Maggie stared into the monitor, as if memorizing the face that couldn't stare back. Though she smiled, the words "talk soon" dripped off her lips like tears. The final words she would ever speak to her brother. Elle had held onto the sendoff like a talisman, vowing to always leave Dylan with the same words.

Elle tried to shake her head to clear the memory and, to her surprise, she felt leather crinkle beneath her. She shuddered, suddenly aware of the danger outside her drugged body. When no hands seized her skin, Elle released herself fully back into the dreamy state.

The longer the medicine played her life back, Elle felt her body return in splices, as if the memories were sinewing her muscles back together, only with more sensitivity.

Colors were more vivid, and she felt her skin prickle against the cold of Modular's chrome walls in a way she never remembered feeling before. Every sense in the playback was heightened, as if when she lived everything the first time, her body had been muted, subdued. She watched the late stages of Cycle 6, cringing as Ellis smashed his deranged body into the unforgiving wall as the Shriek resounded off his walls.

Sawyer's whiteboard countdown, marking the days before the young Legacy would be let out to fulfill the injection-giving purpose she had been believing in for three years.

Elle saw the early days, back when she would catch Dylan staring at an echo screen, entranced. Anxiety crept in as she saw the middle of Cycle 4, a thin scrap of paper shaking between Dylan's fingers as he stood rooted to the floor next to the DLVRD chute. Unease continued to crawl over her skin the further Analepsis pushed Elle into the memories that Void must have dulled, if not eliminated.

She felt the thin muscles of her eyes recoil, protesting the new scene before her. A group of haggard, blue-faced souls through plexiglass, lined up on their gurneys, bloated right arms stretched out. The next flashback swept in and she watched the same haggard souls, flocked together in their community infected pod, holding out their right arms as gloved hands injected a dark blue fluid. The color of the first attempt at a vaccine.

The same color of their blood when it went cold within 12 hours.

It was all coming back too fast, but there was no way to make the movie stop. She watched delirious confusion flash across the Overseer's face as the two of them pored over security cameras and encryption details in Cycle Two: the first time they realized they weren't the only ones who wanted Legacies.

As memories of the first cycle shuffled through, Dewey's infectious grin sent a wave of relief washing through her veins. She'd made it to the beginning. Before the first big groups of Legacies had arrived. Before the lying had become a part of her daily ritual.

Now that the worst was past, Elle gave in to the curiosity, wondering how far back the purple pills would take her.

***

SHE HAD been partly right. The worst part of what she could remember was, indeed, over.

But then the screams shot through her ears, returning lost memories with such detail, she felt like the images were tattooed on her eye lids: prisoners extracted from jails all over the country, strapped down and injected with mossy green serum. The beta tests for what would become the Turnover.

When no animals could be found alive within 100 miles of headquarters, they justified that prisoners were the most fair substitute. Elle would have agreed had she not just been saved from being a test subject herself. How many others, now strapped to lab chairs, were truly innocent, just like she had been?

But she hadn't been able to offer her objections, lest she show a sensitivity that would threaten her new role.

As the bodies convulsed and mouths twitched in whimpers, Elle re-lived the memory but without the desensitized reasonability she'd had the first time.

While the world had been scurrying for shelter that summer and fall of 2016, the core team at Modular had been scampering for a way to forget why. It had been priority one, before the evolution of the ModPod had even begun. Easton knew a vaccine would be a long term mission, and thus, the world needed a way to not just exist, but uphold some semblance of quality of life until a vaccine could be created. Isolated living quarters were a step, but how long could one person live within four walls?

Memory alteration was Easton's solution. The Circle, only four members at the time, objected and debated the notion for a week, precious time that seemed to tick by the longer the group deliberated. In the end, Easton persuaded them all that neutralization—a clean sweep of their memory—was a generous gift.

The screams now echoing through Elle's ears suggested otherwise. With the clarity that only hindsight, and the baffling science of whatever filled the purple capsules, could give, she knew now that Easton's theory had always been wrong.

The erasure of the human mind without permission was an extreme violation of basic human existence, no matter what you believed.

The visions continued to play and she suffered through the relentless film reel, tortured by the realization she had been in a position to have stopped all of it. Bodies rejected their initial concoctions, muscles taut as limbs writhed in pain. Back then, she told herself the inmates were all infected already, that the serum hadn't made anything worse. And some of them were.

But as she watched now, helpless, she realized that many of them had actually been as young as twenty four, free from any Void infiltration at that early stage. The souls' madness was caused by nothing else but Easton and his Circle's own parasitic desire to make scientific history.

Finally the nightmare images blurred past and she saw the empty space of her office, metallic walls glistening with opportunity. She knew differently now, but she still felt the power surge through her veins as it did that first week of joining forces with Easton Hill, fresh out of her cage in Nox.

Back then, everything had felt rich to the touch. She watched herself wander in the space, and the feelings rushed back.

A place of her own where she could have a new beginning. A future before her, untouched by a vengeful society. Her fingers had danced along the back of her new chair, the smooth wood effervescing with hope.

Reliving the memory now, she only felt the sting of a dozen splinters.

The picture before her now faded to black, the transition oddly sudden. Elle felt off kilter, but her body remained limp and rooted to the cushions, as if paralyzed.

The blackness went on for several minutes, if not hours. Time had lost all meaning and Elle wondered if she'd actually fallen asleep.

A shriek pierced through the darkness, more acute than any of the sounds from the previous memories. Elle tried to place the achingly familiar noise... and with a jolt, she realized it was her own voice.

Before she could process the revelation, a scene blinked out of the darkness.

Stark white walls surrounded her, beige linen sheets bundled at her feet and harsh light bounced off gleaming tile. Her perspective within the memory shifted to the right and a hint of color splashed into the scene. Misty gray liquid sloshed harmlessly in the middle of a plastic needle, gleaming in the artificial light for just a moment before it was plunged into her bloated vein.

THIRTY SEVEN

IT HAD been hours since his old colleague had left the chatroom, and, helpless, Dylan had begun attacking every smooth surface in the room with Pine-Sol, scrubbing away his impatience until the scent of lemon made him dizzy.

Link hadn't left him with any sort of plan except to stay alive, which seemed easy enough considering the unyielding four walls around him. Dylan had spent most of the morning in the bathroom, poring over the notes he'd scribbled from the chatroom conversation. Considering the lack of interruption, Dylan was confident his pod was no longer being watched.

But he knew it wouldn't stay like that forever. Elle's gift still rattled in his pocket, and her brief note continued to keep him on edge.

He would feel better once the DLVRD order arrived.

Dylan pulled at the sheets of the bed, finding menial tasks to do as he waited for the chime of the chute. He stopped short as he came to the end of the mattress, staring at the small divot where he had crudely mended the hole where he'd first found the note.

Link hadn't divulged any plans, but Dylan had to believe there would be some sort of insurgence.

Of course, Dylan would never even know, tucked away in this isolated cage. And if his friends failed, Modular would do everything they could to ensure no one in the place knew of the breach, which might include another memory sweep. Dylan couldn't afford to endure this again.

Epiphany striking, he jogged over to the nightstand and pulled out his copy of *Understanding the Shift: Aligning Past and Future*.

Turning to the first page, Dylan scribbled a letter to himself, in the chance that something would go awry. A note had worked once before. He only hoped he didn't have to rely on it working twice.

He ripped the sheet out, folded it tightly and went to the foot of his bed, pretending to pull at some loose sheets. As he did, he slipped the folded piece of paper loosely into the slats of the cheap wood.

A chime sung through the room. Dylan flinched, heart pumping.

If anyone was still watching, he might only have seconds. He had to make this count.

He had to know.

His fingers curled around the smooth metal as he tucked his body in close to the chute and checked the chamber. Loaded. Three rounds.

Still concealing the weapon with his body and cover of the wall, he flicked off the safety and took a breath, helplessness fading away with the exhale. It was time to see the truth. One way or another, he was getting out.

He gripped the handle tightly, one finger on the trigger, and swung away from the chute. One eye closed, the other found the center of the window. He pulled the trigger.

The shot rocketed through the room, deafening in the small, concrete space. But it was the shatter that resounded through his ears like an echo.

He ran forward, pulling his shirt up over his head and wrapping it around his fist as he bounded on top of the desk. Spindly white streaks spread across the window, emanating from the single bullet hole like a contagion.

Up close, the fragments revealed a sheer film that covered the back of the window like a dusty lining. Dylan clutched the shirt tightly and threw his fist into the hole. Misty glass fell like rain and he closed his eyes, waiting for the blast of summer air to hit.

It never came.

His eyes snapped open only to find another wall, covered from floor to ceiling by a giant plasma screen, the outside world only a mirage in front of him.

Splashes of white and yellow glittered before him, nearly as brilliant and real as the sunlight he could barely remember. His eyes crossed in wonder as he let them roam over streaks of painted sky crashing into green hills, a vision he'd only seen in his dreams.

The sparkle of the screen cast a warm glow onto the rest of the room, lighting up a quaint wooden wardrobe, painted bright yellow, a small desk and—his breath hitched as realization dawned—a single wooden stool.

He knew this room. But for the first time, he wished he could forget.

Maggie had been right here. The entire time.

Every muscle in his body went slack and he took a step backward, unwilling to see the truth anymore. His feet connected with air and suddenly he was falling off the desk—as light as a bubble floating away on a breeze.

A deafening thud, but all he felt was the consciousness leaving his body, blissfully taking the grief with it.

THIRTY EIGHT

THE INTENTION of the Analepsis was to inflict flashbacks, but the true power of the purple pills came through the perversion of the mind. The drug made every memory feel as if it was happening all over again, in hyperspeed and with hypersensitivity, and after revisiting nearly a decade of her life within such a short time frame, Elle wondered how much more of it her depleted body could take.

The white walls of the lab room slipped away as the sharp pain from the injection she never remembered finally dulled in Elle's shoulders and neck, leaving only an ache pulsing in her palms. A grungy darkness had misted around her with a chill and as her vision adjusted within the next memory, she realized the gray walls surrounding her now belonged to Nox. Her hands felt heavy and as the perspective shifted downwards, she saw them bandaged and covered by Easton's gloved fingers.

Her ally—the first person to speak to her with a semblance of compassion in more than two years—had kneeled before her, propped her up like a trophy and promised safety, only to send her into neutralized oblivion just like he would the rest of his 'prized' residents.

Anger boiled in her chest and she longed to grab hold of the rocky shard at her feet and smash it into the wiry hand still holding hers.

At last, manipulative fingers drew back and she watched the scene continue to unfold backwards. Easton retreated from her side, strutting back towards the doorway as he took in the entire scene for the first time. Crouched in the corner, Elle perched in a squat, waiting for the intruders to go back where they came from. While she could remember the feeling of desperation she had felt back then, she saw the physicality of the memory now through a vibrant lens. The transformation of Easton's face was unlike anything she remembered, the power of the Analepsis enhancing whatever light Nox had always expunged. As soon as he passed through the doorway, smile lines rapidly smoothed as his mouth went slack. She'd always thought the shock on his face was a result of seeing her, but now she saw the urgency of his gray eyes and they only saw the walls.

Just as she had all those years ago, Elle remembered with a jolt what the stone around her looked like. The blood had dried onto her gouged palms as she had etched the walls with every piece of information she knew to be true. It had been her way of keeping herself sane. But after two years of this, the scratched walls only proved the work of madness.

Within the memory, Elle rose to her feet, anxiously biting the corner of her middle finger, steeling herself. She knew she had to see the walls as the newcomers did if she wanted to make them understand; keep them from walking back out that door.

As her focus took in the stone surface before her, she saw the chaos with fresh eyes. A myriad of etched lines criss crossed over chicken scratch and crudely drawn symbols that would have remained long forgotten in her mind if not for this sudden revival.

But the clearer the memory became, the heavier the burden settled on her shoulders once more.

Her eyes followed the arrows, the spirals of blame, and soon, anxiety turned into cold fear. Dread sliced down her spine and she willed her legs to carry her as far away as possible.

Every time she had recalled this day, the specifics had been foggy. She knew she'd carved into the walls endlessly, the physical effort of mindless etching still made her hand ache. But none of the information she had written down had ever re-surfaced in her memory; she only saw shapes, curves and blurred letters. She'd always blamed Void, and after a year of trying to remember, she'd given up on the hope of finishing what she had started years prior. She knew that more time wouldn't help, but rather just make the memories more opaque.

She had used her anger to fuel her pursuit to rid the world from the contagion that had stolen everything from her. So, with clear eyes, she'd signed her life away, promising to follow Easton Hill to the ends of the Earth if it meant changing the world.

But looking at the wall now, Elle saw with the utmost clarity that she'd been devastatingly wrong.

Because at the very center of the arrows, written in block letters above the etching of a balance scale and circled a dozen times were two evasive words she had never been able to remember: **CUTLESS TECH**.

Her heart rate plummeted as dawning washed over her with ice cold clarity.

Her fading memory had never been collateral damage from Void. Her mind had been targeted.

Eerily on cue, her knees buckled beneath her, and unable to change the past, she felt her weary younger self fall into long, bony arms.

Only this time it felt like falling into the lion's den.

***

MERCILESSLY ROOTED to the floor, Elle's vision within the memory turned towards the monster she'd once considered her closest friend. She saw a smile creep out the corner of his mouth and she felt her body split in two. The isolated, desperate woman she was that day had been filled with hope, mistaking the smile to be one of generosity.

The woman lying drugged on a couch, however, knew the smile had always been a calculation, and she fought against the flashback, bile rising in her dry throat.

As the memory played out, she kept her focus on the jarring letters, blurred behind Easton who was speaking to her calmly, words dripping with empty reassurances. She didn't care to hear the first time she had let him lie to her, and instead, used this second chance to see the evidence in her own handwriting, vengeance hardening her eyes like emerald daggers as the epiphanies erupted in her brain like fireworks.

He could never have let her out of his sight, she had known too much. All he needed to do was alter the narrative.

He'd injected her with global transient amnesia, a light catalyst to fog her memory, make her forget the truth she'd written with her own hands on the walls—but not enough to make her forget she needed his protection.

Easton's face disappeared and Elle had no choice but to keep watching as the Analepsis sent her through a flurry of images that appeared to be a time-lapse of her life in the small cell of Meridian State Prison.

The environment didn't change for several minutes as her hands raked back and forth, words and phrases decorating the walls like kindergarten graffiti. The rapidity of the work seemed to slow down, the words erasing from the walls as the purple pills rewound her time in Nox.

And then the walls were blank again.

She waited, watching through her old eyes, staring at the silent walls, and after a full two minutes, she began to wonder what the point of this memory was.

Then she heard the moans, whispering like a fog through the exposed pipes that had often carried the loud voices of the other inmates. At the same time, she saw her own slender fingers reaching out among disheveled sheets on a grungy cot, closing around a sharp black rock.

Whimpers escalated to shrieks, and Elle felt a slight pressure on her ears where her younger self must have risen her hands to block out the miserable noise.

Yells turned to muffled whimpers again and the pressure released from her ears as she strained to hear the syllables dripping out of the pipes.

"Pain is good, Paige. It means it's working."

Not understanding, Elle listened closer, impatient for the memory to rewind faster, to clear the confusion.

More breathless gasps, and then the same voice returned. The owner struggled for breath but spoke clearly.

"Don't be scared, Paige. Remember what I told you about my old job at Cutless Technologies? This is it. This is what they were working on. I told you they'd figure it out."

The voice sputtered as a hacking cough erupted from the pipes, but by the time it reverberated throughout Elle's cell, the sound seemed to have twisted into a laugh.

"They released Void. I can't believe it's finally happening."

The voices fell away as revelation fell like hammers, dulling the images that continued to play before her.

When Easton Hill found her cowering against the walls of Nox that day, the alarm she'd seen on his face had never been a reaction to the sight of her.

It was because of those two words.

Elle and her small team had been sent down so many rabbit holes over their months of research and digging, but had never found a single entity to blame. The Scale had hidden well behind all sorts of masks, but Elle knew there was a mastermind funding them, and she'd gone to prison before finding out who.

The irony now swelled through her like a tidal wave.

It wasn't until she had made it to Nox that she overheard those women—and was finally shown the truth. And as soon as she'd heard it, she had written it in stone, marking it with her blood for all to see.

But she had never dreamed the mastermind himself would come—and when he did, she'd made her first, grave mistake.

She had confused a smirking grin of opportunity for a smile of compassion.

Because saving her meant keeping his enemy close. Rescuing her offered him the chance to manipulate his biggest threat.

Her mind had gone numb, apathy returning to her medicated body with a vengeance. She felt neither anger nor confusion. Relief nor sadness. The truth of the matter was simple.

You can't feel emotions in a body that was never yours, and she'd given hers away years ago. All the things she'd done— all the things she'd seen and allowed to happen since she walked out of Nox— they had never been her doing them at all. She had merely been a puppet, controlled by a monster she'd tried to warn the world against, twice.

THIRTY NINE

WHEN THE gray walls finally dissipated, she had hoped it would all be over. But then the courtroom shuffled in, the flashing cameras, the countless papers and endless meetings with lawyers. Her basement waffled past, the brown storage boxes and black chat windows blurring in front of her as stress coursed through her younger, tense body. The Elle that laid on Easton Hill's couch, however, still felt nothing except the exhaustion of wishing the resurgence of memories could be over; begging the silent, inky blackness to return for good.

And still, the movie of Elle's life continued to roll, the beige walls of her musky basement now giving way to a scene exploding with such radiance, Elle fought to gather her bearings.

Ornate textures glittered at every turn, shimmering gowns sweeping a long carpet of red shot with gold from the sparkling chandelier overhead.

The gala. The benefit that innocently became the catalyst to it all. Dazed by the dizzying colors, she was unable to prepare herself for the sight looming above her as the point of view shifted upwards, and she felt tears clog underneath her closed eye lids.

Four elegant arms poised on a balcony railing, two shrouded in white sheath and two veiled in black cashmere, cuffed with gold. But nothing was brighter in that room than their grinning faces pointed down in her direction. The apathy shocked from her system, Elle felt a warmth sizzle in her fingertips as she laid eyes on her parents for the first time in a decade.

Adaline Drake held out a sparkling hand, offering her approval of the event Elle had been organizing for months. Just as she had that night, she felt a heat surge to her cheeks in pride as she watched the woman float down the stairs to join her side. They walked in harmony, Elle's blonde bob dusting her shoulders as Adaline's jet black hair refused to move in its chignon bun, their posture the only physical similarity between mother and daughter.

The flashback seemed to slow, and Elle took in every detail of the woman who had always been her mother, just without a birth certificate to prove it. Her own father glided behind them, always content to watch his girls take the spotlight.

Twenty-three years prior, left widowed in a cold hospital room and holding a brand new daughter, Barton Stryck asked Miss Drake— his wife's best friend and Eleanor's middle name-sake— to move in, care for the baby and maintain the home. Adaline never left, and one year later became his wife, her only request that she keep her maiden name so as to not replace Mrs. Stryck.

On Elle's eighteenth birthday, she dropped her own surname; a gift to the mother who had never asked for anything.

Arm in arm with Adaline now, Elle felt the warmth rise up from her toes as she cast her eyes around the ornate hall. Silks, glamour and elegance had adorned her entire life, but her parents had refused to let it define her upbringing. They had kept her humble, teaching her the importance of a work ethic, tethering her to the ground without the leash of an unearned trust fund.

Despite putting her in the best schools, she had learned the most from the two souls who were always there waiting when she hopped off the bus. Her lifelong pursuit of perfection was never a product of parental pressure, but rather an obsession of her own to reflect their glimmering excellence.

Elle had been in Nox when her parents succumbed to the pandemic, and her heart had wrenched when she found their names in the Modular census database. In Elle's eyes, their loss had only elevated their perfection, crystallized in her memory forever.

She would always be grateful her memories had been saved from the sight of her parents, tortured by Void.

The red carpet dissipated as the Analepsis projected more and more memories of a life untouched by the disease, and Elle felt it was both unbearable and impossible not to watch.

She soaked in the scenes, content to watch old high school friends dance in her bedroom, family pets trot alongside her as she walked city streets, the quiet moments shared over the family dinner table.

Elle had been robbed of so many memories that she had never known she was missing, precious gifts the Analepsis was now returning to her. Gifts that could be given to anyone who'd had memories ripped from them without permission.

An image of long skinny fingers clutching a headset, tears glistening in green eyes sprung to her mind.

People who had once been erased, painted right back into minds that had forgotten them.

The idea sent ripples out to her limbs and they began to shake, tingling, reaching for reality even as a quiet poolside scene played on her eye lids. Elle knew there was more to see, and she desperately wanted to stay, but there would always be time to remember. If she waited any longer, no one else might get that chance.

Elle struggled to shake her body awake for what felt like an hour before ice suddenly flooded her veins and her eyes shot open to find a single person hovering over her, an empty water jug hanging loosely at their side.

"Well, you look like crap."

The voice was harsh and yet sang with familiarity. Elle's eyes cinched to slits as she tried to get her bearings, but the face before her loomed cloudy.

They spoke again, and although a white blur seemed to cover their mouth, Elle knew a snarl hid behind it.

"Where is the Elite wing?" the soul asked.

Elle fumbled to sit up and as her fingers brushed against the leather, it was like another bucket of water sloshed against her skin. She snapped her head back up towards the person and willed her eyes to clear, fear surging through her fingers already closing into a tight fist. She didn't dare say a single word before she knew what role to play.

The sharply angled face finally came into focus and her fingers loosened a fraction. It was a stranger, with red lips pursed in concentration and dark wavy hair slicked back into a low ponytail.

"Excuse me, who are you?"

A slight shake of the shoulders was all the woman offered, dark eyes stoic.

"Let's just say, an old friend."

A scene, fresh from the Analepsis's treasure trove, suddenly formed in her mind: a black and white chat window in front of her as a burner phone sat cradled between her shoulder and ear. The breath left her body as she released a single syllable.

"Link?"

"Pleased to finally meet you, Eleanor Drake."

FORTY

"IT WAS you. It was always you, trying to get to Dylan."

Her mind was firing on all cylinders, puzzle pieces notching into place.

"And what fun it was to find out it was always you keeping us out," Link replied, a twinge of hostility biting off the words. "Congrats on being alive, by the way."

Elle squinted at the face she'd never actually seen in person, but long assumed dead. She was still unable to believe the truth so clearly before her.

Link kept talking.

"We don't have a lot of time here, you need to show me where the Elite wing is."

"We?"

"I'm here with two Kiwi operatives who are standing guard outside the door. I don't know what chaos is going on within these walls, but it was too easy to get in here. We snuck up to this wing quietly with the hopes of finding you in your office but we couldn't get past all the yellow tape. So we came here, hoping to confront the Overseer, but then we found you instead, limp and unconscious. I recognized you and sent the other two out. I've been trying for an hour to wake you up."

Dark brown eyes squinted now as Link took a step back and looked Elle up and down, gesturing towards the couch. "What was wrong with you over there, anyway?"

"I'll explain later," Elle said, massaging her forehead. "So Easton wasn't here when you came in?"

"The Overseer? No, no one was here."

Emerging from the Analepsis so abruptly had made her wary on her feet, but now urgency coursed through her veins.

"We need to find him— and now," Elle said, rising to her feet, loath to spend any more time explaining why.

Link shifted in her path, a subtle limp jarring the motion. "No, we need to get to Dewey."

"You don't underst—"

"I understand plenty," Link interrupted, daring Elle to stand down.

An awkward silence seeped into the walls, which were now catching the light of Easton's UV monitor, shedding a hint of orange dawn across the bookshelves. Elle must have been in this room for at least four hours.

Elle was drawn to her old colleague's hands, a slight shake trembling through each finger. Link caught her looking and tried to hide it, suddenly drumming them against the empty water jug.

"Look, I don't care what friends you've made here or the life that you have, but frankly I don't care about any of it. All I need is your clearance," Link said, eyes glaring at the keycard on Elle's chest.

"Saving one Legacy won't make a difference, even if they're—"

Link cut her off, a single brown eye twitching. "You really don't know?"

Elle was agitated now. "Know what? Drop your attitude and just talk—fast."

Dark shoulders fell in surrender as Link caught Elle up to speed everything she had learned from her online reunion with Dylan. Elle listened patiently, already knowing—or having assumed— most of it and waited for the final shoe to drop. But when Link failed to say anything about who Easton truly was, Elle decided to keep that revelation to herself, if only for a little while longer. Her old colleague already looked shell-shocked about the plan for the Remedy.

When Link finished, Elle closed the gap between them and bore her eyes into her friend's, hoping she looked more confident than she felt.

"It's simple, really. We need to shut this place down," Elle said.

Link nodded, already moving towards the door. "You seem to be intent on finding the Overseer, and I have a hunch wherever the Giver is, Easton and his Remedy is, too. You take me to my priority, you'll find yours."

The pair agreed to check the cameras before moving around the rest of the facility. As Link stepped outside to check on her teammates, Elle went to Easton's computer and pulled up the feed to Pod 0017. Her colleague popped back into the room while Elle was shuffling around in the desk drawer, searching for a mic that she knew Easton only used in emergencies.

Link stood behind her as Elle prepared to engage the feed, heart in her throat as she prayed they wouldn't find an empty pod.

Just as Elle pressed enter, Link suddenly yanked the headset off Elle's ears and settled them onto her own, pulling the mic down over her mouth.

"Dewey, it's— it's me. Are you there?"

Shocked into paralysis, Elle sat rigid in the chair, searching the screen for movement, waiting for a reaction. Any reaction.

Link's voice bounced back in reverb through the monitor— the lag a likely result from an overworked system under attack— and then Elle saw him. Dark chiseled shoulders flinched like they never had before as Link's voice touched his ears.

Dewey perched on a padded weight bench in the corner of the room, chin tilted upwards as if searching for the voice. Elle felt warm breath seep over her shoulder as Link hovered over, staring at the screen.

The Legacy looked dazed and Elle wondered if the medical team had already administered transient global amnesia to prepare the chosen Giver for the bloodwork.

Dewey finally stood up, calves rippling with unsteadiness, and as he turned to face the closest camera, she finally saw his eyes, usually twinkling with light, now flaring with white fury towards the ceiling.

"Is this some type of sick joke? Another test?" Dewey cried out.

"No, Dewey. I promise, this is real!" Link replied, inhaling shakily and Elle felt a slight pressure as a trembling hand rested on her shoulder. "Do you know who I am?"

Elle reached up with her own twitching fingers, the moment too heavy to care about the threat of skin to skin contact. White on black, Elle tried to push every ounce of comfort through her veins in the hope it would bleed into her old friend. It seemed like the whole room had been suddenly deprived of oxygen.

The Legacy's quavering voice sliced through the silence, still rife with anger.

"You sound a whole lot like someone who can't be here right now so, no, I really don't."

"Dewey. This isn't a test. Now come on, you know who it is... but I'm going to need you to say it for me, alright? What's my name?"

Dewey's snarl had transformed into a perfect O before two words spilled out, and even though she'd known it was coming, they still sent a shockwave through Elle's body.

"Alex Perkins."

FORTY ONE

SHOCK ROOTED Dewey's feet to the floor and Elle squeezed the hand still clutching her shoulder.

"Alex, you have to start explaining," she said quietly. "And soon. Who knows what kind of time we have."

Alex nodded, and adjusted the mic against her lips.

"I promise, it's me. I can explain everything, ok? Just stay with me."

Taut lines around Dewey's mouth relaxed a fraction, but his stiff body seemed hard pressed to believe his cousin was back from the dead.

"I'm sorry, Dewey— about all of this. I should've told you—" Alex sputtered, breaking off.

Without turning around, Elle rubbed soft circles into dark skin, urging Alex to keep going. Through the monitor, Elle saw a soft smile had slowly begun to pull at the edges of Dewey's lips.

"By the time I came out of the coma, the world had completely changed," Alex said, pain etching her words. "I knew things, Dewey... dangerous information, and I just thought— I thought it would be safer for you if it looked like I had died," Alex's voice wavered.

A soft moan, or whimper, sounded from the pod, and Alex flinched. "I was trying to protect you, Dewey. You have to believe me."

The Legacy didn't respond but began to pace the room, hands clasped together in front of his mouth.

"Keep going, Alex. You're getting through," Elle said, turning to face the woman behind her. Alex offered a reluctant smile but then her eyes swerved to the monitor behind Elle, alarm streaking across her face. Elle swung back and saw Dewey had spun, too. His profile looked stricken, seeing something off-camera.

Elle jerked to the keyboard to change camera views. She knew that pod layout like the back of her hand, and Dewey was looking right at the camouflaged doorframe.

She found the right camera and was startled to see a figure decked out in plastic, emerging from the sliding door built into the wall. Arms shrink-wrapped in neon yellow stretched out loosely towards the bewildered resident, and although the person was completely covered, Elle knew who it was.

She flipped a switch on the monitor screen that muted their end of the feed, and she spun to face a wide-eyed Alex, mouth hanging open at the sight.

"Alex, listen to me, that's the Overseer, Easton Hill. We cannot—"

"How can you tell?" Alex's panic pinged off the walls. "That could be anyone!"

Elle took hold of Alex's hand. "I've never spent more time with anyone in my life than that person in there with your cousin. It's Easton, you just have to trust me."

Elle winced at the suspicion flaring back in Alex's eyes, and Elle pushed the fear out of her own as she glared back. This was not a time for doubt.

Although they were muted, both women could hear the other side, and an airy, resonant voice slid through the audio feed.

"Dewey, I don't want to alarm you, but we have engaged emergency protocols. We need to get you out of here."

Alex's panic was still radiating off the walls and it finally settled within Elle's bloodstream. Her mind spun for ideas as she turned and saw Easton inching closer to Dewey.

"Elle, he's bleeding," Alex suddenly said, motioning towards her cousin as she peered closer at the monitor. "He used to get nosebleeds a lot as a kid, in stressful situations. He faints easily," she said, voice quivering.

Both women leaned over the desk, watching as the Legacy backed up into a corner and Easton flinched to a stop. The abrupt movement made something jolt in a low pocket by Easton's ankle, stealing Elle's attention away from the thin trail of red under Dewey's nose. A hint of color shimmered in a small tube, just peaking out of the pocket and Elle went cold.

If Easton was prepared to send his precious Giver into a Turnover, negating all the work it had taken to get the candidate trained for the Remedy inputs, it meant Easton thought he was out of options. A monster with nothing to lose could bring down an entire planet, and this one standing before her had already done it once.

Driven only by instinct and panic, Elle hovered over the mute button for a second longer, twisting her neck just enough to see Alex in her peripherals.

"You need to keep talking. Make Dewey believe you. If he thinks you're here, he won't leave with Easton."

All she could see was a swift nod and Elle spun back to face the screen. "When I switch this back on to live, I won't be able to speak. Easton can't know I'm here— not yet," Elle ordered, mind spinning in all directions, improvising a plan. "Ready?"

"Wait," Alex hissed. "What are you going to do?"

Elle stared straight ahead. "I was trained to observe, so that's what I'm going to do. Here we go," she said, curtailing the conversation as she clicked the unmute button.

Alex began hesitantly, a hitch to her voice. "Dewey, don't go anywhere." The Legacy's neck shot upwards again, and Alex's voice grew stronger, gaining confidence. "None of that is true. They're not here to help you, only themselves."

On the monitor, Elle switched to a bird's eye view so she could see both the resident and Easton. Dewey darted his head back and forth, from the human standing before him to the disembodied voice of the cousin he had thought had been dead for years, now bouncing off the walls around him.

If Easton was confused by the other voice, he didn't show it. Keeping his eyes on Dewey, the Overseer lightly cast out his gloved hands, palms up.

"That's not them, Dewey. Alex is gone, remember? This is all in your head. Void has breached the complex. Eleanor Drake has infected us all, and we need to get out of here. Now. Please, come with me."

The smoothness of the lie came off so easily that Elle wondered if this elaborate scheme had always been a part of Easton's plan, and the anger began to come to a boil in Elle's stomach again.

They would never reach Dewey by talking through audio feeds. Trust would only come from seeing, and the longer Easton stood there, human and solid, the quicker they would lose Dewey.

The idea rushed in and without thinking, Elle punched the mute button again. Alex threw off the headphones angrily, but Elle bit off the incoming insult.

"The back codes. I saw your username in the coding of Dylan's pod when it was rebooted the other night. Did you actually find a way to hack in?"

Alex recoiled, thrown by the change of subject.

"Yeah, it was our last resort. We couldn't get a hold of him any other way, so we shut the whole pod down, temporarily."

Elle felt a shred of hope sizzle up her back.

"I need you to do it again."

Brown eyes went wide, but Elle turned back to the desk, yanking open drawers.

"You want me to reboot Dewey's pod?" Alex yelled behind her. "That's insane, it will lock every door and cut off our feed— and it's longer than just a reset, Elle. Like, 30 minutes. We can't let Dewey be alone with this guy for that long!"

"He won't be," Elle said, calling over her shoulder as she jostled through stacks of papers and pens, searching for a key card. A small white Advil bottle rolled into view and Elle snatched it, its contents shaking together as she threw them in her satchel.

She could feel Alex's confusion boring into her back and she spun around, slinging the bag over her shoulder.

"I'm going down there," she said calmly, the plan cementing in her mind as she spoke. "All you need to do is keep Dewey in that pod. Keep talking to him, and do not let him leave with Easton before I get there." Elle glanced back towards the screen and saw the gap closing between the two figures. Her fingers burned white against the leather strap. "As soon as you see me on this screen, lock it down. Got it?"

Mystified, Alex held her gaze as if in a trance. "Eleanor. When that pod goes dark, there's no way for any of us to help you. All three of you will be cut off."

Elle looked at Alex, cherishing the concern she saw reflecting back.

"I'm counting on it," she said, offering a grin. Then Elle took a deep breath and on the exhale, flicked the unmute button.

Tiptoeing backwards, she held up a single finger to her lips before turning to wrap her buzzing fingers around the cold door handle of Easton's office. Without looking back, she gently pulled it towards her and heard Alex's commanding voice dimly chase her through the opening.

"Dewey, just listen to my voice, alright?"

***

HER FEET tapped against the tile, and she nodded towards the guard who was blushing again, clearly still embarrassed from the other evening. She hadn't actually stopped to think about the possibility of her being blacklisted across the facility, but the news had seemingly not reached every floor yet. She rushed around the corner and immediately came up on

Pod 0017, noticing a yellow light flashing on the door panel, signaling the lock was not in effect.

She wrapped her fingers around the smooth metal handle, and pulled.

Two faces snapped to attention. One twisted in her direction, drenched in confusion. The other met her eyes with shock, before quickly glancing down the length of her body and Elle knew Easton was looking for a weapon. She kept her fist tight.

A sharp piercing whine seared in her ear, and it was then quickly followed by Alex's voice.

"Dewey, listen to the voice you know. Trust it, please."

Then there was only darkness.

"What the hell—" Dewey cried.

Dropping to her knees, Elle held her breath as she silently navigated the features of the pod that she'd memorized from blueprints and monitors over the years.

She heard Easton's breathing, dangerously close to her own and she felt a moment's temptation to reach a hand out towards the nearby vial. But she stuck to her plan and crept across the floor, the tantalizing coolness of the air light against her cheek as she squinted in the shadows, aiming for the dark, bulky form huddled in the corner.

She finally spoke aloud, but quietly.

"Dewey. It's Ray. I know you can't see me, but that isn't new—"

"Dewey!" Easton's voice hissed from somewhere closer than Elle had anticipated. "That's Eleanor Drake, just like I warned you. Do not listen to them!"

"Alex is here, Dewey, I just saw her," Elle continued, ignoring Easton's shrill warning. She fought to keep her voice steady just like she'd always done when she spoke to her Legacies.

"Your nose is bleeding, just like when you were a child, right?"

The only response was the swish of plastic as Easton moved somewhere in the darkness.

"Listen, Dewey," Elle said urgently, "I couldn't have known you used to have nosebleeds. Alex told me, herself. Just a few minutes ago."

Her eyes had finally begun to adjust to the shadows, and Elle moved silently closer to the lumpy bulk now just an arms length from her. She crouched down and brought her voice to a whisper. "She also told me what happens if you don't take anything within ten minutes of one starting."

Elle was close enough now to hear Dewey's shallow breathing and she hovered a hand above his, her heart racing.

"Do you remember what happens?" Elle asked, just under her breath.

A drawling murmur, twinged with fear, replied, "I pass out."

Elle brought her hand down to Dewey's, which flinched but didn't pull away.

"Neither of us want that to happen right now. Alex sent these with me... she had extras," Elle fibbed, and then she loosened her fist, dropping two pills into Dewey's hand, which wrapped around the offering tightly.

Easton's voice startled both of them.

"Compatriot Perkins, do not listen to this traitor—"

Easton's voice was drowned out by a single gulp and Elle released a lung full of air, offering one tight squeeze of Dewey's hand before it went limp. She heard the shuffle of plastic closing in, and she tried her best to let Dewey's bulk ease back comfortably against the wall as it fell.

"Dewey!"

The hiss bounced off the walls without a response and Elle backed into the corner, pulling out a handheld flashlight from her vest pocket.

"I underestimated you, Elle."

She swerved the torch towards the direction of the voice, and stone eyes squinted behind a plastic hood. "You've got some tricks."

"Learned everything from you, Compatriot."

Easton gestured towards her as she stood, muscles flexed and alert.

"I see you discovered the Analepsis."

Elle shrugged, gesturing towards Dewey's still form. "And I'm going to make sure the rest of them discover it, too."

Easton's eyes flashed for a moment, but then returned to their calm glaze, as if he had always known this moment was inevitable. Elle noticed him glance down at the glint near his ankle, and she followed his gaze.

"You were going to throw it all away, just like that? All of that forward progress this year—erased with the stab of a needle?"

Eyes still downcast, he said nothing, and Elle defiantly held the torch still, light her only weapon.

"What forward progress?" Easton droned, his voice so robotic it didn't even sound like a question. He looked up now, staring through the heart of the glow as if he could see her eyes through the harsh light. He didn't even blink.

"This building has been compromised. Not from Void— but from unbelief."

Easton walked over now to the bed, her beam of light following closely, and with resignation, he unzipped the hood to the suit.

"Every member of the Circle has gone MIA. They're either hiding in quarantine from the disease they think lingers in the halls— or they're backing out from our entire plan. I tried everything to push the Remedy forward as quickly as possible, but there's just not enough time." His slender, puppeteer hands massaged the lines across his forehead. "I know the Kiwis are here—joined up with those stray dogs who have been nipping at our heels all these years. The Legacies themselves don't know anything yet, I ordered the Graduate Facilitation Division to be put under full lockdown, but I expect that to be compromised soon enough."

She kept quiet, finding solace in Dewey's steady breathing and the bright light in front of her.

"And then there's you," he continued, boring his eyes into the light with the same hardness as when he'd stabbed the needle into her arm hours earlier.

But this time, a calm flooded her veins. She knew too much to be afraid.

"What a successor you could have been. I even gave you the keys." He clicked his tongue and looked away, rubbing his eyes. "If not for that one defining characteristic—you could have had it all."

"And what's that?"

He let every single syllable of the word roll off his lips like it was a dessert.

"Empathy."

She glared back, expressionless.

"You cared too much," he continued. "Everything else—the pride, an irrefutable will to adapt and overcome... all attractive qualities I noticed the day I saw you on my television screen after I leaked your information." A sneer crept across his lips. "Sorry about that."

His eyes turned to her again, watching for her reaction, but she offered nothing. Her body had grown desensitized to shock.

"I only hoped that Nox wouldn't break that spirit. All I needed was for it to break the empathetic part. The part that still thought the whole of humanity was worth preserving. When I found you— all those stupid words covering the walls in your own blood and handwriting, well I was a bit shocked at first. But I couldn't help but smile. You hadn't lost the spirit after all. I knew I could use that."

She desperately wanted to remain silent, to offer him nothing, but her lips parted, indignation pouring out.

"I was only ever a tool to you. You used me for whatever purpose you needed that day, and it didn't matter whether I was on your side or not."

"No, you weren't a tool, Elle. Don't you realize that by now? You were my greatest threat. When Dylan started remembering, I knew I couldn't keep you two close anymore. That voice alteration switch really came in handy. I should have put Shawna in charge a long time ago."

Bile rose up in Elle's throat. She had actually been jealous of this monster's attention.

"Then why didn't you blow me up with the rest of the evidence? No one would have missed me."

"I thought about it," he admitted. "In hindsight, it probably would have been the wisest choice. I knew I couldn't have you roaming around spewing all that information that had been on those prison walls. But as I saw you there in front of me, fear coursing through your body like an abused animal, I saw an opportunity. I had been watching you for years— I believed you and I were cut from the same cloth."

Elle's throat burned and the glow from the flashlight flickered as she held up her free hand to cover the gag reflex. Easton didn't seem to notice and plodded on.

"After all the work I'd done to get to that point— all the sacrifices— I couldn't bear to think of what would happen if I succumbed to Void, too. I needed a viable replacement. I needed someone who had the drive to make the world better, but to do it with the level of perfection that I would. Someone who wouldn't stop for anything less. Or, anyone less."

"And you thought I could do that?"

"Of course."

Elle felt dizzy. "I gave up everything to protect the world from— from you, it turns out. How could I have ever become your successor?"

"I'm not a monster, Eleanor," Easton said, adjusting his face to look in her direction without squinting. "I did what needed to be done to justify the end. The Evergreen race was my ultimate goal. Void was not enjoyable for me, I didn't like watching pain."

Elle wanted to be as far away from this shell of a human as possible, but in the locked down darkness, she knew there was nowhere to run. Plus, the longer he talked, the sooner his time would run out and everything would be back in the light.

"You never stopped inflicting pain, Easton. Releasing Void was just the beginning. The Turnover, the Shriek? They were all designed to harm people into doing or feeling what we needed them to." The beam wavered as Elle gritted her teeth, biting back her shame from ever being a part of his plans. "I justified it because I always believed it was a temporary harm; to usher them into a life free from pain."

Easton began nodding his head, a chuckle hauntingly echoing against the walls.

"See, that's why I never told you about the Analepsis. I knew you would demand we use it as some kind of benevolent gesture to our Legacies," he said, holding out a hand in the direction of the bulk in the corner. "Which clearly, I assumed correctly."

"That's exactly what I would have done! Why didn't you?"

"The unknown breeds fear. The Analepsis tears down the veil. It was simply a failsafe, hopefully never to be used. My entire plan revolved around the residents retaining fear of what lied outside the walls. We had to make Equinox and the Modular Communities their only option. Their desire. You knew that. You were a part of that."

"I was a part of helping the human existence survive, Easton! I was a part of ensuring another generation would follow us. You just want a kingdom of puppets, bending to your will. You don't care about humanity at all."

"That's not true, Elle," Easton interjected quickly, head now shaking back and forth, staring down at the sheets of Dewey's bed. "No, I care. I actually think I've been in danger of caring too much."

She opened her mouth to scream, but the anger ripping through her body choked the words. The torch now shook in her hand, every muscle in her body lit up like a fuse.

"You killed 75 percent of the world's population!"

His whole body was rocking back and forth now on the bed, head still shaking back and forth.

"I didn't— I never meant—" Easton stammered.

"Stop lying!"

"The virus wasn't supp—" he gasped for air and he launched off the bed. Elle tensed, following him with the flashlight and keeping her eyes on the glint of the syringe still in his pant leg. He unzipped the rest of the suit and, still heaving, peeled off the protective layers.

Dressed only in a white v-neck and a pair of black joggers, Easton paced next to the bed, fingers scraping through his hair and digging into his skull. Unsympathetic, she kept her eyes sharp and narrowed on the floundering figure.

"The virus escalated too fast," he finally said, the breath slowly returning to him as his eyes cinched closed. "I honestly never meant it to go airborne.

It got out of my control so quickly..." he pressed two fists into his eyes. To the outsider, he shook with grief. Possibly even remorse.

But Elle knew better. He was only sorry for allowing something to spin out of his control.

Elle may not have truly known the person in front of her, but she knew how a person behaved when locked in a cage.

Even if it was a mental one.

Shaking before her now was a tortured soul. While fury still raced through her veins, she knew embracing it would only endanger herself and right now, she was the only person alive that could tell the world the truth.

And to stay alive, she had to keep Easton from becoming unhinged.

Gritting her teeth now, she took a gamble, flicking the light towards the opposite wall, and Easton melted into the darkness. Without the plastic covering, he had the luxury to move quietly and she held her breath.

A soul who thrust the world into darkness is someone who feels comfort in it. She needed him to stabilize, return to his baseline. The thing with Easton was that his baseline was still unpredictable.

Her heart settled as footsteps retreated, the bed frame creaking softly.

"It was never supposed to kill so many."

His voice wasn't wavering anymore, but timidity still echoed off the wall. Now that her eyes had adjusted to his form in the darkness again, she saw his head angle towards the opposite wall— as if fearing the flick of her wrist that could flood him with light again. She drew power from his anxiety.

"Then what did you expect to happen," she stated, biting off the question mark. She refused sympathy.

There was a soft intake of breath, and then a loud exhale punctuated the silence.

"The MW3 Strain, as it was originally known, was only supposed to instigate population control. Clear the pathway for Equinox—a new planet Earth designed to protect its residents. To preserve an evergreen race, designed to withstand what generations before us never have, to last through every season." Easton paused, a twinge of longing lilting his voice. "But it would never work in the world we were living in... there needed to be a reduction of life."

"An extermination, you mean." She saw him flinch.

"Our planet was depleted of resources. You say you want to make a world sustainable for future generations... if we had stayed where we were, there would have been no planet left for our grandchildren."

"And what—you think the world you created is hospitable?" she bit back.

Easton clicked his tongue, and just like that, she knew he was back to his old self, curtailing his own emotions to present a body in total control.

"It was extreme. I knew that. But decades of talk with nothing to actually show for it? World leaders weren't extreme enough. My plan would work. I'd been honing it for fifteen years, setting aside every dime of my investments, inheritance and income and tucking it all into shell companies to be used for the day I knew would come. I already had the framework for the ModPods that would become the foundation for the Equinox Communities. I created my business for the sole reason of practicing my design out in the open, without questions. And I bought the farmland I would use for Headquarters seven years before even hiring the— what did they call themselves? The Scale? Anyway, I just needed to pull the trigger on releasing the virus. Everything was in place, and yet I waited. Do you know why I waited?"

She didn't, nor did she care. Her shoulder involuntarily twitched, the light flickering.

"I was afraid. The virus was to target those 55 years and over, and yet I kept thinking of all that human life. I walked down the street and saw strangers, wrinkles just beginning to etch into their cheeks and I would think of them in the ground, lifeless. I cared, Elle. Because I cared, I didn't release the virus in the winter, like I'd planned. I put it off until I couldn't anymore. One— or maybe both— of your friends continued the work without you, and were on the verge of tracing it back to me. So, in August 2016, I gave the order. The bacteria rifled through its targeted audience within days, but then it changed. In all the experiments, the strain couldn't detach itself once lodged into the nervous system. But, the virus seemed to evolve in heat, and suddenly, it went airborne. It was... uncontrollable."

"Yet somehow, an entire generation was safe. You were within that window in the beginning... was it just a ploy to save yourself?"

"Of course not. You already know all this. MW3 was designed to target the appearance of brain degradation, simple as that. The success of Equinox depended on souls who were comfortable, perhaps even excited, for the kind of social reform this new world would bring. I never intended for anyone younger than the Legacy window to be lost— I had hoped they would just be taught by the generation ahead of them."

Elle had known all of this about Void, but hearing its creator try to explain its purpose was twisting into a nightmare.

"What about all the open-minded sixty-five year olds, who had been dedicating their time to their communities, begging the younger generations to listen?" Elle was on the edge of her seat, the diatribe nearly making her foam at the mouth. "Or the disabled 20-year-old who, by age requirements, should have been saved but fell under your blade because their brain wasn't fully developed?!"

"Please don't yell."

For a split second, she thought he'd actually punched her in the gut. A hollow emptiness formed in her stomach as a seething anger rose up in her throat, sucking the air from her. She flicked her wrist and cascaded him in blinding light.

"You will never tell me how to do anything, ever again," she hissed.

His palms went out in surrender and she slowly turned the torch down to his white sneakered feet. The room was quiet for several minutes, save for Dewey's measured breathing. Elle was about to spit out another argument when her left ear sizzled with the tinniest of buzzes. The pod remained shrouded in shadow, but the sound was undeniable. She had no sense of how much time had passed, but she had to assume that Alex was intent on being an invisible fly on a dark wall for as long as there was no imminent danger.

Easton's voice shook the silence.

"I took the Analepsis, Elle. It's not a gift. I have to remember the world like it once was. Before I had the chance to save it."

His head shook back and forth against his palms, seemingly unaware of the sounds of the rebooted pod. He'd never been acutely invested in daily pod life apart from the initial design, so she wasn't surprised. She just prayed he wouldn't catch on until help was right outside that door.

"Even if you didn't plan for so many people to die, you still planned on mass murder," she said. "Don't try to be a victim."

Easton tilted his head towards her, eyes genuinely puzzled.

"I'm not. What I made happen isn't the travesty of our world, Elle. It's the fact that its people want to undo it."

Elle felt the dizziness float up to her head, just as her heart plummeted to her toes. She may have caged this monster, but she had locked herself in with it.

"You didn't have to see the world suffer," Easton continued, keeping his eyes on hers. "While you wasted away in Nox, the planet just got worse and worse. It's been almost eight years since Void." He paused, frowning at the floor, as if angry that time had had the gall to continue even when the world stopped. "Eight years, Elle. Eight years of molding history, rewriting the future, and all for what? Just for life to go back to the status quo? I had finally forgotten what kind of life that was. And then I took the Anaplepsis."

At the mention of the drug, Elle saw an image of her parents. Pain wrenched through her chest and, voluntarily this time, she shut her eyes to shake the image away. Easton's voice continued to fill the space.

"You know, there was hope for a little while. After the initial wave hit, people came out of their hiding places and just... started helping. All over the world, scientists, innovators, influencers, they were all trying to fix what was left of the world as one harmonious unit—"

"Then why didn't you just let it all be?" she interjected.

"Because, just like before Void, nothing they did was actually working!" Easton yelled back stiffly and he recoiled as the sharp echo bounced off the walls. Elle shifted in her seat, taken aback.

He smoothed his hands against crumpled white sheets.

"I mean, the more time that went by, the more life Void took away, which just continued to extinguish any of their advances. Hope was regressing, and quickly. So I hurried up completion of headquarters and started taking in as many people as we could. The planet needed saving, and I was the only one prepared to do it. The Turnover was never in my original plan, but it revealed itself to be necessary, didn't it? The only way to move forward was to forget the old, and forge on with the new. A future void of conflict, arguments, pain... a place of equality. A place for everyone to thrive."

"Is it thriving if there isn't any semblance of real life?" Elle asked quietly.

"What are you talking about?"

"The Remedy. That is the end that justified all these means, right? To force the human race to eternally coexist in harmony through the elimination of the free will."

Easton shifted his face to look at her now. Despite the shadows, she saw a coy, sneering smile pass over his lips.

"You really know how to sum up an unexplainable idea, don't you?"

Elle brought her eyes to meet his.

"You're right, you know." She saw his eye lids flicker. "It is an unexplainable idea. Because I don't think your precious Remedy would have even worked."

Easton's mouth morphed into a thin line. Strengthened by his irritation, she pushed on.

"I was in Nox for 732 days, and after about three of them, I had no will to live. And yet, as much as I wished for it, this body refused to die. The human will is unbreakable. Unexplainable. Unsurmountable. You might have engineered a way to command the mind to forget about the idea of will, but there's no guarantee the body would have listened."

His scoff erupted off the walls but before the defense could follow it, light flooded the room. Four eyes squinted against the sudden brightness and Elle blinked feverishly to clear her vision, but Easton didn't move. Glancing over her shoulder, she was grateful to see Dewey hadn't either.

Suddenly the door clicked, and Elle's peripherals caught a thin, dark frame slipping through the door and quickly sliding it back closed. Easton lazily lifted his chin to see the intruder.

"Well, I am grateful to see that not all of my plans from back then were successful," he said, and Elle spun now to look at Alex, whose face was contorted in rage. Undaunted, Easton flitted out a hand lazily. "Although, that's on me for failing to vet my employee's ability to aim."

Alex flinched, and Elle saw a dawning break across her face. Alex's hand flicked towards a metallic shadow on her left hip.

"They didn't miss, Easton. And if I didn't want to personally see you rot in jail, I'd show you my own ability to aim."

Easton just stared through the veteran, as if he couldn't even hear her.

"You know, I always had a hunch it was you, toying around our systems all these years. Elle, did you know that? Your old friend here was the reason for all those security breaches."

Elle was on her feet now, but seeing no offensive from Easton, she silently crossed her arms.

"Ah— right I guess you already knew that, now that you're back together again. I'd really wanted to be there to see that reunion."

Easton grated his tongue against the back of his teeth before turning his attention back to Alex, who maintained an equal distance between the door and where Dewey rested.

"When a notice of your expiration didn't show up on the post-Void Census, I started to worry something had gone wrong," Easton said, so casually, it felt callous. "So I started looking for Dewey... you know, as a test to draw you out in case you really had survived the—" he paused, fingers forming into quotations. "—*accident* over there in Kuwait. I assumed if I brought them in, you'd have to be close behind."

Looking between the two figures, Elle couldn't tell whose eyes spewed hatred more.

"But when we finally found Dewey, they explained— in quite vivid detail— your death, which lined up pretty much the way I ordered it. So, I made a note of it in the database, making it official. Still, I couldn't help but check every census brought in from the Void Recon team, and yet, your name never came up. With or without the expired label. For that entire year after we brought Dewey in, I wondered where you might be. But the longer the Legacy stayed in there without you ever showing up, I figured it was all true. I mean, how could a cousin— a sibling, in fact, as Dewey once referred to you— let their own flesh and blood walk right into the arms of the enemy?"

Fingers grazed the metal handle on her hip. "I didn't know then," she said, words raking through clenched teeth. Alex then tapped the small black bud in her ear. "I still wouldn't, had I not just heard the last ten minutes of this conversation."

Still sitting on the bed, Easton dropped his eyes with a smirk.

"Ah. I should know better than to assume someone isn't always listening." He tilted his head back up to stare at her again, eyes slitting in doubt. "But really, Alex? Come on, you knew before any of them."

"All I did was intercept a comms feed that I was never supposed to hear. Believe me, I wish I could have forgotten it."

"Ah, if only you'd come to see me sooner," Easton replied smugly, gray eyes flashing.

Alex lunged forward, words grating through her teeth as she came within a few feet of Easton. "I should have taken you out that day in the courtroom. A hundred eyes trained on the judge waiting for the sentence, and you were just looking around the room as if you already knew what he was going to say. I knew there was something wrong with you, you sick piec—"

Elle launched herself in between her friend and Easton, who was still postured on the bed, mouth hanging open.

To discover that both Dylan and Alex had been with her that day in the courtroom was enough to bring Elle to her knees, and tears began to pool in her eyes as she looked at Alex, mouthing the words "stay calm."

Easton seemed just as startled at Alex's statement.

"All of us were together that day? I knew I'd seen Dylan, but—" he cut himself off, a chuckle daring to fall out of his mouth. "Wow, if only I'd known... the options."

Elle closed her eyes and felt the dampness hit her cheeks. In her lowest, loneliest season, she'd never been alone. When she looked up, she caught Alex's glance and prayed the sentiment was felt in the silence.

Easton sighed behind them. "Just as well. I knew you'd come here eventually, Alex, whether you knew the truth or not. Making Dewey the Giver was simply to draw you out. I knew you would wait in the shadows until they were in danger, and I was tired of always wondering when. I needed to absolve the threat. I had only hoped to meet you when everything was already too far gone to stop."

Easton drifted off, staring idly at his fingers as he steepled them together, like he used to do when eyes looked upon him adoringly.

He took a long breath and then snapped his head up to look at the two women.

"So, what's next? I mean, the world is still in ruin out there. How do you expect to live outside these walls?"

Elle turned towards her old colleague, suddenly burning with curiosity.

"Honestly, we don't," Alex replied, staring around at the gray walls. "Believe me, I wish I could burn all of this down. But, we don't want to undo the work that's been done here."

Elle didn't dare turn to see Easton's expression, for fear that if she saw the pride in his eyes, she'd pull the metal handle straight from Alex's hip.

Her friend's voice called her back to reality.

"Modular operated on the basis of manipulating choice. You told Legacies a version of the truth to fit your needs, forcing their decision in the name of safety. You sold your lies as loving gifts."

Elle bit her lip as shame burned her cheeks.

"New Zealand operated on the idea that the only way to show love was by offering choice. They let anyone in their walls, just as you did here. But living on this installation meant life in an isolated pod, with only yourself and the walls to help you deal with the painful memories of Void. Not only did the Kiwis offer people the choice to endure that, they also let them choose not to. If someone refused to live in a ModPod, they let them walk away, despite knowing it would bring them harm. Love is giving a soul the right to choose their life, even if you know it will bring death or suffering."

The room was silent and Elle dared a glance at Easton. His eyes were downcast, but the arrogance remained.

"You proclaim equality and acceptance as the only way a soul can thrive, Easton, but eliminating the chance to choose those things... eliminates the soul."

Easton looked up, the hardness in his eyes drilling into Alex. "I ask again. What is your plan?"

Undaunted, Alex crossed her arms.

"The ModPod technology is brilliant in its offering of protection, but not on its basis of isolation. You were so afraid of human interaction that you never thought to research what would happen if a Legacy breathed the same air as a Gray, let alone touch them. What you were afraid of, physical touch— life itself— New Zealand realized could be the actual remedy. They have already created mass communities within their installation that harbor both Grays and Legacies, coexisting together, without any additional infection rates. If anything, the rate of infection is decreasing."

Elle's breathing had shallowed and she clenched her fists together to keep her legs from wobbling beneath her.

"The virus you created was meant to separate generations. But, really, all it has done is force generations together. So no, Easton. There is no vaccine. Not yet. But there is still life on this planet. There is still a will to live. Your technology will continue to be used, but instead of your walls separating humanity, they will surround millions of souls learning to be close again."

Elle turned towards Easton. His eyes had glazed over, as if he was in a trance. Speaking to the wall, words trickled out of pale lips.

"Without my help, this planet won't survive. You know that, right? If nothing changes, it's over."

A crass reply died on her lips as all of her muscles suddenly went taut. Easton's long white fingers had stopped fluttering in his lap and were fiddling around the discarded Hazmat suit that she only just realized had been sitting there within arms reach.

He had his eyes down, and she let hers follow his fingers, gauging the distance between them and the vial she knew had to be somewhere among the yellow layers. In her peripherals, she saw Alex still focused on Easton's mouth, daring him to speak further, unaware of the threat.

As his fingers idly buried into the material, the suit shifted and the vial she'd seen earlier suddenly caught the light, illuminating the liquid inside. With horror, she realized it had never been green at all, but a dark blue. Visions of what the Analepsis had shown her mere hours ago bounced back to her: cold bodies on metal tables. Frozen to her seat, she might as well have been one of them.

"I never cared about being a Legacy, you know," Easton mused placidly. "I knew I couldn't live forever. So I made my own legacy. It was perfect, it would have fixed everything." He sighed and shook his head. "What I don't understand is why any of you would want to live in a world that saw the promise of change, and rejected it?"

He was still looking at the floor, clearly not wishing for the question to be answered. Elle couldn't see his fingers anymore, but the vial hadn't moved.

"I just can't allow it," Easton said, now bringing stone eyes upward to drill them right into her. "I won't watch."

And then his arm jolted and Elle flinched backwards, her eyes closed in reaction, but she felt nothing this time. When she blinked, the blue liquid was gone, sunk deep into Easton's bloated right arm.

FORTY TWO

ELLE LEANED in close to the cold body, not sure what she hoped to feel. When unmoving silence came back, she sat down on her heels, her body warring between anger and relief.

Easton Hill was no longer a threat.

He would also never receive justice.

She kneeled there in the quiet for a few more moments, grateful Alex didn't push her. When she finally stood up, she turned to find Alex not even paying attention to her but rather kneeling over Dewey.

"This is what you looked like when I found you," she said, looking up anxiously. "What is happening to him?"

Elle opened her mouth to explain, but Alex was staring back at her unconscious cousin, words continuing to fly out of her mouth.

"You said something about an analepsis? When you were talking to Easton—what is that and why don't we know anything about it?"

Elle fumbled for the words, her mind only focused on the reality before them. There would be a time to look back, to process all that had happened—and now was not it.

"It's too much to explain right now, but trust me, he's going to be fine," Elle responded quickly. "Listen, we need to get this body out, and then we need to let Dewey rest for as long as he needs."

Alex turned back to her and Elle saw the whites of Alex's eyes flare.

"No, I finally have my family back. We can't just leave him here. I won't."

Elle closed the distance between them and rested her hands on her friend's shoulders. "Waking up is only scary when the nightmare doesn't end," she said, glancing over Alex's shoulder at the quiet bulk, still at peace, slumped against the wall. As she turned her eyes back on Alex, she briefly explained the power of the Analepsis.

"Alex, he's not in the dark anymore," she finished.

The woman's dark eyes widened and then drifted back to Dewey's expressionless face, suspicion still evident but she said nothing.

Elle turned to take in the room as her thoughts ran rampant. What was the next threat?

The computer stole her attention and she jogged over to it, checking the time blinking in the corner. 6:05 a.m.

With Dewey under safe lockdown, Dylan was the last remaining priority. Her fingers tapped wildly as she searched her memory. Just before giving her the Turnover, Easton had said he'd always planned on Dewey being the Giver. So where had that left Dylan? Still in the lab room?

"Elle, what are you doing?"

The voice jolted her thoughts and she spun on her heels, an idea forming.

"Alex, when did you last speak with Dylan?"

Dark lines wrinkled on her forehead, eyes squinting in concentration. "Yesterday. Yesterday, like late morning or so?"

"Where was he? How did you connect with him?"

"He had been moved back to his pod, I had hacked into his pod feed."

Relief flooded through her veins. Dylan was only one door down from them.

"Elle, we need to get moving," Alex added, checking her watch. "The cameras here are going to be back in Modular's capable hands in about 15 minutes. We need to put Dewey back in his bed and get Easton out of here."

The two women worked quickly, and as they emerged from the door, Elle was surprised by the sudden appearance of two figures. Both wore black jumpsuits that hugged their toned bodies, their gloved hands taut against the gray hilts of their guns.

"They're with us," Alex gasped, out of breath as she heaved Easton's torso against the wall of the hallway. "Elle, Quinn," she offered, nodding towards the more petite figure, short dark hair peaking out under a dark red cap. "And Barrett, we go all the way back to Kuwait. He was in the hospital room the day Dewey brought me in after the... incident." A wince tugged at her voice, and Elle caught the furtive glance she gave the silent body resting a few feet away.

Elle knew all too well that the scars might never heal.

"Thank you so much for being here," Elle said, nodding to each of them. "Let me just to do a quick once-over of the pod and I'll be back out."

Elle dashed through the open doorway and double checked their work, straightening the sheets around Dewey. She pressed two fingers to his wrist, grateful to feel the steady rhythm pulsing beneath her fingertips.

A smile pulled at her cheeks as she lingered over the first Legacy she'd ever cared for. Seven years, and he'd never looked more at peace.

As she approached the door, a soft ping echoed through the room. An incoming email.

She jogged over to the screen. 6:13 a.m.

She opened up the mail icon to find a new message emboldened at the top of the screen: **Congratulations! Commitment requirements complete.**

She clicked on the message, curiosity burning, and skimmed the text. Signed by the medical team staff, the email announced that Dewey had finished their incubation period early, and the team was making preparations to release them to the Lab Wing for final processing.

Even without the master puppeteer, the lies kept coming.

Elle drummed her fingers against the mousepad, feeling the urgency to leave this room as quickly as possible. Glancing at the clock, she still had five minutes. Elle swerved to log out of Dewey's account and typed in Easton's credentials, praying he hadn't changed them since he'd taken back his position from her.

Her breath released with a hiss as the screen opened before her, the familiar burn of unlimited power surging to her fingertips. She swept them across the trackpad, finding the *Sent Messages* folder within seconds. She called up the filtered search bar and typed: "Dylan, Cavanaugh, 0018."

Hundreds of emails populated, but she clicked on the most recent, which had been sent from Easton to the Graduate Facilitation Division. As her eyes moved down the message, she felt her stomach drop to the floor.

...the fall might have done the work for us. The resident was still unconscious when Medical personnel moved them to their bed. The Shriek is scheduled for the same time as always. If the resident wakes, and appears to remember anything regarding their old colleague, Eleanor Drake, you must release the Expiration drug into Pod 0018. It is with great remorse that I must order this to be done, but we have to remember it is for the resident's own good. Dylan Cavanaugh has given so much to this installation. The least we can do is put them at rest, finally free from their nightmare.

Elle bolted from the room, refusing to read any further. Three blank faces stared back at her, but she ignored them all, running to the next closest door, fifty yards down the hallway. She pounded on the smooth metal, screaming his name at the top of her lungs.

Dim hollers echoed behind her but she pushed her ear against the door, desperate to hear something, anything.

Nothing came back except shouts growing louder and louder as hands grabbed her shoulders.

"Elle! What is going on?"

Dazed, she looked down at her hands, blotchy and red.

But not red enough. Elle flailed out of someone's grip, dashing back to Dewey's door, and skidded next to the limp body resting against the wall. The shouts faded to nothing as Elle let her numb hands unleash her pent-up fury. Knuckles connected with still-warm cheekbones and red began to trickle from pale thin lips. She felt something wet on her own cheeks. Maybe it was his blood, maybe it was her tears, it didn't matter.

Elle didn't know how long she'd been punching before strong, dark arms enveloped her like a straitjacket.

"Elle, you have to stop!"

Elle heaved out syllables, breathless and trying to wrench free.

"Let me— go! He killed— him—"

"What? Who?"

"Easton!" Elle yelled back, spinning to finally look at Alex straight in the face, their eyes just inches apart. "He ordered the FAC Division to release the expiration drug into Dylan's pod! The one we used... the one we used to—" she was hiccuping now, the words refusing to come. "He murdered him. Just like everyone else." Elle turned her head to see the broken face, streaked in red. "And he got off scot free."

Sharp fingernails dug ten small crescent moons into the back of Elle's arms, snapping her attention back.

"Elle, listen to me. If what you said is true about Dylan, you cannot go in there."

Elle twisted and kicked but Quinn and Barrett had closed in around her, offering no escape. Terror still coursed through her body, but she stiffened, bracing herself against Alex as the fight left her.

"Okay, now talk to me," Alex prodded gently.

Elle rehashed the email, explaining everything she knew about the drug they'd always used to "mercifully" let go of the Grays too far gone in the Infected Communities.

Alex checked her watch again. "Dylan's Shriek always came on at 7 a.m., right?"

The relief made Elle double over.

"It hasn't happened yet, Elle. There's still time."

Arms loosened around her body, and Elle staggered backward, blotchy fingers bracing herself against the wall.

"But we can't just waltz in to his room right now—you know that, right?" Alex said tentatively. "They're clearly still monitoring him, and if we walk in, they'll gas us all."

Elle nodded absently, her thoughts too jumbled to come to one clear conclusion.

"Elle, you need to focus now. You're his facilitator, and you know how this place works better than any one right now. Where is the best place to reach Dylan?"

"My office— but you said you already went there. It's been blocked off?"

Alex's eyes fell. "Yeah, yellow tape everywhere."

Seconds passed and although she'd had the idea right off the bat, she kept thinking. Hoping to find any other option.

But there was none.

Hardening her eyes, Elle stared back at the three faces, looking to her for the next move.

"We have to go straight to the source," she said, so casually she surprised herself. "We have to get into the Graduate FAC Division."

FORTY THREE

THEY SHOVED the lanky body into a storage closet at the far end of the hallway. They would return for him, but she lingered at the door, glancing back one more time at the truth before her, shrouded in a sea of gray.

Easton and all of his illusions. His body leaned against chrome shelves adorned with damaged echo screens, unused cameras and broken Ciphers. The only color in the room, the various deep red trails draining down his ashen, lifeless face.

Like dried blood dripping down stone walls.

"You're wrong, you know," Alex whispered in her ear as Elle shut the door behind them. "He won't get off scot free."

"Don't talk to me about him," Elle said curtly.

Alex softened her eyes. "The Analepsis. We will make them all see... make them remember what he did. He may have killed himself, but we hold his legacy."

Elle searched her friend's eyes, and seeing the same anger mirrored there, she set her jaw and nodded, hoping the message was loud and clear.

They jogged ahead to find their fellow team members waiting at the guard desk where an unconscious figure was slumped against a chair.

"Just knocked out for a bit," Quinn said quickly, seeing the concern flash across Elle's face.

They stuck to the shadows the whole way to Level 2 but encountered no one, and within minutes, they found themselves at the door announcing the Graduate FAC Division.

Elle brushed a hand across her hip, feeling the cool metal of the weapon Alex had given her as a precaution. She dropped her fingers back into her pocket and tightened her grip around Easton's plastic keycard, a lackluster substitute for the rock that sat on her desk, unreachable.

A panic attack now could be the end of everything. She dug the corners into her palm, and glanced back at her compatriots, hands ready at their hips. Each of them nodded and she turned back to the door, her shaky breath forming a smoky cloud on the chrome surface.

Elle glanced at her watch. Seconds to 7.

No time for doubt.

Elle held the shaking card up to the panel, and swiped.

The blare of an alarm nearly sent her backwards as the door swung open. Weapon raised, she swept the dim room quickly and caught an image that made her forget about the shriek in her ears.

Six different TV monitors were anchored around the small circular room, each one capturing a different camera angle of Dylan Cavanaugh as he sat rigid against his headboard, staring at the walls of his pod.

Alive.

The Shriek had gone off, but he was still breathing. Still alert. Cohorts forgotten, she stepped closer to the screen to take in the relieving sight.

Then she heard the voices.

NOW

FORTY FOUR

A SHRIEK pierced the silence like a lightning bolt, sparking every dormant nerve in his body. Inhaling sharply, he felt cold, sterile air snake into his nostrils like a ghost. Sluggish eyes fluttered open, only to reveal a sight he had never seen.

A single room, decorated like a lavish, underground hotel suite. Lush white bedding lay haphazardly across his legs in a king size bed. A fresh hint of lemon clung to the four, stone walls around him. Sleek, marbled shelves stacked full with ceramic dishes filled in a kitchenette to his left, a decadent armoire stood to his right. A single coffee mug perched lazily on a nightstand. Sparks of color hung neatly in frames throughout the room.

Another shriek echoed off the stone walls, and his hands flew to his temples as his eyes snapped shut. When he opened them again, he couldn't deny one, alarming truth.

This room was not his, and yet, it screamed someone lives here.

His eyes continued to move across the space, taking in a sheepskin rug that lay at the foot of his platform bed. He squinted at an emerald green velvet armchair in the corner, willing himself to remember the chrome globe reading light hovering behind it. His gaze tilted upward to find the only window in the room, small and square, heavily textured. As he strained his eyes to get a glimpse of what may be on the other side, he realized the window actually looked splintered—like a mosaic of foggy glass pieced back together. A clunky oak desk backed up against the wall just below it.

Questions surged forward in his mind like a rip tide, the lack of answers threatening to pull him under. The alarm blared off the walls again, fracturing his stream of consciousness.

Nothing looked familiar in this room—but there was something else.

Unease crept up his back like a current.

Something was missing. His heart pulsed through his chest, every nerve in his head reaching out for the answer like fingers wrapping around the trigger of a rifle, eager for the release.

Another shriek, but he didn't hear it amid all the synapses firing in his brain. Dread surged through his body like ice as the final detail locked into place. There was no door.

No way out.

***

EPIPHANY SPLIT through him like shrapnel. A sudden tightness compressed his chest. He sprung off the bed, lost his footing in the slats of the cheap pallet holding up the mattress, and tumbled to the floor. The tips of his fingers burned white as he launched himself back to his feet and towards the nearest wall. He put his hands out and started feeling around the surface, searching for any divot, hole or ridge that offered relief from this ever-growing sense of dread. Finding nothing, he began to crawl over to the next wall before his ears split open again. Only this time, the alarm was chased by a strange, irritated voice.

"Turn the stupid alarm off, Reyes—"

The sound cut off, and he gulped in the sudden quiet as if it was oxygen before spinning on his heels to find the voice.

"A little off there this morning, Cavanaugh? Wakey wakey!" the voice cascaded all around him, lilting with amusement.

No one was here.

Muffled garble drifted in behind the voice, and then there was an audible sigh.

"A little compassion? Really, Reyes, do you know what they've done?"

But he heard no answer—only radio static.

.

FORTY FIVE

6 August
7:01 a.m.

FOLLOWING THE voices echoing through the walls, Elle tore herself away from the monitors and tiptoed to a side door of the observation room, kneeling to press her ear against the cool surface.

"A little compassion? Really, Reyes, do you know what they've done?"

Elle didn't hear a reply—only the clatter of something falling onto a table.

"Just get back to the other screens, alright. Do your job and I'll do mine."

There was a pause and then suddenly she heard footsteps coming closer. She tore her eyes around the room, trying to find anything to use as a barrier, but the latch was already turning.

She rose to her feet, pushed her back up against the wall and yanked the gun off of her hip. In the split second before fluorescent light flooded the dim room, she watched the other three poise themselves for the offensive.

The same loud voice from before drifted clearly now through the open door.

"Alright, Cavanaugh, do you happen to remember anything, or rather, anyone—"

The familiar voice was suddenly interrupted by a sharp shriek as Elle came face to face with the young FAC she knew to be Elias Reyes. Just behind their white-jacketed shoulder, Shawna Blake stood with headphones on, mouth contorted into an oval.

"You can't be in here!"

Elle tore into the room, gun poised in her hand as her eyes searched the small area. The set-up was exactly like the one in her own office and she saw the blinking red light, signaling the live audio feed. Elle swiveled back to Shawna who was now gingerly retreating towards a black box mounted on the wall that Elle had never seen. Fear surged her legs forward and Shawna dodged out of reach, the headset dropping to the floor.

"Dylan!" Elle cried out, pleading for the mic to pick it up.

"You betrayed us all," Shawna screeched as she turned her back and ran towards the box. The gun shook in her hand, but Elle couldn't pull the trigger. Shawna had reached the box and was punching keys on the panel next to it. Elle dropped the gun and swerved to the left, looking for a different trigger.

She plucked the headset off the floor and dashed to the monitor, searching for the the one, forbidden button on every FAC's control board.

With only a split second's hesitation, Elle double clicked the icon labeled Door Unlock and yelled into the microphone.

"Dylan! Get out of th—!"

But her words were cut off by the scream of a bullet as it ripped off the walls. She spun back around to see three things happen, all at once.

Shawna's fist smashing into one of two buttons on the black box before falling to the ground.

Smoke twirling out of the barrel of Alex's pistol, still aimed at the knee of a whimpering Shawna Blake.

And on the screen just above them, a haze of white shrouding the body of Dylan Cavanaugh as he crumpled to the hardwood floor.

***

NOT CARING if anyone was behind her, Elle bolted from the room. She was halfway down the stairs to Sector Zero before a hand yanked her backwards.

Alex caught her as she fell, arms holding her captive again.

"Elle, you can't go in there!"

Grief, terror and anger tore through Elle's body, and she flung herself out of Alex's grip, jumping the stairs three at a time.

"Elle! Can you hear me? If they released that expiration drug in there, you'll be dead in a minute!"

She whirled around, staring down her friend.

"There were two buttons on that panel. Maybe it was the Turnover."

"Are you willing to take that chance?" Alex's entire face was contorted in fear. "... for him?"

Elle felt every muscle stiffen in her body, not from reluctance but rather the magnitude of the decision she'd already made.

"He may just be your friend, Alex. But he's my Legacy."

Heavy legs pulled her down the last two flights of stairs like anchors, and as trembling fingers slid the unlocked door open, only one thought remained.

Like all good navigators, the captain goes down with the ship.

FORTY SIX

HEAVY EYELIDS fluttered as the dark outline of a door spliced open with a sudden blast of light.

"Dylan."

He blinked, dark eye lashes flapping against his cheeks as a silhouette emerged from the brilliance. The soothing waft of a voice danced across his skin, its calm tone easing him out of what felt like a comatose sleep.

Wary of finding himself on the floor, he propped himself up on an elbow and pushed a lock of hair out of his eyes, searching for the owner of the voice through the fog of white.

"Hi, Dylan," the voice spoke again, and he heard—rather than saw—a smile pull at unknown lips.

Something warm touched his hand and he flinched, overtaken with its familiarity. He struggled to move, desperately trying to see the stranger his body seemed to know so well, but each limb felt like a separate weight threatening to pull him through the wooden floor.

Now something was being pulled from his limp hands. A dim rattle tingled his ears as he caught a flash of purple, and then long, petite fingers touched his lips, parting them slightly. Two tablets slid down his throat as his reflexes took over.

He was falling.

No, he thought. It wasn't that, but rather every single piece of him was splitting into separate atoms that he could no longer feel.

In fact, he felt nothing. Cared about nothing. And only then did his vision sharpen, details suddenly coming into focus.

Jade green eyes stared down at him as his mind searched for the name that accompanied them, recognition on the edge of his lips like a delicate bubble lost on the breeze. The effort lolled his head uncontrollably to one side and he let it rest against the stranger's legs. With one final glance up, he saw a single pair of pale pink lips play into a tiny smirk before breaking into a full grin.

He let his eyes close, two words ushering him into the kind of blackness that blankets a theater before the movie plays.

"Talk soon."

ACKNOWLEDGMENTS

The first chapter of this story blinked onto the page in the middle of 2020, amid a world turned inside out. Doors, shut. Faces, shadowed. *It takes a village*—a metaphor of the past.

How ironic, then, that if not for a village of people, this story would have never made it out of the quarantine of my own head.

To go back where it all started, Mrs. Crosby of Forest Vista Elementary—I hope the next time you tell a student, "Maybe you'll be an author one day"—they won't wait 21 years to do it.

To my editor, Kylie Lynne. She is the reason you are not still reading ten more chapters, eyes glazed over. Thank you for your careful eye and ability to slice. If ever you choose to leave your editing career, I strongly suggest you consider becoming a surgeon.

Nicole Elizabeth Smith, what a gem to have found in the nick of time. You know, all too well, how much I appreciate your talent, but most of all, your friendship. Thank you for spending your midnights on this gorgeous cover design, I will be enchanted by it forever and always.

For all my early readers, thank you for not only accepting the time burden that comes with 115,000 words, but doing so with the added pressure that the author could be shattered by your thoughts at any moment. Kristen Juett, you pestered me for years to write a book. Perhaps it was so that you could live your dream of reading an unpublished manuscript, or perhaps it was because you've simply always believed in me, but either way, I do believe Monica says it best. Nagging works!

To the woman who always has a million things going at once, and still you found time to read all those early pages—Susan Dolan, thank you for your servant heart.

Alisha Hansen, you and I have always been... *like this*. Thank you for seeing this story with my eyes, and understanding that parallel ending before anyone else did.

Micah Patton, your analytical eye is both terrifying and a blessing. Your encouragement bolstered my confidence in this story right when I needed it. Thank you for investing so much time in making this passion project of mine better—and all the hugs to Kristin, who gave you the time and space away from her to do it.

Ben Hansen—you may never have rescued me from a dark attic, nor have you called me champ, but you gave me the greatest childhood that I could never forget. Thank you for being my Maggie.

To the president of my fan club, Mark Hansen, I do not need an agent for as long as I have you. Although you may not read every word I write, you share them with everyone you know. To have you in my corner is to have the greatest asset.

Without my love for books, I would have never wanted to make my own. So, to the catalyst of my book addiction, my very first reader, Chris Hansen: thank you for reading every work that has ever made it from my brain onto paper. From kidnapped presidents to the tale of how the giraffe got its long neck, you've read every creation as if it had earned a Pulitzer. Thank you for every bedtime story, every lunchbox note and every late night you saw my light on but remained quiet. I love books only because you loved them first.

To my handsome man, you entangled yourself into every phase of this book as if it was your own. You've always had a knack for getting me to check off bucket list items, and only you could have figured out a way to make me cross this one off. Thank you, Jesse, for your gift of challenge—you make me better in so many ways. You turned my "maybe one day" into "I did it." To say I could not have done this without you is the biggest understatement.

To Emerson and Cora, my own sweet suns, my beautiful balls of energy. Your dimples, the freckles just starting to dot your unblemished skin... you two are larger than life, and yet, have only begun to make your mark on this world. I am eternally grateful that I get to watch the pages of your life unfold, and that this project will no longer keep me off any of them.

Finally, to my Redeemer. I will rejoice forever that You chose me, but I will never stop saying thank you for allowing me the free will to choose You back. You are the greatest gift.

ABOUT THE AUTHOR

Renee Dolan is a serial teller of stories. Inspired by her childhood love of books and trained by the Mayborn School of Journalism, her nonfiction work can be found in a variety of newspapers and magazines across the Dallas, Texas metroplex. *Among the Gray* is her debut novel, and the passion project of her first love for fiction. Renee is a Dallas native, but now traverses the country as a military spouse nomad with her husband and two children. Connect with her on Instagram @reneedolanauthor or by email at reneedolanauthor@gmail.com and look for her short story fiction on www.reneedolanauthor.com.

Maybe, Margot
Take Me Back
The Theory of Evergreen